W9-AJU-935

The Sun by Night

For Ken —

With best wishes,
greatest compliments
and in friendship!

4/9/09

THE SUN BY NIGHT

by

Benjamin Kwakye

Africa World Press, Inc.

P.O. Box 1892　　　　　P.O. Box 48
Trenton, NJ 08607　　　Asmara, ERITREA

Africa World Press, Inc.

P.O. Box 1892
Trenton, NJ 08607

P.O. Box 48
Asmara, ERITREA

Copyright © 2006 Benjamin Kwakye
First Printing 2006

All rights reserved. No part of this publication may be reproduced, stored in a retrieval system or transmitted in any form or by any means electronic, mechanical, photocopying, recording or otherwise without the prior written permission of the publisher.

Book design: Saverance Publishing Services
Cover design: Roger Dormann

Library of Congress Cataloging-in-Publication Data

Kwakye, Benjamin, 1967-
  The sun by night / by Benjamin Kwakye.
     p. cm.
  ISBN 1-59221-349-9 (cloth) -- ISBN 1-59221-350-2 (pbk.)
  1. Ghana--Fiction. 2. Prostitutes--Crimes against--Fiction.
3. Businessmen--Fiction. 4. Politicians--Fiction. 5. Journalists--Fiction.
6. Trials (Murder)--Fiction. I. Title.

PR9379.9.K87S86 2005
823'.914--dc22

                                    2005028254

For Sister (Mary) and Mama (Abrafi)
Sisters of amazing grace

CONTENTS

PROLOGUE

THE JOURNALIST'S NOTEBOOK

I am everywhere, but stealthy like odorless air. I confound like the riddle of life and death. But, then again, like the riddle of silence, I am nowhere. And the story I venture to chronicle is rooted in this uncanny ability of mine to be (but not be) everywhere – a skill despised by many, especially the targets of my inquiry, but loved by those to whom I bring my tale. So who am I? Vex not, for the riddle unwinds eventually like the mystery at the end of a long, winding road. That is the road you and I must travel together. There's no other way. Because I'm not omnipotent or omniscient, to dwell on my questionable omnipresence would be misleading. After all, my powers stay encircled in the lives of those in whose stories I lodge for minutes of mutual parasitism. Therefore, my insights are limited, my foresight as useless as impotent talismans dangling visibly to scare but the feeble. Given this, it must follow that my narration's limitations are not entirely mine, being handicapped by the finiteness imposed by the owners of this tale I must tell.

But, what tale? A tale of social meanings and political shenanigans, economic strain and spiritual jests. A yarn of death and the smell of scandal and sex; two lawyers (one a former candidate for parliament, the other a lauded prosecutor); a lady of ill repute (and for her, I will reserve further judgment for now, given my own attachments to be unearthed later); and a businessman and politician. There are equally prodigious appendages to this corpus of characters: a soldier who became a politician, an old man and his enigmatic words, friends, foes, and myriad men and women inextricably attached to the corpus like an octopus and its flaying limbs.

I must confess at the onset that the case excited me because it involved one of the city's wealthiest men (also a former minister of state toppled in a bloody *coup d'etat*) and a poor woman no one had heard of.

As for my excitement, I profess no exception to the susceptibilities of everyday weaknesses. And so the day he was arrested stands luminous like tempestuous bonfire in my memory, its significance a testimonial to the outlandish thrill of the charge itself: the charge of murder. He had it all by any reasonable touchstone: money, stature, fame. Why would he so cruelly murder an unknown woman who seemed to have eked no distinction in life? At first blush, to believe that he was guilty seemed to take common sense to a low, precarious level even uncommon for the arrogance and self-arrogated invincibility of the rich and powerful. And to say that I was shocked like everybody else is to underestimate my reaction: the visceral, almost indescribable reaction that burns inside when normal people appear to do things we deem outrageously abnormal. I mentally re-circled and recycled what I had learned of the case so far, reviewing every detail as though my own fate interfaced with the defendant's (and in a way, it did). And, still, I had no coherent story, no brilliant theory to promulgate except to ask fruitlessly whether a man like the defendant could surrender to such temptation.

Intrigued and beyond shock, I had fought hard at *The Accra Chronicler* to be the sole reporter on the case, and that right was granted me. After all, I was the most seasoned reporter they had (and a frequent editorialist, too). But given the empty bag of expectations in this case, I was a determined man when I tried to reach the defendant for an interview, hoping that the undisciplined temptation to profess innocence would outweigh any pragmatic need to be circumspect. But his lawyer wouldn't let him talk to me, leaving me somewhat trapped between suspense and doubt, expectation and caution. I thought I deserved better from the defendant, given that I'd been through so much with him: the bonding, the fear of execution shared in small confines, our days commiserating on the injustice of a system as arbitrary as it was pernicious, and the nexus of camaraderie in dire circumstances. I thought I would cling to his back, tenaciously as a wall-gecko to a wall, until he caved in to my request, but I presumed he was routing all requests through his lawyer, untrusting of everyone on the outside, even me. And his lawyer was as unbreakable as rock, this despite the day he and I faced the assault and arson of political hooligans. But I appreciated that his professionalism outweighed the personal. Yet, unarmed by my guesswork and absence of a scoop, my empty arsenal trumped my confidence and I cursed his lawyer twenty times twenty times.

I rose early on the day of the trial, nervous as a cat-hunted mouse. I had some sympathy for the defendant who must face his family, his friends, and his nation; accused of a crime that none would have expected him to answer for. My wife David and two children were asleep as I pulled out of the house in my old VW Beetle, the chill of the morning surging strongly over my face like the force of blood I felt within. In hindsight, I should have woken up my wife and asked her to tickle my toes. I find the female fingers on my toes rather rewarding in the confidence it bestows on me. I don't know why.

The air was still brisk when I arrived at the office. I imbibed my first cup of coffee and quaffed down two glasses of water, which I imagined to be alcohol in the hope it would boost my confidence (a confidence I didn't want to impair any more than my nervousness already had). But my imagination was to little avail. I readied my mind for the trial in that dispossessed state of inertia. Perhaps, for that reason, I didn't feel as gratified as I had expected – and that rather nervous instinct kept nagging at me, cautioning me. I was even tempted in one insane minute to turn the entire matter over to another colleague.

But, given the circumstances, I knew I was too mentally involved to let go. I got back in my car and drove to the courthouse, where panoramic events were yet to unfold, secrets long past about to rear their ugly mucus, eject their multiyear-choked excreta. And I had to collect and collate and relate them to ears that would expect coherence out of incoherence. Yes, I am the air, omnipresent; but, like the finite beats of a heart, I am not omniscient. Therefore, I can only offer the labyrinth I am given, out of which I can only hope to weave a complete and coherent tapestry.

Hours later, my palms soaked with sweat, my toes still not tickled, with the double nervousness from what I had observed in court, I began to prepare my report. It was a very formidable assignment, given the two things in the courtroom that particularly affected me. The first was the presence of a distinguished old man in the corner of the room. It was difficult to guess his age, but, judging from his completely white hair and his deeply furrowed face, I knew he was well ahead in years. There he sat like a lucent being; hardly blinking, intense as fire, chin supported in palm, critically observing the proceedings and apparently in deep thought. He seemed to send vibes from a mental focus provoking in me thoughts of erudite literati aggregated into one body. I didn't know what to make of him. But I would keep a close watch, I decided.

The second was whether to reveal to my readers the uncomfortable discovery that one of the jurors was my ex-wife. After all these years, she hit me again, unexpectedly, like a sudden thunderbolt on a sun-burnished midday. I hadn't done my homework well. How could I not have known she was on the jury? But there she was. She teased me with her looks, vividly reenacted in past and present tense like a captivating film. There she was, sitting with the other jurors with her long lashes curving into a thick brush of brows, together like a riddle unsolved, a magical sensual mystery. Her eyes, I had gazed into so many times in the past: a sclera the color of day, iris the color of midnight. They were to me a vista of an endless spiritual and somatic power. Who could resist those lips that had brushed against mine in moments of careless passion? I remembered them heavy and appealing, eternally mysterious to me as mercury. Now I saw them unmarked by lipstick, lined instead with its crimson tint. Who could resist those cheeks raised high by the sensual wingspan of her bones underneath, stretching flesh falling so effortlessly into a stiletto-tipped chin? Her pendulous chests that to me were (or should I say are?) twin *magna opera,* bold like gigantic pyramids from the Divine, a masterstroke, a dual erection over a horizon framing skeletal excellence. She, still painstakingly stippled until the verdant whole is achieved in her living frame. The summa: in front an undulating plateau; and in the back, a mountain range – a road of sweet mysteries. But, alas, I digress.

Prologue

What a troubling coincidence! Was that a warning before me, clear like irate lightening before a thunderstorm in the anguish of the pre-trial period? Would it bias my reporting? Ought I divulge it to my readers? After a little thinking, I decided not to say anything about it for the moment, but to wait and see, patient as a vulture scavenging. Given that resolve, I started my report. And after hours of writing and rewriting, I filed it. Excerpts follow:

OPENING STATEMENTS TODAY IN MANU TRIAL

Lawyers on both sides of *The People Versus Koo Manu* delivered their opening statements today in an intense mood at an Accra Circuit Court. Koo Manu is on trial for the alleged murder of a resident of Dansoman, an Accra suburb. *The Accra Chronicler* has been unable to learn of the deceased's profession before her death, nor could any family member be located for comment. Speaking to reporters before court opened, the prosecutor, John Amoah, insisted on the defendant's guilt. Defense counsel, Ekow Dadzie, issued a terse response minutes later. "I urge you not to rush to any judgments," he said. "We must wait for justice to take its course. The facts will prove my client's innocence."

Once court opened, Justice Janet Ocloo was forced to instill order in the courtroom by objurgating a rowdy crowd into silence. She first invited the prosecutor to deliver his opening statement to the court. His poise imposing, his voice soothing as that of the preacher that he is, Mr. Amoah addressed the jury: "Ladies and Gentlemen of the jury, in this Year of Our Lord, you are part of a monumental team whose sacrosanct duty invokes ecclesiastical authority to deliberate on a matter of utmost eminence, the aftermath of which shall reverberate through and outside of this august edifice. Your hallowed duty is the determination of the intentional killing of a human being with malice aforethought, a vicious and heinous crime that negates, but is incapable of replenishing."

His fists clenched, his face stern, Mr. Amoah continued: "And so your duty shall be performed with me, a facilitator, illuminating the evidence that shall demonstrate the defendant's possession of

7

the requisite *mens rea*. You shall be privy to testimony of witnesses unsullied by bias, above reproach in credibility, who shall demonstrate in sufficient amplitude the inevitable conclusion of willful and deliberate homicide. All consistent with a defendant who perpetrates the deed and *ex poste facto* attempts to obfuscate the seekers of justice. All in the face of evidence mandating the conclusion, and the solitary conclusion, that the defendant in cold blood and intentionally, with malice aforethought, by repeated motional movements of his forelimb, impacted the defendant with a miniature pestle."

(As we know, a pestle is a wooden instrument shaped like a broomstick, only it is much heavier. According to reports, the pestle in question is small in size, being about four feet. Still, it is heavy enough to cause fatal damage).

Now standing in front of the jury, Mr. Amoah concluded: "You shall convict the defendant. Why? Because on the day in question, he, by vehicular means, and later, by oral persuasion, negotiated himself into the victim's habitation, already set in the aim of murder. Having gained entrance into the victim's domicile, he proceeded to strike the victim with the pestle. And as a proximate result of such repeated striking by means of a pestle, the victim expired by this most heinous means. Regards."

Justice Ocloo then invited the defense lawyer to deliver his opening remarks. Mr. Dadzie rose slowly and walked to the jury so that he was standing almost among them. He began: "I welcome you today, dear jurors. I thank you deeply because of the important task before you. We all feel deep pain when a human being dies. It's even worse when that person dies not from natural causes, but at the hands of another human being."

Mr. Dadzie paused, flashed a frown and continued: "I can assure you that I too want the killer to be punished severely. But I'm afraid that the prosecutor is asking us to make a very terrible mistake, because Mr. Koo Manu *did not* kill the deceased. Convicting Mr. Manu will mean sending an innocent person to jail or even death. That would be a double injustice, a travesty, and a cruel abortion of justice. And we mustn't allow it to happen.

"With the trial unfolding, let's ask ourselves this general question: even believing the prosecution's witnesses, are we convinced beyond a reasonable doubt that Mr. Manu killed the deceased? No, this case is full of doubts. And we'll realize after all is done that Mr. Manu, a hardworking, God-fearing and generous man is incapable of murder. And, realizing Mr. Koo Manu *did not* commit the act, we'll have to acquit him.

"So throughout the proceedings, let's pose three specific questions. One, has the prosecution proved beyond a reasonable doubt that Mr. Manu had the criminal intent to kill? Two, did Mr. Manu have the opportunity to do so? Three, do we believe beyond a reasonable doubt that Mr. Manu used a pestle to repeatedly strike the deceased to her death? The answer to all three questions will be no, no and no. An innocent man having put his fate in your hands, we must endure this difficult process to demonstrate his innocence. I'll discuss these with you at the end of the trial. And I trust that you will render a verdict of not guilty. Ladies and Gentlemen, it is the only verdict we can render in the service of justice. Thank you very much for your time. I'm looking forward to working with you."

The Accra Chronicler later interviewed a cross section of the courtroom audience. Asked whose opening statement they liked the most, an overwhelming majority said they preferred the prosecutor's. Asked exactly what they liked about the prosecutor's statement, many responded they did not understand exactly what he had said; however, they said his language was appealing. "His language has a certain exotic charm," said one observer.

Stay with *The Accra Chronicler* for more on the Koo Manu trial.

So there you have it – the first day of a trial ostensibly to find the truth that would prove Mr. Manu's guilt or acquit him for his innocence. The lie, the pretense – all, except the most naïve, knew that innocence was not the practical quest. Lawyers would use facts, fading memories, faulty recollections, oratory, appeal to emotion, and every available tool to convince the jurors of their case. Under this weight of manipulation, where was the truth? In my estimation, Mr. Manu's guilt or innocence was beside the point. The result of the case would simply be the product of the process, a deeply flawed process dependent on human frailties, the sharpness or tardiness of lawyers, the sympathies and prejudices of jurors. Therefore, to appreciate the case meant to go beyond the facts presented in court and to dissect every detail of argument and strategy, two minds in combat, the facts mere arsenal or armor. It meant understanding the larger picture preceding the trial, the context, the relative truths or falsehoods of reflections in court. Like a chameleon's skin, it held no permanent coloration.

But now that the locomotive is in full motion, I repose the question: Who am I? At this juncture, I offer some clues, feeble as they may be. In my estimation, I am part of *The Abused Road*. How can I escape it when it's a part of me? When it's me. So you may see me in black tar, trucks negotiating my curves. Or you may see me standing in lethal dance while taxi drivers traverse me with careless steering ease. But when the drivers corrode my beautiful body with such tireless play, please don't call me a prostitute. Even if you may see my edges lined with repulsive soil and aglow with fires that set my tar weak or caked by droughty hearts and here and there pedestrians abuse my delicate flesh and I groan under muddy footwear, and my abused beauty is tangled in phlegm from chocked nostrils or spittle from sullied mouths or the trash of many months line my landscape with their stench, don't shun me. Instead, when you see my body avalanched by unsightly holes, my pools filled with rain, pray that they be not the tears of my dirge, but the rebirth of my body.

It is that beauty, wearied by the lacerations of injustice and falsehoods, joy and pleasure squeezed into me … it is that contradiction that pulsates in my step, ignites my energies into a conflagration …. And I become privy to stories normally told behind closed doors only, the ear behind the closed door, the eyes peeping through the keyhole, the soaking sponge in the mangrove. And yet who am I, a mere journalist, to hog the entire narration when others have tales told better through their own lenses? I shall return, but for now I yield the stage to she who had held my attention like pleasure (or pain) and haunted me even when I returned home to have my toes tickled.

11

Book One

─────────

THE ABUSED ROAD

*You have picked a quarrel with Earth, but you eat
from the earthenware pot*

–Proverb

THE JUROR

You left work early and went to the beach for the rest of the afternoon, and there you sat on the wet soil and for a long time looked ahead over the vast sea and up at the infinite sky to the flying birds. It was refreshing for you to sit and look into the ocean when it was not too populated with swimmers or lovers or tourists. You imagined the sea forever in love with the sky in the horizon, where they seemed to touch. Just as illusory as the love we live, in which the sight and imagination are more promising than the reality. You spent the remains of the afternoon at your beloved beach which incessantly received the flapping waves just like lovemaking itself. On your way home your thoughts quivered with the thrill of things you imagined would unfold that night in the other trade that only begins for you under moonlight. Unfold like glowing trinkets to be cherished for their value but also their beauty. Unfold in the forbidden lusts of carnal weakness marred in its guilt-ridden waves like the ocean's many secrets.

As you left your bungalow that night you felt gripped by an overwhelming and ravishing force. Gripping like a memory, half-remembered and half-forgotten, that lays siege to all conscious thought. Yet you found resolve to step outside of your Ridge bungalow and walk to the corner of the street where you hailed a taxi. Perhaps you took comfort in the shadows that seemed to have a multitude of sources when they fell on your path even under the onslaught of lights from passing cars. The shadows came perhaps from blotches of human bodies, or the flapping of wings of bats, or images of trees and buildings. Whether animate or inanimate, or nocturnal or diurnal, seemed of no importance. You wondered if you had turned into a different creature that walked outside almost fearless and free from the halo of the afternoon.

You disliked driving on occasions as this because your car might get noticed. Your peers would not take too kindly to the second profession you had chosen, and so far you had succeeded in keeping it secret. But you always dreaded that you would be discovered some day and you had to tell yourself that life itself is a risk. The shadows gave comfort in the belief that you were hard to notice in your make-up of eye shadow and rouge, and in your black tee shirt and black jeans, with your wig taken off to reveal your closely cropped natural hair.

You reached the corner of the street and waved down a taxi. As the car moved away you could see the city resurrected from the day's little deaths for those who would cultivate the first joys of the weekend and garner its harvests the next two days. By the sides of the streets young women seemed to convulse in loud repartee. The cacophonic mixture of horns and screeching ignited the air and returned it to life without the stale brightness of day. You saw peddlers of kebab and fried pork and fried turkey tail and rice and beans selling to eager but impoverished hands. In one far corner you saw a nightsoil carrier treading quietly by, while a group of young boys yelled names at him and a retiring panhandler looked on askance. In one corner you saw a throng gathered in front an open bar, drinking beer to the blast of *highlife* music, while a couple sat head to head under a mounted but almost tattered parasol.

You always made the drivers stop at the mango tree close to your destination because you did not want them to get too close in case they were the suspicious type. Your destination was a rectangular building of concrete painted blue and although it seemed firm, your heart pounded with the itching fear that the building would collapse one day while you were in the act itself. You were afraid your body would be discovered battered in its nudity and that the next day *The Accra Chronicler* would carry an article written by Nii Lamptey himself with the screaming headlines AMA BADU OF MINISTRY OF ECONOMIC PLANNING FOUND DEAD IN A BROTHEL. You wondered what your friends would say if that happened as many of them believed that you were a walking specimen of virtue. You shuddered at what Nii would think and how he would write the article.

Book One: The Abused Road

You entered into the dimness of the building and the first person you saw was Akwele when her shadow fell on yours. You moved along the corridor and Akwele took your hand; and at that point you were like Siamese sisters, understanding and completely trusting each other. You walked on to the main large chamber where two sofas and a number of coffee tables and chairs were sprinkled and a bar reposed at the very back.

Madam Beatrice is a voluptuous, almost obese woman with an equally large spirit but carried her weight with regal dignity. She had a presence that grabbed respect without requesting it. She kept a hotel and restaurant close by that were frequented by the rich. She used this place as an adjunct for her restaurant and hotel clientele who sought more than food and rest. She had an amazing way of keeping track of the time each woman spent with a customer so that she knew exactly how much money to expect at the end of the day. You thought she was kind to the women who worked for her so long as they did what they were told. You thought she liked you because you never gave her any trouble and you always paid her cut without complaining.

Akwele released your hand to welcome two men who had just entered the main chamber, while you looked up slowly because you could not afford to let anyone you knew recognize you. You tried to be inconspicuous until you were sure that you did not know them. These were ordinary men: they were very simply attired and walked into the hall without caution; unlike the rich ones, who approached slowly and looked around furtively as if afraid they would get caught. One was short and stout and the other taller and looked a little shy, and you would have preferred the taller one but in this business you did not have much choice. In the seconds between their entry and your observation the double-edged knife of want and revulsion sliced into you. And you were sure the knife was long enough to reach them as well and connect you to them in that contradictory nexus.

Araba and Akwele had already captured them before the other women could attempt to lure them. While you were observing them you had turned your attention from the entrance and so you did not notice the young man who stepped in and who now tapped you on the shoulder and prompted you to turn around. He was of medium height with a broad forehead and broad eyes and thick eyebrows and heavy lips and a square chin with a cleft in the middle. You could smell the alcohol on his breath and the nervousness in his body. "How are you, sweetie?" You grabbed his hand and then you saw Madam Beatrice winking wickedly at you as you walked to pick up a key.

Then you moved away from the hall into the long corridor as the double-edged sword sharpened in your mind into a bizarre evocation of air to bleed and blood to breathe. Like an enigmatic being capable of giving life and drowning it out. You opened the door and moved on into the bedroom where you both undressed. As you always did with your customers, except on occasions when you simply became careless or were compelled to do otherwise, you made him wear a prophylactic and then you were ready.

His body was heavy and moved with a bird's agile freedom and the unstoppable force of an elephant and the perfect precision of a percussionist. And he went up and down and up and down with sinewy elegance. He never lost his mounting intensity or the uncontrolled rhythm that came with it as he built to the crescendo so that the sweat on his moving body formed a unified stream of glistening wetness, leaking carelessly from his machine of flesh. Then his speed increased and went higher and higher and he began breathing heavier and heavier as his muscles seemed to twitch pleasurably and his eyes seemed incapable of focusing. His lips opened wider and wider and his loud breath came in short gasps and its rhythm was irregular as though forced and strained and tortured. And then with one exhilarative scream his whole body seemed to weaken and came collapsing downward and it was all over.

After the first burst of energy, it seemed he did not want to do anything but talk. "This is an experience," said he.

"Is it your first time?"

"It's my second, unfortunately."

"What do you mean?"

"You have to understand. A man like me shouldn't be in a place like this."

"I can understand that," said you. "Are you a lawyer or a doctor or something of the sort? You look the type."

"Possibly, but I'd rather talk about you, if you don't mind."

"If you pay for the time."

"What's your name?" asked he.

"Mary Magdalene," replied you in jest because you never offered your customers your real name. "What is yours?"

"Jesus Christ," said he.

You laughed out loudly but you knew that he had tailored his answer to fit yours and you could not complain. Most of them never used their real names anyway and you were content to interact incognito. "You're a beautiful woman," said he. "Why are you in a place like this?"

"You are a handsome man, so what are you doing in a place like this?"

"I thought we'd agreed not to talk about me."

"Fine," replied you. "I am here because I enjoy being here and you know that is more than most people can say about what they do for a living."

"I can't really believe anybody would like doing this kind of work."

"I cannot speak for other people, but I mean what I am saying."

He ran his hand over your palm and they tickled and made you giggle. He released your hand and asked: "Doesn't it bother you that all kinds of men walk in here and use you and then walk out, leaving only the memory of their bestial cries? Where is the emotional attachment that you need, that everybody needs, to feel alive, to feel human?"

"Do not I also use them if I get paid for it?"

"It's different," said he. "I come here, get my fulfillment and then I'm gone and I can do whatever I want. Those who come here take whatever you have to offer. They leave little behind. Satisfied, they go

19

home to their beds, their families or wives. But then they have taken a piece of your soul with them. They take and take and take. They never give. Don't they make you feel cheap?"

"But to me it is no different from any other profession, like lawyers who advise their clients or doctors who tend to their patients and feel emotionally drained at the end of the day. Does the engineer who repairs every car feel cheap? Does the doctor who treats every patient including even criminals feel cheap? Does the lawyer who takes on every client feel cheap?"

"It's just that there is really something fundamentally wrong with what you do for a living. In other professions you acquire a deep sense of gratification from your work. A doctor, for example, saves lives. That in and of itself is satisfaction."

"I do not agree that those in my trade do not derive satisfaction from their work. We take care of needs too."

"How about the question of morality?"

"I suppose if you believe that what I do is immoral then I must grant you that view. But on what grounds do we draw that line if not from some sort of arbitrary societal imposition?"

"You surprise me with your intelligence, Mary," said he. "But even if there's reason in your position, why can't we as a society dislike something because we feel it is wrong? Isn't that good enough? I mean it must be wrong if the rest of society frowns on it so much."

"No it isn't ..."

"Well, by your standards then we can make no moral judgments or distinctions. It's all a societal imposition? What a way to argue. There are some things that are simply antisocial, that require no justification for being outlawed, no need to explain why they're wrong. We just know they aren't right. We instinctively acknowledge that they are wrong. Call it instinctive law ..."

"Instinctive law, or whatever you call it, must have limited value in a thinking society."

"You have a response to everything. You sound so educated."

"I keep an open mind."

"What is your level of education?"

"Just primary education," you lied.

"You sound like you have a much higher level of education." He shifted his body on the bed and then he reached over your head and turned on the light and smiled at you. He seemed to be studying you and finding ways to smooth the sharpness of that link of dual impact between us that sullied and strained the relationship while at the same time feeding it with satisfaction. He reached over and turned off the light and said: "I still have to understand why a beautiful and intelligent woman like you would be in a place like this."

So he thought that there was something fundamentally wrong with your practice and yet there he was helping you perpetrate it. You could not stop thinking that whatever else, he was your partner in the deed. The word hypocrite came to your mind. But in another curious sense he had won your respect because he seemed genuinely interested in finding answers to questions that others would not dare to ask. Those who would simply have their fulfillment and hurry away to create as much distance between them and you, so that the only burden they carried wherever they went was on their consciences and perhaps in their inner selves. Some of them would return again and again until perhaps they were freed of the pull of the place. You believed that no one who came to the place ever returned the same. Because once you had been there you were within its shadows, and even if it was hidden inside of you it could never be erased.

Not wishing to argue with him any longer you simply said, "What society thinks, society is entitled to think."

He smiled and then he moved toward you and again you were one with him.

৵৽

He put his head on your belly as if he were listening to something inside; as if in the pulse of your belly and your womb he could find a clue to you. And you slowly ran your fingers over his hair and then you told him how wonderful he had been and when you said that he began to cry. At first it was slow and quiet and you thought he was laughing

21

or something and then all of a sudden his body trembled and he began to sob loudly and sniffle as if he were a baby. You gathered him in your arms and took his pain and vulnerabilities into you without knowing what they were or being capable of living them the way he did. Nor did you interrupt him or say anything because you knew that he had to purge whatever it was that made him break down and cry in your presence. When he stopped crying he started to tell you about himself, although you wished that he would not.

"My name is Kwamena," said he, before you could stop him. "I was born and raised here in Accra. My parents are in business, both of them trade in this and that."

"You don't have to tell me that," said you.

"I want to," replied he. "My parents have been married a long time now. I can't even remember how long. I am the second in a family of five. I'm an accountant. The eldest is a doctor and the one after me is an engineer. The other two are studying history and economics."

"Your parents must be very proud of you."

"They are," he replied. "I left the University of Ghana with a degree in business administration; I took the professional accounting exams and joined an accounting firm, where I still am. My life read like a perfect picture book. I jumped where I was supposed to jump and sat where I was supposed to sit. I have thrived within the system." His voice fell a notch as if there were another person in the room he did not want to hear him. "When I finished school I was about twenty-two. I was lonely and looking for a wife. A mutual friend introduced me to her. She too had just finished university and started teaching at secondary school. We had a good relationship. Every day, after work, I'd meet her and we'd have a meal and spend the night together. If we had any differences then, our love submerged them. We got married nine months after we first met.

"It continued to be a perfect marriage. Then one year later we had our first child and we spent all our energies on that child. We didn't notice our passion beginning to slip. A compliment that might have been paid before wasn't anymore. Instead of a kiss for husband or wife, the baby got all the kisses." He paused a short while and then

22

continued: "Two years after the first child, we had our second. And our attention for each other was diverted even more to the children. Three years later the third child came and two years later we had the last child and things didn't get any better. I realized that instead of bringing us together, our children actually pulled us apart. Sure, we both are immensely proud of them. I knew that our four children linked me inseparably to my wife, but at the same time a gulf grew between my wife and I. We no longer had the ease just to slip a hand over a shoulder, extend the neck and kiss a face."

He did not look that old to you, but you guessed that he was just aging graciously. You tried to imagine what his wife might look like and when he paused you took the opportunity to ask him, "Do you still love her?"

"I don't think I know what that means. I used to believe in love. I believed it was something you felt in the blood and flesh. You were overwhelmed by it. I used to feel like that about my wife before and soon after we were married, but I don't have the same feeling nowadays. I have thought about taking a second wife, but I know it's not the modern thing to do."

"Why don't you ask her for a divorce?"

"My life will not be complete without her."

"But if you must make your life empty in order to make it full why not take that route?"

"I don't know what a divorce will do. Will it make me happier? I don't know. Oh, I wish I knew."

"Are you here then in search of answers?"

"I don't know …."

"Well supposing you found your answers here, would you then be willing to divorce your wife?"

The question seemed to sting him and he moved away from you and sat upright on the bed. He did nothing and for a long time sat rigidly and all you could hear was the rise and fall of his strained breathing. Then he turned to face you and said: "No, I will not leave my wife. I will never leave her. I would rather marry a second wife or

23

keep coming here. But I won't leave my wife." When you did not say anything he said, "I know you won't understand why I can't leave her. You can't just leave whenever you wish. You develop a certain bond. Ask any married person and to varying degrees they will tell you that you almost become one with your spouse. Perhaps even you have been in a relationship where you've felt a certain powerlessness to leave."

"I was married once, you know."

"Then I am sure you'd understand."

You were tired of the exchange and so you replied, "I do understand, my dear."

He turned to you and you knew that he was ready and you were one in flesh again but this time his climax was quite violent. And after that he smiled and seemed to be at peace and you were almost sure that he was happy at least for the moment. There he was in a stranger's bosom and his troubles were for the moment eclipsed by your body and your words within which no demands were made on his soul and no pull was made on his humanity and no questions were asked that he did not want to answer.

But even as you considered the issue you asked yourself if in fact he was a stranger. Is not the stranger the person you met in the street but did not see, or the smile in the dark alley that disappeared in the shadow? Or the brief handshake that gripped you and eased into a memory where it could no longer be retrieved? You said to yourself that strangers did not meet in obscure places to escape from the outside din, and that you did not tell stories in secret to strangers. And a stranger was not this flesh with which you had just become one. So you reasoned that perhaps you were not strangers at all, but rather friends in a spiritual sense with a connection that went past the physical experience.

He stood up and began to dress. "I had a very nice time with you, Ms. Magdalene," said he.

"You say it as if it surprises you."

"Yes, I'm a little surprised. I didn't enjoy the experience so much last time. I didn't think tonight would be any different."

"The world is full of surprises. Is it not?"

He turned on the light and you were blinded by it as he stood there fully dressed and gazing intensely at you. "You are a very beautiful woman," said he.

"This is costing you a lot of money," you reminded him.

"I can afford it."

"Make the most of your money."

"I am."

You were thinking of what his beloved wife might be thinking or whether his dear children would ever imagine that their father would come to the place.

"I'd like to see you again," said he.

"You know where to find me."

"Are you here every night?"

"No."

"Well, which nights?"

"I do not keep a regular schedule, although I am here most Fridays."

"Can't you give me a more precise answer than that?"

"I really do not know when I will be here next."

He frowned. "How do you make any money if you don't work most days?"

"I have my ways."

"Well, can I arrange to come where you live?"

"That will not be appropriate."

"What about meeting in a hotel somewhere? I will take care of all expenses and I will pay you well."

"I am sorry that I cannot do that either, but if you come around next Friday I am most likely to be here."

"You are a very curious woman."

"But are we all not?"

You put on your dress and he watched closely as you slipped it on. You told him how much he owed and he gave it to you without complaining. He took your hand and kissed it, and when you looked at him there was something awkward there. And you did not know if it was desire or passion or something else, and you were not sure you liked what you saw.

"I will see you again soon," he said and then he walked out of the room.

⤙⤚

On the road a few mornings after that, it appeared as I pulled out of my house that there was someone in a red Peugeot parked outside my bungalow. At first, I paid no attention to it. But as I drove on I saw the car moving right behind me. A couple of miles later, I grew suspicious because the Peugeot was still behind me, moving faster when I moved fast and slowing down when I slowed down. I wondered who it could be and for a while I thought it might be a government official spying on me, as I too had heard rumors that some members of the military were planning a coup. But it did not make sense that they'd follow me. What would I have to do with any of that? In fact, I had no connection to politics except for the loud-mouthed colonel who frequented Madam Beatrice's and occasionally boasted that he'd be president some day. Had his careless talk led to some connection to me?

I quickly pulled into a petrol station, although my tank was full. As I did that I saw the Peugeot drive past. I stayed at the petrol station for five minutes and then got back on the street; then I felt something like a heavy weight behind me. And I felt the weight was staying within shadows so I couldn't tell its nature. And yet it was early morning and a time when I thought I'd be safe because of the brightness of sunlight. But that morning the sense that I was being followed was pervasive. I looked into my rear view mirror as I turned a corner. As there were so many cars coming up behind me, I couldn't look for long and yet I felt someone was getting closer and closer. A sensation close to fear began to seize me and I was afraid something dreadful might happen. Instead of driving straight to the office I decided to drive around a little, just so I could be sure whether I was actually being followed.

And as I drove past the Ministries, there was the red Peugeot again behind me. I drove very slowly because this time I was determined to find out who was driving the car, but it was a useless effort. The person was wearing a big hat and his face was covered with huge sunglasses so that it was impossible for me to see anything. I pulled over to the side of the street and stopped, so he had to drive past me; but I managed to see and memorize the numbers on his license plates. I did a U-turn and headed back to work, still looking in the rear view mirror to see if I were being followed. But this time I saw no red Peugeot and I drove to work. Still, I was nervous all day because I had a fear that the door would open at anytime, and someone wearing a hat and shades would walk into my office and yell that I was caught. And if he caught me, what would be the consequence? Would he link you and me?

That night, tormented by the red Peugeot, I assessed my ability to transform myself from a trusted civil servant to a woman of the night. I was looking for answers in what was more of a riddle than night shadows and daylight. I wondered if perhaps I were the walking mirror that reflected whatever was thrown at it so that I become like the shadows that cloud my path and protect me, shadows that left me the same creature that simply changed its skin color but did not change its skin. Or was I a different creature that completely transformed itself in order to carry out the secret trade of the night that is so thrilling and yet so risky and sometimes depressing? Or did I remain the same creature like the snake that sheds its skin for another one? And, if so, did I move from a lower to higher plane or did I glide on the same plateau and exist on its different contours?

Then I began to recall the nights I spent with Nii Lamptey whom I'd not seen in a long time so that his face was fading like a pale shadow in my imagination, like the fuzzy image from a dream hard to remember. He would walk these streets with me when we were married and talk loudly of his love for me and say all sorts of sweet things that didn't mean much. Nii liked to hold my hand and squeeze my fingers or touch my shoulders and rub them gently for long periods or stroke my face as if he were seeing it for the first time. I used to enjoy our strolls under the moonlight when all sorts of thrills were awakened within me. I too danced on my feet like a little girl who finds infatuation for the first time and I said those sweet nothings too.

Nii and I would rush home and consummate the throbbing desire. Only the physical limits of our bodies restricted what we wouldn't do. But after a while I no longer enjoyed our promenades, as it seemed the thrills I felt for Nii were all gone. Like the lost mystery of a dreamy figure now come into full bloom. Then when he touched my face it was like the touch of a brother and the things he said to me seemed boring and lacking in spontaneity. I withdrew from him, and although he tried hard I withdrew more and more. The night I told him I didn't want to go outside and stroll, he withdrew into a corner looking pathetic, but I felt there was nothing I could do for him. How could I comfort him when I felt no desire for him or wish for his companionship after only two years of marriage?

One day when I returned from work he'd left me a note saying he was going to stay with his brother for a while, and that he realized my heart had left the marriage. He said although he wanted to be with me he wouldn't force me to live a life I didn't want. The divorce was not finalized until eight months later. I kept the bungalow because it was mine, given to me by my father when he decided to move from the city. In hindsight, I sometimes thought it was good I'd miscarried the previous year. Even though it sounded devious and selfish, it rid the relationship of any organic link with what once used to be. In addition, because to live is to die, and because of death's sorrow, I had no will to have children.

But all that happened many years before. The last time I saw Nii was about three years ago when we bumped into each other at a party and he told me he'd gotten married again and had two children. Even though I'd not seen him in a long time, I often read things he'd written because he'd become a big shot reporter for *The Accra Chronicler.*

Book One: The Abused Road

I remembered one article about a national monument that attracted so much attention and national interest even outside Accra. The Accra businessman Koo Manu was nominated to have a new rotary being developed in Accra named after him. Many thought that a man who'd risen from nothing to national prominence through sheer hard work and enterprise should be duly recognized. Nii wrote an article about the issue that had by then become a *cause célèbre* of the Accra business community. He wrote: "I too recognize that a man of Mr. Koo Manu's business caliber deserves some sort of recognition, but to name a national monument after him? Is this where our great nation is headed? Let people of true national importance like Kwame Nkrumah, J. B. Danquah, and Yaa Asantewaa receive such recognition. As for Koo Manu, I recommend we pick a gutter and name it the Koo Manu Gutter. That would be entirely befitting." Needless to say, the article generated a great deal of debate with some praising Nii as insightful and others calling him a brash journalist with no respect for his elders.

In any case, why were those flashes of my past life with Nii intruding like an unwanted dream? Why was I always guilt ridden when I thought of him and what he might think of my new profession? Why must I feel guilty if I wanted to break the barriers defined and constructed by others? And why should their truths be mine? Didn't I have the right to reject such imposition so that I could find my own truth and determine my own moral order? Didn't I have the right to determine my own beliefs and therefore define myself in my own light? Did I have to agree when others called me names? Couldn't I change the description with a new attitude capable of enlarging a vision that only yesterday was narrow and exclusive?

But perhaps I was wandering too far afield. Or, as I approached middle age, was I worried and beginning to wish for the comfort of marriage and for the security that it brought those who stayed with it? I'd become more aware that I wasn't as attractive as I used to be and the downward drift of bodily parts that once stood firm and erect had accelerated. The wrinkling had begun, forcing me to wonder how long I could keep up with the younger ones like Akwele and Araba.

29

The Sun by Night

ॐॐ

It was very late the next Friday and business was near a halt. The sound left was the unheard, hollow echoes of clients' demands and moans and the smell left of stale sweat that stays even after a thousand washes. It was time for Madam Beatrice's women to thrust out of tight cocoons since the married men had returned to their wives and the single ones were either spent or seeking other ventures. Most of the women were huddled in groups of twos and threes around the bar counter. As on most such occasions our group comprised of Akwele and Araba and you.

"I wish sometimes that I didn't have to do this. If you know what I mean. I wish that I had a husband to take care of me. And I wish I had lots of money and lived in a posh suburb." That was Araba, who was always complaining about one thing or another she did not like about the business.

You replied, "You do not have to do what you do not want to do, Araba. Marriage is not all it appears to be."

"I'd want to go through it and make the judgment for myself," said she. "I want a man who loves me and no one else."

"Where are you going to find such a man?" asked Akwele.

"Ask and ask again," said you.

"You two have no faith," said Araba. "I will find him."

"Let me know when you find him and ask him if he has a brother," said you.

As you looked at those two women you became acutely aware of your own financial privilege. You had a job that paid you plenty and you had the money and the assets you got from your father. But you believed that the choice was not just economic and that for you it was more spiritual and psychological and emotional. Your financial privilege was perhaps the only advantage you had over Akwele and Araba.

You knew Araba a little but not very well because she was a little bit like you in that she rarely told you anything about herself. But you knew that she had a habit of using illegal narcotics and you were

30

worried about that as it could get her into trouble with dangerous scofflaws. But you never prodded her because you did not want her to ask you any personal questions either. So you shared a few jokes and traded stories that were not important. And then you went your separate ways at the end of it all and because of that you did not know her very well, even though you really liked her. But in the end you affirmed that what mattered was that you shared the space where certain experiences were like molecules expanding to fill every breath and pervading your systems so that you became linked like sisters.

But you must confess that you held a certain special softness for Akwele because she had opened herself up to you and given you the microscope to go into the secrets of her life without asking that you do the same:

She was born a twin in a family of eight children in the Accra suburb of Bukom. From the day she became aware of it, she knew poverty and tasted it: everywhere she looked, naked poverty stared at her unblinkingly. Her father was a fisherman. Although a fisherman does not make a lot of money, the little he made could have helped. But he was a drunkard who spent all his money on alcohol. Akwele recalled that her father hardly came home. Even the little time he was there, he spent quarrelling with her mother or sleeping and snoring.

She detested the constant bickering between her parents, often hearing her father call her mother names so terrible that they need no repeating. Oblivious to the presence of the children, he would throw insults at her with the carelessness of a drunkard and the vigor of a tyrant. And then occasionally he would beat her, and all this time the children watched and felt powerless. Once, Akwele begged her father, "Papa, please don't beat mother." But he simply growled at her and nothing changed. Then she saw the change descend on her mother slowly like dusk. Her mother, who had been the sane one holding the family together, began yielding to despair. It was as if she had become a vessel through which their father cast insults. She turned around and insulted them too, just as he did her. Then Akwele's mother stopped taking care of herself. She had to be forced to take a bath and she would neither cook nor clean up nor do much else.

Akwele was already twelve years old when her mother began her mental decline and neither she nor any of her siblings had ever been to school. So none of the five boys and three girls could read or write.

By the time Akwele was thirteen her mother was incapable of recognizing her children. Her father didn't know how to respond to that except by increasing his insults and beatings. But while her mother had previously argued and barked back at him, she now simply laughed mirthlessly as he beat or insulted her. She seemed not to care about what he did to her, which disarmed and perhaps overwhelmed him. He increased his drinking and stayed away from home for even longer periods.

When Akwele was fourteen her mother walked out of the house and never returned. The children would stay up late waiting for their parents and hoping that one of them would be there. But the mother never came back. And when the father returned, his breath reeked of alcohol and he struggled to hold himself erect before his children. But he had little money for them. It became clear that one or more of the children had to win the family's keep.

Quartey, who was only seventeen, developed a tendency to sit by himself all day and think without finding a solution to the problems facing the family, problems that seemed too profound for him; so that the second sibling took the responsibility upon herself without anyone actually asking her. And she was barely sixteen. Naa would be gone all night and return in the morning's wee hours exhausted, but with enough money to feed the family. No one asked any questions. It was as if they were afraid to find out and her father was perhaps too guilt-ridden to question his daughter, if he noticed her nocturnal absences at all.

Perhaps Quartey was shamed that his younger sister had found a way to help the family while he had failed. Unexpectedly, he too left home and took up with a group of mean-looking young men who were rumored to be thieves who plagued wealthy neighborhoods for items they could resell. Occasionally, Quartey would return home dressed in flashy clothes and carrying a lot of money that he gave to his siblings.

By the time she turned fifteen Akwele was beginning to feel the need to do something for herself. She felt she couldn't rely on her sister forever or her brother who appeared when he felt the need. So she asked Naa about her nocturnal absences and how she too could help to keep the family aloft. But Naa didn't want to say. She made excuses, saying that Akwele was too young to be involved with what she was doing. But Akwele wouldn't give up. Eventually, with tears, Naa explained to her younger sister that she sold her body for money. For many seconds, Akwele was repulsed by the idea and she insulted her sister by saying that she had brought shame upon herself and upon the family's dignity. But Naa asked, "What dignity?"

Akwele found it difficult to believe that her elder sister was a prostitute because she had always imagined that only bad people did such things. But slowly she reconciled herself to it. But it took longer for Akwele to make the choice for herself, even as she realized that she had very few options. She delayed her decision until her twin Akoko got married to one of her father's friends who was also a fisherman and who was old enough to be their father. When her twin sister left home, Akwele felt so lonely that she knew that she had to occupy her time with something to keep her mind away from the world that was unhinging around her and to help make some money for the younger ones in the family.

Akwele told Naa she too wanted to be involved and that she needed her elder sister's guidance. But the elder one would not hear of it, saying everything she could to discourage Akwele. But Akwele cried and begged and cajoled and prodded until finally Naa gave in, and about a month short of her sixteenth birthday Akwele went with Naa and Akwele too started in the trade.

You had wondered several times whether Akwele felt imprisoned in the trade like Araba. Whether she felt she had no choice but to continue in it even though she disliked it, and because she hardly complained about anything it was hard to read her actual feelings.

As you thought through these things, you heard footsteps thudding menacingly and you knew it was Colonel Duah. He walked in briskly looking cleanly shaven and sporting a political suit. It seemed he had a way of picking late hours to make his entrance at Madam Beatrice's when no other men were around. You could empathize in that cautionary approach, given the wish to stay as anonymous as possible while enjoying forbidden fruits. What you did not understand was his ostensible revelations once he was at Madam Beatrice's. "I am the next leader of this country," he'd once announced in his gruff earsplitting voice.

"I thought elections would soon be underway," said Madam Beatrice. "The Head of State said you soldiers are leaving politics and going back to the barracks."

"And return the country to incompetent civilians? What does the Head of State know? I taught him everything he knows. Ask him. He'll tell you himself. These upcoming elections mean nothing. Believe me."

Madam Beatrice knew the man had important connections reaching all the way to the Osu Castle. This was not a man to ridicule for his ludicrous views or challenge for his ambitious stupidity. So Madam Beatrice indulged him with false titters and fake optical glitters of admiration and he seemed to swim in that bogus esteem. On most occasions, the Colonel was interested solely in Araba and Madam Beatrice herself. When he made his appearances, we all knew that in most likelihood Araba or Madam Beatrice would have to accommodate him on the premises. On those occasions, Madam Beatrice had to make exception to her policy of not bedding customers. But as whimsical as Colonel Duah could be he would occasionally pick a different woman. You had the misfortune of being picked on occasion. And you must admit that they were not the most pleasant part of your experiences at Madam Beatrice's.

Before the act itself, he warmed himself up with fifty pushups and fifty sit-ups and the words: "You should be proud that the future leader of the nation is going to fuck you." The Colonel was a poor performer who did not seem to realize his shortcomings and therefore talked vociferously throughout the act about how he was giving pleasure and what a superb sex machine he was. And then he would proclaim a series of crass sobriquets: "I am the lion with steel cock"; "the conqueror of the elephant and the platypus"; "the breaker of men and the fucker of women"; "the soldier with forty balls"; "the man with more love juice than the ocean"; "the hard stick without end"; "the man who eats with a spade and drinks from a barrel"; "the house that kills warriors and the fire that eats water." And then, to crown his unilateral achievement, he would scream like a wounded man and bang his head three times against the wall, and then collapse for exactly three minutes before getting dressed. The only plus in this humiliating and negative experience was that Colonel Duah never had a repeat performance in any one night.

Colonel Duah went directly to Madam Beatrice and asked, "Is the lady of the house ready to service the future president?" And with the reluctance we all knew but Colonel Duah could not recognize, Madam Beatrice smiled and took the man's hand and led him away. In that very moment our sense of powerlessness descended on us like a storm on a day when you would rather have sunlight. We could hear Colonel Duah's yelling of self praises a few minutes later, and then the huffing and puffing and the last violent yell, in contrast to the complete silence of Madam Beatrice. And then we heard the three thuds of his head hitting the wall.

After Colonel Duah left, you knew Madam Beatrice was a little downcast. Araba recognized it too and started humming a tune that you had never heard, and then she began to dance. She danced slowly at first and then she started to move her waist faster and heave her shoulders back and forth. Then she opened her lips wider and transformed her humming into a song and her legs were moving all over the place. Then the other women began to clap or drum on the bar counter to create a collective sound. Madam Beatrice reached behind her and brought out a guitar she kept behind the counter and she ran her fingers along the strings, and then she was thrumming on them and together with the clapping and the drumming created a rather crude but charming song. And soon everyone was on the floor dancing, and at that time the song was simply *a capella* but it did not lose its charm because all participated and bodies convulsed with dance and song. You thought to yourself that truly there were no devils or angels at Madam Beatrice's, but just people.

Later that night a taxi dropped you off at the junction close to your bungalow and as you began to walk home you heard a sound behind you. You turned around to look and it appeared you saw a man wearing shades at that late hour and dressed in a long trench coat, moving very slowly behind a couple of trees; and your chest went into merciless convulsions.

You remembered the man in the red Peugeot who had followed you to work and you started to run. You thought you could hear heavy boots running behind you and that prompted you to run even faster. As you thought of the red Peugeot you also thought of the Colonel and you wondered if he were playing tricks on you. When you got to your bungalow you turned around to see if you could see the man. You did not see him anywhere. You opened the door and quickly locked it and went to the phone and called a policeman that you knew, but he did not answer. You went to the kitchen and took out a knife and went to your bedroom, but you were too afraid and excited to sleep so you sat in the corner of your room and waited for the slightest sound. After a while you were very tired and you knew that you would soon fall asleep, but you were afraid of sleeping on your bed; so you went into your closet and that is where you slept that night.

You later called again the policeman you knew, and he told you the license number you gave him did not exist. Because you were sure you had properly noted the number, you were convinced it was fake. Under the circumstances, you felt you had no choice but to hire a night watchman.

A week later you were still shaken from the experience several nights before as you listened to Kwamena insist that he had to have something of yours. You were not happy with that, but he was so insistent that you had to give him something. You had proposed giving him a ring just so he would shut up but he did not like that suggestion. Instead, he wanted the dress you were wearing that day. It was a beautiful navy blue dress with little sunflowers all over it that won you praises whenever you wore it. "If you won't tell me how I can see you more often, then at least give me that dress," he pleaded, and on and on he went to the point where it seemed he was on the verge of crying.

You told him to come back for the dress next time. The next Friday he waited at the bar counter until you were free from another customer so he could be with you. After an hour of physical exertions he asked you for the dress. You gave it to him and watched him hold it close to his face and then to his chest and smile and look at it as if it were some great prize he had won. You did not want to take any money from him but he insisted. Then he held you very close for a long time, telling you how you were opening his eyes and creating new desires in him he had never felt before and how he felt you were becoming one and inseparable. You told him not to talk like a child, but you regretted that as soon as you said it.

But I couldn't get rid of Kwamena's question of why you were a prostitute, and I asked myself why as well. It was not the first time I'd asked that question, but this time it seemed different for some reason. All I could find was the memory that came back to me whenever I faced that question.

I recalled when I was younger and all the times when I was left alone at home, times when I hoped my parents would be there. I'd look for someone to play with when I felt so intensely lonely. And much as I had tried to run from it, my mind returned to the memory of that friend of my parents who came to visit when I was nine years old. I knew little about him except that he'd come from a very far away place and would stay with us for two weeks. He was very nice to me, giving me sweets and telling me how good and pretty I was, and how he had a daughter like me. I liked to hear him say such nice things at first, but he kept saying them again and again until they sounded saccharine.

A week before he left, my parents had been invited to a party and the visiting man said he wasn't feeling too well. He wanted to stay at home and tell me stories and my parents said that was a good idea. After my parents left, the man asked if I wanted to have some sweets, and I said yes. He gave me some and said he'd give me more if I behaved like a nice girl and did what he asked me to do. He turned off the light in the living room. The only light came from the moon through the slightly opened curtains. I began trembling and he said I shouldn't be afraid because he'd never do anything to hurt me. He came closer to me and started touching me and it felt good but I had a feeling that it wasn't supposed to feel good.

Then he dropped his trousers and underwear so that he was naked below the waist. I closed my eyes and looked away, but the man said I shouldn't look away. He said he would tell my parents I'd been a bad girl if I looked away. I looked at him in the face but he said I should look lower. I was very afraid but I looked lower and he began to touch himself.

When he was finished he wiped himself with a handkerchief and pulled up his underwear and trousers and gave me some sweets and told me stories. Then he said if I told anyone what had happened I'd die a very painful death and go to hell where I'd burn forever. After a while, he told me to go to bed, but I was afraid and felt sick, but at the same time I felt strong and knowledgeable. Due to of all those feelings, I couldn't sleep for a long time and then when my parents returned I heard him tell them that I'd been a very good girl. He said he'd told me stories and I'd gotten tired and gone to bed. It happened two more times before the man left and both times I had the same feeling of power and revulsion.

Even after he left, I was still very afraid and I knew I had to conquer my fear and nausea somehow. At the same time I knew he had awakened a curiosity in me that had to be sated somehow, and that feeling thrilled me a great deal. But I said to myself that it wasn't actually I who had watched the man touch himself. It was you. It was not I who felt pleasure at the feel of his hand. It was you. And I knew that once I found you I'd never let you go.

So it was you who would satisfy the curiosity he had created, and it was you who seduced Anfom that day in secondary school when the party was over and you were alone with him in the darkness behind the tall assembly hall. It was you who told him you loved him and let him go all the way, while in the same month letting Bob and Fiifi and all the others do the same. It was you who went in search of answers to an awakened curiosity and appetite that would go on and on and on. It was as if you could not help yourself and you would change so many boyfriends in school because your hunger never seemed satisfied by any one of them.

You thought you could overcome your male shopping if I got married but you found out that the marriage to Nii was like a weak shield against your powerful force, because Nii could satisfy me but he could not satisfy you. And then after the divorce you felt you had to explore that other self some more. By doing so perhaps we would conquer you. We knew we were taking a big risk but we also knew that we'd never be satisfied with the *status quo* if we did not attempt the challenge.

തരു

For the first time since you started working for Madam Beatrice you accepted an invitation to her house. She invited you to come over on a Saturday afternoon. You were very apprehensive but you felt that it would be an insult to her if you did not accept. She had also invited Araba and Akwele. You felt that a dooming circle was about to close and you had no control over it. But after stalling for a while you finally said yes. You took a taxi to Dansoman to Madam Beatrice's house that Saturday afternoon. It is a sizeable mansion guarded all around by a five-foot wall and shrouded from the inside by mango and guava trees.

"Welcome," said she with wide-opened arms that embraced you for a long time, so tightly as the circle you imagined closing around you. "Come, come let me show you my humble home." She led you indoors and you could immediately smell from the kitchen the aroma of rice and beef and goat meat. She showed you her wall-to-wall carpeted living room cooled by an air conditioner, and the plush furniture; and then the kitchen with its cooking stoves and refrigerators, which opened into the backyard with some papaw and more mango trees. Then she walked you to the front veranda and asked you to sit as she yelled for Akwele over the top of her wall. Akwele popped her head out and yelled back "I'm coming!"

"You are not going to a beauty contest. Hurry up before the food gets cold."

Akwele ignored Madam Beatrice's comment and asked for you to come and see where she lived. You walked around to Akwele's house which was a two-chamber structure without any fence and much smaller than Madam Beatrice's. One room was a kitchen and the other was a bedroom, and in that room she had a long sofa on one end and a table with an old television on top at the other end. There was a small torn carpet in the middle of the room and in one corner she had carefully mounted her mattress. She quickly slipped into a faded yellow dress and said, "It's a small place, this home, but it's cheap."

You thought of your own three-bedroom bungalow as you replied, "It is very nice."

"I do my best. But I thank Madam Beatrice. She lets me have it at a very low price."

"Madam Beatrice owns this building?"

"Yes," said Akwele. "I never told you? She'd wanted to turn this into a guest quarters, but changed her mind. Then she built the wall around her house but she never built a wall for this one." The reality of walled buildings and fenceless ones and imagined circles besieged your thoughts. Akwele was ready. "Let's go before Madam Beatrice gets angry with me."

Madam Beatrice had already brought out the food. Araba arrived and Madam Beatrice embraced her. Insisting you were her three most favorite girls, Madam Beatrice created a makeshift dining room out on the verandah by bringing out four chairs and a small table so you all could sit and eat around the table. "You women are so good, I don't know what I'd do without you," said she.

"Oh, Madam, you flatter us," said Araba.

"It's well deserved. I've never invited any of my ladies home to eat. I try to keep my business and personal lives separate. I think that's the best way to make the business thrive. I made an exception for Akwele when she needed a place to stay. But as she knows, I've been very impersonal about it. I collect my rent from her, I don't meddle in her affairs and I don't let her into mine. That's the way it's been since she moved in two years ago."

"Actually, Madam, it's been three years."

"Three years? I've lost track of the years. You know what happens when you get to be my age."

"You can't be that old," said you to Madam Beatrice.

"I'm not young. I never tell my true age, but I'll tell you if you don't tell anyone.'

You shook your head to indicate she could trust you and Araba promised to keep the secret. "We won't tell anyone," confirmed Akwele.

"I am fifty-eight years."

You said, "You look at least ten years younger than that, Madam Beatrice."

"Mmmh, my daughter, you have a sweet tongue. No wonder all the men like you, and the other women envy you so much."

You all laughed and for a few seconds no one spoke as all you could hear was the sound of your own chewing, and the pigeons in the trees chirping away in the lazy haze of the afternoon heat. A young woman stood over Madam Beatrice's wall and yelled greetings. Madam Beatrice explained to you that she was their nosey neighbor Anaa Quarshie. Anaa Quarshie soon disappeared behind walls and trees.

Araba asked Madam Beatrice, "Do you think you will ever retire from this business?"

"I don't know. It's become my life now. It will be hard for me just to walk away. It's been a long journey and I feel like now that I've arrived, I can take it easy, concern myself with the finances only. It wasn't always like that, you know. I used to have to use my body too, just like you. Believe me, I worked very hard at it. Oh, it's been such a long time. I remember how reluctant I was when I started and how horrible I felt the first time.

"I was born into a poor home, you know. My father was a mechanic. My mother sold fish at Makola Market. They hardly made enough for both of us. My parents wanted me to go to school and they did their best, but it was even difficult to raise enough for my school fees. My clothes were all old and threadbare. I resented going to school and seeing some of the other children wearing nice clothes. I paid little attention to my lessons. When I was home, instead of studying, I had to help my mother with the chores. I was almost always close to the bottom of my class. It was clear when I finished middle school that I wasn't going anywhere with my education. I had to find something to do. My mother had a seamstress friend who agreed to teach me how to sew.

"I had never been happier. I was finally going to do something for myself, something meaningful. But, mind you, I was now only an apprentice who had first to learn the job. I didn't make any money. For two months I went to this place and learned to sew, but I was completely broke and I had to borrow money from here and there. It was harder than I had imagined.

"One day when I left work, wondering what I was going to do, a young man approached me and said, 'For a long time, I've observed you come to this place.'

"I wondered what he wanted. He was sharply dressed in a nicely pressed blue shirt and khaki trousers and he was wearing very nice cologne. He had gold bracelets around his wrists and a huge ring on his right index finger. He looked very handsome to me. I continued to walk on.

"He walked beside me and asked, 'Are you working for that seamstress?'

"'I am learning the trade,' I told him.

"'That's very nice,' he said. 'My name is Kwame Konadu. But most of my friends call me KK, so you can call me that as well.' He looked at me closely and asked, 'What's your name, beautiful woman?'

"I smiled and said, 'Beatrice.' And I must admit that I already liked him. You know, he was one of those men with such good looks and charm that you find hard to resist and you think you can trust completely.

"'Beatrice, will you allow me to buy you some food?'

"I agreed because he simply overwhelmed me. He walked me to his car and drove to a Chinese restaurant near Osu. He said nice things to me. He said he thought he and I could do things and go places together. As I listened to him, I felt as if I was in heaven. He said he knew how to find me and he would be in touch. I hoped I'd see him the next day, but I didn't see him for another week. And then when he next appeared, I felt completely overwhelmed by him. I couldn't resist him that night and he was my first. I was in love and I thought he was the man I'd marry. You should have seen me then, so happy and feeling on top of the world. But I was in for a bad shock

"About a month after we'd met, KK took me to a hotel where he said he wanted me to meet with some very important guests. There were three of them at the hotel and for a long time we sat at the bar. They ordered some expensive liquor they called Chivas. I sipped on a cola drink. Then KK said it was time to go upstairs. I didn't quite understand what he meant but, as I trusted him completely, I just followed all four men up the stairs into a room in the hotel. Then KK fondled my behind and said, 'Now, darling, you are going to do for these men what you've done for me.'

"I thought he was joking or that perhaps I'd misunderstood him. So I said nothing and he started to pull off my dress. That's when I knew he was serious. 'No!' I hollered and began to push him away.

"'What's wrong, darling?' he asked.

"Are you mad?" I asked.

"'Do this for me, darling. For me. No one is going to get hurt. You will be amply rewarded. I will love you forever.' I probably should have ran out of the room then and there, but I didn't. And I'm not sure why. I figure it's because I still was in awe of KK. So I stood there while he took off my dress and then you can imagine what happened next."

"All three of them?" you asked Madam Beatrice.

"All four of them," Madam Beatrice replied, and went on: "I didn't know how to take it. Despite the pain that shot through me, through my womb, I felt tiny bursts of pleasure. I was, nevertheless, awashed in shame. Later as we drove home, KK handed me a bundle of cash and said, 'This is for all your efforts tonight. You were simply wonderful.' I didn't want to take the money, but in the end KK persuaded me to take it. I was quiet all the way home. I felt cheap, used and abused and as soon as KK dropped me off at home, I went to my room and cried like I'd never cried before. But even then I knew that this man held a power over me and I didn't resist him next time he took me away again to service more of his 'friends'. I was confused because he still maintained sexual relations with me. "Will you marry me?" I asked him one day.

"'Marry you? Beatrice, are you mad? You want me to marry a prostitute?' That hurt me badly. He had said it. A prostitute. I had become one. A cheap prostitute.

"It took me another month to embrace my new profession and I realized that I had entered something I wouldn't easily give up. In a way it was easy money. I left the apprenticeship to become a seamstress and moved from home. I stayed with KK for a while. It was then that I realized I was one among many, that I had enjoyed no unique status in his life. I learned that he recruited young women just the way he'd recruited me and then he pimped off them. I worked for him a number of years and then he was killed in a car crash and I was on my own.

"I approached my work with a vengeance. Using KK's contacts, I managed to keep and expand my clientele. I targeted the rich. I seduced them whichever way I could, whether it was getting invited to their parties, hanging around in hotels where they frequented, or even going to their offices to proposition them. I was a sales woman of sorts, and in this I was single-mindedly determined. I made a lot of money because I knew I was beautiful and my rates were very high, and my clients could pay because they were rich. That's the way I made it. I even got one of them to buy me a car. Men are so easy to convince, you know. If you know the right things to say to them, you can get them to do anything you want. Anyway, I used the car as a taxi. I saved a lot and then by the time I was thirty, after being in the business for twelve years, I had three taxis and I began building this house. It took me two years to complete it, but I was in no hurry. Eventually I built my hotel and restaurant and then the building where you all come to work."

Araba and Akwele and you had listened raptly without interrupting Madam Beatrice because she had invited you into a past that until then she had never told. She said that whenever she thought of that day with KK when she had been introduced to the trade she still felt a deep confusing feeling inside and she was not sure if it were pain or sorrow or pride; and she often wondered where her life might have led if she had become a seamstress and found a job, and perhaps gotten married and had children and perhaps become active in a church or some community activity. But those things were denied her and sometimes she was sad that she had not chosen the more traditional route, and yet at the same time she felt accomplished in a way so that she felt her sacrifices were not for nothing. She explained that she kept up appearances still so that officially she was a businesswoman just in case she needed to explain her wealth to someone.

She burst into a long laughter after she had told you her story as if she were trying to cheer herself up or something. "There's so much food left," said she. "I suppose I'm going to have to give it to my police friends when they come here tomorrow."

"Police friends?" you asked.

"Yes," replied Madam Beatrice. "I have to keep them happy, you know. Otherwise, they can close down my business. I have to pay my bribe to them to keep them quiet. There are two that I rely on the most to keep things in control. One of them I've known since he was a child. Many weekends, I invite those two over for food and drinks. Those are some of the things I must do to keep us in business."

"I never thought of all that," said Araba.

45

"I take care of such business so you can work in peace."

As Madam Beatrice spoke you kept asking yourself if you too should try and establish something similar to what Madam Beatrice had. You had the money to do it and you could pull the connections to keep afloat, but you were not sure you could put yourself out for so many to know what kind of business you would be managing. You knew that you would not have the courage to create that kind of enterprise, and that there must always be the likes of Madam Beatrice and the likes of you. You would rather walk in the long shadows of those like her, and for that you were grateful to her and you felt strong warmth for her.

But suddenly Araba's demeanor changed to somber, as if the word peace were a mockery; and then she said, "I don't want to sour the mood, but there's something very important I need to disclose to you. I just found this out yesterday." She paused for long seconds while we waited with bated breath. "About two weeks ago I went to see the doctor for what I believed to be malaria. He did some tests and told me yesterday that I have AIDS."

For a full half-minute no one spoke as the bombshell continued to disseminate its near-fatal fumes. And then Madam Beatrice said, "My poor child, what are we going to do?" The use of the plural suggested a collectiveness that revealed rather than concealed our vulnerability.

"I have been sentenced to death. What can I do about it?"

"How did this happen?" asked Akwele. "Didn't you use protection?"

"I did, but it broke sometimes."

In Madam Beatrice's suggested collectiveness you thought of the risk of your own exposure. You often made your customers use condoms but there were occasions when you had given in to insistent customers like Colonel Duah. When you told him to wear a condom he gnarled at you, saying that he was immune to disease. You knew the other women were thinking of the same things and whether they had been exposed to the virus through the sharing of men. You knew for a fact that Colonel Duah liked Araba and had been with her many times. You knew also that Madam Beatrice would have to consider the consequences of AIDS in her establishment and the potential loss of business.

Araba's bombshell soured the atmosphere, and for the remaining minutes the conversation was constrained and tense. Dusk had settled when you left Madam Beatrice's and you promised yourself you would get yourself tested for AIDS, and you would insist that every customer use a condom even if it were Colonel Duah. You never got the AIDS test, however.

Madam Beatrice's story brought back the memory of the day you made your own decision to enter the trade. It was a long time after Nii and you were officially divorced, leaving you with lonely nights like the ones spent while growing up when Mother and Father were not home and you had few friends. With those memories you felt so lonely that you knew you had to act to pull yourself out of the creeping boredom. You decided to go to a nightclub in Kaneshie that you had heard so much about.

It was a sultry Saturday night when you stepped outside. And the night felt like a mass body panting with insatiable lust that begged to be fed. You felt it in the humid heat and incognito conversations of strangers and the physical agility of bodies abroad. You hailed a taxi to the club and even as you stood on the street outside you could hear the music booming loudly. You bought a drink and sat by yourself for a long time while looking around to see if you could recognize anyone. A pretty hefty man came over and started making conversation, and as you looked him up and down you decided that he was not bad looking except for his oversized midsection.

You encouraged him to sit next to you and then as you started talking a younger man approached and asked you to dance with him. Your initial companion did not like that and told the younger man to leave you alone. But the younger man would not acquiesce, saying that no one owned you, and that you could make your own decision, and that angered your initial companion. All of a sudden someone spilled beer on you and your initial companion did not like that and he was up and going after the younger man. As the two men tried to fight each other, things began to fly here and there so that for a short while it was quite chaotic. But eventually things settled down and your initial companion came back and sat next to you, but you could not see the younger man any more. And the younger man became an opportunity lost to you.

After the commotion passed and you both were calm the man invited you to go to his place. A curious idea came to your mind and in jest you asked him how much he would pay you if you went along with him. He was a bit surprised by that question and it took him a long time to name the price. But you saw the eagerness in him and you felt so much power that you asked him for more money, and he agreed. You would later think over why you had done that and the more you thought about it the more you were baffled by your own actions.

You drove over to his house in Dzorwulu and you could tell that he was wealthy because of his huge house and the Jaguar parked in front of it. You stayed with him all night and the next day he paid you and you told him you had never done this before. He said if you were interested he would introduce you to someone with a great deal of class who dealt in prostitution. You were intrigued by the idea and so you got the directions from him. Said he, "Tell her Paa Tetteh sent you. She will take good care of you."

As your boredom grew you thought of it over and over again until you decided you would give it a try. You had never been without a man for long. Ever since the day when your parents' friend made you watch him, you had gotten a yearning that would not die. Like hunger it could be sated only briefly, but not for long. You had tried marriage and that had not worked and your male shopping had not worked either. At that point Paa Tetteh's suggestion seemed to be a very viable and attractive solution. Plus the sense of adventure to replace the boredom you faced at that time led you on.

You shaved off your hair and put on make-up and followed Paa Tetteh's directions which led you to Madam Beatrice's restaurant. She welcomed you and took you to her place, where you felt at home from the very beginning; and you kept going and going until you felt her place had become such a part of your life that you could not just pull away from it. You got yourself a wig that you wore whenever you went to work, and after a while it seemed the wig was a part of your public persona. And because you had few friends to begin with it was not very difficult maintaining your dual identity. The new life alleviated your boredom considerably, but you also felt even more alienated from the rest of society.

࿓

A few weeks later, a coup struck the country like an unexpected storm. Perhaps I shouldn't say it was entirely unexpected, as Colonel Duah had warned us that it was coming. But who would give much credence to the careless ruminations of a squat soldier so self-absorbed in his self-conjured prowess? But then, with the announcement of the coup that morning, I knew I should have taken Colonel Duah more seriously.

The coup would have had no impact on my own life except for three things. The first was the detention of Nii Lamptey three weeks later. The second was the imposition of a dusk to dawn curfew. The third was that Colonel Duah stopped coming to Madam Beatrice's. It was easy to see why, as he was named by the new government as Liaison Officer with Powers Plenipotentiary between the Military Machinery and The Revolutionary Council. Whatever that meant.

I heard of Nii's detention through his brother, who came to see me asking if I could use any of my connections at the Ministry to get Nii released. He said he didn't know where else to turn, and he thought I would know some important people as I held an important post. It appeared Nii had been detained for an editorial he wrote in *The Accra Chronicler* in which he stated: "With three months to the end of the Military Council's rule, do we need another military government? The Revolutionary Council's intervention cannot be anything but a derailment of the process towards constitutional democracy. We demand the immediate dismantling of this new bogus military apparatus in favor of civilian rule."

I had to be cautious as I didn't know how any attempt to intercede on Nii's behalf would be perceived by a new, angry government.

Instead, I entreated Madam Beatrice to intercede on Nii's behalf through Colonel Duah. "He is a powerful man now, with strong ties," I said.

"These are dangerous times, but I'll see what I can do for your friend."

A day later, Madam Beatrice said Colonel Duah could help, but some people had to be paid off first. Colonel Duah named a pretty hefty price to secure Nii's release. I got the money for Madam Beatrice, although I was afraid she might get suspicious of my interest in Nii and how I could raise such money. I took the risk, however, for the sake of Nii. Luckily, Madam Beatrice asked no questions. Even after I paid the money, it took another two months before Nii was released. I never told his brother how far I'd gone to secure Nii's release, telling him instead that I was doing my best. I felt I owed Nii that much, especially as rumors started circulating that arrested journalists and officials of the erstwhile government were being molested or even executed in detention, and especially after three former Heads of State were shot by firing squad; and especially after seven other officials of the toppled government faced the same fate. In that climate, who could predict what could happen to Nii in detention?

The dawn to dusk curfew was modified to midnight to four a.m. It affected my comings and goings a bit, but I just ensured that I was either at home or Madam Beatrice's during those curfew hours.

In that period you had to make the most of the hours you had before the curfew hours and your time with Kwamena took on a new urgency. Ever since you gave him the blue dress he seemed even more eager to see you more often. You must admit that you experienced the pleasure that he was capable of evoking, especially in contrast to Colonel Duah. Kwamena's performance seemed both a mixture of the most beautiful emotional concern as well as the crassest of bestial expressions, when his face contorted into a frightening portrait of nothing but base energy. "You satisfy me like no other woman," he said.

"You are excellent yourself."

He smiled for a long time and then asked, "Will you marry me?"

"What!" Exclaimed you with complete surprise, because the last thing you would expect from him was a marriage proposal. You thought he was joking and he meant the proposal merely as a compliment. So you said in jest, "It could not have been that good."

He propped himself up on the bed with his elbows and then he asked that you turn on the light. It was only then that you could see on his face how serious he looked as he said, "I mean every word I'm saying. I want you to be my wife."

And this time, because you knew he was serious, you thought of all the arguments you could muster against the proposal. You told him that he was a married man with children and you were a prostitute to be used and then discarded, and that society would never leave you two in peace if you got married. You knew you had to think of whatever ammunition you could to persuade him to change his mind, whether or not you believed in what you said. You saw him get up from the bed and begin to pace the room and then you heard him say, "I know that you're surprised. But I have been thinking about this for a long time. I have weighed things over very carefully and I'm sure I love you. I'm happy when I'm with you and I'm miserable when I'm not. You give me the most pleasant sensations, plus you challenge my mind. I love you. I want you to be my wife, Mary."

You were recovering from your surprise when you said, "I think you are confusing physical desire with love. We give each other pleasure and that is all there is to it."

"No! I know infatuation and this isn't just a little child's infatuation. I feel you in me, in my heart, in my veins, my blood. You have taken possession of me. You are me. This is love."

"But you hardly know me, and you cannot love someone you do not know. You may come to despise me once you get to know what kind of person I am."

"I know you enough. My love will prevail. Can't you see? I love you completely."

You did not know how to argue with this, as he seemed determined to convince you that he really loved you, so that you were not sure he would even listen to reason whether it be yours or his. And yet somehow you hoped you could find the voice to caution him. "I thought you said you would never leave your wife," you said.

"I can change my mind."

You thought of him as a hypocrite who would not care to make and break promises when it suited him. "It will not work," said you. "What will your friends say?"

"I don't care what anybody says. It is enough that I love you. I don't expect an answer from you right now. I know it's all sudden and unexpected. Take your time and think about it. I will be back."

After he said that, you both dressed without talking and then he smiled at you and paid you and then kissed your hand and left you with your heavy thoughts.

రావ

You all heard the news with complete disbelief and shock. You knew her so well and appreciated her vivaciousness so much that you had expected her to be there that day, even if she had contracted AIDS. Murder seemed like an alien disease suddenly injected into your veins. Why would anyone kill Araba, who hurt nobody and just hoped to marry a man who would take care of her and help her raise a family? Apart from her use of drugs, as far as you knew Araba kept to herself. The most troubling thing was that she had been killed right underneath the mango tree, only three feet from the building, with her body stabbed several times. Did it have anything to do with the over-vigilance of the soldiers, who took advantage of the national curfew to molest or rape or even kill those caught abroad in its forbidden hours? Had Araba strayed outside and gotten herself killed? Had the shadows of night so inadequately failed to protect her?

Madam Beatrice's women were quiet and subdued although it felt like a storm was lurking beneath the calm. And even though Madam Beatrice seemed as troubled as all the women, she tried to maintain calm. She walked from woman to woman forcing herself to smile and patting everyone on the back, saying that there was nothing to fear. You knew that to overcome the sadness you had to make believe somehow that the grief and fear were not right. You told the other women that although what happened was terrible, the initial reaction of sorrow must give way to the need to continue with business. You thought you could see gratitude in Madam Beatrice's face.

Said she, "I know this is a very difficult time for all of us. It has never happened to any of my girls. Everything has worked out so well, it's unusual what has happened to Araba. Because she was our friend, we must mourn for her. And as we mourn, I also realize that some of you are afraid for your own safety. You needn't be. This won't happen again, trust me. This afternoon, I hired two guards."

Madam Beatrice called for the two men and they appeared from behind the counter where they had been standing all the time. They were tall and muscular and both wore black tee shirts and black jeans, and they did not smile or show any emotion as Madam Beatrice went on: "These are Eshun and Atta. I can understand if any or even all of you don't feel like working tonight. If you feel that way, I'd prefer that you leave right away. Perhaps you need to sleep over this sad news and return tomorrow, or even later. But, if we can, this place must stay open for business tonight. We must try to keep our customers happy, even if it will be hard."

"I will stay," said you and then you looked over at Akwele with the hope that she would join you in expressing support for Madam Beatrice so that the others would follow. But Akwele seemed confused and she looked back at you as if seeking some help.

You could not sustain the searching scrutiny of her eyes, so you looked away and left her to make her choices by herself. "I'm sorry," said she. "I don't think I can work tonight." And then she burst out into a stream of noisy sobbing that was as loud as a little baby's, and she seemed completely out of control and she kept saying, "I'm sorry. I'm sorry. You don't understand. I'm so sorry. I wish this had never happened."

"Don't worry, Akwele," said Madam Beatrice as she placed a tender hand over Akwele's shoulder. "I understand." Madam Beatrice smiled forcibly and knelt next to Akwele and gave her a handkerchief and then said, "Eshun will escort you out when you are ready to leave."

The Sun by Night

You knew that by choosing to stay you were conniving with Madam Beatrice in the indirect but callous request that the women stay and work that night. But more importantly for you, you knew you had to try to fill the void that Araba's death caused. You needed to do something to keep her as far out of your mind as you could. Akwele said between sobs, "God be with you."

"Sleep well," said you, and she smiled painfully and you watched her leave with Eshun beside her. When they had left, you imagined Akwele walking outside with the shadows awaiting her, as nothing but sadness would become her, and you thought to yourself that today especially she would need their protection. But the haunt of Araba's death returned when your mind got calmer and on further reflection the (un)timeliness of her death seemed too convenient, like a *deus ex machina* of sorts for Madam Beatrice's business. What if the story of her AIDS got out?

That night, with Araba's death still haunting you, you became aware of yourself more than ever before when you asked yourself who you were. It was as if her death had lent you a telescope to look inside where the kaleidoscopic array of your selves was magnified. You began by hoping that perhaps you were a prostitute dirtier and purer than priests. And if anyone would want to know more, then you would tell him or her that you were the eyes that saw visions while you were awake and that dreamt them while you were asleep. You would say that you were the eyes lent to friends who see what you do not see so that you end up seeing what they see. You were the eyes with trifocal vision, and the eyes behind the head that see the knife behind you and not just the smile in front. You were also the sea where all who need comfort could come to rest because you gave of yourself and you took all you could take.

You were the ugly and the wise. You opened eyes like walking on a bleak day and bumping into an old man with elephantiasis in tattered clothes behind the veneer of whose pain lay layers of unquestionable joy and wisdom. You would say that you were where the tired could find rest and the disturbed could find meditation and the sad could find empathy. The unknown hum at night that brought peace and the piercing yowl that broke into sweet dreams, because the sea had its breeze and it had its waves and it had its dolphins and it had its predatory sharks. But you were afraid that asking more questions as to who you were was as futile as a hunger without an appetite. Or asking the question where does the human body begin and where does it end?

You left your bungalow the next day trying your best to relieve the stress you felt pounding away in your head, mostly because of Araba's death and Kwamena's marriage proposal and the possibility that the man in the coat and shades would return. You arrived at Madam Beatrice's and walked over to the corner of the main chamber and waited for customers. But the first person to enter the room was Kwamena and you had an immediate fear that he was going to nag you with his marriage proposal again. But he seemed not to notice you and walked over instead to Akwele. For quite a long time the two of them were in deep conversation, and that surprised you because you did not know that the two had anything of mutual interest. You felt as if they were building a force to which you could lend no energy. And you felt a little jealous even though you believed that you should not. Several minutes later Kwamena walked over to you.

And when you went to a room with him, you asked him against your own judgment what he was talking to Akwele about and his reaction surprised you. He seemed extremely troubled by that question and he appeared a little nervous too. You were not sure of it but he even seemed afraid of you and you could not understand why.

Said he, "We didn't talk about much. We were just making small conversation."

You wanted to leave it there but your annoying curiosity prompted you to ask, "Since when have you been making small conversation with anybody here but me?"

"You are not jealous, are you?"

"You must know that I do not get jealous."

He did not reply to that and you believed then that he had talked to Akwele to find out more about you, so that he would know how to win you and make you agree to marry him. You were sure of that once it entered your mind. It was not until much later that you figured out that they must have been talking about something entirely different. As Kwamena undressed, you tried to determine if he matched the size of the man in the coat but you could not tell because that man was so well hidden in his baggy clothing.

That night Kwamena was a bit tentative and he was not as energetic or as talkative as before and he had an absent-minded look. He paid and left the room unusually early with the excuse that he did not want to get caught in the curfew, even though it was only nine o'clock. That had you so troubled that against your instincts you went to the hall seeking Akwele. You observed Akwele's haggard look and your heart felt heavy for her because you knew she was still struggling with Araba's death, and you tried your best to console her and in that effort you realized that you too were purging yourself of the anguish.

Later that night, Araba's death came back again and seemed to echo in the darkness with an eerie quiet that appeared to permeate the air and foul and stifle it as you walked into the shadows to be protected. The shadows emboldened you and for a long time you were not afraid of what the world thought of you. But the comfort was brief because curiously at that moment the thoughts that came to your mind were of your father and mother. Your father who had started his working life with the Fire Service and then won the lottery and gone on to establish a successful printing business from which he still made sure you got an income every month. And your mother who made her money by selling textiles. And the two of them who were mostly gone on business or to a social gathering, leaving you to a childhood almost devoid of parental attention.

Together they made a lot of money, and they had so much to give away because you were the only child and you were never in need of anything while growing up. And then, when you got your degree in economics and joined the Ministry of Economic Planning, your parents decided they had had enough with big city life. They moved to Koforidua and you only saw them on rare occasions.

"Someone wants to kill me," said Akwele to you a few days later.

"Akwele," you almost yelled, "who wants to kill you?"

She tried to force a smile and asked, "Will you miss me if I die?"

"What kind of question is that? This is no way to talk. Is somebody trying to kill you or are you making stupid jokes?" Akwele did not respond, and as you recalled the man in the coat and shades and the gruesome murder of Araba you said almost desperately, "Akwele, talk to me."

She smiled at you and said, "I was only joking with you."

You did not know what to think because she looked deeply concerned, and although you wanted to believe that she was truly joking you still felt that there was something she was not telling you. "You have to tell me if something is bothering you because I am your friend. Akwele do you hear me?"

"Oh, I was just joking. I know it's nothing to joke about, but I have been acting silly ever since Araba died."

"I understand that and you know that we all are worried, but we are trying our best and you must do the same and not start getting ideas that anybody is trying to kill you, even if you mean it as a joke."

You took Akwele's hands in yours because you were getting increasingly concerned about her and more so because she showed so much weariness. Those were days of fear and intimidation, when soldiers with grievances took advantage of the charge in the atmosphere to settle old scores. So was it possible that Akwele had offended a powerful soldier who threatened her under the new Revolutionary Council's banner of vigilante justice? But you also knew that you could not do much for her unless she wanted or allowed you.

That night you watched her very closely between your sessions and tried to eavesdrop on her conversations and listen carefully to every word she said. You tried to detect the least strain in her voice. But you had no results, and as the night came to a close you realized how desperately you had failed to learn more about this woman who seemed to be changing into a stranger right in front of you.

Atta escorted Akwele and you out that night at eleven so you could beat the curfew, and you continued to try to burrow into Akwele's mind. But still she would not let you and she replied to your questions with very general answers that revealed nothing. You looked over at Atta, hoping in vain that he could add something to the conversation to help you get into the thoughts of your friend; and when he said nothing you looked at him even more closely and for the first time you noticed how handsome he was. Because he was dressed in a tight tee shirt all the muscles of his chest were exposed in your scrupulous vision and you could imagine them pressed against yours. In your imagination, his biceps and triceps stood out like a pair of mountains in need of exploration. You had a powerful yearning to ask him if he would like to take you home, but you realized that you really ought not compromise your professionalism, and so you said nothing.

You were twice entangled in what had become your main form of speech since he proposed to you and you tried your best to discourage him. And he seemed trapped in the extremes where he was either lethargic and uninterested or vigorous and completely absorbed. Twice you joined in the flesh with him where a terrible feeling took control of you and displeasure replaced the ecstasy you had expected. And you wanted to reach with both hands for Kwamena's neck and strangle him. And after it was all over, you felt used and abused and spent. He had not brought up the marriage issue for some time and you thought that he had perhaps proposed in an insane moment of passion and that he did not really mean what he had said. You hoped he had gone home and thought the whole thing through, and realized that a man of his position and means could not marry a prostitute.

But then he said, "You give me the greatest pleasure. The best. I mean it. I've never been so easily satisfied. And I don't see why it has to end. I want to feel you close to me all the time."

"It does not have to end. I will be here when you need me. We can continue this arrangement for as long as we want."

"You don't understand. I don't want to come here every day seeking you, not knowing if you'll be here. I don't want to come here and have to wait my turn. I want us together all the time."

"We can arrange it so that we meet here more often." Against your principles you were proposing to him a compromise because you felt that you must give him something.

"I don't want to share you with anyone else. I want you to be my wife. Mine only, until death do us part!"

Perhaps there was the possibility that you could penetrate his dense wax of insanity and bring him to reason. "Wait a minute," said you. "You thought you loved your wife and now you think you love me?"

"Do you want me to divorce my wife to be with you?"

"That's not what I am saying. What I am saying is that your love is not guaranteed. You may wake up tomorrow and begin to feel that you do not love me anymore."

"That won't happen."

"But it is happening with your wife right now."

"What I feel for my wife is different from what I feel for you."

"How can you be sure that you will not feel a different love for another woman at some time in the future?"

"What I feel is genuine."

"You are going around in circles."

"What if I had no wife?"

"Why do you ask that question when you already have a wife?"

He did not answer that question. "You are afraid to take the risk? Life is full of risks. You are afraid I will stop loving you in the future, but that is the future and we must let the future worry about itself."

"We have consummated what we have and we do not need marriage to sanctify it and then be locked in combat for life. We do not need to spoil what we have."

What we have.

He paced the room agitatedly at an extremely fast pace. Then he stopped abruptly and came to the bed and sat next to you. You could see his face in the semi-darkness, in which he seemed to be studying you as if he were seeing you for the first time and then he asked, "What's your answer?"

"You should not put us in this situation," said you.

"All you have to do is answer me. Yes or no, will you marry me?"

He gave you no choice in the matter and you felt you could no longer be ambiguous. You answered him truthfully. "No," said you softly, hoping that you could water down the weight of what you had said.

He shrunk away from you as if you were a cold object, and then he put his face in his palms and began to massage his face while he said repeatedly, "I don't understand this."

"You do not need to understand anything, darling, because all you need to do is enjoy our moments together." You sat up on the bed so that you were sitting directly behind him and you ran your fingers over his shoulders and massaged them, and then you felt the eagerness in him despite the news you had just given him. He did not resist you and you thought to yourself that everything would be fine. But you were wrong.

ॐ∾⊛

My secretary brought me a pile of paper at the office on a day when I'd rather not work at all. She piled them one on top of the other and said, "The principal secretary said he wants you to review these reports and get back to him by the end of the week."

I rolled my eyes and my secretary smiled because she knew how demanding my boss could be: this wasn't the first time he'd asked me to perform such time-driven tasks. "Thank you, Sissi. This man will kill me one of these days. By the way how was your weekend?"

"It was nice, madam. I spent most of it with my husband and his parents. But these days you have to be careful about these soldier boys. Only last week, my aunt got caught in the curfew. Two soldier boys took all her money before letting her go."

"I know, Sissi, these are dangerous times."

"How was your weekend, madam?"

"Relaxing. Thanks."

She said my boss wanted to see me in his office. "How are you this fine morning, Ama?" he asked when I entered his office.

"I am fine, sir. And you?"

"God keeps me well." He cleared his throat and said, "Have a seat."

I sat on the cushioned chair directly in front of his huge mahogany desk. He walked to the front of the desk and sat on it. "How are you doing with the reports I sent you earlier?"

"I am beginning to go through them, sir ...."

"Good, good. The new Minister wants to talk about them early next week, so I need your analysis as soon as possible. You know how the new government is. They want everything done right away. When you don't get them what they need, you can be in some serious trouble. I know I can count on you."

I wanted to ask him if I had any choice in the matter but instead I said, "You can, sir."

"Good, good. The real reason I asked you here, though, is to tell you that I'm very pleased with your work. As always. You are intelligent, conscientious, hard-working and simply brilliant. I have approved a promotion and a twenty-per-cent pay increase for you, effective as of next month."

"Thank you very much, sir," I said, surprised.

"Thank *you*."

I didn't know how word of the raise and promotion got out, but as soon as I was back in my office a couple of my colleagues came by to chat about the promotion and pay increase. Kwasi Apim said I should take them to lunch and Yaw Kumi suggested dinner would be better. I said I'd take them out for a meal sometime later just to get rid of them. I worked non-stop until noon when I decided to take a break

The Sun by Night

I went over to the Makola Market to buy a piece of cloth I wanted to make as a gift for my mother. I parked and started walking by the roadside, where the traffic was building up and the noise of cars and human voices were at high pitch. Not far off, I saw young schoolgirls playing *ampe*. Closer, I saw someone spit on the road and another blow his nose with precision into a pothole in front and another throw litter on the road. However, I turned my attention to a debate happening behind me. It was so vociferous I had to pay attention. Five young soldiers, no more than thirty years each, in full regalia, with whips held in their hands and AK-47s strapped on their shoulders, were interrogating a market woman about fifty years old.

"You are selling this tin of sardines for how much?" A soldier asked.

"Papa soldier," the woman said, "you can have it for however much you wish."

"Answer the question," another soldier yelled.

A man standing by volunteered the information, naming the price the market woman had quoted before the soldiers arrived on the scene.

"Do you know that selling above the control price is a crime?"

Sensing the imminent danger she might face, the market woman started begging the soldiers to forgive her. One soldier had already asked for the media to be summoned. "You market women must be taught a lesson." The soldiers waited until the national media was represented by at least three newspapers. Then they stripped the market woman naked, all the while as she was begging them to spare her. They lay her across a table, and as one pinned her hands down, two held her legs while one cheered and the fifth flagellated her with vigor and enthusiasm. The media took pictures. I left and returned to work, depressed by the punishment I'd witnessed meted to the market woman, its humiliation, its irreverence, asking myself what morality could be professed in stripping a woman naked in the marketplace and flagellating her. But, worse, I was ashamed of my own cowardice, my own silence in the face of such brutal power. Two days later, I would read about the flagellation in the newspapers.

So that evening you felt you had to cleanse yourself of all that was happening within and without you. The sand slipped through your fingers while the wind blew across the seashore where you went that evening. The wind blasted at you as if hurrying to empty itself and all over the shore was a calmness within the movement of the waves. For a while, you walked slowly and stepped on marbles and broken sticks and shells scattered all over the shore. You walked back and forth like that for a long time until the dusk turned to a dark blanket. And all you could see were the silhouettes of a few people and the coconut trees. And then you felt the first surge of energy run through you like a current of electricity and you felt prompted by that impulse to start trotting along the seashore until the second jolt passed through you. And you reached under your dress and shed what was underneath. But even that did not seem to be enough so you shed the rest of your clothing and you felt the wind blow freely on your bare skin.

You looked out to the sea and you could see a few brave ones swimming even though it was cold, and you too ran to the sea and jumped into its vastness. You began to swim without knowing where you were swimming. A group of people were close by and they noticed you but they did not say anything, and yet you felt the ripples created by their moving bodies and they were pleasant. And yet at the same time you felt as if you were too close to them so that you felt uncomfortable. For a moment it even felt that you could feel their breath on your skin as though carried by the whiff of wind blowing across the sea. You were like swimming to them and embracing them and telling them that you loved them even though you did not know them.

You told yourself that it must be enough that you were all swimming in the same sea, and that you could feel each ripple they created, so that it did not matter what their identities were, nor if you never saw them again. And yet even as you thought those thoughts you were afraid that if you were to make that bold move toward them, you might disturb the silent tranquility that existed between them and you at that moment. And you all were suspended in oceanic oneness between fear and hope, and because of that fear you kept the distance.

Then the group got out of the sea and you saw them walking away and talking happily. You watched the coconut trees rising elegantly into the sky as the tide gyrated and jolted the coconut trees into a flit. The wind gifted a chilling sting brushing your face as you listened to the song of the shore so soft within the breeze. You watched the hollow imprints of the group's footprints on the sands. Then the wind rose again and picked up the grains of sand like little ants in mid-air, then the sands scattered down like a strained gasp in space in the relapse of the wind as though with final breath. You watched the hollow imprints of the group fade away as the coconut trees still stretched leisurely amid the gyrations of the tide; and you felt a weight lifted from you and you too got out and began walking on the shore, and then you began to ran.

You ran like a sprinter who sees the finish line but who never reaches it, like the mirage of the horizon, and so continues at full speed; and you ran like a hunted bird that knows not where to go except to escape its assailants. You ran like a falling star shedding the weight of its glow, and you ran with the force of splattering rain in a thunderstorm. You ran on and on but you did not know your destination – if ever there were one.

৯৽৹

Several months had passed since Araba died and life seemed to have returned to normal at Madam Beatrice's. None of the women protested when Madam Beatrice sent Atta and Eshun away saying that they were no longer needed. You were still wary of the man in the coat and shades but you had not seen him for a long time. Akwele and you formed a stronger bond because when Araba was alive the three of you were a closely-knit group at Madam Beatrice's. Now that Araba was gone it was only natural that the space left by Araba be filled by a renewed sense of friendship between Akwele and you. Akwele lost the earlier haggard look she acquired when Araba died and she seemed to be happy.

Akwele was even happier when she learned that her brother Quartey, who had been jailed for robbery, was going to be released. She said she would help him financially to regain his feet and you had so much respect for her. You felt guilty because even though Akwele had refused to tell you what she had discussed with Kwamena that night she opened up other facets of her life to you. And you began to think that you ought to invite her home for a meal, but were afraid that if you did your secrets might unravel.

The night had been demanding for you and you were exhausted at the end of it all. You could not even talk to Akwele and so she went and huddled with some of the others. You watched with envy as the other women continued to bristle with vim and loud chatter and sparkling eyes. You looked over at Akwele who was grinning at someone else. It was difficult to believe that not long ago she had been so disturbed by Araba's death.

Madam Beatrice started a dance party that night when she turned on a stereo behind the bar counter. She moved to the center of the room and began to move slowly as if to defy the wild rhythm of the music. Her body was heavy and her movements were slow, but she had the right motions. She moved with slow grace and with the calculated movements of her legs. For a while you all watched the rhythmic movements of this big woman and for a full minute she went on alone until she began to wave to us to join her.

You were tired and did not feel like dancing, but the others followed her invitation and soon the floor was packed with dancing women, fat and slim, short and tall, awkward or graceful. But it did not matter what they looked like because together they created a beautiful dancing mosaic, united in that panorama which made their hearts lighter. And as you looked on feeling unable to join in you felt like an outsider for the first time. The feeling went deep so that you felt alien both spiritually and physically. Meanwhile, the women of Madam Beatrice were lost in that dance in which they found so meaningful an expression for one another. And soon they seemed to move in your mind, limbless as shadows of dusk scattered like air and occasionally as shadows of ghosts seeking persona in the dusky wind.

৯৯

About a year after Kwamena proposed marriage he did it again, and you turned him down again and he paced the room as he often did when he seemed disturbed. Only this time he seemed unusually perturbed, so that when he turned on the light you could see that his face was in despair. But there was also such a clear earnestness in his voice that you began to feel sorry for him. You wished he could will himself out of such imprisoning emotion and you were not sure if he loved you or simply wanted to love you. You made yourself believe that he simply wanted to love you and if he could do that he could want not to love you anymore.

"I am getting tired of asking you to marry me," said he. "But even you must understand that I won't give up easily. Can't you see that? I will make you a happy woman. I promise you that. I will give you a life free of want. You shall have anything you want. Why can't you just say yes and relieve me of this misery?"

"We have gone over this so many times and I have told you I do not want to get married."

He looked completely defeated as he said, "Is your answer no, again?"

"My answer is no."

He was quiet for a long time and then asked, "Do you love me at all? Do you have any love for me?"

"No," you said. "I do not love you."

Miserably he said, "Well then, I must leave."

You wanted to say something to make him feel a little more at ease because you knew you had brutally assaulted his ego, all the worse because you were a prostitute. But you did not want to say anything that would give him false hopes and prolong his suffering. He had to deal with your answer sooner or later, and the sooner the better for him. So you said nothing as he got dressed and you also got dressed, and he paid without saying anything or even looking at you; and it was as if he were afraid that if he looked at you he would only be reminded of his failure. He hurried out of the room, and when you looked at him you thought you could see a tear drop from his eye. And you were so uncomfortable that you looked away.

Book One: The Abused Road

After he left, you went back to the main hall and you felt drained and did not feel like working again that night. You went around talking with some of the women and trying to make light conversation when your heart felt so heavy. Akwele came and sat next to you later, and you had a strong feeling to tell her how you felt at that moment so that you might give her a chance to console you just as you had so often consoled her, and let her love you the way you loved her. And you told Akwele of Kwamena's marriage proposal and how you had turned him down and how you felt bad that you had done that. Akwele put a hand over your shoulder and said nothing and you buried your face in her lap and cried as she silently took your burden unto herself.

That night the pursuer was back after a long absence and I knew that I had to do something drastic and do it immediately, but I didn't know exactly what. My room had been ransacked by the time I got home and I suspected it was he. I asked the watchman if he'd seen anyone come around and he said he hadn't. I kept wondering when he'd had the opportunity to ransack my room.

As I stood there thinking and wondering what to do next I heard someone drive into my driveway, and I looked outside through my curtains and saw the pursuer step out of his red Peugeot even though my night watchman was sitting outside. He walked out of the car in his shades and baggy trench coat and confronted my watchman saying he wanted to see me. I overheard their conversation and I was so frustrated by the man's stubbornness that I yelled to my watchman to drive him away. But he wouldn't budge and as I looked through my curtains I saw my watchman point his stick at the pursuer and yell, "You will go or I will have your blood for my drink tonight!"

The pursuer leaped forward and punched the watchman who took a few steps back and retaliated. They went at each other and I knew I could either call the police or watch them and hope that the watchman triumphed. But what would I tell the police without possibly leading them into the other lifestyle that I'd tried so hard to keep a secret?

I was desperate for solutions and in that state of mind I took my car keys and stealthily opened the living room door. The men kept fighting, one on top now the other on top another minute. They didn't see me sneak outside. It was only when I'd started my car that I saw the pursuer look over and shove the watchman to the side and start running in my direction. But I was way ahead of him and driving off by the time he could close the distance.

It was a half-hour to midnight.

I didn't know where I was going, but I wanted to get away from home as far as I could. Without thinking about it, I realized that I was looking in my rear view mirror. In it, I saw a car approaching from far behind on the deserted streets. I slowed down, thinking that the company of a car was better than the terrible feeling of loneliness on the night streets.

I looked in my rear view mirror again and this time I realized I had made a terrible mistake, because right there behind me was the red Peugeot. I stepped on the accelerator and my car shot forward with the pursuer speeding behind. I turned corners as quickly as I could, as my car screeched and seemed on the verge of turning over. But the pursuer kept coming right behind me and I could neither lose him nor widen the distance between us. I feared that I'd die if he kept up with the chase and yet I felt there was nothing I could do. I drove to Medina turning on and off roads I didn't know. Then I made a quick turn and another quick one and zoomed forward going back towards Legon. This time when I looked behind me I didn't see the red Peugeot and I wondered whether I'd finally eluded the pursuer or if he were playing with me. I drove to the University of Ghana campus and parked in an obscure corner.

I stayed there all night until daybreak when, feeling extremely tired, I drove back to my bungalow and approached it very cautiously to find the night watchman sleeping outside. I woke him up without yelling at him for sleeping on the job because I wasn't in any confrontational mood. "Madam, your friend is very strong. He almost killed me. He left me here when he saw you leaving. I think I scared him off."

I went back to my room to think what to do next when the phone rang and my friend the policeman told me they'd found a red Peugeot in Medina. The license plates matched the ones I'd given him a while back and he wanted me to know that the driver was dead.

"How did he die?" I asked.

"You should see the car. It's a complete mess. He drove right into a building in Medina. He must have been driving very fast, made a turn too quickly and lost control. He must have been a drug dealer or something because we found a lot of illegal drugs in the car and a stack of cash, too."

I sighed. I looked back on the events and remembered the death of Araba and how closely I had come to perhaps becoming a victim of the man in the red Peugeot. I wondered what might have happened if he'd actually caught up with me. And the fear that had for so long been simmering inside simply boiled over despite the knowledge that the man was dead. For one thing I couldn't tell for sure that he was acting alone and I couldn't convince myself that this was the end of it all. I decided to end my visits to Madam Beatrice's or suspend them until I was convinced it was safe.

To do that, however, I knew I had to tell Madam Beatrice in person and I was shocked by her reaction because she wouldn't hear it. "There's no way I will let my most prized possession walk away just like that," she said.

"Prized possession?" I asked. "Prized possession?"

Madam Beatrice showed a side of herself I'd never seen before. She frowned at me and in a determined voice said: "The clients have told me how much they like you and I have plans for you. I have tried to give you some freedom, but I want you to work for me more regularly, get away from this irregular schedule you keep here."

I was becoming angry when I said, "You don't own me and I'm free to do whatever I want and you can't stop me."

"Oh, but you are very wrong, my child. Do you think I am stupid? I haven't come this far by being ignorant. Or do you think I have not had my investigation done, Ama Badu?"

At the mention of my name my heart sank, because I knew then that she knew who I really was, and in my shock and sudden fear of her I couldn't speak.

Madam Beatrice went on: "My child, the day you first came to see me, I knew you were different. I saw no desperation in you. I saw no convincing reason why you wanted to join with me. I couldn't exactly tell what it was, but you didn't seem the type … I have been in this business a long time, you know. I can tell these things. So I had to question your motive. I had to have you investigated. I had to keep an eye on you. So rest assured that I know who you are and where you live and what you do. I know you are a very intelligent woman, so all I want to tell you is this: if you leave me, I will have to share my knowledge with the world."

"Are you threatening me?"

"I think I've said enough."

I was trapped and I knew Madam Beatrice knew it and there was nothing I could do about it except go along with her, and because of that I got a sickening feeling inside. Hoping to find some freedom in this trade by escaping the rules out there, I was now faced with its own rules and circumscriptions, and I felt so overwhelmed by it all that I don't remember much of that night except my great worry and fear. I couldn't stop wondering how far Madam Beatrice's knowledge extended.

I wasn't feeling well the next day and I didn't do much all day except sleep and clean around the house a little and watch television and worry. With the reported death of my pursuer I felt, perhaps stupidly, that I didn't need my watchman. So I let him go, although Madam Beatrice's threat continued to ring in my ears.

I still felt a little lethargic the following day as I drove to work at the Ministry of Economic Planning and picked up a copy of *The Accra Chronicler* on the way and folded it up without opening it until I got to work. And then I sat down at my desk and opened it and began to read the front page first which was filled with the usual political news that did not interest me. In any case, almost a year after the coup, with the upcoming elections and the handover to a civilian government, the political news was getting duller.

I kept opening the pages until I got to the middle page, where I saw the frightening headline WOMAN FOUND DEAD. I looked at the photograph next to the headline and my mouth opened with shock when I realized that the woman in the photograph was Akwele Oddoi.

Your Akwele. But quickly, she was becoming my Akwele, too.

For a while I could read no further than the headline as shock and disbelief washed over me until I felt completely defeated, and my heart beat faster and sweat broke across my face even though it was a cold morning.

Then after a while I managed to read on as I thought to myself what a cruel way she must have died. The shock of Akwele's death rendered me numb for a long time. I felt as if I'd die also and I couldn't function normally all day. I went to Madam Beatrice's, but I couldn't do anything that night and I could hardly hear Madam Beatrice as she spoke to me. But even she was clearly affected by Akwele's death and she spoke softly and with great effort. I felt so betrayed by her that I hardly cared about how she felt anyway.

I was angry and wanted so much to know who had been arrested for killing her. The article simply said that a man was taken into custody by the police for the murder, but the man's name wasn't given. I thought to myself that anyone who'd kill a sweet and innocent person like Akwele had to die too, and the more I thought about it, the more I became even more infuriated. And the more I became infuriated, the more I convinced myself that I had to become involved in the trial and bring whatever resources I could to it, to ensure that Akwele was avenged. Under the circumstances, I could think of no way better to do this than become a juror in Akwele's trial, if it ever came to that.

Once I got that idea I couldn't contain myself as it revived my low spirits and gave me some hope. But I knew that I couldn't just wait and hope that I'd be called to do jury duty if the murderer was brought to trial. I had to insert myself in the process by using my connections and whatever influence I had amassed in my position with the government.

A month later I started making phone calls as I learned more about the details of the case. I did it as subtly as I could in order not to arouse any unwanted suspicions. I knew then that the defense lawyer wouldn't oppose me because I recalled that I'd testified on his behalf once in a trial when he was just beginning in the profession, so he would be favorably inclined toward me. Although in this case he would not have known that I was even angry with him for taking the case on behalf of the murderer. I had no issue with the prosecutor because I was certain that he didn't know I'd ever testified for the defense lawyer and I revealed nothing to lead him to that fact.

And true to my hopes and efforts, I was summoned for jury duty; and I was sure that those like Madam Beatrice who didn't know how hard I'd worked to be on the jury would think it an unlikely coincidence. But I supposed they'd attribute it to the belief that sometimes the stars align perfectly to produce bizarre twists of events and Fate's random hand points in unlikely places. I was fully aware of the risks I was taking by going on the jury but I said to myself that she was worth it. I knew I would do all that I could to ensure that the defendant was found guilty: someone had to pay for the innocent blood of Akwele shed so brutally.

THE JOURNALIST'S NOTEBOOK

Like a python waking from sleep with tenuous venom, I rear my head again and retool my journalistic pen, ready to unleash controlled floods (if the floodgates will break). I come again because events, malevolent and benign, beseech me from my dreamless stupor to rise and vent memories like puke from poisoned entrails; a stupor imposed under the threat of imminent bodily harm, even death. Before I yield time and space to the defendant's tale, an introduction is altogether apropos. It isn't an introduction that clears mists and paves transparent ways where opaque ones existed. It isn't the introduction that leads from one obscure way to cleared paths. It is rather the introduction that sets a spiritual milieu and seeks shared connections amid unhinged forces that shock our *status quo ante* beyond precedent.

To begin the introduction, I must step back in time to the day of the coup that toppled the Military Council and replaced it with the Revolutionary Council. It began with an early morning broadcast (preceded by a spate of thundering gunfire) of a voice over the Ghana Broadcasting Corporation radio airwaves, announcing the overthrow of the Military Council and the dismissal of all members of Government with the refrain: "We have suffered for far too long." The coup leader, who would become the new Head of State, requested members of the toppled government to report to the nearest police station immediately, with an entreaty for Ghanaians to stay calm. He warned all resisting military regiments to surrender in order to avoid further bloodshed. Marshall music followed.

This wasn't the first coup to which I'd been privy. In 1966, I was a young man when Afrifa and Kotoka jettisoned President Kwame Nkrumah's Government, ending the First Republic and introducing the country to its first coup since independence on March 6, 1957. That coup lingered in my memory when about two years later the reins of government were handed to the Second Republic under Prime Minister Kofi Busia. About two years later Busia's Government would be sacked by Colonel Acheampong, who would himself be dismissed in a palace coup, installing General Akuffo as Head of State. The list continued.

While the country had seen many such military interventions, this was the first time a massive coup had been conducted successfully by the military against the military. I feared it would be bloody. I told my wife David not to go to the office and to keep a close watch over the children. This was a day to stay indoors. No school for them. She didn't want me to venture out either, but I overruled her with the excuse that as a journalist I had to go out and test the climate. We could hear sporadic gunfire even then, and despite her repeated attempts to detain me at home, including tickling my toes, I went outside. But I admit it was reckless machismo that pulled me outside, not wanting to appear weak before David and the children.

I smelled the tense air of the Asylum Down morning, entered my car and headed towards downtown Accra. And there and then, I came into contact with my first roadblock. A series of cars were backed up, as rifle-totting and shade-sporting soldiers inspected vehicles without discrimination. I inched my car forward until it was the second in line. The Jaguar in front pulled up to the roadblock. Two soldiers converged on the car, while many others stood by, scooping the surroundings. I could hear, but barely, the conversation ensuing upfront. "You be Minister of the Military Council," one soldier who seemed infatuated by his fleeting power announced. "I know you."

"I am not a minister," the driver protested. "I am just an accountant. I have a meeting downtown this morning, that's all."

"You think I craze?" the second soldier questioned. "You think I no know you? Step out! Step out now! Accountant can't get such nice car."

The driver stepped out, displaying a three-price suit ironed stiff like a tree. One soldier pricked his back with a rifle's butt and kept it there for a few seconds. Without being told, the driver had raised both hands; but he remained calm, perhaps with the confidence of his societal stature as evidenced so visibly by his Jaguar and attire. But as we would soon realize, these were new times, where stature and status symbols had to be suppressed in order to survive the dawning current of bloodletting. The soldiers began their physical interrogation by first frisking the man, whom I now recognized as Paa Tetteh, a highly successful Accra businessman.

As Tetteh was being frisked, another soldier searched his Jaguar and retrieved a briefcase. The soldiers forced Tetteh to his knees. They compelled him to open the briefcase, which he did reluctantly but with fear as a couple of strikes to his buttocks shook him out of the stupor of his wealth. In the briefcase were stacks of cash, which the now enthused soldiers caressed with relish. "You be hoarder of money? You dey run somewhere plus this money? How one man fit grab all this money? How one man fit chop all this money?"

Feebly, Tetteh announced, "It's for a business deal I need to close this morning."

"Kalabule man," one soldier yelled as he kicked Tetteh to the ground. Tetteh tried to get up, but his ribs encountered boots that doubled him over in ostensible pain. The soldiers forced him up and stripped him to his underwear. A few yards away stood an open-back truck. "You dey go barracks, corrupt man. Bad man." Tetteh was shoved into the back of the truck, where he joined another half-naked man, blood oozing from a swollen eye. I noticed that the briefcase of cash did not make it to the truck.

The soldiers now motioned me to drive up to the roadblock. I was afraid, cursing myself twenty times twenty times for not listening to David. If God spared me, I vowed, I'd listen to David always. I had just witnessed the uncompromising vehemence of new-found power, although Tetteh had driven into the wide opened jaws of anti-establishment with such a status symbol as a Jaguar and a three-piece suit, in contrast with my beaten VW Beetle and almost threadbare shirt and old jeans. But who could tell how wide the jaws of this new creature were opened? I drove up in sweat.

"Hey, who you be? Why you dey sweat like that? You be some big kalabule man or wetin?"

"Officer, I just be paper man."

"What you get for inside the car?'

"I no get nothing for inside, officer."

Two soldiers checked the car and found nothing of interest. "You get some kola for your brother?" one of the soldiers questioned.

"Sorry, my brother," I said, "I no carry money for my skin today"

The soldiers' spokesman debated my response for some tormenting seconds. "I go make you pass this time. Next time make you carry some kola for your brotherman."

I drove to the office with relief, my heart taking several minutes to return. The office was almost empty. I couldn't blame the no-showers, given the heated climate and the potential risks of venturing forward on that day. I turned on the radio to await any news of developments as I processed what had happened. Marshall music continued to dominate the airwaves, occasionally punctuated by a repeat of the earlier message announcing the Military Council's overthrow. I presumed that the coup was now a *fait accompli*. I sat down to write an editorial. My brain could not organize all the thoughts I wanted to express. I needed a break, but I was afraid to go out in view of the morning's happenings.

As I struggled with my ideas in response to the takeover, a new but familiar voice reached us on the radio. It was the army commander of the previous government announcing that the coup attempt had been foiled. He said a few disgruntled members of the Armed Forces had decided to rebel and illegally acquire control of the government. The attempt was unsuccessful. He urged Ghanaians to be calm and stay by their radio sets for further instructions.

This seesaw of events confused me. I had been critical of the Military Council's regime, but I was looking forward to the upcoming elections (about two weeks away) and the refreshing transition to civilian rule (scheduled to occur in three months). It disturbed me that all the preparations would be rendered nugatory with a change in government. Nine or so years of military rule were sufficient.

I decided not to editorialize on any of the happenings for the meantime.

Three hours later, I heard again on the airwaves that the Military Council was kaput. The voice of the uprising carried more urgency, demanding that all resisting elements surrender to avoid further bloodshed. Gunfire fouled the air throughout the day. At six o'clock, I left the office, convinced that we had a new government. I was cautious, hoping to avoid the unpleasant interrogation of the morning. Luckily, the new soldiers at the roadblocks (now increased to two on the short trip from downtown to Asylum Down) were more professional, inspecting cars quickly and waving drivers on.

That night, we heard that the Army Commander had been killed, riddled in a barrage of bullets in his attempt to quell the coup. The whereabouts of the Head of State were unknown, but the Air Force Commander was in custody. The Chief of Defense Staff would later broadcast an announcement acknowledging that the reins of government were now firmly in the hands of the Revolutionary Council. As a member of the ousted regime, he was urging all who would be planning further resistance to desist and acknowledge the new Government. For his efforts, he would later be rewarded with a position in the new Government of the Revolutionary Council.

I wrote an editorial a few days later:

One military government has replaced another, the ostensible purpose of the new coup leaders being to clean house before returning the country to civilian rule. With three months to the end of the Military Council's rule, do we need another military government? The Revolutionary Council's intervention cannot be anything but a derailment of the process towards constitutional democracy. We demand the immediate dismantling of this new bogus military apparatus in favor of civilian rule. Any housecleaning of the military is a matter for the military. The whole country cannot be held hostage to internal bad blood.

Without denigrating the call to accountability, it must not come at the expense of imminent constitutional democracy. And if we are to be honest about accountability, the very soldiers under whose auspices the housecleaning will occur are sullying their hands already. Witness the indiscriminate use of new-found power to intimidate and harass and settle scores. In only a couple of days, we have seen looting, detention of civilians without regard to guilt or innocence, some charged and some not. Witness the beatings and even rape of civilians. Accountability must begin with a clear timetable for handing over to civilian rule and an immediate cessation of the hostilities directed against civilians.

Given my editorial, the state-owned presses had a field day. One paper's response was to publish its own editorial with the heading 'An Apology for Corruption.' The paper blasted me for apologizing for a government that had illegally amassed wealth on the back of the common man. My words, the paper claimed, were tantamount to sedition. Another paper labeled me a 'reactionary bourgeoisie who deserves to be purged as an example to the elements of society tainted by their connections to the previous corrupt regime.'

I knew some form of danger was lurking, but the die was cast. Soon, the former Head of State and former Army Commander were shot by firing squad. The shootings were broadcast on Ghana television to wide applause. The body politic was enamored by the allure of compelling phrases, bewitched by the wizardry of tall promises, ensnared in the fiery seduction of power within reach, and seduced by the charisma of idealist leadership. The country drank deep as they might a beauty potion promised to the self-asserting hideous. Caught in the national vertigo, like shark after wounded flesh, students of the University of Ghana organized a rally in support of the new Government with the cry "Let the Blood Flow." Some would say the need to feed the occasional human hunger for bloodletting held sway. And the blood flowed a few days later when two other former Heads of State, together with five members of the erstwhile regime, were also executed by firing squad.

I may have gotten away with my first editorial, or postponed reckoning day, but my second got me into trouble. After the second spate of executions, the pressure from some clergy and some foreign governments grew in their appeal to the new Government to halt the killings. To this, I added my voice:

Let us not, in our search for justice, be unjust. What kind of fairness could be accorded to the recent victims of executions? These men obviously were executed without trial. Is that just? We applaud accountability, but justice is equally, if not more, important. The lack of transparency in the process is troubling. We need it to winnow the dregs from the upright. We call on the Government to halt all executions and institute clear procedures for holding trials. What is being done in the name of revolution is as dastardly as it is barbaric.

Two days later, I was in detention. They came for me at dawn. I knew they were there even before they knocked on my door. I woke up to the sound of boots. I didn't want to wake up David, so I tiptoed to the window and peeped out of the curtains. Outside, in the dawn light, I saw at least five armed soldiers apparently moving to surround my house. I feared the worst and it seemed my heart was in my mouth as I was forced to wake up David and tell her what I'd seen. I saw the panic wrecking her body and did my best to calm her.

The knock came seconds later. I opened the door.

"Na you dey write nasty stuff for your paper?"

I made no response.

"Make you come plus us."

"Give me a second," I said, "I need to put some clothes on."

A soldier followed me to the bedroom. I whispered to my wife, David, to tell my brother I had been taken away. She nodded, but was too afraid to speak. The soldier accompanying me pushed my head and ordered that I hurry up. I thought I'd never see her again and at that moment I reached for her lips and drunk deep from the salivary gourds of her mouth. The soldier ordered me to stop such nonsense. I complied. As we were stepping back into the living room, my nine-year-old daughter and seven-year-old son emerged from their room. "Daddy," said my daughter, "who are these men?"

"They are friends. Go back to sleep. I will be back soon."

My children stared on with incredulity. Even in their inexperienced youth, they must have known something was awry. I was led to the army jeep and driven to Usher Forte. There, I would share a cell with Koo Manu, businessman and former minister without portfolio, now political detainee. But, perhaps, alas, I digress.

Book Two

THE ECLIPSE OF MOTHER

The land was lost as in a whirlwind A whirlwind
of confusion. And the stage was set for The Eclipse
of Mother

THE DEFENDANT

1

A young man met us at the door. He looked about seventeen. He was bare-chested and very muscular. He wore a little cloth wrapped around his waist. "The Great One will be with you soon," he said. "Please come in."

We followed him into a little wooden structure. It was very dark inside. We stood there confused. Then our eyes adjusted to the darkness. And we felt more comfortable. The young man said he'd be back soon. He went through another door and we couldn't see him. He was gone for many minutes. I turned to my son Kubi and said, "Everything will be alright. They say this one is very good." Kubi forced himself to smile. I knew he didn't have much hope. I couldn't blame him. He couldn't be hopeful. Not when all promises had failed so far.

The young man appeared again. "The Great One will see you now. Please follow me."

He led us through a door. We came into another room. The room had a strong smell. It was an unusual smell. I looked ahead of me. The priest was sitting on a raffia mat in the middle of the room. His head was bowed. He didn't look up when we entered. I noticed that he wasn't wearing a shirt. He had on only a short raffia skirt. In the corner of the room was a carving. It looked like a very short person in a seating position. In front of the carving were a number of objects: there were some coins; also some grains of corn, I think. I noticed that there were some unfamiliar drawings on the walls. I tried, but I couldn't tell what they were. I looked at my son, Kubi. I could tell he was frightened. His face was tightly squeezed. He looked as if he wanted to run away. I wanted to tell him not to be afraid. But I didn't say anything. Even *I* was afraid of the priest, the Great One. But I tried not to show it.

The Great One was silent. For a long time. The young man who had led us to him went and stood behind him. I began to wonder if the priest could speak at all. But I knew better. I still said nothing. And Kubi was also quiet. After about five minutes, the priest spoke. Actually, he yelled. I flinched a little. Kubi took a step back. Still, the Great One didn't look up. And I didn't understand what he had yelled. I looked at the young man. "The Great One says he knows what brings you here," the young man said.

"I'm glad," I replied.

The priest yelled again, but he did not look up. The young man said, "Your son is ill and you need help."

"That's correct," I said. "How did he know that?"

"He knows everything," the young man said. "He is the Great One who kills lions with his stare, who eats the intestines of ants and drinks the blood of crabs."

I turned to my son Kubi and said, "You see, I told you he's great."

Kubi smiled, but he didn't speak.

Then the priest looked up. Now I was truly afraid. I noticed that he wore a beard. And a moustache. And the sides of his face were also full of hair. His hair fell to his neck in locks. His eyes were like eggs. Big and white. He didn't seem to have any pupils. He looked very fearful indeed. He stared at me. I felt as if he were looking through me. It was like I was there but not there at the same time. I smiled at him. He didn't smile back. My fear got worse. But I felt comforted because he looked confident. There was no sign of doubt in his face. The priest got up. He was lean. And muscular and tall. I noticed that he had a flywhisk in his hand. He said something in his strange tongue to the young man. The young man left the room. He returned with a calabash. There was water in it. The priest dipped his whisk into the water. He sprinkled the water around the room. I suspected that there was something in the water. It had a strange smell. The priest's body twitched. His face contorted. It was as if he were in pain. He began to chant some incantations. Then he moved from one side of the room to the other. We all moved back to give him more room.

The priest leaped up and down. When he went up, his head almost touched the ceiling. He danced a jerky dance. All at once he seemed to be everywhere. Moving here and there, chanting and dancing. He did this for a while. Then all of a sudden he calmed down. He sat down on the raffia mat. His body was covered with sweat. He put the whisk in front of him. Then he began to move his shoulders around. His head moved with his shoulders.

He spoke his strange tongue again. The young boy translated: "The Great One says your son has a big problem. Another man has put a curse on him. It's a position at work that will soon open up. To that man, your son is an impediment. He thinks he should get the position. Not your son. So the man wants to eliminate your son. That man has gone to a *jujuman* and put *juju* on your son. If you hadn't come to me, your son would be dead in a week. You are a lucky man. Your son is lucky."

The Great One let out a scream. I jumped back in fear. Kubi ran to the door. But he didn't open it. The young man told us not to be afraid. He continued to translate as the Great One spoke. "I will cure your son! I will take the juju from his head. Let me tell you the things you must bring me that I can use to cure your son. I need a live hen, a male sheep and a bottle of Schnapps."

"Understood," I said.

"I need them by tomorrow evening."

"I will have them by tomorrow evening."

He told us how much his services would cost. It was a very big amount. But I didn't complain. My son's health was more important. We left. I called my friend Kwamena to help me collect the items.

We went to the priest the next day. The young man we'd met the previous day collected the items. He inspected them slowly. He wanted to be sure we had everything. After a while he was satisfied. He asked me for the fee for the Great One's services. I paid him. He led us to the backyard behind the building. There was a large carving of a strange looking man. The carving was covered in places with palm leaves. The carving itself was under a palm tree. I stood in fear. I knew that Kubi was also afraid. The young man left us. Soon, the Great One and the young man came outside. The Great One took the hen we'd brought by the wings. With both hands. Then he chanted some strange words. He looked at the sky. His face looked fearful indeed. The Great One raised the hen and twisted its head. Then he broke off the head. Blood came out. The Great One aimed the neck at the carving. The blood poured over the carving. The hen struggled. Then it stopped struggling. The Great One put the carcass in front of the carving. He looked hard into the ground and said some strange words.

The young man said, "He says he's done a lot of chanting. He has spoken with the powers. Your son will soon be cured. If you do everything he tells you to do."

"We thank him dearly," I said.

He asked us to follow him. He led us into his room. He crouched over the carving in the room. Then he reached for a bottle from next to it. He gave the bottle to the young man. Then he spoke more strange words. The young man translated: "He says you should take this bottle. There is some mixture in it. He has prepared it himself. The gods led him to the forests where they showed him which herbs to pick and how to make the drink for your son. It's very powerful. Every morning your son should drink a cup after he eats his breakfast. The Great One will make more sacrifices with the things you brought today."

The young man handed us some herbs wrapped in paper. "This Sunday, your son must go to the beach at midnight. He must take a bucket with him. He must fetch some water from the sea and pour the herbs into the bucket of water and bathe with it. Your son will be cured in a month."

Kubi frowned. "Tell him we thank him very much," I said.

I took the bottle and we left. The next morning, I watched to see if Kubi would take the drink. After breakfast I saw him drink a cup. He squeezed his face. I knew that the medicine was bitter. I wished so hard. That I could give him milk. Grandpapa's milk. Just as Grandpapa had given me.

ॐ

2

We went to see Pastor-Lawyer John Amoah the next day. Kubi and I. "Pastor," I said, "My son is suffering from a strange sickness."

Of what nature, he asked?

"I don't know. He gets a lot of bodily pains. And sometimes he just vomits. I have taken him to the doctors. They haven't been able to help him."

The pastor said we should affirm our faith. "Faith motions mountains," he said. "God's poignancy permeates the impermeable. All if your spiritual predisposition to Him is amenable."

Pastor-Lawyer Amoah invited us into his living room. There was a big, white crucifix on the wall. There was a big Bible nearby. He asked us to sit. Pastor Amoah looked at my son and asked a question.

"Pardon me?" Kubi asked.

"How are you?" I said. "The pastor wants to know how you are." That is one thing with the pastor. It's often hard to understand him. Unless one knows him very well. Then maybe one will understand him. Also, Kubi was in discomfort. I didn't want him to strain his mind.

"I'm well," Kubi said.

"So you've been assailed by ailments of malicious characteristics?" the pastor asked Kubi.

"Yes, Pastor," I answered for Kubi. "He has been in severe pain."

"Are you rigidly unequivocal in your certitude of Divine prowess?"

"He believes and trusts in God," I said.

"In the Holy Trinity?"

"Yes, Pastor."

"If your reliance is unfaltering, you shall anon be cured. Join me in adjuration."

We did as he'd instructed and knelt down. Except Pastor-Lawyer Amoah who remained standing. He went and stood under the crucifix. For a long time he stared at it. Then he spread out his hand. He asked us to close our eyes. The Pastor began to pray. As far as I understood him, I paraphrase. He pleaded with God to use His power. To cure Kubi. To take the demon of illness away from Kubi. Then he started to speak in tongues. It was strange to me. I couldn't understand a word. I opened my eyes. I saw Pastor-Lawyer Amoah's body go into spasms. He rubbed his palms vigorously over Kubi's head. I was afraid for Kubi's neck. Then the Pastor stopped. He was calm again. There was a lot of sweat on his face. He told us to rise.

Kubi got up. I got up also. The pastor said that Kubi would be well. The Lord had blessed him. He asked that Kubi read Psalm 23. Every day before going to bed. He asked me to make sure that Kubi said his prayers. He said the Devil was knocking on our door. We had to take our lives away from the Devil. "Be sober, be vigilant … your adversary the Devil, like a roaring lion walketh about seeking whom he may devour." He gave us a bottle. He said it contained holy water. He asked that Kubi rub himself with it every evening.

I had a warm feeling inside as we drove back home. Like one feels after hearing good news. I was confident in the pastor. He believed. I also believed. "Did you drink the medicine the priest gave you?" I asked Kubi, as I remembered The Great One.

"Yes," Kubi said.

"We must do all we can to get you well. Your health is the most important thing now. I know it's difficult for you. But you must do what is necessary."

"But, Papa, do we have to see all these priests at the same time?"

"Whatever works works, Kubi. Now is not the time for doubts."

My son sighed. I knew that he did not agree with me.

I knew an old friend. A *mallam* with renowned powers. I drove to his house. Kubi protested, but I went anyway. My mallam friend was dressed in his smock. He was a rather tall, elegant man. He welcomed us warmly. We spoke a little and then I told him about Kubi's illness. He looked at Kubi. Then he brought out a Koran. He read many words from the book. Words I didn't understand. He prayed to Allah. He said Allah would hear our prayers. He told us to do good. To give alms to the poor. Then he prepared a drink for Kubi. Kubi drank it reluctantly. He said things would work out fine: "Insya Allah." I thanked him and left.

On the way, Kubi complained to me. "Papa, you don't need to take me around like that. I am old enough to have my own family, you know. Why do you treat me like a child?"

"Kubi," I replied, "I am your father. No matter how old you are. It is my duty to see that you are well. You think I am treating you like a child? Just because I ask you to come with me? To see a priest or a pastor or a mallam?"

"Precisely. You can't hold my hands like a little baby. I am my own man."

"Kubi, someday you will have children. No matter how old they are, to you they'll remain your children."

"Yes, they will be my children, but they will not be *children* forever."

"Someday, you will understand."

He sighed. I knew he disagreed with me. He was only showing me deference. And respect as his father. I knew I could not push that too far. Who knows what he might do if I did? I was hopeful at that moment. I had convinced him to come with me. Where I wanted to take him. He fell back in his seat. As if the conversation had exhausted him.

I just about begged Kubi. To take the bath at the beach that Sunday. As the priest had instructed. This he had to do alone. He was a grown man. I couldn't go to the beach with him. And watch him bathe. He said he would do it. It seemed more for my sake than his. I had faith as I saw a friend drive him off.

And yet I was worried for Kubi. My eldest son, Kubi.

འ~ད

3

It was Christmas Eve exactly two months later. And Kubi was fully cured. I stared proudly at him as we prepared for church. He looked sharp in his dark blue suit. He was having trouble with his tie. "How long will it take you to make that tie?" I teased him. "You can't do anything for yourself, you modern scholars."

"I'm almost ready, Papa," he said.

"Good," I said. "I will go and get your mother. Make sure your brothers and sister are ready."

I was very happy. Especially because Kubi was well again. I felt a special affection for him after what he'd been through. I left my son's room. And went to our bedroom. I saw my wife Akua Nsiah getting into her clothes. "You women take forever to dress," I said.

She smiled and asked, "Is everyone ready?"

"They will be ready soon. Let me get the schnapps for the libation."

I got the schnapps and went outside. I waited for my family. Kubi came out first. My first-born. His sister Akosua followed him. She was the second born. We waited for a while. Then my wife Akua came out. Then my other sons, Kwame and Kofi, came outside as well. They were the third and fourth children. They all stood behind me.

I remembered my father. I recalled how he used to pour libation to the ancestors. Now it was my turn. And I hoped my sons would follow when I passed. I poured a little drink on the ground. "Great God, a drink. Asaase Yaa, a drink. Nananom Nsamanfuo, accept this drink. Great Nana Kotoku, accept this drink. Nana Atakora, you the mighty one. Feared by men and women. You, whose house no one dares insult. Accept this drink. Nananom, we thank you. We thank you for seeing us through the year safely. We thank you for our lives and our health. We thank you endlessly. Accept this drink. Today, even as we thank you, we ask for your blessing. We ask that you bless us and our relatives and friends. Let no evil befall us. Open our eyes and our hearts. But as for our enemies, let them not say that they have conquered your house. The house of Nana Atakora, the mighty one ..."

I took a swipe of the schnapps after I finished pouring libation. My wife took just a little. But I was alarmed at how much Kubi took. But it was Christmas, so I didn't complain. I took the bottle from him and took another swig. "You will go to church drunk," my wife said.

"I don't get drunk," I quipped. "I am of Nana Kotoku's blood."

We went back into the living room. My wife looked at me. Then she looked at our eldest son, Kubi. She said, "You both look very nice tonight. You look like twins. You are getting to look alike more and more everyday."

She was not the first to say so. My son Kubi was twenty-five years old. I was fifty-two. Yet it was difficult to tell us apart. Perhaps I flatter myself a little. Kubi looks much younger. He has no wrinkles and no gray hair. But I do. A little gray around the temples. Yet we were the same height. We had the same facial features. A broad forehead, cheeks that look emaciated, and a square jaw. And a cleft in the chin. Neither of us had a moustache. Our shoulders were the same big and broad length. And we were both flat bellied. After studying Kubi and seeing my reflection in him, I said, "We'll be late for church. We should get going."

We went outside. The night was very dark. But the stars were bright. I decided to drive my Jaguar. My wife Akua sat in the front with me. My daughter Akosua and my son Kwame were in the back seat. There wasn't enough room in the Jaguar. Kubi and Kofi drove in the BMW. We left the Mercedes at home.

The church service was very good. A few passages were read from the Bible. We sang a few Christmas carols. Then Pastor-Lawyer Amoah delivered the sermon. His message was powerful. I think. It was difficult to follow him. But I think he spoke of the need for change. He asked us to do away with our evil ways. He said we must rededicate ourselves to God. He had given his only begotten son to us. To die so that we might live. He didn't know of any greater love. That is the message I got. But I don't know whether I got it wrong or right.

I went back home after church and slept. We went to church again on Christmas day. Kubi had to go somewhere else. So I packed the whole family into the Jaguar. Pastor-Lawyer Amoah appealed to us for funds. He needed to expand the church. I gave him a check after church. It was for a very large amount of money. He looked at the check for a long time. Then he said I was a very generous man. God would bless me. My donation to the church would be multiplied. He even went to my wife to thank her. "Are you coming to the party this afternoon?" I asked Pastor-Lawyer John Amoah.

"Without equivocation," he said.

I had invited Lawyer Ekow Dadzie to the party as well. I wasn't sure it was wise to do that. I knew that Lawyer Dadzie and Pastor-Lawyer Amoah didn't get along. It is very sad. I knew that they were very good friends once. Then Pastor Amoah went to America for another degree. His friendship with Lawyer Dadzie fell apart after he came back. But both of them were my friends. So how could I invite one and not the other? I went to Pastor Amoah's church. But I used Lawyer Dadzie whenever I needed a lawyer. Pastor Amoah was also a lawyer, but he worked for the Government. Since he was a pastor and lawyer, I often called him Pastor-Lawyer. I was hoping that they would become friends again. Maybe the party would give them the chance to shake hands.

Guests began to arrive around three o'clock. I asked my son Kubi to organize the party. He would see to it that drinks were available. He would organize to have food served. And he would organize the music also. I would devote my time to talking with my guests. Lawyer Dadzie arrived early. He was boisterous as ever. My son Kubi came over and asked him if he wanted a drink.

"Give me some whiskey," Lawyer Dadzie said. "Your son looks more and more like you everyday," he added.

I smiled proudly.

The party was fully underway by five. There were already about thirty people. They were all gathered on my lawn. My son Kubi had

Book Two: The Eclipse of Mother

some songs playing. He had a perfect mix of local and foreign songs. Lawyer Dadzie was with a large group of women. The lady's man that he is.

I noticed Pastor-Lawyer Amoah arriving. Looking from the corner of my eye. He got out of his Peugeot. He started to walk around. I walked over to him. "Welcome, Pastor-Lawyer," I said. "You know, Pastor, I have often wondered. How can you be a man of God and a lawyer at the same time? You know what they say. There is a special place in hell for lawyers."

The pastor answered that it all depended. On how one went about it. He practiced law in the spirit of God. He recalled Moses. The lawgiver and prophet. He who brought the secular and the spiritual together. He said he had to help enforce secular laws. If they were not inconsistent with God's law. The Pastor-Lawyer wasn't making much sense to me, I must confess. Perhaps, I just misunderstood him. "Alright, Pastor," I said. "But for now, why don't you enjoy yourself?"

My son Kubi came to us and asked the Pastor-Lawyer, "What will you drink, sir?"

The Pastor-Lawyer requested something soft.

"Oh Pastor Amoah," I protested, "have a little hot drink. It's Christmas."

He said drinking was not right. I said it was right if one didn't abuse it. The Pastor shook his head. But he didn't smile. He disapproved of my comment. My son brought him a glass of orange juice. The Pastor took a sip. Then my maid Aba came over with some fried meat on a tray. The Pastor and I took some meat and ate. Meanwhile, I was thinking. How could I get Pastor Amoah and Lawyer Dadzie together? I looked around. Lawyer Dadzie was still with a group of women. He seemed lost in their company. He was talking and laughing loudly. Presently, Pastor Amoah requested that we play something spiritual. He said we must glorify God always.

"But, Pastor," I said, "We sung many spiritual songs in church. Can't we play something else, for fun?" He shook his head again. But before he could speak, I said, "Pastor, there is something I want to discuss with you. Will you come with me to the living room?"

He nodded and followed me. We entered the empty living room and sat down. "Pastor," I said, "I heard your plea about expanding the church." The Pastor-Lawyer thanked me again. For my generous check that morning. "That is only the beginning," I said. "I want to help even more. I want you to call my accountant. Tell him how much money you need in total to expand the church. I shall give you half of that money. Whatever it is."

The pastor was surprised. But he looked very pleased. "This act shall invoke God's consecration and sanctification."

"God has blessed me. That is why I must give Him something back."

The Pastor-Lawyer said that not all who are blessed thought that way. We spoke for a long time. Mostly, Pastor-Lawyer Amoah continued with his case for change. He thought I was good at heart. I had the potential to become a better man. A true child of God. He urged me to give up worldly things. No more drinking. No bad music. I promised him I would change my ways. I had no intention to do so. But I didn't want him to keep lecturing me. I had heard all that before. He seemed pleased by what I said. Then I knew I had to act. Because he was in a good mood.

"Pastor, I have a request. It involves another man."

"Who?"

"Let me go and get him," I said.

I went and got Lawyer Dadzie when the Pastor didn't protest. He had his arms around two women. It was difficult to get him to follow me. "Where are we going?" he kept asking me.

I didn't respond. We entered the living room. And then I saw Pastor Amoah's face fall when he saw Lawyer Dadzie. I looked at Lawyer Dadzie. He seemed surprised too. I said, "You two were friends once. It's Christmas. Please reconcile in the spirit of the season. It makes no sense to keep this tension between you. Shake hands. Embrace."

Lawyer Dadzie said, "I am not the problem. This man went abroad where he thinks he found God, so he came back and decided he was too holy for me, his friend. I am too sinful to be his friend. This man with whom I chased women. This man with whom I drank. Now he thinks he knows God and so I can't be his friend."

Pastor Amoah replied in a stern voice, "Of time antecedent, I too strayed. Nevertheless, prospectively, I cannot countenance licentiousness."

"Licentiousness?" Lawyer Dadzie protested. "Licentiousness? You hypocrite! Or are you afraid that if I'm around you I'll reveal your secrets to the world?"

"Don't quarrel, please." I begged. "At least shake hands. Start afresh."

Lawyer Dadzie took a step forward. He staggered a little. Pastor-Lawyer Amoah said, "Degenerate and befouled by liquors imbibed senselessly like a beast. What a corrupting sight, *sans* redemptive potential."

Now Lawyer Dadzie shot back. "Very well, son of Jesus. I am a bad influence. I drink. I chase women. And you know what? I enjoy it. So why don't you get rid of your self-righteous, holier-than-thou attitude? Shake hands with me and I'll take you to a nice prostitute like I did before you left for America. Didn't you enjoy it then? I know one who is even better now and she will ..."

"Lawyer Dadzie," I interrupted.

I looked at Pastor Amoah. His face was filled with horror. Maybe he was even ashamed. I had never seen him like that before. He quickly got up and thanked me for the party. He said he could not sit there and be insulted. By a "nincompoop." I begged him to stay. But he had decided. He excused himself. Then he shook my hand and left.

"Why did you act like that?" I asked Lawyer Dadzie.

"You should have told me you'd invited him. I could've spent my time with women and not waste it trying to talk to that man."

"With an attitude like that, he will never talk to you."

"Believe me, my friend, my friendship with John Amoah is beyond hope. Perhaps he is truly repulsed by my lifestyle. Or he may be afraid of me because I know too much: I have seen him at his worst. Or perhaps he fears that I will corrupt him."

"You speak too harshly of him."

"Let me. In the name of God he has become God. But he's only like you and me."

"I will talk to him. I will get him to come talk to you."

"Don't waste your time. And why are we wasting the party? There are women out there waiting for me."

We walked outside. It was getting darker. The guests had started dancing. I went to find my wife, Akua. I led her to the dance floor. We started dancing. Lawyer Dadzie brought a woman to the dance floor. They started dancing next to my wife and me. I moved closer to Lawyer Dadzie and asked, "Is it true that you took Pastor Amoah to a prostitute? Before he left for America?"

"Oh my friend," Lawyer Dadzie replied. "That's a story for another day. Another day."

ॐ

4

I came home late a few days later. It was almost midnight. I parked in the garage. I thought there was a snake in the corner. I needed something to kill it. I couldn't see anything in the garage. I went to the living room. Then I decided that I needed help. Perhaps my son Kubi could help me kill the snake. I went and stood outside his bedroom. I knocked. Once, twice, thrice. There was no response. How deep could he be sleeping? I knocked louder. Still, there was no response.

I tried the knob on his door. It wasn't locked. So I opened the door and stepped into his bedroom. It was dark. I turned on the light. I was surprised that he wasn't in bed. I knew he had to work the next day. But he was twenty-five years old. I could no longer tell him what he must do and not do. I also noticed that he had a Bible and Koran in his room. The Bible and Koran were lying side by side. In the middle was a flywhisk. It was a curious sight.

I stepped out of his bedroom. And went to the living room. Then the door to the living room opened and my son Kubi walked in. "Papa," he said, "I didn't expect you to be up so late."

"Nor did I expect you to be out so late," I said.

He didn't reply. But I could tell he wanted to tell me something. He seemed to be thinking. Maybe he was trying to make up his mind. "I thought I saw a snake in the garage," I said. "I wanted you to help me kill it."

"Can't we do it tomorrow, Papa?" he asked.

"Tomorrow? You want to leave a snake in the garage all night?"

"I'm very tired, Papa."

I looked closer at him. He did look tired. His hair was disheveled. His eyes looked weary. "Have you been out drinking?"

He laughed a fake laugh. "Drinking? Drinking what, Papa?"

"I don't know. You look exhausted."

"I'm just a little tired."

"Are you doing drugs?"

"Papa, have you ever seen me do drugs?"

"No, that's why I'm asking."

"No, I haven't been doing drugs."

"Kubi, you are an adult. You can do whatever you want. But if you have a problem, you should tell me. You hear?"

"Papa, I am fine. I was just out with some friends, that's all. Let's get the snake in the garage."

We walked to the kitchen and got two pestles. Then we went to the garage. I turned on the light. We looked for the snake. Cautiously. But we couldn't find it. Maybe my eyes had deceived me. We went back to the kitchen and put the pestles away. "Sleep well," I told Kubi. I smelled strong cologne on him. And there was another smell too. I couldn't tell what it was. It was something stale. The cologne made it very difficult to tell. Kubi went to bed. I went outside and found the night watchman. I told him I'd seen a snake in the garage. I told him to look out for it. Then I went back to the living room. I still tried to figure out that lingering smell on Kubi. I wasn't successful. I found myself thinking of Grandpapa's milk. The milk he fed me.

After a while, I too went to bed.

కా ్

5

My recent troubles started when I married a second wife. Not to mention my involvement in politics. It's hard to know where to begin. Maybe I am old. But there were days when things were different. When a man could take many wives. And nobody complained. In fact, they praised one for it. And then they respected one when one had many children. But these are modern days. So called. They are getting in the way. It is like a tree that falls in one's way. And suddenly one can't use the road one is used to. So here I am, walking the road I know. The path of my fathers and their fathers. But now it is an abused road. Yes, used and abused and mislabeled. And yet, after all, the elders said it. Even if the back of your teeth tastes sour, it's there that your tongue licks. But now they lecture me like a child. They say one should do this and not do that. But perhaps I am a ranting old man. I need to go back and start from somewhere.

It was raining heavily. Thick, like grains of rice. On rainy days like that one can't do much. One stays indoors close to the fire. Or one keeps close to a woman. I had been in the city for many years. And I didn't like city girls. They were too arrogant. And they were spoilt. I had tried a couple. And I decided I needed an authentic woman from the village. A woman not spoilt by the ways of the city. The city with all its corruption and bad modern ways. I had sent word already to my mother in the village. I told her to find me a wife. She sent word back that she was looking. But it was taking too long. I knew my mother was trying to find me a perfect woman. Mothers! They are never happy with our women. I decided to go and try myself.

Book Two: The Eclipse of Mother

So I went to the village. It started raining badly on my first day there. The gods were against me. I thought so as I stood inside and looked outside. This was the room where I used to sleep before I left for the city. I was trying to remember all the things I'd done in there. But I couldn't think for long. Because I saw her.

What a woman she had turned out to be. She was trotting outside in the rain. I could tell she was struggling to make it through. The darkness played games with my vision. Yet she stood out. She ran like a star at night. All my previous desires were coming back. And I knew I had to meet her. She was moving away quickly. I had to act. I ran outside. I didn't care that I was getting wet. I ran towards my gem. She didn't see me at first. But she noticed me as I approached her. Then she stopped running and turned around. She seemed to be afraid of me as she wiped her face. I couldn't allow her to be afraid of me. I had to take her fear away. Before it became a bridge between us.

"Lady," I said, "I saw you running in the rain. I wonder if you're lost. Or perhaps you're far from home? Maybe you can come inside and wait until the rain stops."

"I'm on my way home." Her voice was seductive as fire. It sounded like a thousand flutes. She turned and prepared to leave me.

"Wait," I said. "You don't have to run in this rain. You could become ill. How far are you going?"

"Zongo," she said.

"That will take you a long time." I pointed to Mother's house and said, "Please come in until it stops raining."

"I have to go. Thank you for the offer."

"Why don't you want to come in the house with me?"

She hesitated a little before saying, "I don't know you."

My heart beat badly. The evil and mistrust of the city had come to our town. I said, "Lady, do you think I will do you harm? Don't you know my father, Opanin Mensah?"

I could tell she recognized the name. My father was quite famous in the town. She wiped the rain from her face again. She looked at me carefully. Then she seemed to smile. "Oh, you are Koo Manu. You've changed a little," she said. "I can wait on your verandah."

We walked back through the mad rain. Through the loud thunder and the flashes of lightening. I led her on home. We went to the verandah in front of my room. I took out a towel I had brought from the city. I gave it to her. She took it and wiped her body. I turned on the light in the room. It shone on the verandah. I saw the full presence of her. Before, I had seen an outline of beauty. But she was like an immaculate ornament in the light. I couldn't help it. My eyes traveled slowly from her plaited hair downward. I looked as she busied herself wiping her body. Her eyelashes went up one by one. Isolated by the wetness. Like something in prayer to the sky. Her eyebrows were full. Her eyes did not glare carelessly like the sun. They were elegant. Like the full moon. Full and red-bright lips contrasted with skin that was the darkest charcoal in color. Her skin was smooth. Smoother than the back of a calabash. Pardon me, if I am crass. But how can I stop now? I went down to the breasts. The rain plastered her dress to two firm fists. A flat stomach, a pair of rounded hips. She had youthful splendor. Vigor. Vitality.

She finished wiping herself and gave me the towel. She still stood in the middle of the verandah. I walked behind her. I pretended I was looking for something. Now I saw her from behind. I caught a good glimpse. Her behind moved away from her waist. Her waist was thin like the neck of a gourd. And her behind was full. I was making plans already. I could spend one million years with her. She had grown well. From the earlier years when I had noticed her. She had potential even then. So long ago. Now, the potential was fully fulfilled.

"Please sit down," I said. She sat on a stool and thanked me. "What is your name, lady?" I asked, pretending I didn't know.

"Ama Owusu," she said.

"I'm surprised I haven't noticed you before," I said, still pretending. "A woman as beautiful as you." She didn't say anything. But her face glowed. And I knew she was happy. "Maybe it's because I've been gone from the town for so long."

She looked at me with interest. "Where have you been?"

"I have been in Accra for the past few years."

"No wonder. I thought I could easily recognize just about everybody in the town."

"It's a big town," I said. She shrugged. I added, "May I ask you how old you are?" I guessed it already. But I wanted to be sure.

She seemed surprised by that question. Still, she answered: "Eighteen years."

She had matured a lot in the years while I was gone. Eighteen was good for me. I was only seven years older. "Lady, may I ask you who your father is?" I knew the answer. But I wanted confirmation.

Again she hesitated. But she answered, "Kofi Appiah." That was all the information I needed. I would win her and then I would talk to my mother. I only had a week to do that. I listened to the joyous music of falling rain. And I was still planning. Later, I looked on as she walked into the night. The night was like a morning cast in glorious sea. Abundantly beautiful because she was in it.

Forgive me if my sentiments seem impertinent.

৵৶

6

I knocked on the door to Mother's room. She told me to come in. "City boy. How are you?" Mother was a very large woman. And looked bigger because she was short. She was very good-humored.

How should I answer that question? I was burning with desire. I had gone through four days of serious courtship. Four days of emotional heat. Ever since I met Ama Owusu. I had seen her several times since. We'd spoken for long periods. The more we talked, the more I liked her. I was eager to marry. She seemed perfectly suited to be my wife. I didn't want to delay. So I had to make my intentions known.

Now my mother smiled at me. And I smiled back at her. "Maamie, I have something important to tell you," I said.

"Come and sit down then, city boy." She pointed to a spot on the bed next to her. I sat. I suddenly became nervous. Why should I be nervous? Mother had been telling me to get married. She had warned me not to be tempted by city girls. "They will suck you dry and then leave you," she said. Now I had found a wife in the town. What she wanted. I was convinced that all would be well.

"I have good news, Maamie," I said and paused. It is always good to build tension. News is always better if told little by little. Mother's eyes flashed curiously. But she said nothing. I continued, "Maamie, you know how you want me to get married? How you always say I'm growing old and should take a wife?"

"Don't worry, son," Mother said. "I think I have found you the perfect woman."

I hoped she was joking. I didn't want her to be disappointed. To learn that I had made a choice over hers. I knew she had my best interests in mind. She wouldn't pick a bad woman for me. But it was too late now. I put my hand over hers and said, "Maamie, I have found a woman I like. I want you and Papa to ask for her hand."

"You young men are very impatient. Just when I thought I'd go and knock on the door of Agya Baako for her daughter Akua Nsiah's hand in marriage for you. Now here you are telling me you have found a woman by yourself. But what can I say? If you have made a choice, I must bless you and give you my help. But even you know that there are rules we must follow, so you must tell me who this woman is. Who are her parents?"

"Maamie, she is a very beautiful woman. Her name is Ama Owusu and her father is …"

"Huh!" Mother frowned. "Ama Owusu? The daughter of Kofi Appiah, the mechanic?"

I knew something wasn't right. Mother's face told me plenty. "Is something wrong?" I asked.

"Everything is wrong. You can't marry her. You can't marry a woman like that."

"But why, Maamie? I can marry any woman I want."

102

Book Two: The Eclipse of Mother

"You will not marry her! I forbid you!"

I was getting angry with my mother. "But, Maamie, why?"

"Ama Owusu has a reputation." My heart sank. A reputation!

Mother said, "She's very disrespectful. Everybody knows her for that."

My heart rose. I had feared something worse. That she was of loose virtue or something. But merely disrespectful? She was beautiful. It didn't matter if she was disrespectful. I laughed loudly and said, "Is that all? She is disrespectful? She can overcome that."

"You don't want a woman like that for a wife. She will bring you nothing but trouble and shame."

"Maamie, those old ways are over. The days when parents' every command was obeyed. These are modern times. All you can say is that she's disrespectful. That's nothing. And, I don't care. I will marry her."

"Don't be foolish. You don't have to pick a woman like her. What is it about her that you like so much? Is it her beauty? Don't let that deceive you. Beauty is not what it takes to be a good wife. I have found you a good woman. Marry Akua Nsiah. Forget Ama Owusu. She has no character."

"I can't, Maamie. I love her."

"Love? You young men nowadays are very stupid. Love. What is love? You see a beautiful woman and you think you love her because you want to sleep with her …"

"Maamie …"

"Shut up and let me speak. Love is what you feel after you've married a woman and felt the warmth of her bed, the sweetness of her meals, the comfort of her character. It is not that feeling you get in your manhood. A marriage built on that will not last. But a marriage with foundation is the one where your wife, your husband, has a good character."

It was ironic. Mother's own marriage wasn't a perfect model. She and Father were not divorced. But they lived in different homes. Like strangers. If she knew so much about marriage, why this? I told her what I was thinking. "I know my marriage is not a very good example. But sometimes the best teacher is not the best player. I have lived longer than you. Your generation thinks it knows everything, that it has the answers to all our problems. You think your elders are backward and even stupid. You think we belong in an age long gone. Foreigners have come and taught you things, their ways. And you have accepted their ways wholesale as if you have no minds of your own. We were doing well on our own before they came, if you don't know. Don't throw away the wisdom of your ancestors."

"But Maamie, I've not done anything wrong. I'm doing exactly what you have asked. I want to get married. I haven't done what some do these days. There are some who marry without even telling their parents. Or they tell them when it's too late. But not me. I want you to help me, Maamie."

"You have done the right thing. By coming to me you have averted a big error. I will ask for Akua Nsiah's hand for you. Forget Ama Owusu. You'll see, everything will be perfect."

"Maamie," I protested. "I don't want Akua Nsiah. I don't even know who she is."

"And you know Ama Owusu?"

"Yes. I have seen her. I have spoken with her."

"And you think that is enough? Be careful of appearances. The elders say that you see the crab's eyes and you say they are splinters of wood. You don't need to know a woman to marry her. What you do is investigate until you know she has a good character. I've done all the work for you. I've asked a lot about her character. I know Akua Nsiah is good for you. Everybody speaks well of her. She has character. That is what you need."

"But, Maamie, what if I don't like her?"

"You will learn to like her. You will like her if she's a good woman. And she is a good woman. Plus Ama Owusu's mother is a Northerner. You need a full-blooded Asante woman."

"That's the real reason why you oppose her, isn't it? You don't like her because she has Northern roots."

"Don't be silly … but even if that were the case, what's wrong with marrying one of your own? You want your children to be with you as you grow old, not far away somewhere."

"Maamie, she was born here …"

"But her mother is from the North. Asante's are matrilineal; therefore, she isn't Asante."

"I don't care."

"I have spoken."

"But …"

"I know this is difficult for you now. Why don't you take a little more time? Go back to the city, think about it and come back when you are sure."

That seemed reasonable. I was still very disappointed. But I would think about it a little. I wouldn't even say anything to Father for now. The sun was beginning to rise. The household would soon be filled. My sisters, three of whom had children. The other two were unmarried yet. And my three brothers. I walked out into the early weather. And I resolved that I would return for Ama Owusu. I would marry Ama Owusu. No one would stop me.

I went to see Father. I didn't mention Ama Owusu. The old man was growing even older. It bothered me to see him dwindle so. This man who used to be so vigorous once. He'd lost most of his hair. The rest made his head look funny. Like an abandoned football field. And the hair left was completely white. Once he was a burly man. But now he seemed scorched, like dry corn. Once his voice boomed like angry thunder. But now it wavered like trickling water from rooftops. I knew he was dying slowly. But that is another subject. We spoke for a short time. He wished me a safe journey back to Accra. I left, feeling a little sad. And very afraid that he would die soon. I thought of Grandpapa. I found myself wishing for some of his milk.

7

The trip back to Accra was short. I missed the adventure of it. The street peddlers as they assaulted the passengers at a bus stop. Those with whom I often made conversation. I would talk with them or buy an orange or doughnut. But that day, I didn't notice them. My mind was troubled. So I kept to myself. And I kept thinking. I had a headache by the time we got to Accra. I went home and slept for two hours. It was evening when I woke up. I knew that it would be dark soon. I needed release from my lonely thoughts. I went to find my friend Kwamena. He had married once. His wife had left him for another man. He said he'd never marry again. "Only fools marry," he'd say. "I was a fool once. I won't be a fool twice. After all, you don't step on a fool's balls twice."

I found Kwamena sitting in front of his house at Because. He shared it with his brother Kuuku. "You didn't go to the park today?" I asked him.

"No. I'm a bit tired."

I sat next to him on a stool. "How is it?"

"We dey inside," he said, "contrey broke or contrey no broke."

I moved closer. "Listen, Kwamena, I need to talk with you."

"How much will you pay me for that?"

I ignored his question. "Let's go get something to eat. I will tell you while we eat."

He didn't hesitate. Kwamena liked to eat. But he never got fat. Some people are like that. We walked to Abeka Lapaz. We entered Paradise Chop Bar. In front were multicolored bead curtains. The curtains sang a rustling song as we entered. Trust Emilia to have something going on. At any hour. She knew how to make money. It was empty when we entered. The room was like a long passageway. On each side were rows of tables. And chairs. Emilia was at the very end of the passageway. She was preparing *fufu* in a mortar. A young man was pounding the *fufu* with a pestle. His body was covered with sweat. Pounding fufu is not easy.

Playing the fool, Kwamena yelled "Hey, Emilia, why is this boy sweating into the fufu like that? Can't you buy him a towel to wipe himself? With all the money you make?"

"Kwamena, don't disturb my ears," Emilia said. To me she said, "Tell me what you want, my gentleman."

"But you, Emilia, you know what we want and you must still ask," Kwamena said. "Give us the usual." Usual meant fufu and palm soup with goat meat.

Emilia said, 'It will be ready soon, please be patient."

"Get yourself more help, Emilia," Kwamena said. "You can't keep people waiting all the time. What kind of business is this?"

"The best," Emilia replied. And she was right. She made the best *fufu* in town. "Two minutes, my gentlemen. I promise you."

We chose a table at the back of the room. We sat facing each other. Kwamena was silent. I knew he wanted me to tell him what was on my mind. But my mind was a mess. I didn't know where to begin. "Why are you so silent, Koo?" he asked me. "Don't you have something to tell me?"

"Yes, yes." I tried to gather my thoughts. "Kwamena, I don't want you to laugh."

"I won't laugh."

"My friend, I have found a woman."

"And so what?"

"You don't understand. I love her."

Kwamena laughed. "Only fools fall in love."

"Be serious, Kwamena."

He waved his hand. As if dismissing me. "It is all in your mind. If you allow it, your mind will make you fall in love."

"That's nonsense. This is a matter of the heart, not the mind."

"Not true."

"What are you saying? That we love with our minds?"

"That is where it starts. It tells your heart what to do."

Emilia's assistant approached us. "What do you want to drink?" he asked.

"Give us two bottles of beer."

"Beer?" Kwamena protested. "I don't have money for that."

"I will pay."

The assistant left us.

"Who is this woman you say you love?" Kwamena queried.

"I met her when I went back home. To visit my parents. I knew of her a long time ago. Before I left the town. I don't think she noticed me in those days. She's grown so beautiful. Kwamena, you should see her. Mmmh… mmmh… I said to myself, this is a woman."

"Such women bring trouble."

"You sound like my mother. I don't care if she brings trouble."

Emilia's assistant brought us the beer.

"You are being a fool. But if that is what you want, then go for it. What's the trouble? Or is your mouth dead you can't talk to her?"

"I want to marry her."

"My brother, I have told you several times that …"

"Only fools marry," I completed the phrase for him.

"You know that I was a fool once and got married. I will never do that again. If you like a woman, take her to bed and get what you want. Then leave her. Or if you don't want to leave her, keep taking her to bed. Then when Christmas comes, leave her. Otherwise, you will have to buy her a gift. After Christmas, get back with her. It's that simple. It saves you a lot of trouble."

"For you, not me. I need some good advice, so stop talking nonsense."

"I've warned you. I don't think you should marry her."

"I feel her in me, Kwamena. I want her."

"You've heard my view."

I was silent. And then I said, "There's more, Kwamena. I told my mother I wanted to marry her. And Mother said no."

"I don't blame her. She must have told you to take your time as any good mother would."

"That's not what she said. She said I shouldn't marry her. Why? Because she has no character, Mother says. That she has a reputation for being disrespectful. Also, she's not a full-blooded Asante. And you know how the old ones are. They fear their progeny will be lost."

"Your mother lives in the town with her. She hears things … she knows. Listen to your mother, my friend."

"How, Kwamena? How? I love this woman. Ama Owusu."

"Don't be foolish. You are behaving like a child."

I felt defeated. My face sunk. My chest heaved and fell with disappointment. I didn't know what to say. I smiled. But it masked my concern. It didn't reflect joy. We sat in silence. Emilia brought us the food. And we ate without speaking.

Then Kwamena started to make small talk. But I could hardly hear him. My responses were short. I felt miserable. Kwamena put a hand on my shoulder. "Don't be sad," he said. "Your mother wants the best for you. I am not that old, Koo, but I am older than you. I've seen more life than you. If that counts for anything, let me advise you to be careful. Listen to your mother. Sometimes when you are in a particular situation, you don't see the road ahead of you. You have to listen to others to point out the pitfalls, the thorns awaiting you on the road. Especially those who have traveled that road ahead of you."

I waited a long time and replied, "Kwamena, your advice is reasonable. But I won't take it."

Kwamena shrugged and repeated that I should be careful. He said he knew what was right for me. Exactly what I needed. "What?" I asked. He wouldn't say. He just asked me to follow him. And I did. We went to rectangular building of concrete painted blue. "What place is this?" I asked Kwamena. He said nothing. Instead, he led me inside. It was only then that I knew. It was a brothel. Kwamena took full advantage. I was tempted. But I felt it wasn't right. I left Kwamena there and continued on my way.

తోళ

8

Three weeks later. It was getting worse. I couldn't get Ama Owusu out of my mind. I didn't have her in Accra with me. So I relied on my memory. The images were vivid. I could recall every detail. At work. At home. With my friends. She was always on my mind. Even *I* questioned myself. I couldn't believe that I would fall prey to such emotion. But it was happening. And it seemed I couldn't help it.

She was in my dreams. Coming to me surreptitiously with a cat's stealth. Jingling her living jewels. Like bells. She smiles coyly but boldly. And rolls her eyes like dice. She stops and peers at me. My tongue is glued and can't move. She walks forward with a queen's air. Like a seesaw she sways her hips. Silently, like a crab, she steps. Then she smiles, coyly but boldly. Again rolling her eyes like dice. She squints at me. My heart drums badly. She extends her hands and pauses. They hang like claws over my head. Will they descend and touch me? She smiles, her eyes roll, she looks. Sweat befriends my face. She glides her hands and touches. She rolls her eyes again, smiles again. My knees jerk outward and I collapse. Into the ground like chopped wood. I struggle. But for now I can only await her return. But will she? I hope so. But I bear the risk. Love does not promise security.

I began to think of ways to get her. Although I had my fears. Would she reject me? That thought bothered me. She seemed to like me. But one can never know for sure. What if she were interested in another man? Or became interested in another man? I decided to go back home and win her completely. I would get Father's help this time. He had to see things my way. He was a man. He would know how I felt.

So I took one week from work. I went back home.

Book Two: The Eclipse of Mother

The first day I said nothing. But I arranged to meet with Ama. I needed to tell her my plans. I needed to know what she thought before I took further steps. We met around seven in the evening. We met in a dark junction. It was quiet, except for insects making noise. I started by asking her if she was well. I knew she knew what I was thinking. But I had to be tactful. She was very nice and polite. And she said she was well. Then I asked her what she'd been doing. With her time. Not much, she said. I walked around the subject for a long time. I told her about Accra. Its people, the climate, the culture of the place. She listened eagerly. I finally decided to tell her. My heart beat savagely. I was afraid. But it was now or never. I told her that I had to be frank. I didn't want to waste time. When one sees something one wants, one goes for it. My heart wouldn't rest. Ever since I met her. I wanted to marry her.

For a long time she said nothing. It was dark. So I couldn't tell what her face said. I feared the worst. But finally she spoke. Not to reject. Only to question. "I don't know if I can take you seriously, or if you are like all the other young men who come from the city promising marriage, only to deceive the women who listen to them and leave after they've got what they want."

I heard her well. "I do not intend to touch you until we are married. You can trust me."

She was silent again. Then she said, "You know where I live. I am not the one you should be talking to."

I was happy. Happy!!! She had invited me to ask for her hand. I intended to do that. I went to see my father the next morning. My mind was made up. Afia, my second mother, met me at the entrance. She greeted me politely. She went and got my father. He was surprised to see me so soon. But he was happy. I sat next to him.

"Everything is fine with us. How was the journey?" He asked.

"The journey was fine, Papa. As you will recall, I came to visit three weeks ago." I decided to go straight to the point. "I met a young woman when I was here. Papa, you know that I'm growing older. This young woman I met, she's very nice. I have decided to marry her, Papa. I want to give you some grandchildren."

Father nodded. His face was pleasant. "So you like this woman?"

"Yes, Papa."

"That is well. You have done your part, Koo. You have done the right thing by coming to me. The rest, you must leave to your mother and me. We will ask about her for you and then we will do what is necessary, perform the customary rites, so that she properly becomes your wife."

"You will like her, Papa."

"I know I will, Koo. But we must still inquire about her so that your home will be blessed and not filled with trouble. This young woman, what is her name?"

"Ama Owusu."

Father rubbed his hand over his face. It seemed he was trying to place the name. "Who is her father?"

"Kofi Appiah," I said.

Father's face grew grim. And I knew that all wasn't well. "Now I know who the woman is," he said. "My mind is weak these days and my memory isn't as good as it used to be. But if I recollect correctly, this woman you talk about has a reputation as a bad girl. She doesn't respect anybody, not even her elders, and she goes about insulting everybody. The elders say of certain things: they are beautiful, but they excite no envy. I didn't want to mention this to you, because I wanted to hear what you had to say, but I must tell you now. A few days ago, your mother came to see me about asking Agya Baako for his daughter's hand for you. The way to marriage is a long one that is walked with care. But the elders say that when a way is long, we cross it with our feet, not our machete. From all my inquiries, his daughter Akua Nsiah is a very good woman. That is what you need, my son. A good woman."

My world seemed to sink. What was Father's real motive? That Ama Owusu was a bad woman? Or was it her ethnicity? My hopes crushed. I couldn't shout and argue with Father. I didn't like what he was saying. But I had too much respect for him. I felt tears coming to my eyes. It took great effort to keep them away. "I've heard, Papa," I whispered.

And then we spoke about other things.

જ્જ

9

I couldn't go against my parents. I thought about the matter a long time. Then I reached a very painful decision. One of the most painful in my life. I would not marry Ama Owusu. I was too ashamed to face her. I hurried and returned to Accra. I was a very unhappy man. I kept thinking about her. I couldn't go against Mother and Father – yet how could I just turn off my feelings? Kwamena tried to cheer me up. But I still felt very sad and lonely. I thought I would go mad. I went back home the following weekend to talk to Mother. I needed somehow to quench my thirst for Ama. Maybe it would help if I had a wife. Mother was happy when I told her my new plans. I would marry her choice. The woman called Akua Nsiah. Mother praised her. She was a good woman, Mother said again and again. She was from a good family. Her reputation was perfect. There was no history of infertility in the family. No bad illnesses. She'd provide me with a good home. We would have many children.

Mother didn't waste any time at all. The next day she went to see Father. She roused him to go and see Agya Baako and Eno Yaa. I felt guilty dragging Father into this. I knew it was hard for him to walk. But what had to be done had to be done. And I know he was proud doing it. I had to return to work in Accra. So I wasn't with Mother and Father when they went. They told me about it later. All I knew about my future bride was that she was twenty years old. And she'd finished St. Monica's Secondary School.

Mother and Father were led into the family room. The furniture was austere. They were offered water to drink. Agya Baako asked of their mission. "The elders say we know and yet we ask," he said. "Here, all is well. You are the ones who've been walking."

Father didn't waste much time. He said their mission was a good one. He explained that they had come on my behalf. About their daughter. Father had forgotten her name. Mother whispered it to him. Father said, "Your daughter Akua Nsiah. We have all known her since she was a little child and we have watched with admiration as she's grown into a beautiful, well-mannered young woman. We are hopeful that the union of our son and your daughter will also unite our two families. We will be honored." Father paused to catch his breath. Then he continued to talk about me. I had turned out to be very resourceful.

Agya Baako took it all in. When Father was finished, he nodded his head. He said he'd heard. They were proud to be the parents of Akua Nsiah. They were glad of the interest in her. Agya Baako said, "We have heard you speak. We will have to ask Akua what she thinks. If she says yes, we will let you know."

Mother spoke next. "We have heard and we know that nothing must be done in haste. After all, the elders say that hasty things fly away." Agya Baako nodded. He assured my parents they would move with speed. Father and Mother gave Agya Baako a photo of me. And they got a picture of Akua Nsiah to show me.

Mother and Father sent me word in Accra. They included the photograph of Akua Nsiah. It wasn't very clear. I couldn't tell if she was beautiful or not. But there was no turning back. I waited for two months and got no word. I sent word to Mother. That I thought Akua Nsiah was taking too long. Mother sent word back. "Maybe," Mother said. "But what can we do? The elders say you don't go to the black fetid ant's door and tell her she stinks."

Three days later the word finally came. Akua Nsiah had agreed to be my wife. I sent word to Father. That I was ready to perform the marriage rites. A date was set. I took leave from work and went home.

I was between sadness and joy. In the next two days, I wasn't sure what I was doing. I wasn't sure I'd like Akua Nsiah. What if I hated her? What if she hated me? This was the wrong way to think of it. I reminded myself, I had to believe. Things would work out well. They had to. Mother had done her investigation. Papa, too. They trusted Akua Nsiah. Her parents, no doubt, had done theirs. They were assured I would be a good husband. That which both parents blessed had to succeed! After all, marriage should be stable. It is not just for satisfying the loins. That is a small part of the whole thing. Important, yes. But still a small part. The larger part was how we would behave towards each other. How we'd create a secure and safe home. Make the other have peace of mind. Marriage is raising each other until death. Not just exacting sexual pleasure until that pleasure was gone. I reasoned: to succeed, marriage must be spiritual first, sensual second. So I put all reservations away. I looked ahead. I still loved Ama Owusu. I often thought of her. I still wanted her. And wished she was the one I was marrying. But I couldn't have her. So I yearned silently. In pain. In dying hope.

The day arrived. It was a Saturday. Father gathered our entourage. To Agya Baako's house. It comprised my siblings and aunts and uncles. And our *Abusuapanin* or Head of Family.

When we arrived, Agya Baako and Eno Yaa were waiting. They were there with a number of their relatives. We exchanged greetings with them. Shaking hands. After this, they served to us water. Then Agya Baako spoke. Loudly to the hearing of the gathering. But his spokesman had to say it again: "Agya Baako would like to welcome Opanin Mensah and his entourage to his humble abode and would like to know their mission this afternoon."

Father also spoke through his spokesman. My uncle Anane. "We have come here this afternoon with love and in absolute peace. My son, Koo Manu, has seen a flower of fragrance and beauty in your house and wants to transplant it to my house."

Agya Baako's spokesman: "May we be informed who this flower is?"

Anane: "Your beautiful daughter, Akua Nsiah, is the flower."

Agya Baako's spokesman: "The elders say no one drinks medicine for the sick. Call Akua Nsiah here."

Agya Baako turned to his wife. "Eno Yaa, call your daughter here."

Eno Yaa yelled: "Akua Nsiah!"

Akua Nsiah answered from the gathering, "Maamie." I hadn't even recognized her.

"Come here," said Eno Yaa.

Akua Nsiah walked shyly to the middle of the group. My fears were unfounded. She wasn't ugly as I had feared. But she wasn't beautiful either. I could have found one like her easily on my own. She looked very simple and average to me. She didn't arouse me. Like Ama Owusu aroused me. But I had no choice. She would be my wife. Hopefully, until death. Therefore, I had to put away any bad thoughts. If I didn't like her, I'd have to learn to. I'd have to live with her. In a peaceful way.

Agya Baako's spokesman asked, "Is this my daughter that you are talking about?"

Father turned to me and asked aloud, "Koo, is this the beautiful flower for which we are here?"

I smiled and responded, "Yes, Papa."

Agya Baako's spokesman: "Akua, Opanin Mensah wants to engage you in marriage for his son, Koo Manu. Do you agree to marry him? Should we accept the marriage drinks?"

Akua Nsiah bowed her head. She looked furtively at me and smiled. She answered slowly. "I agree, Papa, to the proposal." Her voice was soft but certain.

The audience went into spontaneous laughter.

Agya Baako cleared his throat. Then he said through his spokesman: "Ah, Opanin Mensah, how have you come?"

Father replied through Anane: "May I ask your permission to open the way for me to perform the customary rites?"

Spokesman: "With all pleasure, permission is granted."

Anane: "In these modern times, we would like to shorten the ceremony, with your indulgence, by presenting the following." He called to my brother. My brother carried forward a box. Anane opened it. "Here are two bottles of Schnapps, one carton of beer and two crates of soft drinks as head drink. Here is cash to cover the customary rites including the share of Father, Mother, Grandmother, Grandfather, aunts, uncles, brothers and sisters-in-law and other relatives. I humbly plead that you arrange the distribution of this cash in your own wise way. Finally, and additionally, I present one bottle of Schnapps, one carton of beer and two crates of soft drinks and this cash for the gathering."

Agya Baako's spokesman: "We have accepted the presentation. The flower is now ready to be transplanted." The audience laughed. Father and his entourage went round. To shake hands with Agya Baako's relatives. And thank them for the honor. The honor done our family. Then Agya Baako and his relatives went round. To shake Father and his entourage. For the performance of the marriage rites.

Agya Baako's spokesman spoke. He said one bottle of Schnapps would be served. For all to partake in the marriage rites. Plus one carton of beer. And two crates of soft drinks. He opened the Schnapps. He poured a little into a glass. And drank it. The *Abusuapanin* of Agya Baako's family held out a glass. The spokesman poured some drink into it. In three installments. To almost fill the glass. Their Abusuapanin would pour libation. For the success of the marriage. He raised the glass up and down. He said, "Almighty God, without whose help nothing can be done, here is your drink." He poured a little drink on the ground. He called the family god by name. "Asianoa, here is your drink." He poured a little drink on the ground. He called the names of noble ancestors. Who had gone to the life beyond. Then he poured a little drink on the ground.

He continued, "This afternoon, the purpose of calling you all is that your granddaughter Akua Nsiah has been married to the son of Opanin Mensah called Koo Manu. We ask you to stand firmly behind the marriage, guide and protect them in all ways and make the marriage a successful and memorable one. Endow them with plenty of children who will grow up to be responsible citizens. Let them live to see their grand- and great, great grandchildren. Protect them from evil influences. We leave anyone who will wish the marriage a failure, or who will think evil of them, for to you to deal with as you think fit. Protect and give health to all who have gathered here this afternoon. Here is your drink." He poured more drink on the ground.

Some of the elders responded by saying, "Well spoken."

The spokesman poured him some more liquor. He gulped it all at one go.

Meanwhile, Agya Baako had broken the gathering's cash into small denominations. He distributed it among the gathering. In proportion to their status.

It was almost evening. The drinks were served. My wife's family had prepared some little food. This was also shared. Agya Baako's spokesman spoke again. He called for advice from anyone present.

Our Abusuapanin said, "*Agoo! Agoo!*" When he got the audience's attention he continued, "I am happy that God Almighty and our ancestors have made it possible for me to see the day when Koo Manu has been married to the daughter of Agya Baako. My plea is that they should remember that they come from families with outstanding reputations. Nothing should be done to untie the strong bond which has been laid between the families today. Settle any misunderstandings that you may encounter peacefully with love. Don't let a day pass over it. Remember that the success of your marriage depends on the two of you alone. Beware of bad friends. Don't listen to bad advice. May the Great God bless you and your marriage."

Father spoke. He said he was very proud. Of my choice. He encouraged us to be open with one another. To share our successes and failures. To learn from them. And to grow from them.

Yaw Mensah spoke next. He was a relative of my wife. "My best wishes to the married couple, Koo Manu and Akua Nsiah, for a successful marriage. May the Lord give you everything you wish for yourselves. Remember always that marriage is an institution from the Creator. You are now one flesh. Let no one therefore tear you apart. Trust each other at all times. Have patience for each other."

Book Two: The Eclipse of Mother

Then Kwame Asempa, my uncle, said, "Marriage is a hard road to travel. Someone has described marriage as a burning house. While some are running away from the heat, others are rushing in. With understanding and love you will be able to extinguish all flames that may erupt in your marriage."

My uncle's wife, Yaa Fofie said, "My humble advice is to both parents of the bride and groom. Do please allow your children to have a peaceful marriage. Don't interfere in any way in their affairs. This applies to the other relatives as well. Don't go to spend endless weekends with them. Don't stand behind your son or daughter in cases of petty disagreements that may occur in the marriage. Each family should treat them as son or daughter as the case may be."

My oldest uncle spoke. Kofi Boateng said, "My advice is to the bride. She should avoid gossip with her friends. If she has friends, and they should be picked with great care, she should never discuss any marriage problems with such friends."

Many more came forward. And gave us some advice. I was glad to hear them. But after a while, I got tired of them. Although I knew they meant well. Then it was time to celebrate. A singing group began to sing. I drank some palm wine. Then I moved to the middle of the compound. With Akua, my wife. I don't know if it was the drink. But as I danced with her, I got feelings for her. Others joined us to dance. We danced for a long time. I spoke to Akua. I don't remember what I said. I kept drinking. And dancing. Slowly the crowd thinned out. I too left and went home. After saying my thanks and farewells.

Akua Nsiah came to my home in the night. Around eight. Her sister accompanied her. Her sister left us. That night we consummated the marriage. I enjoyed it. And I finally slept thinking that everything would be well.

I woke up the next morning with a headache. I had drunk too much. And exerted myself too much. Akua returned to her parents in the morning. At five. She sent food in the morning. Her mother brought it. I ate merrily. I returned to Accra two days later with my wife.

119

10

My first child Kubi was born. That was a year after Akua and I were married. He was born on a Thursday. So he was a Yaw. He was named Kubi after his great grand-uncle, who was said to be a very great farmer. I never knew him. But his reputation was sufficient. I asked Father for his permission. To give my child that name. Father said that was a great choice.

I wanted a simple child-naming ceremony. Both Mother and Father came to Accra. I invited Kwamena. And a few relatives and friends.

My wife brought out our son, wrapped in a white cloth. Father poured libation. He prayed to God and the ancestors. He continued, "Koo, my son, who sprung from my loins has given me this child whom I name after our great uncle. He is to be called Kubi. Yaw Kubi Manu. Please guide him well. Let him grow up into a good and strong young man whose sweat I shall enjoy. Let him be brave but respectful of his elders. Give him long life which will be full of joy...."

I took Kubi after Father finished. I placed him in Father's arm. He looked at Kubi for a long time. Father then inserted his right forefinger in a cup of water. Father put the finger on Kubi's lips. Father continued, as Kubi tasted the water: "Kubi, when you say water, you mean water." He did this three times. Then I brought a cup of liquor. Again, Father dipped his right forefinger into the liquor. He put it on Kubi's lips. "Kubi, when you say liquor, you mean liquor." He did this three times.

I gave some money as a gift to my son. Then I gave gifts to Akua. For the safe delivery of our child. It comprised of cash and three pieces of the finest textiles. She thanked me. I poured some of the liquor used in the naming ceremony into a glass. I passed it around for all to taste. Then refreshments were served. A little later we had some food. And we made merry.

I had never been prouder in my life.

ॐ

11

I now had a new purpose in my life. My son Kubi. And I had to work harder than ever. I was working for Mr. Oppong in those days. He was a wealthy man with a big business. I worked in the salt division of his company. I supervised the export of salt. Mainly the export was to Burkina Faso. He paid me quite generously. But I needed more money. I went to see him. "I would like to accompany the drivers on their trip," I told him.

Mr. Oppong looked at me. As if I was crazy. All his seventy years showed. He moved slowly and spoke softly. But his mind was sharp. "Why do you want to do something so difficult, Koo? Believe me, it's not easy driving in a truck all the way to Burkina Faso. It is not a job for a gentleman like you."

"Sir," I said, "I have a plan to make you more money. But I need to go on a trip first. I need to make sure the plan will work."

His eyes widened. "What is this plan?"

"Sir, we need to be more disciplined. We have to get the drivers back sooner. Improve our turnover. Pay them generously if they meet goals we set for them. And notice how they come back, sir? With empty trucks? We can load the trucks with food. From the North. And sell it in Accra. Or we can rent the trucks for that purpose. It will increase the money you make, sir."

"You want to make more money for me? Is that why you want to do this?" He was frowning when he asked that.

"Not entirely, sir. I have some personal interest, too. I just had a son. I have another mouth to feed. I need more money. Sir, give me this chance. If my plan works, all I ask is a pay increase. If I fail, sack me."

"That's all you want?"

"Yes, sir."

He thought for a long time. All the while puffing on his cigar. "Mmh. Alright. You have a month to show me something. If I like what you do, I will reward you. If I don't, you have set your own fate: you won't work for me anymore. Are we in agreement?"

"Yes, sir."

"Let me know if you need anything. I will make sure you have it."

"You won't regret this, sir."

"I won't. But you may."

I put all my energy into work. I saw this as my destiny. I was there when we bought the salt for export. I was there when we loaded the salt on to the trucks. And then the four trucks set out for Ouagadougou at five a.m. I sat beside the driver in one of the trucks. It was a long journey. We couldn't make it all in one day. We had to rest in Tamale for the night. I went out that night. I asked around. And I struck a conversation with a local farmer. His name was Mumuni. I asked him how he got his crops to the south of Ghana. He said that he hired trucks. They were very expensive. And the costs cut deeply into his profits.

I offered him a deal. To organize those who needed transportation. I would haul their crops to Kumasi and Accra. At a reduced cost. He could be my first client. He was suspicious. Why this deal? He said that it sounded too good to be true. I went and showed him the trucks. Eventually, I convinced him. "Get ready," I said to him. "We will be back in a day."

We continued the next day. We crossed the boarder at Paga into Burkina Faso. And then on to Ouagadougou. The salt was unloaded. And sold to our clients. The drivers wanted to gallivant. I said no. We had to go back. They grumbled, but I insisted. So we drove back. We stopped at Tamale. I got Mumuni's rice and yams loaded into the trucks. He came with us to Kumasi, where we unloaded the first batch. Then we continued to Accra. We unloaded the rest there. He was thankful. I made arrangements with him to transport his crops next time. I wanted him to get his fellow farmers together. I would offer the same deal to them.

I went to see Mr. Oppong later. "You are back from Ouagadougou already?" he asked. "It takes them about a week to make the trip and come back."

"It's my plan in action, sir," I said. I handed him the paperwork, showing our profits.

His face glowed. "Good work, my boy. Very good work."

"Sir," I said, "May I ask a small favor?"

He frowned but said, "Go ahead."

"Sir, I pushed the drivers very hard. I didn't give them any rest at all. May I ask that we give them a bonus? For their hard work?"

He nodded. "Yes. By all means. We need to keep them happy."

"Thank you, sir." I turned to go.

"Koo," Mr. Oppong called. I stopped to listen. "How much do you expect from this for yourself?"

"Whatever you deem fit, sir."

"You will be rewarded. Keep up the good work."

I did. The drivers were surprised when they got a bonus. "There's more if you continue like this," I told them. I set up a rigorous schedule for them. They were rewarded generously when they met it. They got nothing if they didn't. And I was in constant touch. With the farmers in the North. Their numbers grew. I was sure to meet their demands. I provided additional trucks when necessary. And I accommodated their schedules. Business boomed. Mr. Oppong took notice. He created a new position for me. I was officially Director, Salt Division, Oppong, Inc. My pay increased dramatically. I was financially comfortable for the first time.

I gained Mr. Oppong's confidence. He consulted me a lot on his business matters. This way I gained insights into other aspects of his business.

So life became more comfortable. It was hard work. But I managed. My wealth grew in the next seven years. I had my daughter, Akosua. My sons Kwame and Kofi came later. I wanted the best education for my children. And now I could afford it. I sent them to the best private schools. I was happy to wake up to the many sounds of children. My wife Akua took care of them. I was proud of her. She didn't work otherwise. I had the money to take care of her. Mother was right. Akua was a perfect wife. She didn't complain. Nor did I demand much from her.

Even my friend Kwamena got jealous. "You have an excellent wife. See how she takes care of you and the children? I wish I had had such luck myself when I got married."

"So now you see that it's not fools who marry." He shrugged and said nothing.

Everything was going well. And then I got bad news: Father died.

Father's passing was painful. But I tried not to show my pain. I bore it quietly. If only I could find the strength of Grandpapa.

I went about doing my business. More intensely than ever. That helped. But the pain lingered. Mother came to Accra often. I think because she missed Father. It was always good to have her. Except when she told stories to my wife and children. About stupid things I did when I was little. Meantime, time passed. I didn't notice it. We moved into a new home a year after Father died. It was two-story building in Labone. I bought a car. A Nissan. I wanted to have more children. My wife Akua said children were expensive these days.

"I want to work," she said. "If I work, we can have more children."

"Why? Don't I take good care of you?"

"You do, but I want to do something by myself. I don't want to depend on you for everything."

"I want to take care of you. Your every need. That's why I work so hard."

"I know, but I don't feel right about that."

"Akua, take care of the children. I will take care of the rest."

"The children? They are all grown now."

I insisted I didn't want her working. That I wanted her to take care of the children. They deserved her time. All of it. She wasn't happy with my decision. But she didn't protest. I sat by myself a long time. I was wondering if I had done the right thing. But she was such a good mother. And a good wife. She was such a good caretaker of the home. Why should we change that? Hadn't I provided her with a good home? Provided her with all the clothing and jewelry? Given her four children? So why was she dissatisfied? The next day I bought her clothes. Very expensive ones. Then I bought some jewelry too. I also gave her a huge cash gift. I told her I appreciated her work at home. "Let's get a maid. She can help you with the housework. You deserve some rest."

"Don't worry. I can take care of the housework without the help of a maid."

"I insist. I want you to have more free time. To be free to relax and enjoy yourself. Let's get a maid."

"If that's what you wish."

We sent word around for a maid. We got one the following week. A fourteen-year-old called Aba. She was still in school. She would stay with us. Help my wife. And continue with her school at the same time.

"Have I done my wife wrong?" I asked my friend Kwamena.

"No. I think you have done well by her. But if she wants to work, let her. Didn't your mother work outside of the home? And her grandmother? Our forefathers never kept their women at home. Women always worked outside of the home. It's part of our heritage."

"The times are different."

"Maybe," Kwamena said, sighing.

I didn't know what kind of sigh it was.

Kwamena was still staying in the same place at the Accra suburb of Because. He still worked as a Customs agent. Which could be quite lucrative. But it wasn't for Kwamena. No promotions, no demotions.

He was still poor. I remembered all the confidence he used to have. And I remembered what the elders say: The blind man said he would grow eyes when he got older. He is grown, but he still bumps his head. I don't know how he felt about me. He had watched me gain in wealth. Move beyond his circle. "Let me go get you a drink," I said.

"That's why I like you," he replied.

⊱⊰

12

I bought my first Mercedes three years later. It was a mark that I had arrived. Business was booming. Mr. Oppong was now almost completely retired. And he was confident in me. So he turned the business over to me. I was rewarded very well. One day he said to me, "Koo, when you first came to me, I didn't know what kind of person you were. But you sounded so confident I decided to give you the opportunity, to see if you could deliver. You have more than delivered. Now my business is more successful than ever. I am in charge now, but only in name. I am an old man. I want to retire completely at the end of the month. As you very well know, I have not been able to have any children of my own. In a sense, you have become like a son to me. I want to turn over the business to you. If you can buy me out."

My time had come. I put my funds together. Then I borrowed money from the bank. It took some doing. But I prevailed. I bought Mr. Oppong's business. And I was in charge. I worked harder. I paid off my loans. I was getting richer. Because of that, I attracted people to my house. I now had three nephews and two nieces living in my house. And I was putting them through school. I gave Kwamena some money. For business. But he never seemed lucky. He lost the money for one reason or another. He kept coming to me for help. I kept helping. And he kept failing.

Some asked me, "Why are you doing all this?"

I responded: One walks into an empty living room. One has nothing but the empty room. One can stand there alone. And die alone.

126

Book Two: The Eclipse of Mother

Or one can invite others in. One of them will laugh. That laughter will make one laugh also. One will dance. And the other will want to dance too. One will have yams for your hungry belly. Another's handshake will warm the heart. I can go on and on. I know that the wages of kindness is to be surrounded. By the scavenging presence of the needy and greedy. But I know the gift of cruelty is eternal solitude. So let me reach out. Each one brings something to the room. Something new. Something fresh. I take from them. And I give to them. I can't take unless I give. So I have to give a little of myself. Die a little, so I will live fuller. Otherwise, I shall have gained all. But lost all.

I know that if I have six yams I can't keep them all if another has none. If he shall say to me, "Brother, I need your help." He is family. I can't turn him away. I have to share. And I will have less. And so it goes. If I am the one with no yams, I will ask. I will ask those who have. I remember the saying of the elders: When every bird dies, its wings come back to the earth.

So let me not stand alone.

My wealth grew even more. I was invited to many functions. Because of my wealth. I had to make very many donations. I got the opportunity to meet important people. Other business people, lawyers, engineers, doctors, politicians. I met them all. I grew in fame and influence.

Because I had made money, I could make more. It's true money makes money. All I had to do was make a phone call. If I needed a contract. Unlike the days past when I had to sweat, day in and day out. Days when I lay awake, thinking. And I realized that people, especially women, found me more interesting. When I stepped out of my car, they were awed. Previously, I had been too busy. But now I could take some time for leisure. But I didn't want to be unfaithful to my wife. My friends called me a fool. "Take advantage," they said. "Enjoy life a bit. We struggle only for death."

127

But I would think of my wife Akua. She was not a very pretty woman. But she was a very good woman. I didn't love her when I married her. I couldn't because I'd not seen her before. But I had grown to love her. She had gained it over the years. It is not the kind of love one sees in films. Nor hears mentioned in bad poems. Where one wants to take somebody to the moon. And life is all-sweet. Just because one has that person on one's side. This was a different love. But still a powerful one. Steadfast. One wishes the other person will always be there. One smiles inside. When one notices she is happy. No insane urges to touch heaven in sexual bliss.

But an anchor that will not move! Certainly more than a state of mind. A spiritual love!

෬෬

13

Twelve years had passed since I moved to Labone. Then I received word that Mother was ill. Worse than ever before. She had been ailing for a while. We had tried traditional medicine. But the herbs she drank didn't help. I had her brought to Accra. And taken to the best doctors. But to no use. I wanted her to stay in Accra with us. But she insisted that the city would kill her. So she went home. There, she got weaker and weaker. Her eyes sunk in. Like crushed shells. Her face withered like a turkey's neck. Her face got white like the moon. And she shrunk in size into a lithe stick. She could barely speak or walk. Later when my son Kubi got sick, I got worried. Somehow his illness reminded me of Mother's.

I drove home as soon as I got the word. What I saw brought tears to my eyes. Mother's eyes were now just tiny slits. I couldn't tell if they could even see. But she seemed to notice me. When I walked into the room. Her body seemed to have lost all blood. And she looked like a dried branch. There were deep wrinkles across her brow. Wrinkles I hadn't noticed before. Her room had an alien smell. Like a bad sneeze. I associated it with death. Mother mumbled something. I looked at her in horror and disbelief. At first I couldn't understand what she was saying. So I went closer, my heart clobbering my chest. Fearful at the sight of her. Then I realized she was calling my name. Faintly, she was calling out to me.

"Yes, Maamie," I said. "It's me, Koo."

I wanted to say something. But I couldn't think of anything to say. Sadness rose inside of me. Mother raised her hand. Very slowly. I knew she wanted me to take it. I was afraid to do so. I didn't know this creature. This grotesque approximation of a person. But her hand hung in the air. Suspended with effort. So I took it. And my tears dropped on my cheeks. Mother held my hand tightly. I knew she did so with much effort. Her hand felt cold. Like death. And then I wasn't afraid anymore. Except I was sad because I was losing her. And proud that she'd been my mother.

"Koo," she whispered. "My son, Koo. I am leaving. I am dying."

"No, Maamie. You are not dying. Don't say things like that."

She forced a smile. But it looked more like a frown. "Koo." She spoke haltingly. "Take your grandfather's coat. It's in the corner over there. I have had it for a long time. But now I want you to have it." Then she stopped speaking. And for a long time the room was in silence. Mother's forced breathing struggled with the silence. Mother raised her head. As if preparing to rise. But her head fell heavily back down. Her grip loosened. Her hand fell on her side. I knew then that Mother was dead. I bent her arms so her hands rested on her bosom. I shifted her head to make her face look up directly. She looked dignified to me at that moment. I stared at her for a long time. I wiped the tears off my face. Then I went outside to tell the others.

Mother's death hung with me longer than father's.

I had to find refuge. And I found it in my wife and children. And nephews and nieces. And brothers and sisters. In the memory of Grandpapa's milk. And in my work. I expanded the business. Our exports included just about everything. From food to local textiles. I imported. I sold. I bought. I invested in other people's businesses. I was everywhere. Making deals and making sure they succeeded. It was non-stop. For three years. Three years during which my children grew. I got them private teachers to make sure they did well in school.

I wanted them to do better than me. If education would help, then so be it. My wife was wonderful. She continued to raise the children well. While I was away making money for the family.

I built a new house in Labone. It was grand. The main three-story house had eight bedrooms. It had three bathrooms and two living rooms. And a very large kitchen. The guest quarters had four bedrooms. It had its own kitchen and living room. Between the two was a big compound. I had grass planted on the compound. My daughter Akosua said she wanted flowers. I had her pick them up. We planted some on the compound. And she was happy. I hired a night watchman. I was afraid now that I lived in such a big house. I sold my old car and bought three more. A Mercedes Benz for myself. A BMW for my wife. And a Honda for the children. Later, I would replace the Honda with a Jaguar.

ॐ∼ॐ

14

I was surprised. Six months to the end of military rule. I was invited to join the Government. Why me? I had finished secondary school. But that was it. I had not gone to university. I had not done any great thing in academics. All I had done was become a successful businessman. Was that sufficient preparation? Of course, I was a savvy businessman. And I had to make use of all my contacts. That included my military contacts. A number of times I had met the Head of State. Because of my business influence. In fact, the Government once wanted to name a monument in my name. But there was too much opposition to the idea. I would have liked that honor. But it didn't bother me too much. When it didn't happen.

And now they wanted me in the Government. I tried to make sense of it. This late-term appointment. Why? Was it a gift to the business community? A last gesture of goodwill? After all, some years back, there had been nationalizations. The Government took over several businesses deemed corrupt. That antagonized many in the business community. But why now? I asked the Head of State. I said I didn't understand his appointment. He said he'd reflected a lot. He would be

leaving power soon. He wanted to be remembered well. By all. He said
his predecessor had not started off well. He had antagonized business
people. He wanted to end well. By rewarding business people.

I asked what post he wanted me to assume. "Minister without
portfolio," he said. Without portfolio? He said he knew I was busy.
He didn't want me too occupied with government business. He would
call on me from time to time. To deal with issues as they developed.
And he might ask for my advice from time to time. That was all he
expected. The appointment was announced without much fanfare. The
public was apathetic. They were looking forward to the future. Not the
past. Who cared what the Government did in its last three months in
office? But three months later things would change. No one expected
it. The Head of State would be dead. I would be in detention.

I didn't do very much as minister without portfolio. I was given
a small staff. And an office at the Osu Castle. The Head of State
summoned me once in a while. He asked me my opinion. Of the state
of the nation. What was our biggest problem? I told him I feared the
brain drain was serious. All our qualified young men were leaving.
Either going to America or Europe. "We can't build a country this
way." I helped the Head of State launch Operation Stay Home. It
was a mass appeal to young professionals to stay in their own country
and help with nation-building. We made the appeal through radio
announcements, speeches and symposia. We invited academicians to
pontificate. The Operation had no visible consequence. But at least we
were seen to be doing something.

I also advised that we had to address AIDS. The Government
launched a preventive campaign. It promoted the use of condoms and
abstinence. It educated people about the disease. The Government's
campaign was praised. The Head of State congratulated me.

As far as I was concerned, I'd done my part. I wanted to return to
what I did best. Run a business. I eyed the imminent elections without
interest. I didn't care who won. The politicians' stated differences
seemed hollow. I contributed money to both major parties. I wanted
to maintain influence in both.

And then the coup happened. I heard it in the morning. At home on radio. Just like everyone else. I stayed at home and waited for news. By evening, I knew the coup had succeeded. I decided to turn myself in the next day. As requested by the new leaders. I had nothing to fear. I had done nothing wrong except work hard. And then do some public service.

My wife Akua thought otherwise. She argued that they would kill me. She said they'd shot the army commander. Therefore, they'd shoot me. "No," I said. "He was killed in battle, trying to quell the coup. I am a civilian. I'm not involved in any battles."

"Wait a little while and let's see what happens," she cautioned. She convinced me to leave the house. That night, my driver took me away. We went to a distant cousin's house. There, I hid and waited for news. A week later, I heard of the first execution. A former Head of State and army commander were executed. I knew there couldn't be any meaningful trial. The Government had been in power a few weeks. No fair trial could be that short. I decided to try to escape. This was real. I felt danger creeping closer. How far would the executions go? I couldn't trust the new leaders for a fair trial. I would first go to my hometown. I would hide there a little. If things got better, I would return. If not, I would leave for another country.

I shaved my hair. I borrowed my cousin's car. At dawn, I drove outside. The curfew had just ended. I passed the first three checkpoints without incident. But at Nsawam, one soldier recognized me. He first went through the car. Then he shone his torch in my face. "What be your name?" he asked.

"Kumi Pratt."

"Na who you want fool? You tink I no know you? Make you commot from de car one time."

I stepped out as he'd requested. He announced his finding to the other soldiers. He knew my name and position. This was a sharp soldier. Despite my disguise, he knew me. I protested that I was not I. But they didn't listen. They made some phone calls. Then they drove me back to Accra. At Usher Forte, I was beaten. And then I was put in detention. My cellmates changed on occasion. Sometimes, I had no cellmates. When Nii Lamptey arrived, I didn't know what to say. But I found he meant well. So we shared a lot of memories. I knew I couldn't expect any better after his trial.

I too was tried before a group of seven men. All in dark glasses. Even though it was quite dark in the room. But severe beating preceded my trial. I was punched and kicked. I was lashed and pulled. I was slapped. I was chopped and head butted. The trial itself was a bit hazy. I had been caught trying to escape justice. What did I have to hide?

"Nothing, sir."

Two slaps.

"Why were you trying to escape justice?"

"I have no reason."

"You have been found guilty of illegal acquisition of wealth."

"On what grounds, sir?"

Two slaps.

"Guilty or not guilty?"

"Not Guilty."

"Prove it."

"How, sir?"

Two slaps.

"Prove it."

"I can't, sir."

"Your sentence will be announced in due course." I was taken from the room. And then I was beaten again. I felt numb. I was taken back to my cell. I nearly died. Nii Lamptey begged the guards. He said I would die without medical attention. Two days later, I was taken to see a doctor. He treated me and gave me some medicine. And then, unexpectedly, I was released. I was given twenty-five years. Suspended sentence. I was barred from ever holding public office. Two of my buildings (at Tesano) were confiscated to the state. I was fined a huge chunk of money. But I had survived. With bruises. And fewer assets. But I was alive. I would later find out how my wife secured my release.

I felt tired and used. I realized I needed some time off. So I decided to take a vacation. Alone. I wanted time away from the city to rest. I hadn't gone back home since Mother died. I thought it would be a good time to go back.

⊱⊰

15

I drove home. Many came to see me. I wanted to rest, but they wouldn't let me. Some expressed sympathy. Over my detention and sentence. They had all sorts of problems. Most of them were financial. I felt obliged to help as many as I could. But I couldn't help them all. Two days passed quickly. Before I knew, it was Monday already. That evening, I decided to walk around town. Just to clear my head a little. And it was a beautiful sight. The sun was falling in the horizon. A beautiful glow. I stood and watched it. Gasping breathless, I imagined. After its full day's run. I enjoyed the lull. Because, soon, the sky would be full of flashing stars. Like sparkling crowns of the night. I felt a strange calm feeling. As if transformed by the ghosts of Mother and Father and Grandpapa. And I felt very peaceful. So, still, I watched the sun. It was like a seduction of the twilight.

And then I saw her again. After about twenty-five years. For a long time, she was there, but lost. Just like a dream remembered without a face. Now, here she was in face and flesh. And she still had the same powerful beauty. The same power that had aroused me. Almost thirty years before. She looked almost the same. Only a little heavier. The same beauty the rain had introduced to me. I saw her as she walked towards me. She didn't seem to notice me. I couldn't blame her. Perhaps I had aged too much.

I stared at her. I couldn't help it. Then she looked at me. She smiled faintly. I watched her walk past. Something stirred in me. And I said, "You don't remember me?"

"No, sir," she said. She still had the beautiful voice. Of birds singing. Flutes in harmony.

How could she not remember? Had I changed that much? Was it my bald head? "My name is Koo Manu," I said. The recognition came instantly. But there was no smile. I thought I saw anger in her face. "You remember me now?" I asked.

She nodded, but she did not speak.

"How are you?" I asked. "It's been a long time."

"Hmm mmh."

"What have you been doing?"

"That is none of your concern."

"Why are you being rude?"

She spewed out her anger. "Why am I being rude? Who are you to ask me such a question? Do you even remember what you did to me? Do you? I'm sure you don't even remember because you didn't care, giving me the impression that you were going to ask my father so you could marry me. What a fool I was then to believe you, not knowing you were after another woman all the time! I had even gone around telling my friends about you and looking forward to all of it – and next thing, I hear you've married and gone back to Accra. And you didn't even say a word to me. Now, over twenty years later you ask me why I am being rude to you? Maybe you've forgotten, but not I. I still remember."

She spoke in clear anger. I was completely surprised by that. But she was right. I had not treated her well. To leave a woman with hope. Not explain anything to her. And then marry another woman. But what could I have done then? "Lady," I said.

"Don't call me lady!" she yelled. But she didn't walk away.

"Please calm down. Please listen to me."

With anger on her face, she said, "I'm listening." She crossed her arms under her breasts.

"It wasn't by choice that I married another woman." I continued to explain. In detail.

She was a little less angry after I was done. "You could have told me. You could have let me know what was happening instead of keeping me guessing all this time."

I apologized to her. I said that I'd done the wrong thing. The anger left her. She said she'd heard about me. That I had become very prosperous in Accra. Her charm came back. And I wanted her. One way or the other.

"So who is your husband?" I asked.

"I don't have one," she said. "I got married a long time ago, but my husband died."

"I see."

"I have to go now," she said.

"I would like to see you again."

"It all depends on what you have in mind."

"I want to get to know you again," I said.

She smiled. And then she told me when and where to meet her.

I walked around a little. Darkness had descended. Here and there the pests roamed with the wind. As if unsure. Whether to disturb or calm us. I could hear the sound of pestles on mortars. Alternating with whistles. Perhaps of lovers stealing some moments to woo. And I could hear the crickets too. I walked on slowly. I could see a household come alive. In a compound, I saw little ones and adults. It looked as if they had gathered to tell a story. I was curious and so I went and joined in. It was a family I knew well. I greeted the children and their cousins. I said my greeting to the parents. And the grandparents. Who were all gathering into a semi-circle. In the background, I saw they were roasting corn. The firewood crackled. I could smell the burning wood. A mosquito attacked me. As if teasing the hill of fire close by. With the smell of burning wood. With the evolution of sun to moon. I knew stories would come to mind. Tongues would unwind. And sweet stories would be told.

৵৶

16

I awoke the following morning. To the sound of a cockerel's crow. As it drowned my last snore. I also heard the chirping of birds. Who sung away the night's slumber. I heard bleating sheep too. The cockerel crooned on. As though in response to a sparrow's song. I walked to the window and looked outside. I saw the silk tree's leaves ruffling. I saw the grass shivering. As the running wind swept along. Farther away, the wind drew sandy twirls. Into fists of gods. Who had become artists of the morning. And then I saw farmers. Walking paths to their farms. Hunters were toting polished guns. Dogs crept abroad. Bent and looking sleepy-eyed. Traders gathered baskets for the market.

But all I could think of was Ama. I waited all day for her. Anxiously.

We sat under the tree behind her room. The white moon hung above us. Like a dislodged egg. Suspended in mid-air.

"I come here when I want to be alone," she said.

"It is a very nice place. I like it here."

She smiled at me. She was knocking on my door now. Her eyes were wide open. I said with a smile, "You are beautiful. And you have a sense for what is beautiful."

"Thank you," she replied. Her eyes moved to the side. Slowly. She was inside the room now. She could do whatever she wanted. I couldn't fight it. That feeling between the legs. How could I fight it? Next to this woman? And it was like the day I'd taken her home. So many years before. In the rain.

She asked me about my wife. And my children. How many did I have? What were they doing? Was I happy with my wife? My children? I answered her as best as I could. I was happy with my wife. Of course, there were bad days. Days when I was tired of her presence. But those days were brief. I loved her. That couldn't preclude me from

137

loving other women, could it? Was it wrong that I had feelings for this woman? When I had a loving wife at home? I told Ama Owusu the truth. And she wasn't angry. Her face continued to beam. Seductively. The longing for her grew intensely.

I looked at her closely. I just looked and looked. She felt uncomfortable. So she looked down. She smiled a little and I was thinking. Thinking what I would do. What I should do. I tried to think of my wife Akua. She, and only she, could stop me. And she came to mind very strongly. I saw her leaving for the market. Coming back to prepare the meal. And I thought of her in the kitchen. Making a meal for the family. Happily singing a tune as she stirred the soup. I could see her washing dishes. Cleaning and wiping. All that, she'd done by herself. Until we got the maid. I saw her breast-feeding our children. Each one when he or she was a helpless infant. And I thought of her beside me in bed. Every day for the past twenty-six years. Loving my body when I needed loving. Comforting me when I was in doubt. Counseling me when I was confused. And as I thought of all these, I got stronger. And I knew that I had to flee from Ama Owusu. Flee from her as fast as I could. And go back to Akua Nsiah, my wife.

"Why are you so quiet?" Ama Owusu asked me. She said she'd heard how well I'd done. As a businessman. She said she'd also heard of my appointment. But she tried to avoid news of me. It hurt her too much. And then suddenly my wife fled from me. And I faced my challenge again. I didn't know what to do. But I held her arm. Then I stood up, forcing her to do so too. I put my hand behind her. And slowly I pulled her towards me. Until I could embrace her. I kissed her on the forehead. And then I embraced her tightly. She stepped back. Then she reached for my wrist. Holding it, she led me to her room. And I let her lead me. But a terrible sense of guilt took hold of me. Before I could go any further I said, "I can't do this. It isn't right."

And I surprised even myself.

17

I went to see my friend Kwamena. When I returned to Accra. I picked him up at Because. We went to the Paradise Chop Bar. For the sake of old times. Emilia was still running it. After all these years. She had expanded it. And the place was very popular. She had grown older. But still active as ever. She wanted to make small talk. But I wasn't in the mood. She didn't push me. Kwamena noticed my mood. "What is wrong with you, my friend?" he asked. "Is it this coup palaver and all the mess they've caused you?"

"Kwamena, I have fallen in love."

"Good. When you've been married for so long it's a good thing that you have fallen in love with your wife."

"I am not talking about my wife."

"Oh hoh. Trouble."

"I don't know if you recall. You remember before I married Akua. I had another woman in mind. I wanted to marry her."

"Yes, but your mother said no."

"Yes. I met her again. When I went home for vacation. It started all over again."

I told Kwamena the entire story. Except I did not tell him I had promised Ama Owusu I would marry her. After I had said no to marital infidelity. She had looked at me. And I couldn't stand the disappointment. Nor the accusation in her eyes. It was as if things were happening over again. Leading her to the brink. And then leaving her dangling. I told her that I had to do it right. It would insult us all if we had extramarital or premarital sex. It would insult her. It would insult my wife. It would insult me. It would taint us all. We had to get married first. So I told her I would get things started. And we would be married soon. And then we could go all the way.

For that moment, I just told her I would return soon. To make her my second wife. She didn't believe me. But I was steadfast. In the end she said she'd wait for me. But I didn't tell Kwamena that detail.

"You can't do that!" I heard Kwamena say. "Don't bring any palaver to your home by bringing another woman into it. Akua has been a good wife to you and a good mother for your children. How can you spoil all that? Pour scorn on your mother's ghost?"

"I don't want to spoil anything."

"She will be very unhappy."

"Why? Because I want to marry another woman?"

"Yes. Women don't like that."

"Nonsense. Didn't my own father have two wives? And didn't Grandpapa have three?"

"Those days are gone, Koo."

"Then we should revive them. It must be good for us if it was good for our fathers."

"Our fathers did a lot of wrong things."

"And a lot of good things."

We went back and forth. "Kwamena, don't you think a man can love two women? At the same time?"

"I think that happens all the time. It's just by accident that we define our love relationships. See, one meets someone he likes or loves and one gets into a relationship with that person. One ignores his desires for others. One doesn't act on them because one wants to devote his attention to the one he's professed his love to. But there comes a time when the relationship is old and those desires that don't go away come back strongly, and that's when people begin to fool around. If one had met those people before one met his wife, one might have married them instead. But whether we marry more than one person is another matter."

"You know, I love both women. I love my wife. But it is the love that is tender. It resides in the spirit. More than in the flesh. When I see her I am happy. Just knowing that she is there. It is soft love. It is subtle. It doesn't rush. But I love Ama Owusu also. My love for her is raw. It is bold. It boils in the blood. It wants attention. Now. The feelings seem at odds. Yet both feelings have a place in me."

"The decision is yours."

"I have decided, Kwamena."

"I will support your decision, but you know where I stand on this issue," Kwamena added, after a little thought. "You know you don't have to marry this woman to make her happy. You can bring her to Accra and find her a place to live and good work to do. Just keep her on the side. That way, you don't have to disrupt your home life."

"I don't think that is a good idea," I replied. "I respect Akua. I won't lie to her. Better I tell her. Than hide and get caught."

"You are being selfish, my friend."

Later by myself, I thought of the matter. Reconciling my love for both women. Words came to my mind. What was my love? A contradiction co-existing? Maybe ... A serene thunderstorm! Hotter than the sun at midday. The shivering soul of a cold night. The fiery cacophony of the storm's cry. That taps gently like a dying rain on the roof. Louder than a million motional hooves. The calm wind of the evening's soul. That rises like the angry tidal wave. Only to lull itself into burning calm. The cruel demon of torment. As kind as the angel of serenity. Sharper than a canine's canine teeth. And softer than the sheep's wool. Weary as the warrior's muscle. But unscathed like a child's skin. Burning. Soothing. Healing. This ... this must be my love for them. Reconciled. Or no?

☙❧

18

"You know I love you deeply. I won't do anything to harm you. And I don't want you to be unhappy. I have tried my best to be a good husband. And a good father to the children. I have toiled day and night. To provide you with everything you need. Now, see. You have a big mansion. You have cars at your disposal. Clothes, jewelry, money. I never turn down any request you make. I have looked at other women. But I have never fooled around. Even though they've thrown themselves at me. But, Akua, now you must understand. That I am a man. And sometimes I have feelings. For other women. Last time I went home, I met a woman. I had met her before. My feelings for her were renewed. Now I want to make her my wife. My second wife. And I want your blessing. As the elders say, it is the one who loves you who begs of you."

Akua listened quietly. She didn't show any emotion on her face. But when she spoke I knew she was sad. "Don't I satisfy you?"

"You do! You do! But it's not that."

"Then what is it? You say you've tried to be a good husband to me and a good father to the children. I know you try. But a good husband isn't someone who gives you food and clothes. A good husband is there for you as well. Both spiritually and emotionally. So how can you expect to be a good husband if you split yourself between two women? And, in any case, haven't I, too, been a good wife to you, and a good mother to the children?"

"You have."

"Am I too old for you, then?"

"No!"

"Then what is it?"

I didn't know. Except that I desired Ama Owusu. I dodged her question. "Sleep over it. Let's talk later."

The next week she came to me. "I was very hurt when you told me you wanted to marry a second wife. I must admit that to you. Think about it. Put yourself in my position. If you've been married to your husband for over twenty years and had four children with him and then suddenly he tells you he wants to marry another woman, you won't be happy. You will question yourself and wonder what is missing in you that would make him want to marry again. I know that it was common with our forebears. But there were practical reasons why they did that. To have more children so they could have extra help on the farm, for example. Or even as a sign of wealth and power in the community. But not so nowadays. The number of his wives or the number of his children no longer measures a man. There are new status symbols now. And you have them all. Beautiful and expensive

142

cars, two big houses and a lot of money. So I haven't slept properly. I only have one request. Let her not live in this house with us. Get her another place to live. But not in this house."

I didn't know whether to cry or jump. My feelings were mixed. Akua had been most gracious. I should have given her better. But what I felt, I felt.

However, I had more challenges a week later.

They were already gathered. Seated in the living room. I froze when I walked in. Because they stared at me coldly. I greeted them. I tried to sound cheerful. I smiled. But they didn't smile. So I stopped smiling also. "Why is everyone so sad?" I asked.

"The children want to talk to you about something," my wife Akua said.

"Good. I am listening." I sat.

"Papa," my daughter Akosua began. "We don't think you should marry that woman."

"So that is what you have on your mind?" I asked. The elders say it's difficult to chop a tree leaning against a rock. My wife had a rock in the children. I had to be careful.

"It is, Papa," said Kubi.

"But I have already talked with your mother. That issue is settled."

"I told them so," my wife said. "But they wanted to talk to you themselves."

"You really shouldn't marry again, Papa," Akosua said.

"She will do no harm to you," I explained. "She won't live here with us. So you won't even have to see her. Everything will be fine."

"Papa, you shouldn't do this." That was my youngest son, Kofi. That surprised me. He hardly said a word against me.

"It will be alright. You'll see."

My daughter said, "Why must you do this, Papa? Isn't Ma good enough? You have been married for almost thirty years now. She's had four children with you. She's been a good wife to you and a good mother to us. Through everything she's been here by your side. Now you want to jeopardize all that and marry another woman. Why? I just don't understand this."

"Listen," I said. "These are adult matters. Your mother and I will settle this."

"Papa, you treat us as if we were still children," Kwame said. "We are all grown now. We are not children anymore."

"I don't see anything wrong. With taking another wife."

"This is such a primitive practice, Papa," Akosua almost yelled.

"Primitive? Why is it primitive? You call the ways of your grandfathers primitive? Don't you have any respect? For the ways of your forefathers?"

"Then I suppose you will have no problems if Ma marries a second husband," my daughter said.

"What impudence!"

"Why am I being impudent?"

"Shut up!" I snapped.

My daughter Akosua shut up. But she was very angry.

"Look. You children think you know everything. Don't criticize things you don't understand. Things that are different. Don't call them primitive. What an insult! One day you will understand. You may think you're grown. But you are only children. I have been a good father to you. I have provided for you. I have cared for you. Now you accuse me. I haven't gone and killed anybody. Should I sit here and be insulted? By my own children?"

"Papa, we are only …"

"Shut up and listen!" I stopped my son, Kwame. "All I am doing is taking a second wife. It will not diminish you. It will not diminish your mother. I will continue to be your father. I will continue to provide for you. I have been considerate. And I will not bring her to live here. She will not bother you. Now what more do you want?"

They were all silent. I could tell they were still unhappy. But I didn't care at that moment. "Do you have anything to say?" I asked. I knew my outburst had silenced them.

There was no response. "Kubi?"

"No, Papa."

"Akosua?"

"No."

"Kwame?"

"No, Papa."

"And Kofi?"

"No, Papa."

"Then this is over," I declared.

They all left the room. Except my wife, Akua.

When the children were gone I asked her, "Why did you go behind my back? To call this meeting?"

"The children wanted it."

"Children today are spoilt."

"They are not spoilt. They made a lot of sense to me."

"So now you're saying I shouldn't marry her?"

"Do what you like." She was clearly angry.

"I want your blessing."

"What good will it make?"

"It will mean a lot."

She shrugged. The anger never left her face. Nor the sadness.

But the shrug was sufficient blessing for me.

Looking back, I know it was a not a blessing.

She was not blessing it. But I wanted to read it differently. In my own favor.

"Everything will be fine."

I stood up and walked to the backyard. I stood there thinking. Grandpapa, where are you? I asked. The milk of your chest. That had given me such strength.

My decision was final. I would marry Ama Owusu. My children didn't like it. They had said so. But they felt obliged to leave me alone. I reasoned that they would get used to it. My heart belonged to my wife Akua. But it also belonged to Ama now. They would have to share it. There would be no other way.

The next day I had more horrors. My daughter Akosua left the house. She was gone by the time we woke up. She had packed her things and left. I contacted the police. They searched for her without results. My wife seemed a little relaxed about it. My sons were clearly worried. I felt guilty. I knew she left because of my decision. I became very afraid for her safety. And gravely concerned by her protest. Something like an unhealthy silence descended on our house.

あ◦ん

19

I faced more opposition that Sunday. After church service. Pastor-Lawyer Amoah was aghast. He insisted that I shouldn't marry Ama Owusu.

"What do you mean, Pastor?"

"Polygamy flouts divine credo. Bigamy is a spiritual dysfunction." My face dropped. And for a while I couldn't speak. Pastor-Lawyer Amoah said that a man molded from God's kingdom "cannot countenance such licentiousness. It is a transgression against His will."

"How can it be? Didn't Solomon have many wives? The wise King Solomon?"

"Affirmative. Nonetheless those archaic modes of multifarious conjugality were subsequently negated. Mathew 19:5: A man shall leave his father and mother and be joined to his wife and the two shall become *one* flesh. One!"

"You know I respect you, Pastor. But I have already decided."

"Alter your intention."

"I can't, Pastor Amoah."

"You can't or you won't?"

"Pastor Amoah, even you must understand. These are matters of the heart. Haven't you ever felt like that? Where a woman lives inside you? Where you just need to have her? We are men, Pastor. We can be honest with each other."

"Sensuous cravings, being invitational nonetheless, and consummation or the lack thereof of lust are distinct. Resist evil."

"Evil, Pastor? This is evil?"

"Lust does not love equal." The Pastor asked me to come to his home. For prayers so I could resist temptation.

"I don't need prayers," I said. "I need blessings."

"I won't anoint or sanctify behavior so depraved," he said.

"You make me sad, Pastor."

"Your resolve is indecorous, unbefitting and unacceptable. Beware the *Dies Irae*."

"God will forgive me."

The Pastor said God didn't work that way. He forgives only when we repent. But one couldn't live in sin. And expect forgiveness. I told him my mind was made up. He said that was unfortunate. He had known me a long time. As a friend. I wasn't perfect. But he'd always had hope. That one day, I would get better. But now I was insulting his church. With polygamy. He said he couldn't accept that. Then he said it clearly. I would no longer be welcome in his church. The day I married a second wife.

"What are you saying, Pastor Amoah?"

He repeated his warning. I shouldn't step foot in his church. The day I married a second wife. It was that simple. He said. The choice was mine.

That shocked me. I tried to speak. But no words came out. I turned my back on Pastor Amoah. Then I walked away. My family was waiting. "I will never come to this church again," I told them.

"Why?" my wife asked. I told them everything. My wife sighed deeply. But she didn't say anything. Neither did my nephews, nieces or maid. But I knew what my daughter would have said. If she were with us. I was still trying to find her. But she was lost without a trace. Where could she be?

I went to see my friend, the mallam. He was his usual self. Quiet and contemplative. He looked at me and said, "My friend, you look like you have much on your mind. You don't look too well."

"Indeed," I said. "Can I take a little of your time?"

"Ah!" he exclaimed. "But must you even ask? You must come and visit me more, my friend. I haven't seen you in a long time. I knew the new Government gave you plenty of trouble. These young men have no respect for their elders."

"I think I can put that experience behind me."

"You must!" He took some cola nut from his pocket. He offered me some. I declined it. He bit a little cola. "How is the family?"

"The family is well, thank you?"

"The madam?"

"She is well."

"Oh, and your son … is he well now?"

"Yes. You remember? He is very well."

"We thank Allah."

We spoke about general things. Then I got impatient. I told him of my intentions. To marry a second wife.

He was silent for a long time. He pulled on his heavy beard. Then he bit more cola. He put his hand on my shoulder. "My brother, that is a heavy responsibility. 'You may marry of the women who seem good to you two or three or four, but if you fear that you cannot observe equity between them, then marry but a single wife.' The Holy Koran; 4:3. Think about it, my brother."

Later, I would think about it. I knew what the old sage was saying. The part about equity. But I was too far gone. I could not turn back now.

രൂ

20

I was shocked. That he would do it again. I saw him once, you know. A long time ago. He was about sixteen then. I had come home from work. My wife wasn't home. Nor were my other children. I parked the car in the garage. I opened the door to the living room. There, I saw him. He was admiring himself. Like one does when one has new clothes. He looked at his feet. Then at his behind.

I stood staring. Surprised. That he would dress up in women's clothes. And be so happy with it. He had on his mother's dress. And her high heeled shoes. He had put on lipstick. He even had rouge on his face. I stared at him a long time. Then he looked up and saw me. He looked shamed. For a long time I did not speak. Nor did he. But his mouth was opened. In embarrassment.

Finally, I asked, "Kubi, what are you doing?"

"I was ... I was ... trying ..." He stammered badly.

I felt sorry for him. But I wanted to know. Why he dressed up like a woman. "Why are you wearing your mother's clothes?"

"Papa, I ..."

He couldn't go on. He was so ashamed. He looked at his feet.

"Do you want to be a woman? You are a man. You shouldn't dress up like a woman. You hear?"

He nodded. Still, he didn't look up.

"Go to your room and change. And don't do this again."

He left quietly.

I didn't think much of it afterwards. Children do silly things. Especially when they are teenagers. But that was a long time ago.

149

When he was a mere teenager. I didn't expect him to do it. At age twenty-five.

It was as if history was repeating itself. It was a Friday afternoon. I felt tired. And came home early. I parked the car. It was quiet all around. I walked into the living room. There, I saw my son Kubi. He was dressed in a navy blue dress. It had little sunflowers all over it. Kubi was looking at himself. And admiring the dress. And touching it in different places. The dress fitted him quite well. I knew it wasn't his mother's. It was too small. Could it be his sister's dress? I had never seen her wear it before. But then, I probably just hadn't noticed. After all, I had a lot on my mind.

I stood staring at my son. For a long time he didn't see me. I watched his face. Painted in rouge and lipstick. Then he turned around. And saw me. He was surprised. But not ashamed. As he had been before.

"Papa," he said.

"Kubi."

He laughed a little laugh. It had no mirth.

"What are you doing, Kubi?" I asked.

"Nothing, Papa."

"Nothing?"

"I'm just standing here."

"Dressed up like a woman?"

"I was just trying it on."

"Women's clothes? Can't you dress up as a man? Why a woman's clothes?"

"I don't know, Papa. I just felt like trying it on."

"Whose dress is it anyway?"

He was quiet for a while. It seemed he was thinking of an answer.

"I bought it," he said finally.

"You bought it? You bought a woman's dress? What is wrong with you?"

"There's nothing wrong with me. There's nothing wrong with wearing a dress, Papa."

"There's something very wrong with it." He didn't respond. "And the lipstick. Why the lipstick, Kubi?"

"It's nothing. This is harmless. It doesn't hurt anybody, Papa."

"I think you need to find yourself a wife. Soon, Kubi. You are not a young man."

"I will marry when I am ready, Papa."

"I hope soon. A wife will ease your mind. Take it off such foolishness."

"Papa, this isn't foolishness."

I shook my head. In disgust. And yes, in pity. I wanted him to be a man. Not a man who wants to be a woman. "I do not understand you."

"This is nothing."

He walked away calmly. He was not ashamed. I wanted him to be ashamed. To feel guilty. But it was as if he didn't care. Was I just too old? Making noise over nothing? My head ached from it all. I got a bottle of beer. Then I drank it. I was increasingly tormented by the disappearance of my daughter Akosua. I drank too much. To help me sleep. As for Kubi, he was a grown man. What could I do? Sometimes, one just waits. And hopes for the best.

ॐ

21

I got married to Ama Owusu three months later. It was done quietly. I rented a little house for her. In Dansoman, near Accra. I couldn't go to Pastor-Lawyer Amoah's church again. He had asked me not to. So I had to find a new church. Jericho Church of Christ. That's where I went. My wife didn't come. She wanted to keep going to Pastor Amoah's church. I granted her that wish. So she continued to go there. With the rest of the family. And our maid Aba.

The Sun by Night

I had gone to see my friend Kwamena. I told him about Pastor Amoah. Kwamena laughed for one minute.

"What is so funny?" I asked.

"Oh, my friend. Why are you worried just because Pastor Amoah will not let you into his church? Churches these days are as abundant as flies. If he won't let you into his church, find another one. In fact, why don't you come to my new church with me? You will like it."

"What kind of church is it?"

"You will see."

So I waited till Sunday. I went and picked up Kwamena. The church was in a worn-out building at Because. The building was very small. In front was a big black cross. We entered. I saw drums and a conga in the church. On the far corner. And a guitar, a maraca, and a piano. We sat down and waited. It was eight thirty. There were only about eight people there. But by nine, the room was full.

Then suddenly we heard a loud yell. A yell of pleasure. With plenty of energy. Clapping followed this. A group of people entered the room. All were men except one. They were all in blue gowns. Only the female wore a red gown. They began to sing as they walked in. And they were dancing also. Everyone got up as they entered. The church was in a frenzy. For five minutes. The singing and clapping and dancing were intense. One of the blue-gowned men picked up a maraca. One got behind the piano. And one picked up a conga. Three got behind the drums. The music they made was loud and sweet.

By now it was clear who was in charge. The red-gowned woman raised her hand. The music stopped immediately. "My friends," she said in a powerful voice, "Why are we here today?"

"Because God wills it," a blue-gowned man said.

"Amen," she said. Then she started another song. And she shook herself loose. Shaking her body wildly. Moving here and there. Jumping up and down. The congregation began to imitate her. Everywhere, people jumped and shook their bodies. Some moved into the aisle. She ordered the music to stop after a long while. She launched into a sermon. Without notes or a script. She spoke about envy and greed.

And lambasted those not content with what they had. She continued for ten minutes. It wasn't her message that shook you. It was her zeal. Her passion. Her sermon was punctuated by the blue-gowned men. "Amen" or "That's true," or "Praise the Lord" or "Hallelujah."

Abruptly, she commanded, "Prayer!!!"

And the church was transformed. Into a marketplace of prayer. Many yelled loudly. Some spoke in tongues. It was hard for me to concentrate. So I ended up listening to others pray. Suddenly a woman fell down. Her body was seized with spasms.

"Praise the Lord!" the leader said.

"Hallelujah!"

"I said, Praise the Lord!!!"

"Hallelujah!!!"

"Look here!" she yelled.

And the congregation looked. She pointed to the fallen woman. Then she went and stood over her. "Devil that dwells in this temple of God. I command you in the name of Jesus Christ to leave this woman alone. In the name of Jesus. Jeeeesuuuus!!!"

"Amen!"

The fallen woman shrieked.

"I say come out of this woman. Now!!!"

The fallen woman went into more spasms. Then she was still. "Take her outside," said the leader. "She needs room to rest now that the Devil has left her."

The woman was carried outside. The leader smiled. "This is God's house. There is no room for evil. This morning God spoke to me and told me that the Devil was going to send an emissary here today. God told me to be strong. He said he would be with me. The woman you just saw taken outside was possessed by demons. She thought she could cast an evil spell on this church. She came here to test me. But now the evil in her has been defeated. She has been redeemed. We must keep her in our prayers. Praise the Lord!"

Then the singing and dancing started again. I was inspired. The drum and conga beat. The guitar was stroked and the piano played. I too danced wildly. There was something here. The force of energy and power. The collection box was put out for the offering. And we all danced our way to it. The leader had her eyes closed. Chanting all the time.

After the church service I went to her. "I enjoyed your service a lot," I said.

"Thank you, Mr. Manu," she said.

"How do you know me?"

"Everybody knows you. You are a famous man. Or don't you know that?"

"I didn't realize that."

"Money makes you famous. Be careful, Mr. Manu. But I'm not speaking to be critical. How are things going with you?"

"Everything is fine. I just got married."

"At your age? You waited a long time."

"Oh. This is my second wife."

"Congratulations, Mr. Manu. A good marriage is a blessing of God."

"Thank you."

"Come again next week. We are happy to see you here."

Akosua returned three months after she left. By then, the country had a new president. I was overjoyed to see her. But I was afraid to ask her questions. She said a mechanical hello. And went to her room. She hardly spoke to me. I had to learn from my wife. That Akosua had simply gone and stayed with her friend. I didn't ask why. I knew the answer to that question. I was deeply hurt. I had lost the ease with which I could interact with my family. Even my wife. She was more silent now. Perhaps even cold. It seemed some distrust had grown between us all. I spent more and more time with my new wife. I discovered what

Mother and Father had mentioned. About her character. She did have a very sharp tongue. But I learned to live and deal with it.

I had done damage. I had to repair it. I didn't know how. I hoped and hoped the damage was not permanent.

ॐॐ

22

I saw Grandpapa today. I swear we bought the casket he'd always wanted.

I saw him the day after I was released on bail.

The casket was expensive. But we respected his wishes. The wishes of the dead. That's the way it goes. Mother and I went and got it. Exactly as Grandpapa had specified. So why did I see him? It couldn't be because of the casket. We all thought he would like it. And the funeral was grand indeed. Mother and Father outspent themselves. They even hired mourners. The drinks were abundant. Many people attended. And all spoke good things about Grandpapa. My mother's father. What more could the dead ask for?

Grandpapa, who taught me the ways of the world. Even before Mother and Father. He had me close to him most of the time. He would tell me things. He taught me respect for my elders. He taught me courage. And he taught me love. Yes, Grandpapa taught me a lot. I really loved him. Perhaps because Grandmama died before I was born. So Grandpapa was both Grandmama and Grandpapa in one. "Nana," I would say as I approached. Then I would see the smile. His smile. It took control of his face. And truth is, the smile was always there. Even when he was angry. For that reason, I didn't fear him. I went to Grandpapa. When Mother or Father said something I didn't like. Grandpapa would gather me. And put me on his lap. Then he would say something sweet. And I would be happy. Mother would complain that Grandpapa was spoiling me. But Grandpapa kept smiling. I always remembered the smile. Even after he died.

And that makes things even more confusing. When I saw Grandpapa today, he wasn't smiling. I saw his white hair. I saw his wrinkled face. But no smile.

"Nana, is that you?" I asked. He said nothing. "Nana?"

All Grandpapa did was shake his head. He pointed to the coat he was wearing. It was the same coat Mother gave me. The day she died. Mother passed it on to me. Just as Grandpapa bequeathed it to her. It was sewn from the *kente* cloth.

I have often wondered. Why would Grandpapa make a coat out of kente?

Did I need a new one? I asked myself.

If I need a new one, I will get it myself. Or I will sew it myself. I don't need someone else to tell me. They say the coat of another man's Grandpapa will fit me? What if it's too big? They say I will grow into it? Maybe I will. Or maybe I will die trying. And what if it is too small? They say I will lose weight and fit into it? And what if in trying to lose weight I die from the effort?

And then it was as if I was being transported. Transported to my childhood. All I could think of was Grandpapa's milk. I felt as if it was many years ago. I was just a little boy. I went to Grandpapa in the night. Everyone else was asleep. I felt weak and tired. I entered Grandpapa's room. Neither of us spoke. Grandpapa just reached out. Then he held me and brought me close. To his exposed chest. Then he offered me his nipple. And I took it in my mouth. Grandpapa squeezed his chest. Then they lactated. I drunk hungrily from Grandpapa. I went back to bed refreshed. Reinvigorated. Later, I would wonder. Whether it was a dream. Or whether it actually happened.

In an instant, Grandpapa was gone. I should have been happy. To see Grandpapa after all these years. But I was sad. Because Grandpapa looked sad. How do I know? Because he didn't smile. All the time he stood there. He stared and never smiled. Not once. Grandpapa? Yes. I swear I saw Grandpapa. He wasn't happy. He was angry.

Yet I swear we bought the casket he'd always wanted.

THE WITNESS-IN-CHIEF

1

Talk to me, my nana Daughter of my daughter Let the oil of your saliva lubricate your words Woman to woman I want to hear your voice unencumbered Unshackled from its maddening experiences Speak to the depths of your experience Draw from its wells with the spacious bucket of your anguish I want to know It is your voice that offers me the light I need for my hind vision I walked the road but I walked it in my present tense Now I shine your voice like light on the road already covered But I am not simply seeking to retrieve it or gaze at it I can juxtapose that road with your lighted voice against the road without it.

It will help still my curiosity Yes But it will also show the possibilities I could have had, the options Perhaps it can help you, as well For it will show you the benefit of my search The this or the that.

Because I live in you, you owe it to me as much as you owe it to yourself I want your vision to be clear as wind Your voice strong as experience And I will hear you clearly as my own voice But I can vow no understanding of equal clarity Difference is difference But because the left and the right hands work better together than alone, we have no choice Therefore, I beseech you Unfurl the flow of your tongue.

Nana, mother of my mother, please hear my call. Or is there a prayer I can make before even you? I know you have joined the ancestral pool, but, Grandmother, how are you treated over there? You, who shared her matrimonial bed with two other women. Do you even hear me? And if you hear me, do you understand me? Or are they telling you over there to order me to shut up? Are they asking you to tell me to take it without complaint the way I recall you doing? Nana, although you died when I was only thirteen, I don't recall you ever mentioned it. You never complained that grandfather had two other wives. I was puzzled a little even then because I did not understand why father had only one wife and grandfather had three.

Nana, please forgive me that I call on you for such selfish reasons, but I am hurting. My husband has decided to take a second wife. There's nothing I have against the woman, Ama Owusu. I don't know much about her, so how can I hate her? And how can I hate her for wanting something I have, when I know that what I have is good? Isn't it natural that others would want a good thing?

But, Nana, how can I live in the same house with her? Have I not kept Koo's house all this time? Was it not I who raised the children while he was away making money? When a child was sick and vomiting, wasn't it I who made sure that the vomit was cleaned up or the medical attention gotten? When the rooms needed cleaning, wasn't it I who did it? And when Koo himself was ill or needed consoling when he was down, was I not the one who fetched the patience and wisdom of you and mother and gave it to him? Wasn't it I who struggled to get him released from detention? Is the sharing of my home with another woman the reward? Nana, I make recall you had your own quarters, but still you lived in the household with my other grandmothers. How did you do it?

But I ramble on. I have traveled far on this road. I must reclaim the joys I felt in the journey. I must draw from that so I can stay strong. I cannot tell him how I feel. My words will get lost in the emotion. I may say something I don't intend. So perhaps it's best that I accept it. And, Nana, what if I protest too strongly and he makes a decision to leave me? I possess no skills except childrearing. What will I do at this stage of my life?

I reach far back to the day Koo and I got married. When Mama and Papa called me and told me his parents had asked for my hand, the idea disgusted me. I'd just completed secondary school, Nana. I was neither the best nor worst student. Granted, my grades were not good enough to get into university right away, but I wanted to try again. I was confident I could do it. So when Maamie and Papa told me of the proposal, I said no. "I want to go to university," I said.

"Listen to me, Akosua," Papa said sternly. "You don't get very many chances like this. You are not young. You are already twenty years old. Need I remind you of that? If you want to be book-long, go ahead, but you will regret it when one day you wake up and realize that you're too old for any man; when you realize that no man wants you."

"But Papa, it will only take a few years."

"And you think he will be waiting for you? Akosua, he comes from a very good family. And he is a good man, very resourceful. He will make a good husband for you. You know I won't be here forever to take care of you."

"I don't even know him, Papa," I said.

"Listen to your father, Akosua," Maamie said.

"Maamie, I just want to finish school."

"Akosua, please don't be stubborn," she said. "We are doing this for your own good."

I was silent for a while as I didn't want to say anything they would consider disrespectful.

Papa asked, "So what is your answer?"

"I need time to think about it," I said.

"To think about what? What do you need to think about, Akosua? To me, this is a simple matter. Either you want to marry him, or you don't."

Maamie whispered something in Papa's ear. "Very well," Papa said. "It's only fair that we give you some time to think the matter over. Think very hard about this and let us know. I know you'll make the right decision. After all, you are my daughter."

And I thought over it a long time. I must admit that Koo, as I then made recall of him walking around town, wasn't bad looking. I knew he had left for Accra, but I'd given him no attention before he left and, as far as I could tell, he'd given me no attention either. But with the marriage proposal made, I spoke with people I thought might know him. Everyone I spoke with said good things about him. Under different circumstances, I wouldn't mind getting married to a man like him, but finishing university first was important to me. So I stalled for two months by either avoiding Maamie and Papa or telling them I was still thinking about it. But I couldn't do that for too long.

Maamie came to me and spoke with such deep concern I knew she wanted the best for me. "Akosua," she said, "I know this is a difficult choice for you. Marriage is not a small matter. In my days, a woman would jump at the opportunity to marry someone like Koo Manu. Your father and I have inquired about him. He is a good man. And he comes from a good family. I know times have changed. These days you young women want to make your own decisions. I don't quarrel with that. But think about it, Akosua. Ask yourself if it's going to get any better for you. A woman is dealt very few marbles. She has to play them very carefully. One false move could be disastrous. Akosua, we don't have the same leeway as men. School is good, but school will not raise a family."

"Maamie, is it then your point that raising a family is all we need to be concerned about?"

"When you have your own children, Akosua, you will realize that there's nothing more important than giving birth to another human being. That, my daughter, is our greatest advantage over the male species."

Those times have changed, I wanted to tell Maamie. A woman's education doesn't have to compete with her marriage or her choice of whom to marry, I wanted to tell her. I wanted to let her know that her way of thinking belonged in the past. But I recognized the honesty and earnestness with which she'd spoken and I could hardly speak back to her. And I rethought my position. I knew I couldn't try to pursue an education when my parents wanted me married. Plus, I had to be realistic in that it was possible I could never get into university. Also, that I wasn't the most beautiful woman in town, I knew. If I let this opportunity pass and I didn't get into university, where would I be? Although I'd been confident before, Maamie's words and Papa's warnings made me very nervous. I was very confused, but I knew I had to make a choice soon.

After much thought, I made the decision to marry Koo Manu. Nana, as you can imagine, it wasn't a very easy decision. And even after I made the decision, I stalled a little until Papa got angry and said, "I need your answer one way or the other." I said yes. "You will not regret this decision," my father assured.

Once the formal decision was reached, I made a vow to be a good wife to Koo Manu. I would be loyal and dutiful, take care of him and raise our children as best as I could. As best as I had observed you and Maamie do it. Nana, I was a resolved woman on the day I got married. And Koo made me happy on our first night together. He was so kind and thoughtful and gentle. At first, I was a little shy and looked away from him when he wanted to consummate the marriage. And yet he didn't rush me. Instead, although it was clear that he was drunk, he started talking to me, telling me about Accra and its fast life. He said that day was a very happy one for him because he'd gotten married to me. He wanted me to be happy, too. He said I should have no concerns for he would always work hard to provide for our children and me. Then he asked me what I liked to do. I told him how I sometimes helped at my father's pottery shop. As he listened to me speak, I lost some of my shyness. Then, when he started his second attempt to consummate the marriage, I wasn't afraid.

And so it flows like a river bending through the trees eternally like birth Granddaughter, to find a companion for life is as natural as the raindrops of a storm It is like a handshake prolonged We walk its roads with wide-opened arms, receiving its lashes and drinking its weight deeply.

I hear your voice booming under the weight yet to come For that which is fresh is blind to the rust of the far sights, with eyes not trained to view the stench underneath the mighty tree that seems to bear the storm without shudder So these are the blinds you wear as you enter this relationship The smile is yours, but it belongs to him more than it belongs to you.

So your hesitation is like a natural reaction to a stimulus you don't know Almost like a child tossed to the wind The beat in your chest drums for the sake of the sheath you will need Listen to it great blood of my blood Listen to it like you listen to the sound in the dark forest Know it like the habits of your enemies You will need that cautious heartbeat.

But, my nana, I shall not be the bad kernel that spoils the soup You are wise and therefore you know what I mean So let these moments enfold you like a warm wrapper on a cold night Feel it and let it transport you into its world where at least for moments magic flashes for you and you can dance into the twilight Renew the feeling in the watered dusk that leads to the long night of rapture and excess But don't let your soul be debauched by its attractions.

In the dawn, keep this wrapper the way you will keep a beautiful bead For when other nights fall, you will hold it the way a mother finds comfort in the life of her children amid the threats unfolding before them And those mishaps she doesn't know yet.

৵৻৵

2

Nana, our first days in Accra were blissful. Koo did not possess of a lot of money then, but it was still the happiest time. He spent a lot of time at home with me, talking with me. In fact, he seemed to want to hurry home from work to be with me. I looked forward all day to seeing him. I would make him the best meal I could and it was a pleasure to see him eat and enjoy my meals. I would take a bus to Makola Market and shop for my husband. Nana, it was a sight to see: downtown Accra with so many people in one place. The human traffic as well as the cars and trucks made for a very noisy afternoon of shopping. Once I got to the market, I was assaulted by voices calling me to buy tomatoes or onions or beans or this or that. Often, I was faced with the whiff of heated air, redolent with fried fish and the aroma of boiled beans and fried plantains and boiled yams mixed with the perfumed and sometimes choking sweat of market women's sweat. The noise was a bit too much for me, but I shopped happily in anticipation of the meal I would make for Koo.

Sometimes, especially at weekends, Koo would take me places. The beach was his favorite place. We would go there and sit, talk or swim. And we were together most nights and Koo was always patient and tender.

Nana, as you can tell, I had little feeling for him when I heard he was going to be my husband; I married him out of duty and fear. But he made me love him by the way he treated me. Nana, isn't it love when you miss your husband so much you want him to come home and be with you? Isn't it love when you want him to be with you all the time? Isn't it love, Nana, when you take so much pride in seeing him happy, and being happy because you make him happy?

And then I became pregnant. Nana, I'm sure you'll understand when I say that the day I realized I was pregnant was one of the happiest for me. Tears came to my eyes, while I cried your name many times. I'm not sure why I invoked your name that time, but it was a cry of joy that seemed to want you there with me, perhaps to see that I, your beloved granddaughter, was to give you a great grandchild. I was so determined to be a good mother to the child. You should have seen Koo then. I had never seen so much excitement in him. The day he found out, he invited his best friend Kwamena over for a meal. In the following days he went about bragging to others that he was going to be a father. I thought he overdid it, but can you deny a man his pride? Me, he treated like a goddess. And for the nine months the child was carried by me, Koo spent a lot of time by my side.

But that changed when I had the child. Koo was even happier, and so was I. Nana, I had never imagined the power of the joy of actually holding a child that was your own. I'm sure you'll agree that the feeling is too deep and complex to describe. Koo organized a small party and ceremony to name the child. But then a new zeal to work harder possessed him. "To make sure my wife and child are well taken care of," he said.

So he was gone most of the time. He would arrive home exhausted and try to play with the child a little, and then fall asleep. Early the next morning he was gone before I even woke up. I tried to understand. After all, he had a lot more responsibility. And how could I argue that he stay at home when he insisted he had to work especially hard for our child? So, Nana, I was left most of the time with my Kubi. Maamie traveled to Accra for a while to help raise the child and teach me how to take care of Kubi. I was so glad when she came. But she couldn't stay too long because she was ailing. I insisted that she spend more time at home because I knew she was happier there than in Accra. So I was left alone once again with my Kubi.

I treated Kubi like a part of my heart, Nana. I loved that child so much, I didn't know what I'd do if something happened to him. I watched over him with extreme care and attention. He was the only source of joy at that time as Koo was almost always gone, even at weekends, and sometimes on long treks.

As you can imagine, I was so delighted when Asantewaa and her husband Kuuku moved next door. They were a very nice couple. Like Kwamena, Kuuku also worked with Customs. Like me, Asantewaa stayed at home to take care of their little daughter. I had a companion now and, Nana, I cherished it. We bonded very quickly and most days I would go to their home or Asantewaa would come to mine. We would make long conversations and talk about our babies. As time went on, when we got bored, we invented a game. Nana, it was a silly game invented by two mothers who wanted to add excitement to their lives.

We called the game *Your Baby, My Baby*. I made pretend that Asantewaa's daughter was mine and for hours I would be responsible for taking care of that child. I would hold her daughter and call her my son. Asantewaa did the same with Kubi, holding him, carrying him and calling him her daughter. And then we went a little further and started dressing them in each other's clothes. For the next couple of years, Asantewaa's daughter and Kubi grew up together and played together. Kubi seemed happy whenever I took them over or they came to our home.

As for Koo, he was almost always exhausted from working. Occasionally, in the middle of the night, he would find some energy. And from those occasional surges, I got pregnant with my daughter Akosua. I had her just about the time Asantewaa and Kuuku left the neighborhood. I got even busier now that I had two children to raise and I devoted the next few years to doing that. What intrigued me a bit was that by the time Kubi was six, he'd developed the habit on occasion of asking to wear his sister's clothes. He'd cry when I refused until I relented. Nana, I didn't make much of it and I attributed it to a little child's exploration. And a couple of years later Kubi stopped asking me altogether to wear his sister's clothes.

Nana, all this while Koo was staying busy and amassing wealth. We would soon move to a very big house in Labone. Nana, I wish you could see the house. It was massive, beyond anything I could have imagined. It had nice flowers in the front, mostly planted because Akosua wanted them. And, Nana, you should have seen the respect we got when Koo drove us around in his Mercedes Benz. Yes, we had a lot of wealth.

Koo only had time to try and make more babies on the few occasions when he found energy in the middle of the night. And that is how I got pregnant with Kwame and then Kofi, two pregnancies and births that happened very close to each other.

The life of children A currency of the species Explosions of joy In the haggle with life for better terms of existence, children are an indispensable leverage But pray that death or its agents do not diminish that leverage.

Theirs is a joy of shared experiences evoked in lives not yet trampled by the seasons of a road riddled with its own shattering disappointments You might say disgusting as a maggot that feeds eternally on feces But before I condemn the maggot too much, let me step back a second and take another look. It is its own existence at stake? Is it so disgusting if it feeds on excreta in order to draw its nutrients? The waste of others from which it must draw existence and attempt to perpetuate itself? Look closely, my nana Here you will find many lessons to last a lifetime.

There are many options But they are not parallel paths clearly compared This is one option So let the children rise like mushrooms to taste the dropping rains of life Hold a child here and another one there Stroke a hair Nurse a wound Soothe a pain Suck out phlegm with your mouth and taste its innocence Wipe soiled behinds Prepare that meal Make that bed Feel the bite of neophyte teeth on your lactating breasts.

And let the children rise.

And yet in all these, my granddaughter, never forget the lesson of the maggot and his feces. It is as much a road of the future as any.

But it is a road whose thorns rise like angry mushrooms Poisonous in their venom It is a road trapped in its camouflaged potholes and those wide-opened like gaping sores with more overwhelming stench than excreta at its worst.

So, step carefully when you see the tar that lies like a mirage across its vastness Teach the children too Tread wisely when you see the trees lining its edges like a protective sheath See who resides on the trees shaking its rotten fruits loose Teach the children too Hold hands across its width and then raise them to pluck the ripe fruits Reach deeper down to fill the potholes and then step forward The tar is your friend Yes the road is the road of the past And the future.

ॐ∙ॐ

3

Nana, I don't know what happened, but as I paid more attention to raising my other children, I may have neglected Kubi a little. You see, the way I reasoned, he was much older and, therefore, needed less attention than his younger siblings. But, Nana, I couldn't believe it when one day I went with our driver to pick him up from school and I was called to the headmaster's office. Kubi was only thirteen then. "Madam," the headmaster said, "your son was caught smoking marijuana. That is an offense we can't condone in this institution. I have no choice but to expel him."

"Expel him?" Nana, I was shocked. That Kubi was into drugs, I had no clue. Besides, how could I sit by and let him be expelled from school? Nana, if I had one regret, it was forgoing my education in order to get married and raise a family. I would do anything to ensure that my children reached as far as they could go. "Kubi, is this true?"

I asked him. I knew it was true when he looked down. I turned to the headmaster and said, "Please reconsider this decision. It's a rather harsh one, if you consider that this is the first offense."

"But, madam, that wouldn't be fair to the other children who have been expelled for the same offense, would it?"

"Teacher, is there anything I can do to make you change your mind?"

He was silent when I said that, eyeing Kubi instead. I asked Kubi to leave the office. When I was alone with the headmaster I took some money and gave it to him.

He counted it and said, "Now you have spoken, madam. As you will understand, I too must eat. But I must do a token act and suspend him for a week, otherwise my teachers will be very angry with me."

"I can understand that, but I must request that you keep this between you and me. I don't want anyone else to find out."

"That is an additional obligation, madam." I gave him more money. "You have spoken well, madam," he said.

"Why did you do that, Kubi?" I asked him.

"Where is Papa?" was his response.

"You'd better pray he doesn't find out. He will be very disappointed, very angry."

"What does he care? He's never around anyway. He's not going to care what happens."

"Don't say that. Your father works very hard to make sure you get everything you need. This is what we are going to do. For the next week, we will pretend everything is normal. You will pretend you're going to school and no one but you and I will know what has actually happened. I just want you to promise that you will never do this again."

"I promise," he said.

Nana, I thought the failure was mine. Wasn't I the one responsible for raising him? How would his father feel if he knew that I had failed? Nana, that is how I felt and that is why I came up with that scheme.

๛

4

So Koo had made the decision to take a second wife. Nana, this was when I needed your help the most. I wanted to call on you for guidance. I wanted you to teach me how to cope. As best as I could make recall, I had three grandmothers on my mother's side. Nana, how did you do it? Did you not feel betrayed when grandfather married a second and then a third wife? How could you bear to share a husband with other women? It must have taken the greatest act of selflessness. And the grace with which you did it, Nana, amazed me. I could make no recall of complaints or rancor. I could only recall how well you all got along.

But *I* felt an upheaval in my chest that was so powerful I didn't know what to do. Nana, is it that times have changed or is it that I possess the wrong attitude? Grandfather had three wives, yes; but Papa had only one. I asked myself, why? I recalled the day Baffour came to visit Papa. I recalled Papa being asked by him, "Now that you are so successful, Baako, how many more wives are you going to take to help Eno Yaa around the house? She needs some help, you know."

"She hasn't complained. And one is enough for me, Baffour," Papa said.

"What is wrong with you?" Baffour asked. "Are you impotent?"

"Why am I impotent? Because I want to stay with one woman?"

"Didn't your own father have four?"

"But those times were different, Baffour. In his days, wives bore you children that you could use as labor. It was a way of raising human capital. I don't need that kind of labor. My stores are doing well without the need for many children to help."

"It's not that. If you take another wife and you can support her, it will show your wealth, cement your social status."

"But I have two houses and three stores. I think that's enough to show I have done well for myself."

"Baako, listen to me. You need to take another wife, first for your own survival. You don't think our forefathers knew what they were doing? You never know which of your children will survive. The more you have, the more you ensure you would leave some behind by the time you're dead. Not only does that ensure the continuity of your blood, but that of the human race. Second, let me talk about gratification. The more children you have, the more gratified you are. Each child brings a new character to the pool, adds to its dynamism. In and of itself, that's enough reason to be fruitful and multiply. But what can a man do on his own? A man can't naturally bear and have children, only women can. It makes sense, therefore, for the man to help as many women as feasible to bear children."

"How about love, Baffour?"

"Love has nothing to do with it, Baako. Marriage should not be based on love. Look, Baako, our forefathers were wise. They realized that for a marriage to work, you had to unite families, not just a man and a woman. You need the centripetal influence of the extended family, its support systems. You can divorce a man or a woman very easily, but not so easily families. If you unite families, you build a marriage on solid ground. If you marry simply for love, what happens when that love is gone? My friend, you need more than love. So, if you marry with expectations of love everlasting, then you have no need to stay in it when you think there is no more love. If you marry for other practical reasons, like having children, supporting each other in times of need, then you are looking at a long-term marriage."

"If there's no love, I don't see how you can support each other or successfully raise children," said Papa. "Besides, marriage is not worth it if husband and wife don't love each other."

"You can't be serious. Societies have been successfully raised on marriages that had nothing to do with mutual love. I don't think I can say the same for marriages that are supposed to be based on love. That's why our children are getting divorced at such an increasing rate these days. In any case, what's all this noise about love? We are by nature meant to want more than one woman. Our forefathers recognized this basic truth and they were not hypocritical about it. They created institutions to reflect this natural condition. So tell me which is better: to marry more than one woman and be faithful to them, or to marry one and stray? Or which is better: to marry more than one and be faithful or to marry and divorce, and marry and divorce, and on and on?"

Papa made a deep sigh and I could tell he was getting tired of listening to Baffour's lecture. "Baffour," he said, "you've stated a number of reasons why you think I should take a second wife. That's your opinion. I have mine. But let me just say this. In all your talk, you neglect one basic fact: equity. First, the relationship between a first wife and the wives that follow is necessarily inequitable. Either the first wife enjoys a higher status or she is unfairly relegated to a different status in favor of younger women. It is just not possible for a husband to treat them equally. Second, the institution itself is not equitable. Why must a man be able to take more than one wife and not the woman?"

"Ah! But by nature, custom and tradition, that is not permissible; although I hear that in some places, even here in Africa, they allow women to marry more than one man. Even here in our country, there's no law against it. As far as I know, that is."

"The nature thing is subject to debate and dispute. Forget custom or tradition. Just ask yourself whether it's fair."

'My friend, you can't ignore tradition or custom."

"Even if it's unfair? Even if it's wrong?"

"It's not wrong or unfair. Traditions count a lot, they speak to the cohesion of the people, and they reflect the soul of the people. You are asking for trouble when you upturn them in favor of things not natural to the people. Plus, women are different from men."

"Oh, Baffour, you are living in a sad world."

Nana, they went on and on. Papa shrugged off Baffour's accusation that he was impotent and that Maamie had either bewitched him or given him some *juju*. That day, though, I was so proud of Papa, much prouder than I had ever been. Years later, as I stood ready to get married, I would recall that conversation and forgive Papa. I could see him as a man affected by his times, but not consumed by them.

Granddaughter, If you haven't used another road you hesitate to abandon the one you are used to It is the story of order The natural inertia of humankind It takes the adventurous to strike out to new roads But it is not necessarily a good thing.

My nana, I know the lump that lodges like a bone in your throat as you recall these things But do not point fingers at we who came before you We had our times We did what we could with what we had We turn back time to secure a mandate to participate in the future That is what you seem to be doing I like that.

The selflessness of reaching for the arm of your other sons and daughters (borne by your husband's other wives) is as sweet to me as the joy of birthing my children Remember the fruit sprouting to the call of the rain It is a noble calling, to share without rancor It is not a difficult task if that is your familiar path And remember the independence of being one among many The freedom to come and go.

Having said that, I too would rather be the tree But failing that, there is something to be said for being one of many branches Never completely free, but with some room to breathe But to be a seed in a fruit That's another question For if the fruit rots what will happen to the seed? These are difficult matters that have no easy answers.

My nana, I am not attempting to justify anything Nor do I intend to apologize for anything New roads have been cleared for you Paths that were barely noticeable in our times are becoming clearer You must do as you wish with it But do not be surprised that these are roads whose thorns rise also.

Koo made the decision to take a second wife at a time when I thought the family would stay even stronger together to lick its wounds. Nana, when Koo got involved with the Government, I was happy for him, but also a bit apprehensive. That politics can be a very dangerous thing, we all know. But with only a few months left before the Government would be taken over by the civilians, who would have thought a coup would interrupt the process like a massive hiccup at the end of a speech? But it happened, Nana, and we were all swept into its whirlwind.

I heard of Koo's capture through Kubi. He had a friend in the army, a colonel who was appointed Liaison Officer with Powers Plenipotentiary between the Military Machinery and The Revolutionary Council. Whatever that means; your guess is as good as mine. When Kubi told me, I got very anxious. What could I do to get my husband out of detention? Through Kubi's colonel, I learned that Koo was being held at Usher Forte. I went to see Lawyer Dadzie, who soon would be busy running for parliament. He tried to use his influence, but to no avail. They wouldn't even allow me to see Koo. Once, Lawyer Dadzie accompanied me to Usher Forte. He demanded in his legal jargon that we needed to see his client. The soldiers brought a machine gun to his chest and said if we didn't leave in thirty seconds, the only thing we'd see would be his lifeless body. Nana, how can one argue with a gun? We left the place in fifteen seconds.

My only hope was Kubi's colonel. Kubi arranged a meeting between us. I went to his office at Burma Camp. He had left word that I was coming, so the soldiers let me through checkpoints without harassment. He offered me beer when I arrived. I politely refused. He said he knew why I'd come to see him. "We will take care of your husband, but it will be very hard, madam, very hard. You know there are some in the Government who want him finished off."

"But papa soldier, what has he done?"

"Oh madam, don't you see? He was captured trying to escape. He flouted direct orders to surrender to the nearest police station."

"But he has done nothing wrong."

"Madam, I won't argue whether he's done wrong or not. This is a revolution. It is the power of the people. It is the justice of the masses. Your husband is in serious trouble. People have been executed for lesser offenses."

"Can you help him?"

"Now you're talking, madam. Now you're talking. Your son is my friend. I wouldn't do this for anybody, you know. My neck is on the line. I will help him. But you have to help me help him. This will cost a lot of money."

And then we started to bargain. It seemed like that day I bailed Kubi out in school. I tried my best to cut down his colonel's asking price, but he only went down an insignificant notch. After that, it was take it or leave it. I decided to take it before he changed his mind. He came over, and with his beer-polluted lips planted a kiss on my lips. Nana, if it weren't for my fear of his power, I could have done him murder there and then. And then as I was leaving, he smacked my behind. Nana, we were the only ones in the room, but my mood was stained for weeks by the humiliation I felt. I would learn later that although my bribe secured Koo's release, he had to pay an additional price in beatings and a suspended sentence and confiscated assets before his detractors would be satisfied. They also barred him from any future involvement in politics.

6

Although I was disappointed, when I called my children to me, I told them I was accepting Koo's decision. Nana, I may have been stupid for doing that, but I didn't want them to think me unhappy. Nor did I want to do anything to turn them against their father. I could have done that very easily, I'm sure. I am the one who raised them, after all. And they listened to me most of the time. All I did was tell them their father was going to take a second wife, that we should wish the marriage well, and that all I wanted was for his second wife to live elsewhere. Nana, I was shocked by my daughter Akosua's reaction. Yes, that she'd not like the idea, I'd expected; but not the storm of anger that took control over her... Your great granddaughter's voice shook as she said, "Are you going to sit down and let this happen? What nonsense!"

"Calm down," I said to her.

"No, you can't let him do this."

"What do you propose?" Kofi asked.

"Tell him no," she said.

"And if he goes ahead anyway?"

"Then ... leave him."

"That's nonsense," Kofi said. "She can't leave just like that."

"Yes, she can!" Akosua yelled. She clenched her fists and moved towards Kofi. "What do you mean that's nonsense? Are you condoning such behavior?" Akosua was in such a rage, I was afraid she would hit her brother.

"There's no need for this," I said.

"So what now?" Kwame asked.

"What are you going to do?" Kubi asked.

"Leave everything to me," I said. And just then Koo walked into the room.

Akosua's anger notwithstanding, I knew Koo couldn't be stopped. I had to resign myself to it. I knew he would entertain little opposition. I knew the children were too deferential to oppose him. I was impressed by Akosua's performance, but even she couldn't go too far.

It came as no surprise when Akosua left home. You see, Nana, she'd told me about it. I tried to dissuade her but she said it had to be done. I knew where she was. I knew she was safe, but she swore me to secrecy. In all this, Nana, I thrived. Because I insisted Ama Owusu live elsewhere, I didn't have to contend with seeing her. Koo spent time with her, but he seemed guilty, so he spent some time with me as well.

He would even make time and take me to the beach like we used to do when we first got married.

હ~ઈ

7

Nana, oh Nana, Kubi and I could have used your help. He had always been the most difficult child for me. Akosua had an occasional temper, but that was it. Kofi was very bright and never gave me any trouble. Kwame was very quiet, so quiet his friends used to tease him: "As for you, Kwame, you don't know how to speak." And later, when he became slightly more talkative, they said, "Kofi is teaching you how to speak now?"

Nana, a false picture of domestic bliss is not what I want to paint, but it was the closest you could get. Surely, the children fought when they were younger, but which siblings don't? But Kubi seemed to drift and he couldn't be reined in. You see, in that week when we conspired to keep his suspension from school secret, I think Kubi lost some respect for me at a very profound level. Nana, he didn't tell me himself, but call it a mother's intuition. I could feel that he was very disappointed in me. I don't know if he felt I had betrayed his father by keeping it a secret, or if it was something else. Nana, Kubi seemed to withdraw from me. I tried to talk to him, ask him what was troubling him, but he said nothing.

I was so worried I knew I had to do some detective work of my own. One day while he was at school I passed by to observe him. Nana, I saw him playing with his friends, laughing and clowning even. I was happy to see him so alive with his friends but it troubled me that he didn't behave the same way around me. I decided I had to give him some time.

And then when he was sixteen or so he got his first girlfriend. Nana, it was the best and worst thing that happened to him. His girlfriend Boahemaa was very sweet and kind and generous and intelligent. She even reminded me of you. Naturally, we all liked her. Kubi was so enamored he seemed to have become a new man. He was so ebullient around Boahemaa that I always invited her to come home for something or to go some place with us. In fact, she became like a part of the family and Kubi's siblings even teased him about it.

Two years later, Kubi came to me and said he wanted to marry Boahemaa. "Are you sure, Kubi?" I asked. "Why don't you finish school first?" He insisted he had to marry her at that time. He said he was in love with her. "And what if you change your mind? Marriage is not a small step, you know."

"I will never change my mind," he said. "I can guarantee you that."

I remembered when my own parents wanted me to marry Koo and I didn't want to. It made me recall how angry I was that they wanted to dictate my life to me. Only this time, Kubi was running toward what I had tried to run away from. In any case, I didn't want to put undue pressure on Kubi. "We will have to discuss this with your father," I said. "You must promise me that if you get married you will finish university."

"I promise," he said. "I don't intend to quit school just because I am married."

But Koo was angry. "That's out of the question! Kubi, you are too young to get married."

"I am eighteen, Papa," Kubi protested.

"And you think you're grown? I am not allowing you to get married."

"And if I do?"

It was the first time I had seen Kubi so confrontational with his father. "You will defy me? If you marry her, don't come to my funeral when I die."

Kubi shrugged and left. Nana, I think even Koo realized he was walking on very dangerous territory. He called Kubi back. "I know you're not a child, Kubi," Koo said. "But you are still very young. You have your whole life ahead of you. I can understand that you want to marry Boahemaa. I think she's a good young woman. But, believe me, it's a little too early for you. Marriage carries a lot of responsibilities, Kubi. Why don't you wait a little?"

"Papa, she is the woman I want to marry."

"You have just been accepted to the University of Ghana. Are you willing to jeopardize that?"

"This will not interfere with my school."

Koo thought for a few seconds and said, "I propose another course..."

"But, Papa..."

"Listen to me! Instead of marriage, get engaged to her. That is almost like marriage. Only it's not as final. But you'd have declared your intention. The world will know you are serious. When you finish school, you can marry." Kubi was about to speak when Koo said, "Don't say anything now. Think about it."

I went to Kubi later and asked him what he'd decided. He said he still wanted to marry Boahemaa. "Your father has strained his pride to propose a compromise," I said. "I think you should take it."

He said he'd think about it. I went and spoke with Boahemaa. "I will support whatever decision you reach," I said. I proposed the idea of engagement to her. Perhaps she didn't want her potential mother-in-law to be offended. She agreed with me. A week later, Kubi said he'd postpone the wedding until he finished school. We organized a big engagement party for them. It would be a very long engagement, but we averted a potential family schism.

8

Nana, we thought everything would be smooth from then on. But only four months after they were engaged, Boahemaa left Kubi for another student at the university. I had not ever seen my son so broken. Nana, he wept in front of me like a child when he told me about it. "How can a *woman* be in love one day and out of love the next?" he asked me. But I had no answer to give him. And for a whole month, he withdrew from the world. He grew quiet and introspective and my heart was broken too and I wished there was something I could do to help him.

Then, after a month or so, he reemerged and reengaged the world, but it appeared he was doing so on his own terms. Nana, after he was suspended from school and promised me he'd not do any more drugs, I thought he'd stopped. And maybe he did, I don't know. Perhaps the pain of Boahemaa's rejection pushed him in that direction again. Whatever the reason, I suspected he was doing drugs. He was almost always gone from home and when he was home he was often reeking of alcohol and other substances. At least, I could recognize the smell of marijuana on him.

I say in shame that one time he was arrested for drug possession. And I was called to the police station because his father wasn't home. I managed to get him released after I pleaded and paid a hefty bribe. I knew it was wrong, Nana, but I couldn't let my son be charged. I spoke to him and begged him to change his ways. He said he would. I don't think he meant it.

Nana, I wish you could have seen the friends he brought home with him. There were two in particular who stood out. One of them Kubi referred to as Pornomuscular. Nana, even you speak, what kind of name is that? But the name aside, that young man had some very weird dressing habits. He always wore a black leather jacket without regard to the temperature. He also wore dark glasses all the time. One day, when I asked him why, he replied that, "I am one of those the sun shines on twenty-four hours a day." In addition, he always had a cigarette between his chapped lips. Nana, that man was a sight to see. Later, Kubi would tell me that he had become some sort of private detective.

Then there was the one Kubi called Zogomi. Nana, what a character! He walked as if he owned the world, with shoulders raised, the right one slightly higher than the other. He seemed to have no fear of anyone or anything and no respect either. Can you believe, Nana, that once when Kubi wasn't home, he came to me and asked for money?

"I don't have any," I said.

"Come on, lady, I know you're rich. Why you wanna sweat me?"

"Do you think money grows in rivers?"

"Oh come on, I'm gonna work for it, if you catch my drift."

"What do you mean?"

"I got an idea, old lady. You and me together, you know. I service you, you gimme a little something, you know. See, the way I figure, your hubby's gotta be so old he can't even get it up. You gotta be hurting for some. What you say?"

Nana, can you imagine the audacity? I must admit that I was amused by his fake American accent and forced lingo. I ran him off and later told Kubi about it. He just shrugged and said Zogomi was being stupid and meant nothing by it.

Nana, apart from all that, it seemed Kubi was on a woman spree. He went through one woman after the other, like they were clothing or something. Nana, your great grandson had become something like a gigolo. And he seemed not to discriminate. He had tall women and short women and women in between, beautiful women and ugly women and those in between, fat women and thin women and women somewhere in between... I tried my best to talk him out of his new hobby, but he wouldn't listen.

His father was still so busy with his growing business, he probably didn't notice what was happening. And since Kubi could be as normal as the next person when he chose to, he probably managed to keep his father from any suspicion.

When Kubi finished school, I thought he had performed a miracle on account of all the distractions he imposed on himself. He seemed sobered by work a little, but not much. I wasn't very surprised when he fell seriously ill. How much abuse can the body take? Anyway, Koo thought it was some *juju* or something. I think a priest told him that and gave Kubi some medicine to drink. I advised Kubi to rest. That was my prescription for him. He rested and took the medicine and got well.

9

Nana, we had come a long way, Koo and I. We had survived his work that took him away from home for so long. We survived the death of Koo's parents and of my mother. We had become rich and achieved considerable social status. We survived his political activities and the tumult of his detention. In all, Nana, I think he'd been a good husband and father. Not a perfect one, but a good one; especially when compared to his peers. Yes, he'd spent a lot of time away from home and left me to raise the children. In a way, I take that as a declaration of faith in me and as his way of demarcating our roles in the household. He was kind and generous to me. That the children and I lacked nothing, he made sure of. He gave me gifts abundantly. He asked my advice from time to time. Nana, I think he'd made me love him. When he married again, he shook my faith and tested my love, but I persevered.

But, Nana, to have him face trial … Nana, that I had never expected. How could anyone even suspect him of such a thing as murder? It was not my intention to tell the world he was innocent just because he was my husband. I wanted to tell the world he was innocent because he was innocent. He had to be.

"Lawyer Dadzie," I said. "You have to let me testify. I know my husband is innocent. Now let's go and convince the rest of the world of that fact." But first we had to go through the language of lawyers before we could reach the rest of the world. And by the time we would reach the rest of the world, mine, as I would soon find out, was only one muffled voice in a cacophony of voices.

My nana I have not closed my ears against your words Your laments Your tears Your joys But now I am just like a receding voice in the cave that mixes with the other sounds of the forests And often drowned by them.

You belong to the sound of the forests The present You must find your voice and let it roll out from the depths of your belly Therefore my intercession on your behalf is futile if you let my voice stand on its own without adding the power of yours You lift up my voice by lifting yours.

It is now a long night and in its cold whiffs I urge you to reach for the wrapper that became you when you started that journey And you can't blame him alone You too were complicit Your father and your mother as well He is also a victim in many ways.

Except it is like an enclosed cave He stands at the top of the cave and therefore you who lie at the bottom take most of the cold wind before it rises to him By then it has lost a lot of its chill By then you have warmed it.

But still the roads are widening New ones being constructed New possibilities opening up Take your wrapper, Granddaughter Find the best one for yourself

Work with that choice

It shall be your sun by night.

THE JOURNALIST'S NOTEBOOK

I returned from jail to a mixed climate of optimism and uncertainty. The country had risen and stuttered and felt fatigued after the high wattage of emotional shock. But it was more aware of itself, perhaps: its ability to see a side of itself it hadn't witnessed before – like looking into a mirror so clear it magnifies every blemish, every attribute whether flattering or not. The country was on the verge of electing a new president for the next republic, having seen the first two republics aborted through *coups d'état*. In 1966, the first military intervention dismissed the country's first president; in 1972, the second coup sacked the prime minister.

Both civilian leaders would live in exile, their political demise cheered by masses opening their arms widely to the unknown embrace of the new leaders; leaders celebrated by the body politic in a mad, enthusiastic frenzy. The dismissed civilians would both die in exile and return stiffened by rigor mortis to mass applause and mourning. When Nkrumah went, the coup leaders were welcomed with jubilant crowds in public places; and when Busia was toppled, market women and others demonstrated their support for the young leader of the coup, sometimes resorting to *ad hominem* insults on the ousted leader. The climate of support for the new protagonists of instability was something akin to that kind of support previously witnessed, especially after the Government announced a timetable to continue the return to civilian rule. The elections and transfer dates were merely postponed. A new republic was in sight.

But, alas, I digress.

I was released two months after my detention and I reach back for those two months with regret and some gratitude, my gratitude rooted in the pleasant moments I shared with my cellmate; the regret lay in the manner I was detained without any recourse to due process of law. I remembered being abducted at dawn from my wife and kids, being driven in a jeep, shoved outside, and made to strip. These were dangerous men. I could even smell alcohol on their breaths. These were not men to argue with. When they barked their orders, I obeyed.

In the cold of that dawn morning, naked before my unnamed arbiters, I would be kicked, slapped, pinched and lashed. My crotch would be kicked several times and I would retch twice. I would then be shaved, and made to wear damp-smelling prison clothes, and then shoved into a semi-dark cell. In one corner of it another man was lying quietly. After the door was locked and we were alone, he welcomed me with the words, "What is your crime?"

The voice was a whisper, as though fearful of the jail keepers' prodding ears. I found my nervous voice stifled in the wounds inflicted on me, wondering if perhaps this man's voice was also lowered in the pain of the physical, the threat of somatic pain. "Expression of opinion," I said.

"Freedom of speech?"

"You could say that."

"In a revolutionary time, don't you know that there is no such thing?"

"It's incumbent on the gatekeepers of freedom to guard it, regardless of the risks."

"What manner of gate-keeping is that?"

"Journalism."

"Mmmh, one that I've heard of?"

"Nii Lamptey."

"How could I have forgotten? You wrote an article about me a while ago. Remember your opposition when it was suggested a national rotary be named for me?"

Gasping with surprise, I said, "You are Koo Manu."

"The one and only."

"I meant no offense by that article."

I was surprised I hadn't recognized him, given that I had known of him first as one of the most prominent businessmen and second when he assumed the post of minister without portfolio. I was surprised he'd taken the job and become so openly involved with a Government that was about to hand over power. But, then again, are the promises of additional fame and power not often irresistible?

I knew why he was in the cell: he was a member of the previous Government and therefore among those expected to be detained. He shook my hand and said, "Welcome. It gets very lonely in here. The last cellmate I had was taken away. One of the guards told me he'd been shot. I sit here not knowing my fate: release or execution?"

"They will not execute you."

"And why not? I have been in here a while, but the guards are kind enough to tell me of the executions of former members of Government."

"Only soldiers have been killed. They haven't killed any civilians."

"Not yet. But if they've killed, they can kill. Whether you're a civilian or soldier will not matter."

"They won't touch you. You have an upright image. Those killed were all tainted by corruption."

"Are you so sure they were corrupt? What kind of corruption? By whose judgment?"

"You don't always have to put people through a trial to know they're corrupt. Sometimes, it's self-evident."

"Is that so? In that case, where do you draw the line? Can one man's self-evident truths appear entirely unreasonable to another? Isn't that why we need neutral judges? Isn't that why we have courts?"

"Don't misunderstand me. I believe no man should be sentenced without a proper trial. I will defend that to the last drop of my blood; but that shouldn't stop me from expressing my own judgment."

"Very well, but what I need now is my lawyer. And yet they won't grant me access."

"You will need a superhuman lawyer under the circumstances. These are not times for the rule of law. These are times for the rule of the gun. You need to know someone in the military, someone with access to power."

"I hear you. But if any lawyer can help, it's mine. He's one of the best in the country. Ekow Dadzie. Perhaps you know him."

"I do, indeed. He is running for parliament, isn't he? As head of the CUSBP Movement?"

"Yes. He'll be good for the country."

I learned a great deal about Koo Manu. We had nothing else to do in those days. Food was sparse. We got about two ladles of porridge in the mornings. On Sundays, we got the benefit of a thin slice of bread. Lunch comprised of *gari* and a ladle of light soup, whether or not we got fish or meat was unpredictable. Dinner was a ladle of rice and a small spread of fishless stew. Occasionally, our staple was varied a little with beans. We both lost weight. I believe our conversations kept us going – they were the only healthy servings we got. Koo Manu vowed that if he got out of the place alive, he would never return to politics. He would keep a low profile, tend to his business affairs, and raise his children in peace, away from the vicissitudes of the limelight. I could make no such promise, but I promised myself to be more circumspect.

A month later, I got my trial. I was called out of the cell late in the evening. I was blindfolded and shoved into an army jeep, reminiscent of my day of abduction. As we drove, my companions started laughing. "Have you said your prayers, countryman?"

"Your time has come. We dey take you for Teshie go shoot you."

Ha ha ha ha...

"Na who go fuck your wife? I go do am for you. I fit satisfy am well well. I get big soldier prick."

Ovation and laughter.

I thought of my wife David and how she would survive without my income. I recollected images of my children and let them play continually. I thought of my mother and brother. I remembered my father who had died in Burma fighting at the behest of the British when Ghana (then the Gold Coast) was under British rule. At that moment, I was convinced I was on my way to join him. I decided to exit with dignity, show these soldiers no fear. Sooner than my forced bravery could last, the jeep came to a stop. My belly melted as I was pushed outside. I started praying to God to deliver me. I would be a better person if he spared me. I would sin no more.

Instead of being led to a post, I found myself shoved into a room full of mixed odors of food, stale sweat and tobacco. The blindfold was removed. In seconds my eyes had adjusted to the occupants of the dimly lit room. I found that I was facing seven men, all in military garb, seated behind a huge table. Most of them were smoking and they were all wearing shades. In front of each was a pistol of sorts, many of which were being caressed like love objects by the men.

"State your name for the tribunal." A voice flowed at me from the indistinguishable panel of arbiters.

"What tribunal is this?" I asked.

I was made aware of the two soldiers behind me with two massive slaps on both cheeks, delivered from behind. I stumbled forward, but was steadied by the two soldiers. I got the message.

"My name is Nii Lamptey."

"State your profession for the tribunal."

"Journalist."

"Count One. You have been found guilty as follows: failure to pay compound interest on your house at Asylum Down. Guilty or not guilty?"

"What compound interest? I don't know about any compound interest on buildings."

I had violated the amoebic rule of the court. Two slaps made my ears ring, and I nearly fell. "Not guilty."

"State your case. Refute your guilt."

"Gentlemen, I am not guilty."

"Prove it."

"I have no idea what compound interest on a house means. I have paid all property taxes levied against my house …"

"You are not aware of compound interest on your house and therefore you have not paid it and therefore this tribunal finds you guilty."

I knew better than to argue with the judgment.

"Count two. You have been found guilty, through your seditious editorials, of conspiring and conniving to undermine the Government and the rule of law. Guilty or not guilty?"

"Not guilty."

"State your case. Refute your guilt."

"Sir, if you could point to anything in particular I've written that you find seditious, I could refute the charge. I have nether connived nor conspired with anyone to undermine the government …"

"Prove it."

"How, sir?"

"By failing to refute the allegations, you have not convinced this court of your innocence and so therefore you are found guilty."

One soldier who'd been quiet all this time interjected: "Guilty! You conspired all by yourself."

"Sir, I thought by definition a conspiracy required more than one person."

That soldier stood up from his chair and barked, "You making booklong for my front? He picked up his pistol and pointed it at me. "I be better man to shoot you like dog."

I trembled as the soldiers behind me delivered blows to my midsection, sending me to the hard floor. The offended soldier walked up to me and bent low. He used my ears as his ashtray and I could feel the burn of the smoldering ashes in my ears. He kicked me in the stomach and seemed satisfied with my yells. When he returned to his seat, I was forced back to my feet.

The spokesman announced: "Your sentence will be proclaimed in due course. Case dismissed."

It was about three days before I could find the courage to tell Koo Manu what had happened. But I got off easy compared to what he had to face. A week after my "trial," he got his. I have never seen a man so defeated as he was when he returned to the cell.

I was released two days after Koo Manu. He was found guilty of illegal acquisition of wealth with mitigating factors. Because of those unnamed mitigating factors, he was given a thirty-year suspended sentence and ordered to pay a huge fine to the state, among other things. For my part, I got a suspended ten-year sentence. We both got off easy compared with others whose assets were confiscated to the state for illegal acquisition of wealth, in addition to jail sentences ranging from about twenty years to life. We both escaped jail, but we had huge internal bruises.

My first political act after my release was to attend a rally organized by Ekow Dadzie. I had observed the young man's carrier for a while, especially after an impressive performance that got a girl off for murder when most people thought she had no chance. After that performance, his reputation kept growing from strength to strength. My interest in the young lawyer multiplied after Koo Manu mentioned him to me in jail. I had seen him orate in front of judge and jury; I wanted to see if he could transfer his skill and confidence with equal measure to the unpredictable political gallery. Until then, I had dismissed his run for parliament through the CUSBP as a mere publicity stunt. I decided to find out more.

It was a normal burning afternoon, only some three hours past midday. The rally was within walking distance from home. Against the advice of my wife, David, I decided to go (I still hadn't learned my lesson). "You are still within their jaundiced radar," David said. "You don't want to be seen as even vaguely interested in politics." I countered that I was going as a mere observer and nothing more.

I feel obliged at this juncture to explain my wife's name, lest my sexual proclivities be unclear, or it be wondered how David could give birth to two children by natural means. David's father liked the name, enamored from childhood the day he heard the Biblical tale of David slaying Goliath. He swore to name his first male child David. His first child was male and accordingly the father named him David. The second was female, as was the third and the fourth. Then the first male died. He had no David. Panicked that he would leave no progeny with the name David, he re-swore to name his next child David. My wife was the next child, hence the name David. But, alas, I digress.

I brushed aside the plea in her pouted face and went to the rally, feeling as though I had to rendezvous with an inchoate destiny.

The gathered crowd was massive, at least three hundred in the aggregate. A brass band was piping a tune at the one end while a dancing troupe gyrated at the other. At the front stood the dais and, a little behind, the tiny head office of the CUSBP. I observed many enthusiasts carrying placards: Ekow Dadzie for Parliament; Ekow Dadzie is your man; Vote Ekow Dadzie for Parliament. Despite my growing interest in the young man, I couldn't help but wonder whether he was truly serious about capturing a seat in parliament. He was appreciably wealthy, I could surmise, but he was up against Colonel Duah, who had abruptly announced his candidacy for parliament. Colonel Duah had resources and easy access to power. Did Ekow Dadzie stand a chance? His reach was short, even as the leader of the Citizens United to Save Bottom Power, or Bottom Power for short.

Ekow Dadzie emerged from the CUSBP head office dressed in a *batakali*, waving a flywhisk. He walked up to the mounted dais as the crowd's ovation and cheers mounted. Then he began to deliver his address. His charisma permeated the crowd, beamed from his energetic personality like a fusion of a million candlelights. "Ladies and gentlemen," he began. "In a few weeks, you will be casting your votes for the next leader of this constituency. And who will that person be?"

"Dadzie… Dadzie…" the crowd chanted for minutes, quieting only when he raised his hands and begged them to. He explained that his resources were minimal, that he was up against entrenched forces, but that he still had confidence in the people and expected them to see the integrity he'd bring to the parliament. He explained that his credo was simple. "Let us refuse to be bogged down in the minutiae and rigidity of ideologues. My credo is my country, which I love dearly."

Ovation. The crowd was approaching something close to a frenzy. It was difficult not to be infected with Ekow Dadzie's energy and optimism and even I found myself drawn to his simplicity and daring.

Just then a van drove along, blared a disturbing horn and stopped. Then a voice droned out of the van through a loud microphone: "Ekow Dadzie, shut up or we will shut you up." Startled by the intrusion, Ekow Dadzie paused to stare at the intruders. From behind the van, a huge kite was unveiled. Before the Dadzie supporters could summon their energies to respond, the van was gone. But the kite continued to linger, its decoration clear to all now: a drawing of a woman's buttocks, grossly exaggerated in size, with the inscription: Bottom Power Ha Ha Ha.

Ekow Dadzie asked the crowd to be calm. "We shall not be moved by such senseless interference by our opponents. My friends, they are afraid. Despite all their resources, they are afraid. Why? Because we have introduced a new energy, a new force, a new power into national politics and they just can't take the heat. So they resort to such cheap tactics as sending a bunch of rogues and hooligans to cause commotion here, in their crass minds redefining Bottom Power as Buttocks Power, refusing to accept the inevitable need to let power reside with the people who now lie at the bottom of the society. But that won't be for long, countrymen…"

And then from behind him clouds of smoke began leaping into the air and with it came the smell of burning property. Something like an ululation of fear and defeat emanated from the crowd and Ekow Dadzie turned to look at the head office of CUSBP going up in smoke. "Oh my God," he muttered. "What have they done?" And as though waiting for a cue, a group of men seemed to retrieve truncheons from their baggy trousers and leap into the crowd, hitting randomly. That was when the pandemonium started as supporter ran into attacker,

attacker ran into supporter, making it difficult sometimes to distinguish between riff raffs and supporters, while many a supporter made quick retreats from the battleground.

I managed to find my way to the nearest house and convince its owners to let me call the fire and ambulance services from there. I returned to the fringes of the battlefield, still as an observer, not a participant. Within minutes, only a few supporters were left to battle, but even in their dwindled numbers, they outnumbered the attackers. Yet these were no ordinary thugs. They fought fiercely and resolutely. I saw Ekow Dadzie himself entangled in blows with a boy much younger than he and my admiration for the parliamentary candidate increased exponentially.

But these were boys who seemed to have their commands and obeyed them to the last letter, for they were soon disentangling themselves from the battle and fleeing it, leaving behind the bleeding wounds they had delivered. Within seconds, there was not a single attacker left, just damaged bodies, some bleeding, others bruised. The CUSBP building continued to burn in the background. I went over to Ekow Dadzie. He was seated on the dais, his left eye swollen shut, blood oozing from the lump. His lips were swollen as well. "Are you alright?" I asked him.

"I will be. You seem to have escaped it all unscathed."

"I wasn't involved in it."

He looked at me with his open eye. "Don't I know you somewhere?"

"My name is Nii Lamptey."

"Oh, the journalist. Last I heard, you were in detention. Well, well, you have some news for your papers."

"I'm not here in that capacity. I've taken leave from work."

"I'll like to hear about your experience in detention sometime. Now let's see what we can do for these injured people."

We walked to the rally field and tried to talk with the remaining supporters. Most of the injuries were relatively minor, except for an older man who lay on the ground, blood all over his face and shirt.

"We need to call an ambulance," Ekow Dadzie said. I told him I already had. "Then why aren't they here?" he asked. 'We need to get him to a hospital as soon as possible." One supporter volunteered his car. We helped carry the injured man into the car and returned to the field. Already, people in the houses surrounding the CUSBP house were trying to douse the fire with sand and water. A large makeshift fire service had developed, trying to stop the fire from spreading to their houses. "Has anyone called the fire people?" I told him I had. We found another gentleman who lent us his phone. We called the fire service again. They were busy, they said. They would dispatch a service as soon as possible.

We could only join the makeshift fire service and do our best to quench the fire. Despite his injuries, Ekow Dadzie worked hard, carrying buckets of water and sand. The ooze of blood had stopped and dried on his face. I did my best, too. Two or so hours after we'd called for the fire service, the fire truck arrived. By then, the fire was under control. Despite its lateness, we were relieved to see the truck turn into the yard, expecting that the servicemen would finish the last flashes of fire. Four men jumped from the truck and retrieved the hose from the truck. But as they aimed it at the fire, the only thing coming out was air. The firemen seemed stunned by it and they were soon talking to one another. "What's going on?" I asked.

"We have no water in the truck," one fire serviceman replied. Just then, the ambulance arrived.

Book Three

THE RAIN OF SNOW

Now it rains snow in the land of the sun

THE COUNSELORS

1

There's no denying the valuable impact of good music, which cuts deep to the bones even in the absence of sobriety. Irrefutable... this assertion? Case in point: I was dancing as a madman, one hand moving eastward and the other westward, a leg thrusting that direction, the other kicking this way. My rotating head jerked my body around like a spinning bottle. Knowing, even then, that such movements spelled a lack of coordination and the presence of idiocy, I, nonetheless, was too deep in the throes of booze to care. Looking over at John Amoah, I registered he too was in similar bad shape: seemingly with his arms bending in one direction and the rest of his body turning in a different direction.

As I was dancing with Grace, John's girlfriend, he pranced solo, yet he didn't care. Pointing to John, Grace laughed. My own burlesque-like movements, in contrast to Grace's, must have been striking. She was moving carefully: flexible and agile, she seemed imbued with discipline. Combining for a poignant impact were her slender face, dimpled cheeks, full lips, firm breasts, flat belly, long elegant legs, small waist, and crescent behind. I, almost ensnared, wished she wasn't my best friend's girlfriend. A wish ... inconsequential?

"Ekow," Grace said, "I think you need to cool off a bit."

"Huh?"

"You need to take a rest."

"I want to dance!"

"So do I, but I'm tired. And you are drunk."

"I'm not drunk. Never! You go rest. I will dance."

Abandoned by Grace I, still, was without shame, continuing, as John, to dance solo. For long moments, we were practicing acrobatics on the dance floor until, dehydrated and fatigued, I staggered to the table where Grace sat, almost falling over her.

"You two look so silly when you drink," Grace said. "I wish you could see yourselves."

"Perhaps your boyfriend looks silly. Not me."

Approaching the table, John yelled, "Grace, my love, why have thou forsaken me?"

"I forsake thee not," said the replying Grace. "Thou art the master of thine own inebriation."

John and Grace attempted conversation, but I, especially as it was so loud in the nightclub, was prompted to focus more on my beer. Then, the music changing to slow, John, in failed but gallant efforts to appear sober, escorted Grace to the dance floor. I, on the other hand, was beginning to plot a move on a portion of the seemingly available ladies, until the warmth of a palm on my shoulder injected some sobriety into me. "Your turn again," Grace said.

Looking on with approval, John said, "Go dance with her." Slumping into his chair, John seemed exhausted while I, concentrating on every step, went with Grace to the dance floor. There, my hands encircled her waist. The placing of her arms on my neck being platonic, I was holding her only loosely. My drunkenness notwithstanding, I knew enough to hold back, lest John get jealous. Still, a little later, perhaps my instincts rejecting my reason, I was pulling her even tighter to me.

"So how is law school?" Grace asked.

Desirous of enjoying her body, I was reluctant to speak. Nevertheless, I managed to say, "It's alright."

"So you really want to be a lawyer?"

"Very much so." Feeling obliged to reciprocate the interest in conversation, I asked, "How's school. Are you studying hard for your exams?" Not the kind of conversation I'd have liked to make at the time. How inappropriate.

"Yes. It's so hard, though."

"What do you want to study when you get into the university?"

'I don't know. Now all I think about are my exams."

"You'll do well."

"I hope so."

Seemingly, the short conversation melted any distance between us. Grace rested her head on my chest and my arms rubbed her back slowly. Then, with John tapping my shoulder saying it was his turn to dance with Grace, I reluctantly disengaged from her. Fed this feeling to dance with a woman, I walked to the nearest table and propositioned a lady to dance.

"Can't you see she's with me?" her escort shot at me.

"So what? Do you own her?"

"My friend, if you continue like this, I will have to discipline you."

"Don't talk to me like that," I retorted. "Foolish man!"

From the clouds of my drunken eyes, I saw the escort shaking his finger at me. "I am warning you!"

Behind me by then, John attempted to shoo me away from the escort. I resisted, however. Because my movements were awkward, my hand carelessly struck a beer bottle and spilled the contents on the lady I had propositioned to dance. That was it. Her male escort moved forward while John tried to stall him. Struggling to my feet and reaching for a beer bottle – with a drunkard's carelessness – I flung the bottle, which flew past the man and struck someone behind him. I soon heard yells and saw more bottles flying in the air. John so forcefully shoved the man that he staggered, falling into a group nearby. The scene in the club being pandemic, bodies were rising and missiles flying. John, Grace and I bolted, the brawl still unfolding in the club. Reason, being lost in alcohol and anger, I heard the yowls of pain from objects hitting flesh and fists pummeling bodies. But we were leaving the scene behind us, we who'd started the whole trouble.

Grace asked to drive. "I can drive!" John insisted.

"Let me drive," I said. They both ignored me.

"Wake up!" Turning on my side at the intrusion, I futilely attempted to ignore it. The wake-up call continued, nonetheless. Eventually, opening my eyes a little and pretending still to be sleeping, I didn't move. John wouldn't surrender, however. "I know you're awake, Ekow, so stop pretending."

Opening my eyes fully, I turned to face him, wincing as one would who's in pain. "Man, it's still early yet."

"It's Sunday. Papa wants to go to church."

"I don't want to go."

"Neither do I, but we have to. Get ready. We'll leave in an hour or so."

In those days, I seldom desired vacations, my preference being to spend all the time in school. I was loath to travel the distance home to Saltpond for the short Easter break, accepting, instead John's offer to vacation with his family. As John and his family were perfect hosts, I was disinclined to complain about his father's insistence on church attendance. This notwithstanding that, after the night's drinking, I wished to prolong my morning sleep. But crawling out of bed, reluctantly taking a bath, and getting dressed, I sauntered to the dining room to join the rest of the family for breakfast.

"You should invite Grace to church with us one of these days," Genevieve Amoah, John's mother, suggested at table.

"She doesn't like church," John said. His younger brother James shook his head, seemingly disapproving.

"Make her like it," his father said.

Their argument filled the time: John adamant that he saw no reason to force her against her will, and his father insistent he needed to learn the art of persuasion. "What kind of an advocate will you be if you can't convince your own girlfriend to go to church?"

Later, their Mercedes rolled, rather leisurely, down the road, emphasizing the calm of the Sunday morning. John's parents occupied the front while I, sitting in the back between John and James, emphasized to myself my gratitude for such friends. Later still, John, complaining while we lingered in front of the chapel contemplating the young women coming to church, said, "I really don't like being dragged to church on Sundays,"

"It's for your own good," his brother James said. "Put your faith in God and you will want for nothing."

"Put my faith in God?" asked John "Why? What has he done for me? Why not put my faith in myself? I'm going to go in there and listen to gibberish. Where is God when there is so much suffering in the world? If he's omniscient and omnipotent, good and holy, where is he?"

"Count your blessings," James replied. "And it will surprise you what the Lord has done."

"Don't fight, you two," I said. "Come on, let's go in."

John, James and I sat at the very back of the church, which was frequented by the wealthy, as evidenced that day by expensive suits and the finest *kente* clothes. "None of the women here arouse my interest," I, bored, whispered to John.

"It's getting worse. It used to be much better. Those were the days when coming to church was a little fun. These days, it's as if all the beautiful girls have decided not to come."

John was getting restless midway through the service. "Hey, Ekow, do you want to leave? Walk around a little?"

"How about your parents?"

"They won't know. They are so eager to get to heaven, they think they'll get there by sitting in front of the pastor."

Seeing us walk outside, James stared with disappointment.

As it was getting sunnier and warmer, we removed our neckties and folded them into our shirt pockets. John and I stood roadside. "Yesterday was something, wasn't it?" John asked.

"Oh, I'd almost forgotten about that. I was so drunk, I can't believe I'm standing here sane right now."

"You think you were the only drunk one? I was completely gone. Man, it's a miracle I was even able to drive."

"Why didn't you let Grace drive, then?"

"And abdicate my manhood? No way."

Street peddlers dotted the roads, one of whom we saw approaching, carrying fried plantains and groundnuts atop her head.

"Lady," John called for her, requesting groundnuts. Upon receiving the groundnuts from her, John said, with a straight face, "Oh, I just realized I have no money. So what are we going to do about that?"

Frowning, she said, "What are you saying? How can you buy groundnuts if you have no money?"

"I was wondering the same thing," John said. Busy chewing down the groundnuts, he seemed to have lost interest in the woman.

Checking my pocket, I found some money and paid her but, disappointed, I yelled at John: "Sometimes you act as if you are mad! Why did you do that?"

"Leave me alone. I'm really hungry. The groundnuts won't fill me up." Rather than express remorse, he checked his watch. "Church won't be over until another half-hour or so. Do you want to get some food around the corner?"

"I don't think I have enough money."

"Don't worry, I have some."

"But you told the groundnut seller you had no money."

"That's what I told her. That doesn't make it fact, does it?"

"You surprise me."

"Come on, let's go get some grub before church is over."

Although suspicious, I followed him as he turned the corner where hawkers abounded. Before reaching them, however, John stopped and pointed a finger. "Manna from heaven."

Looking in the direction of his finger, I saw a man kneeling on a mat in prayer. Puzzled and looking closer, I saw beside the praying man, a bowl of rice and stew. Now aware of what John contemplated, I gesticulated in protest. Before I could act, though, John had run past me to the man and seized the bowl. Without more ado, he was already eating the food before I could protest further. The praying man, realizing that his meal was under consumption, increased the pace of his prayer, moving up and down more rapidly. Noticing this, John increased the pace of his consumption. Although he asked me to join him, I had my limits. I declined. After finishing the food, John turned the bowl upside down and we bolted, the second time in as many days.

"How could you do such a thing? Don't you have any respect for other people's religious practices?"

"What do you mean? I didn't insult his practices. I just took advantage, that's all."

Church being over just about the time we returned, I was delighted to leave all that had happened there behind us.

Desirous of adventure, however, John and I went to visit Grace in his mother's Toyota Camry. On the way, he contemplated his future. "Daddy wants me to join him after I finish law school. To be honest with you, Ekow, the thought of practicing law with my father thrills me, but it troubles me too. He is a brilliant lawyer, doubtless. I know he's won some of the most difficult cases in the country. Plus, his practice must be interesting because it spans all sorts of matters, from civil to criminal law. To learn under such a mentor should thrill any aspiring lawyer. Except if that mentor is your own father."

"But what's the problem? I asked. "Are you feeling rebellious?"

"Not the kind of rebellion where you argue and fight all the time, not that open and senseless type. The tension between Daddy and me is more subtle, but I fear it can blow up at any time. I don't like being bossed around. Like this morning, for example, before I came to wake you up to go to church, he came and woke me up. I wanted to tell him to leave me alone and to go to hell. But I had to control myself. As it stands now, he and I spend most of our days apart. When he walks into a room, I find an excuse to leave. I don't know why he can't be like Mommy. Anyway, what I'm trying to say is that I'm not sure I want to practice with Daddy."

"You will be a fool not to. What are you going to do?"

"I hope I get into the Masters program at Harvard Law School."

"Oh, that. Will you really leave us here and go do that if they accept you? Leave Grace here by herself?"

"It will open up a lot of doors. Plus it's only one year."

John blew the car horn as we pulled up to Grace's house in Dzorwulu. Smilingly, Grace answered the door, a friend accompanying her. "I see you two survived the toll of last night," she said.

"Hey, we went to church to atone for our sins," John said.

"Who is your friend?" I asked Grace.

"Oh, this is Cynthia Agyemang. She's my schoolmate. We were studying."

I concluded that although Cynthia wasn't the most fetching female, she had ample appeal for my tastes. Soon after, I commenced a conversation with her, which I was enjoying until John asked, "What are you two doing tonight?"

"We'll be studying," Grace said.

"You can't study all the time. Let's do something tonight, the four of us."

"Suits me. But what?" Asked Grace.

"I'll think of something," John said.

Picking them up that evening, we drove to Ringway for a meal. Even though my interest lay in Cynthia, my envy was targeted at John. He had Grace: intelligent, beautiful and articulate. But that, being another story, need not be told yet. Following a late film, John whispered to me that, although desirous of bedding Grace, he didn't know where. His parents were home, and Grace's too. "How about Abob?" I asked.

"Abob from school?"

"Yes. He lives with a brother in Labadi, a young guy no more than thirty. They have plenty of room. You should be able to arrange something with him tonight."

"My friend, you are a genius," John said.

But when Grace flatly refused to grant him his wish in a strange bed, I couldn't get lucky with Cynthia either on account of our having to take them both home.

"Women," John lamented afterwards. "I don't understand her at all. What is the difference whether we're fucking in my room or in another man's room? Huh, what difference does it make?"

"You have to respect her wishes."

"I really need some tonight."

"That shouldn't be too hard. If you are willing."

"Willing? Willingness, I do not lack, my friend."

"Willing enough to pay for it?"

"Now that's something else."

"It's up to you."

"No, Ekow. I can't do that."

"All it takes is a few minutes and it's all over and you have what you want and everybody is happy."

"I've never done such a thing. You mean you have?"

"Yes, and I am still alive. It's up to you."

"I can't do it."

Driving back home, however, John grew restless, saying he was in need of a drink. So inspired, we went to a bar close by, where we sat drinking for hours. It became clear to me that John was drunk when he returned to my previous suggestion by asking delightedly, "How do you know about such a place anyway?"

"When you don't have a steady girlfriend like me, you find out quickly."

I saw John's resistance dissipate after I led him to a place Abob had shown me not too long before then. It was a rectangular building of concrete painted blue. Inside, John perspired nervously, but I told him not to worry. There were numerous women lounging in the room, a large room accommodating sofas, chairs, tables and a bar at the end of the room.

"Welcome," one said. "Is this your first time here?"

"I've been here before, but my friend hasn't," I said.

"Well, then, you know the procedure."

"Yes."

Afterwards, as John and I were driving home, he laughed carelessly as if he'd accomplished a great deed. "I suppose you have to try everything at least once."

Lying in bed later, I contemplated the friendship between John and me. Our friendship spanned a long period: since secondary school, stating it precisely. Having transferred from Mfantsipim to Presec I was in Accra, alone. My parents, hardworking but poor, remained in Saltpond where they kept a farm. John and I bonded immediately. Taking me home with him sometimes during the weekends to his friendly and sympathetic parents both facilitated and cemented our friendship, which was almost as exists between brothers.

John and I were always vying for the top status in the class. If he came first one term, I'd be first the other. Still, though, there seemed no sense of competition between us. Studying together, sharing ideas, and holding nothing back, our friendship grew even sturdier. Nothing could change it, I thought in those days.

కావ్

3

Harvard Law School at last for John Amoah. Irresistible ... this summons? Having watched him zealously work on his application, I was thrilled for him. What I recall about his days in the United States is what John himself told me, either orally or through letters. Having completed law school and captured the admiration of many, John kept saying, nonetheless, he thought something wasn't quite right – he needed a certain *something* to complete himself. Not understanding why, I clarified for him his luck: he had Grace, his father's practice if he wished to obtain good training, and the wealth of his family.

It started during the last year at Ghana Law School when John, contemplating the actual practice of law, seemed to panic – no more a carefree student studying, partying, chasing after women and living carelessly. Then there was Grace, hinting marriage to him ever so subtly. Was John ready for all that, however? Having toyed with applying to law school abroad, he would be advised by the Dean of Ghana Law School to consider Harvard. He possessed the grades, the guts, and the determination. Why not attempt it? So inspired, he applied to Harvard's Masters of Laws program. The application completed, he hoped for and awaited the opportunity to leave, at least for a while, all that seemed to be trapping him.

Not long after finishing law school, a large, brown envelope arrived for John. Opening it with nervous hands, he delightedly read he'd been accepted. John, though wonderfully happy, had to contend with a few hurdles. First was overcoming his father's opposition. "No!" Amos Amoah exclaimed, hearing the news. "You don't need another law degree. What for? What you need is not a string of degrees in front of your name. What you need, John, is experience. The law is nothing but a trade. Experience and determination are what make an average lawyer a great one. Here I am, one of the best in the country, offering to bring you under my tutelage, show you what it means, what it takes, to be a great lawyer, and what do you want to do instead? Throw a whole year away in America."

Explaining it was imperative, he needed to leave for America for personal growth, John literally begged. Having spent all his life in Ghana without exposure to foreign cultures, he reasoned, he'd be an improved person if he spent some time away. Besides, he might learn a few legal tricks at Harvard. But his father wouldn't budge. Not then. Given that the older man would be financing the expenses, John couldn't go without his father's approval.

Failing to prevail, John next appealed to his mother. If Genevieve Amoah couldn't persuade her husband, no one could. She subsequently brought subtle pressure to bear on her spouse. After dismissing her in the first few instances, he soon succumbed to her patience and relentlessness. John's father would shortly thereafter approach him solemn-faced, seemingly defeated. He reckoned John would be better served staying at home and starting his practice, but perhaps it wasn't such a terrible idea for John to earn a degree from Harvard. It'd only take a year and John could learn substantially from the foreign experience. John was his son, as brilliant as he, and would become even more special with this experience abroad. That was the basis for his conclusion that it was a wholesome idea after all. The older man, thus convinced, spoke as if he was the one who'd conceived the idea, now reminding John repeatedly how he'd benefit from the education abroad. He would be glad to pay the fees plus all other expenses.

The most formidable matter for John being his love for Grace, it was obvious he would miss her. He told me repeatedly he didn't think he could find another woman who pleased him as fully as she. A love … boundless? A year away from her was a very long time, he kept saying, though he'd no doubt he'd return and marry her. "No doubt?" I asked John.

"No doubt! None!"

Nonetheless, he was concerned she might not wait for him. He confided in me: "Who knows what will happen if she comes across some charming guy?"

"You have to have more faith in her than that."

"Will you look after her, Ekow? Will you keep an eye on her for me?"

"Sure, my friend. Absolutely."

"I can count on you?"

"Without question."

Book Three: The Rain of Snow

Then there was John and me. I, truly happy and proud of him, knew nonetheless I sorely would miss him. "Ekow," he said, "if you don't want me to go, tell me. You are the only one who can stop me. I like my parents, but they don't see things from my perspective. My brother James won't tell me how he truly feels. I love Grace, but romance is hardly enough to keep me here. It can play tricks on your judgment. Friendship, Ekow, that is what matters in the end. True friendship. So tell me, do you want me to stay?"

"Don't be silly. We'll all miss you, but only a fool will tell you not to go. I'll be angry with you if you don't go. After all, it's only a year."

"You are a brilliant guy, Ekow. Would you like to work with my father?"

"Are you mad? Who wouldn't want to work with the celebrated Lawyer Amos Amoah?"

"You will get an excellent job, no matter what you want to do. You are outstanding, my friend. Both you and I. But, then again, sometimes connections are stronger than brains. If you want to work somewhere, either with a company or the Government, my father will help you get a job easily. He has the connections. But if you want to get into private practice, there is no better place to start than with him."

Not letting the opportunity pass, I prevailed on John to speak with his father, who was delighted I wanted to work with him.

The night immediately preceding John's departure for America, his father organized a party for him. Notwithstanding the pleasantries, the company, and the entertainment, there also abided a melancholic mood. The night waning and the guests leaving, I knew that I would miss him even more than I'd thought, this friend who was my brother. The next day, while bidding him farewell at the Airport, I had no idea how significant his journey would become.

The cold cut through his skin. Even though he'd seen photos and movies of the snow piled up into iced packs when he was in Ghana, he never fully had imagined its savagery. Walking away from Ames, across Everett Street to Massachusetts Avenue where he was meeting his friend Dave Shriver for lunch, John contemplated how a good friendship could develop from a mere chance encounter. He recollected the day he'd gone to the Harvard Cooperative to purchase books for the semester's courses. Orientation week having passed too slowly for him with its endless speeches, receptions and meetings, John was shopping in anticipation of classes. He'd acquired all the books he needed for his classes except Corporations.

Dave Shriver, probably by instinct, thought he discerned John's confusion. "You're looking for something?" Dave asked.

John, looking up, said, "Pardon me." Still not fully familiar with the American accent, John nonetheless managed to figure it out before Dave answered. "Yes, I am looking for the textbook for Corporations."

"Who do you have?"

"You mean which lecturer?"

"Which what?"

"Which lecturer? Which teacher?"

"Yeah, which professor?"

"Jones," John said.

"Oh, really? That's great, man. I've got Jones, too. Here, let me show you. You're looking in the wrong place."

And so it commenced. A second-year student, Dave Shriver lived in Ames as well, a floor above John. Born and bred in Columbus, Ohio, he'd obtained his Bachelor's at the Ohio State University, graduating second in his class. Then he'd been admitted to Harvard Law School on the strength of his academics and his extra-curricular activities: he'd played varsity volleyball, headed the student assembly in his final year, participated in the debating society, edited the college newspaper, and belonged to many a charity organization. Strengths ... unassailable?

After having shown John where to obtain the Corporations textbook, they met in class the following day and lunched afterwards. John, finding Dave Shriver's curiosity to know Ghana impressive and his general knowledge of Africa appreciable, spent more time with his new acquaintance until, slowly, acquaintanceship evolved to friendship. John spent his first Thanksgiving holiday with Dave in Columbus. His parents being divorced, Shriver's father had resettled in Las Vegas. "To get away from this hell," he'd told his family. He meant the hell that, from his perspective, was family life. His mother, a lawyer working with a leading law firm in downtown Columbus, lived in a grandiose Victorian mansion in Bexley with Dave's only sibling Mike, as curious as his older brother.

John and Dave, departing Cambridge the Wednesday afternoon before Thanksgiving, had boarded the subway to Logan Airport and flown non-stop to Port Columbus Airport. Meeting them were Marge, Dave's mother, and his brother, Mike. Marge, a petite, blond-haired woman, embraced Dave immediately they met, implanting a kiss on his cheek. Mike, standing behind Marge, gave his big brother a little nudge in the belly. "Hey big guy, how're you doing?" the older sibling asked.

"Pretty good," Mike said.

"Well, won't you introduce us to your friend, Dave?" Marge asked. "Or do they teach you to forget your manners at Harvard?"

"Oh, sorry, Mom."

Shaking John's hand, Marge smiled broadly and said, "Nice to meet you. Dave's told us quite a bit about you."

"Yeah, he says you're from Ghana," young Mike said.

"Yes," John said.

Mike began asking John questions: "Does it get really hot in Ghana? What kind of clothes do they wear? What are the schools like? What kind of cars do they drive?"

"Mike, you've got till Sunday to know all you want to know about Ghana; but we've got to get home," Marge said.

Driving from Port Columbus to Bexley, they entered the huge mansion John had seen in photos. Marge pulled her Lexus into the garage. They spent most of the remainder of the afternoon conversing: Dave educating Marge and Mike about life at Harvard and Mike desirous of knowing more about Ghana.

Before the night aged irretrievably, Dave suggested they visit a club. His mother, cautioning care, permitted Dave to borrow her Lexus. After driving down Broad Street to High Street and heading south to German Village, they encountered their choice of bars. They commenced the night with a couple of beers, listening to a band playing rock and roll, and watching a few dancers on the floor. "I need to get laid tonight," Dave said. He eyed a couple of women. "Plenty of babes," he said.

Dave, unsheathing his smoothness, which he projected especially after he'd gulped a few drinks, said, "Come on," and walked towards two fetching brunettes. John, following, had not a clue in matters of dealing with American females. Dave whispered to one of the two women. She smiled faintly while John stood by frozen.

"Hello," John said to the other woman.

"Hi," she said and looked away.

Embarrassed, John wanted to escape from the bar. "How come I haven't seen you around?" Dave asked the women. "You just moved here or something?"

"No, I grew up here. You? Just passing through or what?"

"No, I grew up here too. I've been gone a bit, though. Just got back today."

"Yeah? Where've you been?"

"Law School. Harvard."

"Really? You go to Harvard?"

She, who'd ignored John, turned to him with interest. "You go to Harvard too?"

"Yes," John said.

"That's so cool."

After speaking with the women a while and purchasing them drinks, they danced and conversed some more. John got attached to the one who'd ignored him, as she seemingly became intrigued to learn more about him. Not knowing Ghana, and her knowledge of Africa being extremely limited, she said, "I want to go visit sometime. I think it'll be so cool, with all the animals, you know. I really want to go, like, on a Safari or something."

Deciding to continue the party at the women's apartment – they were both students at Ohio State University – the group of four left shortly. John and Dave didn't return to Bexley until about 4 a.m. "We need to call them tomorrow," John said.

"Forget them. They're bad news."

"What do you mean?"

"You don't want women like that," Dave said.

"Why?"

"Hey, we'll talk about it later. Right now, I'm so fucking beat all I want to do is crash."

John would later ask Dave why he didn't want to contact the women. "I'm not about to get into a relationship now," Dave said casually. "You have your fun and then you move on." The answer perplexed John a little, but that was all he could get out of Dave.

Mike helped Marge prepare the turkey and the rest of the Thanksgiving meal while John and Dave worked in the backyard. Later that afternoon, Dave and John picked up Dave's grandmother from a nursing home. Later still, John would ask Dave, "Why do you keep her in a nursing home? Why can't she stay at home with your mother and brother?"

"Who'll take care of her?" Dave replied.

"What do you mean, who'll take care of her? God, Dave, she is your grandmother, the mother of your mother. How can you put her away like that ... like a commodity? Somebody has to take care of her. Are we not each other's keeper?"

"Maybe in Africa. This is America. Each one for himself."

"Even family?"

"Even family."

During dinner, John enjoyed the turkey a little, the potatoes and gravy were passable, and the stuffing acceptable, but he found the food mostly bland.

John's grandmother didn't say much, except when she asked, "Where's Dan?"

"Ma, you know we're divorced," Marge said. "Why do you always have to ask?"

The grandmother shook her head, "Such a nice man."

And there was a lull of silence in the room.

❧

5

John increasingly craved female company. Thus oriented, he was expecting positive results when a professor of African Studies at Harvard invited him for dinner. There, John met another student studying for her masters at the School of Divinity. Being extremely attractive, she grabbed John's attention immediately and, therefore, his ear all night. A beauty ... enticing? Getting along quite well, they began spending more time together: mostly studying at the library and having meals. Then: "What are you doing on Sunday?" she asked him.

"I have nothing planned," he said. His mind still on Grace, he, nonetheless, was willing if Natalie wanted to ask him on a date, figuring it could cause no harm. Besides, what would Grace expect? That he stay celibate all this time?

"Good," Natalie said. "Meet me in front of the Hark at eight. I'm taking you to church."

Church! That was the last place he was inclined to go, but, not knowing how to extricate himself, he felt obligated to accept the invitation.

It was a small racially mixed church in the Boston suburb of Somerville, near Cambridge. The first service passed without much activity for John, during which he daydreamed and focused the bulk of his attention studying the females present. It took a couple more invitations and his acceptance in the hope of pleasing Natalie so he could bed her, before he listened to the sermon. Even then, his interest was mainly confined to discrediting mentally the logic, or lack thereof, emanating from the pulpit. Once engaged in this intellectualizing exercise, John could not stop listening. On his fifth visit, however, something happened that he couldn't explain, something that simply transcended the intellectual.

"Signs of the end of the world," the preacher started. Pausing, to pick up a huge Bible, he continued: "It is clear that the end is near," he warned. "For those of us who will heed the Word, the reward is everlasting life. John 3:16. For God so loved the world! Yes, he so loved the world that he did what? He gave his only begotten son. And whosoever believes in him shall have what? Everlasting life! Yes, my brothers and sisters, life forever. Blissful life. But for those who do not heed the word, what awaits? Hell. Believe it! That lake of fire where you shall burn forever. There is no gray here, it's as clear as night and day. Either you accept Jesus as your personal savior and choose heaven or you deny him and choose hell. The choice is yours; the choice is yours, my friends."

Leafing through the Bible, the preacher went on, "Please turn in your Bible to Mathew 24. When Jesus's disciples asked him 'What shall be the sign of thy coming, and of the end of the world?' Jesus said these words: 'And ye shall hear of wars and rumors of wars ... For nation shall rise against nation, and kingdom against kingdom: and there shall be famines, and pestilences, and earthquakes, in diverse places.' Please move along to verse 37: 'But as the days of Noah were, so shall also the coming of the son of man be. For as in the days that were before the flood they were eating and drinking, marrying and giving in marriage, until the day that Noah entered the ark.' Finally, please move on to verse 44: 'Therefore be ye ... ready for such an hour as ye thinketh not the son of man cometh.'"

Pausing briefly, the preacher looked into the congregation. "Today God sends out His word again. He has given us signs to watch out for the second coming of Christ. And all that was prophesied is coming to pass. Turn on the radio and there's a war somewhere. Turn on the television and see all the pestilences. Read and weep of the hunger afflicting many. These are the signs foretold long ago. The end of the world, brothers and sisters, is at hand. Repent!

"The Lord tells us that no one knows the hour when He shall come. But He has given us the signposts. Therefore, I say repent. The Devil, says the Bible, walketh about like a roaring lion seeking whom he may devour. It is a very bleak hour, my friends. The lake of fire is opening and it is wide. But there is hope. Yes, because Jesus died to save us. He is the light, the truth and the way. No one goes to the Father but by him. Please do not delay. Tomorrow is promised no man. Therefore, now is the time to turn your life to Jesus. He will take care of the rest."

The preacher's shaking voice clearly was full of emotion. "Friends, all you have to do is surrender yourself to God through Jesus Christ. Open your heart and ask Jesus in as your personal savior. He has done all the hard work for us. He who died in order that we might be saved. I now ask those of you here who haven't accepted Jesus as your personal savior to raise your hands. If you want the gift of eternal life, please raise your hand. Don't delay. Tomorrow is promised no man. Please do not go to hell for any reason. Please raise your hand."

Then the pianist started a tune and the congregation started singing:

All to Jesus I surrender
All to him I freely give ...

214

While the congregation sang, John's mind flashed back, recollecting the night in Columbus, the drinking, and the sex. He recollected the night he'd spent in a brothel in Ghana ... memories that flooded him and began to torment him. And the song, entreating him to surrender, calling ... calling ... ever so gently, so strongly ... a soothing call to a pricked and, therefore, troubled conscience. John was fighting it but, nonetheless, the song was finding a way to enter, seemingly filling a void in him. He was thinking back to all his yearnings in Ghana and the wish to travel abroad. They all seemed to be finding meaning at that very moment in that they seemed so inconsequential in the surge he felt within. Slowly his spirits were soaring until, feeling elated, he raised his hand, and the preacher invited all who'd raised their hands to step forward. John was feeling a weakness in the belly, an overwhelming feeling of complete surrender to a higher force beyond description. Going forward, John knelt in front of the preacher and opened his heart to Jesus.

ॐ

6

It wasn't easy for John to stay steady on his new path, realizing it was one thing to profess a spiritual commitment and another to live it. Anyone could agree to the commitment, but not all could put it into practice. The path from the former to the latter wasn't coming readily for John. A path ... nebulous? The next day, he questioned his commitment, unsure he'd taken the right step. He attempted to avoid Natalie. Seemingly, however, she stalked him in her own subtle way, determined not to let this one escape redemption. She would be waiting by John's door until he came home, even at late hours. He would have wished to tell her off, but he liked her, especially because she was so attractive. She was taking an incremental approach, first asking him to Bible studies once a week. And he was having a hard time saying no to her. After going once a week, she prevailed on him to go twice.

Attending Bible studies every Tuesday and Thursday, John gradually developed in the Faith. But even then, Saturday nights were too tempting. He still would go out with Dave partying or chasing women. Acknowledging this challenge, Natalie interceded by inviting John to her apartment for dinner or other social events most Saturdays. She was sharing the apartment with two other students, both equally committed to religion. John, finding their company on Saturday evenings extremely relaxing, was inclined to keep going. They would have dinner, chat or occasionally watch a religious movie. Given the circumstances, John was compelled to start refusing Dave's invitations to visit nightclubs. Trying to explain he was turning away from the ways of the world and building his fortune in heaven, John worsened Dave's confusion. "You've lost your fucking mind," said Dave.

"God loves you my friend," John said.

"I don't give a rat's arse. You've got to stop this crazy shit before it gets too late."

As it was, the two friends spent less time together. Instead, John got closer to Natalie, a sensual relationship with no sexual expression because she wouldn't let it. She, an African American woman from Brooklyn, he an African from Ghana, searching for spiritual growth and thereby transcending their differences and finding their common interests. John's cohabitation with his old desires persisted. He would want to go out drinking or lie with a woman but, instead, he prayed. Once in a while, he slipped, but Natalie and her friends had helped create a will to succeed. Over time, finding that the more he read the Bible and studied, the less he felt tempted in the ways of the world, John did more of the former. He was particularly drawn, too, to the language in the old King James Version of the Bible, in which he found a poetry and diction seemingly on the verge of being lost to the world. John Amoah immersed himself. It took time, but gradually he seemed to be living in a different world, a world that demanded a complete change in habit and even in speech.

John's letters home were assuming a more serious tenor. His letters to me before his conversion had been replete with descriptions of the bar scenes, the women. Now, writing about the Second Coming of Christ, he made mention of his spiritual growth and entreated me to surrender my life to God. He wrote of the need to avert spending eternity in hell.

He wrote of a life filled with God and spiritual renewal. I, on the other hand, wrote to tell him I was readying more women for his return.

Grace intimated to me John communicated with her from time to time. "I don't know about all this faith stuff he's started professing," she said.

"Well, I don't think there's much to that. He's just lonely and going to church makes his life full. I am sure he's very homesick. He must miss you a lot."

"I can't wait for him to come back," Grace said.

"Make sure he makes me his best man at your wedding."

"Wedding? I don't know about a wedding."

"Come on, Grace, you know it's a matter of course."

Smiling, she said, "I will know when I see the ring on my finger."

ॐ∽

7

Graduation arrived. An occasion ... eventful? After the litany of speeches, the presentation of honorary awards at Harvard Yard to graduating students observed in pompous gowns, the diplomas finally were awarded at the law school behind Langdell. John, having no family present at graduation as most of his American colleagues did, borrowed Dave's parents, his father Dan being there for the event. Notwithstanding the tension abiding between Dave's parents, the party thrived. Dave told of John's discovery of God and endeavored further to make jokes about it. John bore the veiled taunts, not amused but resolved. That night, John, holding his diploma in his hand, soared with pride: Master of Laws from Harvard. He immediately was infused with two convictions at the time: with his master's degree, he could successfully launch a legal career on his return to Ghana; and with his spiritual rebirth, he could effect much good with respect to the Gospel.

In the quiet of his room, he plotted his future, the duality of which unfurled before him like a vision. He would bear the cross that

Christ left, but he also would need a secular foundation to ground himself. He would hold the sword aloft – the sword of the Lord Jesus Christ. The Bible would be his armor and the powers of state would be his second sword. To meet his goals, he would establish a church while working with a state agency. The Attorney General's Department seemed an excellent choice. Following the formulation of his goals, John now increasingly anticipated his return home. That would be in three days, which he spent refining his plans, bidding farewell to friends and packing.

Even though still religiously sturdy, the temptation abided to attempt sexual intercourse with Natalie before departing for Ghana. After all, he was only human. God would forgive him. That night, however, he read in his Bible that God would spew him out of His mouth if he was lukewarm: he had to be either completely cold or hot. He resisted his urges. Natalie gave him an autographed Bible, on the first page of which she inscribed these words: "Stay with the Faith. You shall be the vessel of the Lord."

It was a King James Version – and John was buttressed in the belief that God had a plan for him.

Facing three paramount difficulties upon returning to Ghana, John had to address each in turn. The first was his father. The older man, intending for John to work with him, turned furious on learning of John's plans. "Why do you think I spent so much money to send you to America?" he fumed. "I want you to bring your experience and background from America to our practice. If you don't want to practice with me, then what do you want to do? Teach? Ask your friend Ekow. He is doing very well working with me. That young chap will go places. Mark my words. You should plan to be like him."

"I want to work at the Attorney General's Department," John said.

"Did Harvard teach you such foolishness? What can you gain from working for the Government? What kind of money can you make there?"

Intervening, John's mother said, "Give him some time. If he doesn't like it there, he can always come and work with you."

It took a long time to convince his father. Though not wanting to irk his father, John knew, if America had taught him anything, it was to push his will forward, almost without compromise. "The unshakable individuality!" he barked. Reckoning John wouldn't yield, the older man made peace. Amos Amoah pulled on his connections: John's application was reviewed in record time. Less than two months after his return from America, John gained a job at the Attorney General's Department.

ॐॐ

8

In expectation, Grace welcomed John back. I could without reservation attest: neither her beauty nor character had waned even a minor notch. In fact, if I could discern any change, she'd become even more charming. Two nights following his arrival, she invited him to her home for dinner, the rest of her family being away and leaving her the house to herself. Refusing the wine she served him at dinner, John explained he'd stopped drinking. "Just a little for me, John." Without budging, however, he said he was a transformed man. Grace, pursing her lips, wouldn't push her will on him. Then she heard John ask her to surrender herself to God. She replied she already had God. When was the last time she read the Bible? She couldn't recollect. When did she last pray? She couldn't remember. "Why are you speaking in such strange language?" she asked him. What strange language? He shot back.

Insisting it was clear she didn't have God in her life, he maintained she had to accept Jesus Christ and be born again. Christ was knocking. She said she would think it over. They conversed over other issues and he told her his plans. She was not excited that he desired to work for the Government. But she was appalled when he intimated he wished to start a church and preach. "A preacher? That is so boring."

He couldn't fathom why seemingly she took such umbrage at his doing the work of God. "What happened to you in America?"

she asked. He found God, he replied. She seemed distressed. They discussed other matters over a long duration of time.

Then, rising and indicating he was leaving, John headed to the door. "But why?" she asked. "Won't you stay the night? You haven't even kissed me since you came from America. Why?"

He did not want to fall into temptation, he said.

"Kissing me is falling into temptation?"

He said it was.

"Have you found another woman?"

No, he just found Jesus.

"You don't love me anymore?"

He loved her.

"Then kiss me."

No, he said. They should resist such temptation.

"Am I not your girlfriend? Kiss me. I have waited a whole year for you to return. I need you. I really need you."

No! He exclaimed. They couldn't do that anymore. To fornicate was a sin against God.

"Do you intend to stay celibate?"

Yes, he would stay celibate until he got married.

"But you have been with women."

But he was now reborn.

"And what of marriage? Are you planning on it?"

Yes, he was. But he had to get married to the right woman.

"Am I not the right woman?"

She first had to accept Christ and prove herself capable in a probationary period. He couldn't marry a woman who lived in sin.

"And if I don't?"

Then they would have to go their separate ways, he said.

That was how it started. Without equivocation, he informed her that her acceptance of Christ was a necessary condition to their getting married. "Sine qua non," he said. Without denying his love for her, John insisted God must come first. Without reaffirming his love for her, he insisted he couldn't condone sin by marrying a woman who wasn't saved by the blood of Jesus. Grace literally was bathed in tears when she informed me about it the next day, following John's decision to condition his love, which in effect terminated their relationship. He believed it was a conclusion willed by God: she wasn't ready for God and he wasn't ready to deny God for her, despite his feelings for her.

Feeling for Grace, I recollected the numerous nights I'd spent with her talking about John and all her hopes, summoning back to memory all the encouraging words I'd said to her. Knowing she'd turned down many a suitor as she awaited John's return, she now had lost much more than she deserved to lose.

While John was away in America, I did what I could for Grace. Not wanting her to be so lonely that she'd stray from him, I endeavored to include her in many of my social activities. I have done many a terrible thing in my life, but I knew I couldn't romance my best friend's girlfriend. Thus, for a year, I listened to her discuss John. Then following his return, she complained to me John was obsessed. "I too believe in God," she said, "But I also need to live life. I really love John, so I have no choice. I must accept his condition."

"What do you mean?"

"I will accept Jesus, whatever that means."

"Because you want to, or because John wants you to?"

"What does it matter?"

Much as I desired to see them both happy, I rubbished such sad, dishonest acquiescence. "Grace," I said, "I know you love John. Everybody can see that. But you need to think this through. You both will be miserable if you do that just to please him. How long do you think you can deceive him? How do you think he will react when he finds out your commitment isn't genuine?"

"But I love him. What else can I do?"

"There's not much you can do. You just have to be yourself and hope he accepts you as you are."

"And if I lose him forever?"

"There is no other viable choice."

That, however, was Grace, and feeling another's pain is not the same as feeling your own. Needless to say, it was even worse when his uncompromising righteousness was visited on me. I expected he'd take it more in jest than in seriousness when I told John I thought his religious rants were tantamount to gibberish. An expectation ... unrealistic? I was thinking he'd change, but the more I listened to him, the more I realized his seriousness. Desirous of showing him he couldn't surrender the good life, I attempted to get him to accompany me to a nightclub.

"No!"

"Why not?" I asked.

He informed me he'd left those things behind. They were things of the flesh and he couldn't do them anymore. That is what he said, if I understood him correctly.

"You are not a spirit. Did God not give you flesh? What is wrong with satisfying the desires of the flesh he gave you?"

John said God despised such things.

"Fuck you," I said in frustration. "You've gone to America and come back so you think your shit doesn't smell? Wasn't it you and I who chased after women and drank like horses?"

He said those were different times and he had changed. He asked me if I believed in God.

"Yes, but he doesn't have to be a Christian God. He doesn't have to be a Muslim God. He is God. The God that our ancestors worshipped before foreigners came and changed our minds."

"A primitive and pagan God?"

"Ah! Are you a foreigner now? Calling the God of your heritage pagan and primitive? You have been brainwashed, my brother."

We went on thus, John fierier and I more agitated, with no altered opinion on either side. We did not, however, terminate our friendship then. The week following our debate, I returned to see John, two women accompanying me. Going for a drink, I asked John to join us. John was angered. I insisted, however, until he boldly stated he didn't want me to visit him anymore. It was clear, he asserted, that Satan was using me to tempt him. "A vessel of temptation," he said. He'd tried to be reasonable, but I wasn't respecting his wishes; therefore, since our lifestyles were completely at odds, it would be better if we brought our friendship to an end. More than surprised, nay shocked, I left, trying to convince myself he was simply joking. Or I thought perhaps I had misunderstood him, as I often did ever since he returned from America. The next day I tried to call him – he didn't return my calls. I went to his house, but he stayed in his room and wouldn't come out to see me. Realizing that he was serious, I knew nothing now would stop him.

9

As I would later learn, building the church entailed extreme difficulty for John, mainly because he was preoccupied all week at the Attorney General's office and only had weekends to plan and work on his church. First, he needed a building. Knowing it would be difficult to attempt the construction of a building at that point, he had to lease. How and where would he secure the money, however? Seeing no other choice, he borrowed from his father, and, reluctantly, the older man lent him the funds. Leasing a simple, square structure in the Accra suburb of Kaneshie, John prevailed on a carpenter to build a huge cross, which he erected in front of the structure that would become his church. Then he had a signboard constructed saying: WELCOME TO THE NEW CHURCH OF CHRIST. He erected the sign by the road so it was visible from afar. He purchased a used piano and had the carpenter construct some pews. It was a small beginning, but a beginning nonetheless.

The Sun by Night

The first Sunday was nerve-splitting for John, the self-proclaimed pastor. He'd no idea how many would appear for service. One? Twenty? Fifty? Having had pamphlets made, he'd gone from door to door after work, introducing himself and distributing the pamphlets – he would be glad if they showed up to his new church, he said. Some were receptive, some not, and it was John's faith that sustained him through it all: the cold stares, the insults, and the sarcastic remarks.

Notwithstanding his tribulations and fears, the first Sunday was a success. He received a congregation of no less than one hundred – about eighty more than he'd expected. There not being enough pews to seat a hundred, many were forced to stand at the back of the church. The first offering was handsome. John Amoah had begun well. Three months later, following the establishment of a volunteer choir, John would proclaim that he'd "Saved at least sixty people from the Devil."

With John's fame as the pastor of the New Church of Christ growing, I went about investigating. Everyone I questioned seemed charmed by this young preacher. What does he preach about? I queried. That question caused a pause: members of his congregation seemed in agreement on one thing only: he preached about God and Jesus Christ and the Holy Spirit and Salvation. Beyond that, there seemed no consensus as to his message. Not understanding how one man could invoke so many different opinions with regard to the subject matter of his sermons, I went to see for myself.

Going late, I stood at the very back of the church, not wanting John to see me there. Admittedly, John projected a charming image behind the pulpit, in his sharp suit with a large crucifix behind him. Additionally, his profound seriousness once he started speaking conferred on him a daunting respectability. But, despite this image, his language was almost beyond my comprehension. Granted, I am not the easiest to understand either, but he belonged in a class of his own. I found his diction obtuse and his syntax overly complex. Thus, I was beginning to understand why each left his church with a varying impression of John's message, or simply pretended to understand him when in fact none did. Who, after all, desires to admit incomprehension of that which seemingly charms and is understood by everyone? Such mass make-believe.

With John's fame as a lawyer growing, he began to prosecute important, though relatively small, cases. With time, however, he seemingly gained increasing responsibility at the Attorney General's Department, which amplified his fame nationally. Listening to him argue a few cases, though, I honestly couldn't comprehend why he was becoming so famous. He surely had an imposing and determined air. However, his language ... Who could appreciate such an inscrutable style?

Two years having elapsed, John's father told me he was getting worried. His older son was too devoted to the church, apportioning no time for socializing. On the female front, John certainly had numerous opportunities. Seemingly, however, he was searching for the perfect woman who would neither tempt nor corrupt him. "He keeps saying he wants a woman who is saved," Amos Amoah said. "He wants a woman as committed to celibacy before marriage as he is."

"Where would he find such a woman?" I asked.

In the person of Stella Offei. Noticing her sitting in the congregation a number of times, John recognized how she stood out even though she was of average appearance. But he didn't notice her because of her looks; she was outstanding because she seemed constantly to beam with a certain ... *je ne sais quoi*. Knowing he had to converse with her, he awaited his opportunity, which arrived one Sunday after church when she visited him after the bulk of the congregation had departed. "Pastor, I have been thinking. You need to keep the momentum of your church going during the week."

Intrigued, he wanted to hear more.

"Wouldn't it be nice to have Bible studies at least one day in the work week? Our souls need the Word as often as possible."

Smiling, John reckoned he should have forethought that himself. Recalling the Bible studies he'd experienced in America with Natalie and, knowing that he had to start it here too, John classified her a Godsend.

"I can lead the Bible study if you are busy," Stella Offei said.

Looking at her closely, John knew she carried conviction; but, unless he was also convinced of her knowledge, leadership, faith and ability to preach, he couldn't turn the study over to her. He invited her to sit with him for a while. John would learn she was studying at the Institute of Journalism. She'd been born again while in her third year at Accra Girls Secondary School. The more they conversed, the more he became convinced she was the chosen woman for him. Of utmost importance, she seemingly was surefooted in her faith and genuinely interested in growing spiritually. When speaking about God, her conviction became manifest and John was affected. Although they were co-leaders of the Bible studies, John allowed Stella Offei to perform the bulk of the work. Attendees had glowing praise for her.

Asking her out for dinner later, he confessed his love for her. Thrilled, she nonetheless cautioned against the temptations of the flesh. John, utterly impressed that she would raise the issue, was in complete agreement. This commitment … impeccable? Keeping their relationship strong through mutual visits as often as they could, they were nonetheless careful to keep physical contact to a minimum. They undertook long walks during which they deliberated over the church and their future. Stella, struggling to juggle her studies, her responsibilities at the church, and her new friendship with John Amoah, thrived nonetheless.

ॐ

10

Unlike John, I, having few options after graduation from law school, could attempt to seek work either with the Government or by entering private practice. Choosing private practice became more viable following Amos Amoah's request that I work with him at Amoah & Associates. Theirs was a challenging mode of remuneration. You were guaranteed a minimum salary at the end of the month, which was a pittance. Your bonus, being the bulk of your remuneration, was contingent on your work input and the quantity of business you generated. Formidable as it was, it formed the foundation of my entrepreneurial success. Desirous of obtaining a higher bonus, I endeavored unflinchingly to grow business. I was a rookie lawyer trying to garner trade, I had no track record, I was unknown; but I was determined.

Making it a point to attend every function where I could meet potential clients, I even attended parties for business reasons: mingling with and informing people I was a lawyer with Amoah & Associates, which always impressed them. I offered business cards without restraint. John's father, being supportive, would refer potential clients to me when they called on him and he was too otherwise occupied to handle their legal matters. He had his big clients and he didn't need the little ones that I so welcomed. In the first instances, most of the cases I handled were insignificant civil ones. Drawing up wills and drafting assorted contracts occupied my time, but was hardly the type of work to confer on me fame and wealth. I was in dire need of a break, which came about five months after John returned from America. His father, referring the case to me, said almost nonchalantly, "Take care of this, Ekow. It may be an important case for your career."

It was a murder case, wherein my client, Ama Anane, stood accused of shooting a former minister of state, Osei, a powerful politician in his time and considerably influential until his death. In the sight of numerous eyewitnesses, she allegedly had shot him. She, being a fifteen-year-old girl staying with the ex-politician and his family and working as their maid, had every powerful force arrayed against her. A distant relative had sought her rescue by hiring us to represent her. The politician's furious family brought all their resources to bear in an effort to secure my client's lengthy incarceration or death. It became my duty to save her from that fate. Since the story entailed the death of an influential man, it received enormous attention in the newspapers and my name piggybacked on that. *The Accra Chronicler* described me as "a young, unknown lawyer with the high-powered law chambers of

Amoah & Associates." Many newspapers were declaring the case lost for me even before it started. A case… formidable? *The Accra Chronicler* posed a series of questions:

> How can such an inexperienced lawyer withstand the combined forces of the state's prosecutorial apparatus and the wealth and influence of the deceased's family in the face of facts so glaring? Would the case of the accused not be better served if she pleads guilty and begs for leniency? We have seen the facts, and the facts tell a story of cold-blooded murder. The question most people on the streets are asking is how could a girl taken in by such a generous family reward her benefactors with such a cruel crime?

The prosecution presented a slew of witnesses who testified one and all as follows. On the day of the homicide, a quiet Saturday afternoon, they were playing checkers outside the house of the deceased. Suddenly, they saw the accused run out of the house. She stood outside with a pistol in her hand. Seconds later, the deceased, Osei, ran outside. "Give me that pistol," he demanded. My client stood there staring at him, motionless, saying nothing. Then the deceased moved towards her, apparently to take the pistol from her. She raised the pistol and fired once into his chest.

In cross-examining the witnesses, I asked them if they'd ever seen the accused argue with anyone. No. Had they ever seen her fight or beat anyone? No. Did she sometimes come and sit with them while they were playing checkers? Yes. Was she amiable? Yes, but … "No buts," I said. Was she amiable? Yes or No. Yes. So all they saw that day was a woman bursting out of the house with a pistol in hand? Yes. Before then, had they ever heard any ruckus? Any noise that was unusual? No. Out of the many people I interviewed, only one neighbor, Ama Badu, was willing to testify that sometimes in the afternoons, she would hear cries from the house.

The prosecution, trying to impeach the witness's testimony, assaulted her with all manner of sophisticated tactics. The prosecution failed, its relentlessness notwithstanding. Having no personal interest in the case and holding a respectable position at the Ministry of Economic Planning, she projected sophistication and respectability, truthfulness and conscientiousness. Had she ever seen the woman bruised? Yes. At least three times, she'd seen her walking around with bruises.

I subpoenaed the family doctor. I asked him what my client had told him. Not much, he said. Had he treated her for severe bruises? Yes. Could they have been caused by someone engaged in, say, a fight? Yes. So she was actually battered? Yes. By whom? She had said by some neighborhood friends, the doctor said.

Having established the groundwork for my client's testimony, it would all hinge or unhinge on her credibility. Commencing slowly, together we told a coherent story to the jury. She had lived with the Oseis for three years. She'd first moved in with them because they needed a maid to help with the household chores. At first everything was alright and she was treated very well. Then a year later, the deceased started propositioning her. It all started one day when the deceased and my client were alone in the house. He had demanded sex. She had refused. He beat her. Mrs. Osei was surprised to see the swellings on her face. My client lied to her, saying she'd gotten into a fight with some truants in the neighborhood. She lied to her because she didn't want to cause any trouble. Mrs. Osei was angry with her for getting into a fight and slapped her.

Things returned to normal immediately afterwards until Mr. Osei propositioned her again and she again refused. He beat her and forced himself on her. Mrs. Osei called her a bad girl when she returned and saw her swellings. After that she would beg, yell sometimes, but she was afraid to resist because she knew Mr. Osei would beat her. Only once after that did she resist. He beat her so badly she had to be treated by the family doctor. Yes, she'd told him she'd been in a fight, because she was afraid of what the truth might bring.

The day of the shooting, when she was alone with Mr. Osei, he'd come to her again. She'd told him she was pregnant, that she was carrying his baby. Taking out a pistol, he threatened to kill her if she told anyone. He said they'd get the baby aborted, but she said she couldn't do that. He walked towards her with the pistol in his hand and she was afraid. She pushed him back and he tripped over some books on the floor and fell on his back. The pistol slipped out of his hands when he fell. She picked it up and ran out of the house. He pursued her outside. That was when she fired the pistol.

The prosecution's objections, ranging from hearsay to lack of relevance, were mostly overruled. The prosecution attempted to shake my client, trick her into changing her testimony, but those efforts were unavailing. I presented testimony and test results establishing the deceased as the father of the fetus.

The case went to the jury. Following long, nerve-splitting hours of deliberations, the jury returned late with a verdict of not guilty. In one evening, I achieved stardom as a legal genius. If I could assist an unknown accused walk away with murder, they said, I could do anything. *The Accra Chronicler* put it this way:

> A bedazzling output by a young man who demon-
> strated that intelligence, skill and sheer determination
> can tower over wealth and fame. Whether his client
> is guilty or not, Mr. Ekow Dadzie has today paved
> the way for a monumental legal career.

11

Following my triumph, John's father gained great confidence in me. He said to me, "It disturbs me that you and my son are no longer on good terms, but I have to look beyond that now. I don't blame you. Someday, I hope you can settle your differences." I started performing most of the older man's legal duties. He invited me to his important meetings and, within months, I became almost indispensable to him. It was around that time that he introduced me to Koo Manu, the businessman whose star seemed on the rise. The man, and his rise from nothing to opulence and influence, impressed me. Koo Manu, not being a highly educated man, nonetheless was intelligent and sharp, with an abundance of business savvy. As nothing escaped him, I was careful to manage his legal affairs with utmost care. He, impressed by my victory in the Osei case and gaining even greater confidence in me, insisted I work almost exclusively on his legal affairs, most of them being corporate matters.

Seemingly with a prefect home, I must confess I was a surprised he'd marry a second wife. Not that I was opposed to it, but, nowadays, people seldom do that. His eldest son, Kubi, almost a replica of his father, persuaded me to attempt to dissuade the older man. I tried, but Koo Manu wouldn't listen.

A little earlier, a group of people approached me, asking that I run for parliament. The country was on the verge of civilian rule: party politics had been reintroduced by the Supreme Council following years of military rule, and the soldiers were returning to the barracks. In my opinion, that's where they belonged. When the Revolutionary Council seized power, it had no choice but to continue the transition to civilian rule. Being busy with my legal work, partisan politics was the last thing I contemplated. Nevertheless, I listened when the group, comprising mostly of political aficionados recently disqualified by Government fiat from running for office, expressed concern that the seat could go to the Revolutionary Council's choice – Colonel Duah. He'd announced his candidacy after the Government reopened the elections to new candidates. Meantime, the leading candidate was disqualified from running and held in "protective custody" pending investigation of the nebulous charge of 'illegal acquisition of wealth.'

Thinking I had the stature and wherewithal to thwart the outgoing Government's effort to steal people sympathetic to it into the parliament, the visiting group entreated me, pointing to my recent unanimous election as president of the Ghana Bar Association. Calling him "nefarious and cantankerous," I, they said, owed it to the country to defeat Colonel Duah.

Skeptical at first, especially in the face of what was happening around me, I refused, especially considering that Koo Manu had just gone undergone an ordeal because of his foray into politics. Increasingly enticed, however, by the possibility of a seat in parliament,

I reconsidered. Believing myself more competent than Colonel Duah, whose only achievement seemed to be his association with the Revolutionary Council, I eventually agreed to run for parliament. The group suggested that I run as part of a *bona fide* organization that would lend legitimacy to my candidacy. Following hours of deliberation, I suggested forming a movement to be named Citizens United to Save Ghana. Demurring, another, speaking as though in jest, said instead: "We need something that those at the grassroots can dig. How about Citizens United to Save Bottom Power?"

Although the name appeared ludicrous to me and I said so, I liked it nonetheless. It was the kind of catchy name capable of generating instant interest. Aware I was in need of as much interest as possible in the short period I had before the elections, I agreed to the name. Receiving financial support from the group, the movement and my candidacy were born under the banner:

EKOW DADZIE FOR PARLIAMENT
CITIZENS UNITED TO SAVE BOTTOM POWER

The response was amazing. Many seemed magnetized to the banner and within days hundreds joined in the movement. Others, however, seemingly were taking matters to an extreme. Someone, with either a warped or great sense of humor, organized a competition – The Bottom Power Contest – under the banner of the movement, ostensibly to reward the one who could shake his or her buttocks the most in an allotted time of one minute. Reliable accounts reaching me indicated that a panel of judges had observed as contestants lined up and shook their behinds to the cheer of admiring fans. The winner subsequently was awarded a cash prize in the name of the Citizens United to Save Bottom Power. I objected when I heard, but it was too late. Regardless, immediately following that event, we received a flood of applications to join the movement.

Book Three: The Rain of Snow

Although there is more on that point, I, for now, return to Koo Manu. I had attempted, although unsuccessfully, to win the return of his assets from the Government. That, however, was in a civil trial, when all that was at stake were his assets and bank accounts. Soon, though, things would become more serious.

After Akua Nsiah Manu, Koo Manu's wife, called on me to handle his criminal case, I sat down alone at night, internally deliberating the matter. The case against him being mostly circumstantial, I wasn't convinced he'd done it. I wasn't even convinced he was capable of committing the crime, although you never know, with absolute certainty, people's capacities for harm. Knowing a jury could find him convictable based on the facts, as I then knew them, I was concerned. In fact, I'd witnessed convictions on less compelling facts. There existed always a chance. Thinking that if I could stop the case from going to trial, Koo Manu would be better off, I attempted to persuade John to drop the case.

Not desirous of going begging, given our sour relationship, I nonetheless put my client's interests first. "Why would you want to prosecute a case so weak? You know it won't go far. A jury will never convict him on the basis of the evidence you have. So why don't you drop the case?"

Smiling, he said that was for the jury to decide.

"But you don't want to waste the Government's money, and you don't want needlessly to expend your own reputation on a case like this."

He said his case was strong enough.

"We all were friends once, John. For goodness sake, I am asking you as a favor to me to drop this case."

He said he couldn't do that.

"Alright, why don't you do it for Koo Manu. He used to come to your church once. Don't you have any feelings for him? Do you really think he is capable of murder?"

John said sternly that Koo Manu was a polygamist, which was a sinful practice.

"Yes, but let God deal with that."

John said polygamy was a primitive practice. Until the people learned to move away from such practices, the country would continue to wallow in backwardness.

"You speak like a foreigner. Even worse."

He replied, "Your jingoistic sophistry is enmeshed in the expedient fabric of tradition and feudatory sycophancy. No bogus atavism or transcendent pride in cultural asymmetry forbids importation of superior notions." He went on to say that he didn't care what he spoke like, so long as he spoke the truth. Such pagan practices had no place in a modern world or in the eyes of God.

"You sound like you are condemning him for polygamy and, therefore, murder. Is that the logic?"

John simply said that he was convinced of my client's guilt.

"Very well, we will meet in court." I walked to the door. "I regret that we are not the friends we used to be. I truly regret it. John, you have changed."

He said something full of bombast.

"What does that mean?"

He said nothing.

Appearing all over the newspapers was the arrest of Koo Manu and his release from jail on bail. The facts, presented sensationally and lopsidedly, made it seem my client, without question, had done murder in cold blood. Knowing actual facts are often many steps behind their initial presentation, I had to be patient, concentrating on the heavy work ahead. Desirous of devoting all my attention to winning the acquittal of Koo Manu, I dropped or delegated all other matters. In fact, I'd never in my career wanted to win a case as badly as I wanted to win this one.

THE JOURNALIST'S NOTEBOOK

1

As I said, I am everywhere, but then again, I am nowhere. Therefore, I reenter like a waterfall diving into the river below, eternally pushing into it, but one with it. The elections were over and the civilians had taken over. The country sighed collectively with the exhalation of new relief, the luster of the self-arrogated revolutionaries dimmed by time, although the electrifying shock of the Revolutionary Council's short reign still hung its specter over the new regime. On a more personal scale, Colonel Duah had defeated Ekow Dadzie for a seat in the new parliament. The official result was shocking in that Ekow Dadzie had not received a single vote. I mean ZERO, which would indicate that neither he nor anyone else had voted for him, which was outrageous to believe. I had voted for him; therefore, at the very least, he should have had one vote.

Ekow Dadzie ranted about the result. He called for a recount and took his case to court, but the court rejected his case in a very terse opinion: "Mr. Dadzie alleges fraud in his contest for parliament against Colonel Duah. We find no proof of fraud. His case is dismissed." Lawyer Dadzie blasted the court, labeling the decision as "inane." The court threatened to find him in contempt if he continued impugning its integrity. That ended his quest.

But he was soon again embroiled in the limelight of court dramatics, this time at the behest of his long-time client Koo Manu. Despite his avowal to avoid the public spotlight, Mr. Manu challenged his suspended sentence and sought the return of his assets and bank accounts as soon as the soldiers returned the country to civilian rule.

Ekow Dadzie argued that Koo Manu was not tried and, therefore, his suspended sentence of thirty years was an infringement on his fundamental human rights. Similarly, he had been deprived of his

235

assets and bank accounts without due process of law. The Supreme Court heard the case and concluded by a slim margin that even if there had been no actual trial, there seemed to have been a purported trial. Transitional provisions in the new Constitution barred the Supreme Court from reversing decisions made by the Revolutionary Council, whether actual or purported. Therefore, said the Supreme Court, because Mr. Manu received a purported trial, the Court couldn't reverse his sentence. The Court's conclusion that there was a purported trial was derived from the following testimony of Colonel Duah (who, we found out, had participated in the Revolutionary Council's military tribunals):

Dadzie: What transpired at this trial you claim took place?

Duah: It was such a long time ago. I don't remember much of it.

Dadzie: Are there any transcripts of this so-called trial?

Duah: No.

Dadzie: Was Mr. Manu allowed a defense counsel?

Duah: No.

Dadzie: Why not?

Duah: He didn't bring one with him.

Dadzie: Was he allowed any witnesses?

Duah: No.

Dadzie: Why not?

Duah: He didn't bring any with him.

Dadzie: How many people tried him?

Duah: Seven.

Dadzie: What are the professions of those seven?

Duah: Soldiers.

Dadzie: All of them?

Duah: Yes.

Dadzie: Who are they?

Duah: I don't remember.

Book Three: The Rain of Snow

Dadzie: Did you issue an opinion?

Duah: No.

Dadzie: What was he accused of?

Duah: Something. I can't remember.

After the Supreme Court's decision, Ekow Dadzie stated that it was "another inane decision in a series of inane decisions by jurists who have abdicated their senses". He was blasted and chastised for being so critical. There was even some talk of disbarring him, but that came to naught. After the trial, Koo Manu disappeared from the public arena. But some months later, he would be back, charged with murder.

And as that trial started, I had to face new intriguing matters; the distinguished old man, for example, the one I'd seen in the courtroom on the day of the lawyers' opening statements. He walked very slowly, pausing now and then to take in the view. I wanted to ask him who he was, this man to whom I found myself so inextricably drawn. But as I got closer, I realized I didn't know what I'd say to him. I tried to think of something, but my mind failed me like a stranger's futile knock against shut doors. A little sadly, I turned around and walked away, determined to do better next time.

The vexing question remained even after I had filed my first report on the Manu trial: I was still struggling with whether Koo Manu was the actual killer or a falsely accused man. The question haunted me so much that, smelling blood like a hungry lion after bleeding prey, I decided to find out as much as I could.

I drove to the house of the deceased, Akwele Oddoi. It was a rather small house and it looked quite cheap to me. I stood by the street and observed the house for a long time. It seemed to have the distinguishing hollowness of death hanging around it, as gloomy as sadness. As I stood there, a man approached. He stared at me and, as if pulled by a magnetic force, I walked up to him and asked him if he knew Akwele Oddoi. I was casting my net wide, just in case. He

237

shook his head and hurried away, as if I shouldn't have asked him that question. I stood there for minutes in resignation, thinking what to do next, when a younger man approached. He too looked at me carefully and asked, "Are you the one who's asking about Akwele?"

"Yes," I replied. "Did you know her?"

"Who are you?" he asked.

"My name is Nii Lamptey. I work for *The Accra Chronicler*."

"You are a newspaper man?" The man frowned. "Are you going to put me in your paper?"

"It depends on what you tell me," I said.

"What are you looking for? Akwele is dead."

"Did you know her?" I asked again.

"Did I know her? I *knew* her." And his pun was clearly intended.

Still, I asked, "How did you know her?"

He frowned again (reminding me of a bulldog). "If you want information, my friend, you must pay." He held out his hand. "Give me some cola." I gave him a little money. It wasn't much, but he seemed happy with it. Perhaps I was throwing money away, but at that point I was quite desperate for information. "Now you are talking." He seemed more relaxed but made me vow I would never mention him in my newspaper. "I hear they've put that rich man, Koo Manu, in jail or something for killing Akwele. That is so foolish. It makes no sense why Koo Manu would kill her. Anyone who knew Akwele knew she lived a dangerous life. Anyone could have killed her."

"What do you mean?"

"She was a woman of the night. Understand? Selling her body …"

"She was a prostitute?"

"Need I say the word? I told you I *knew* her. All you needed was some cash and she was yours."

"I see. But why would anyone kill her?"

"It's a dangerous profession, you know. Too many crazy men get involved with that type. Anyone could have killed her."

"Including Koo Manu?"

"Yes. But why? His wife lives right next to Akwele's. Do you think he would get up one day and kill a prostitute living next to his wife?"

"It's possible."

"But how likely is it?"

"Have you spoken with the police?"

"No. No one has asked me anything. I don't think it's my business."

"Thank you for the information," I said, as I walked over to my car. Then a question came to my mind and I yelled it at the man as he walked away. "Do you know any of Akwele's friends, relatives, enemies?"

"No," he replied. "Except she once told me she was quite close to Madam Beatrice."

I ran to the man for more information. "Madam Beatrice?"

"Yes." The young man breathed heavily but uncomfortably, like a gear abruptly shifted into higher gear. "Do you know Colonel Duah?"

"Of course."

"Don't tell anyone I told you this, but he was one of Akwele's customers."

I let the news dissolve like bitter medicine before asking, "How do you know?"

"I saw her with him at least twice. His car was parked about two hundred meters from here, over there around the corner. The first time I saw them, I was coming from a night outing. It was close to ten. As I walked home, I saw Akwele and the Colonel standing by his car. They seemed to be arguing. I recognized the Colonel's voice. I had just watched him give a speech on TV the week before. Imagine my surprise when I saw him again, this time with Akwele. She seemed to be protesting that he was manipulating her. He was insisting he could do whatever he wanted with her. I sneaked by quietly. At least one other time, I saw him drop her off around the corner. I think he was being cautious."

I extrapolated as much information as I could. My mind was like a swing, as if it had been propelled into a vertigo-inducing swirl. Did Colonel Duah, now retired, Member of Parliament, have anything to do with Akwele's death? With many thoughts running through my mind, I prepared my report late that night:

TRIAL WITNESS SAYS "I SAW DEFENDANT BUT I WAS DRUNK"

The trial of businessman Koo Manu for the murder of Akwele Oddoi continued today at the Accra Circuit Court. The sultry weather did not deter a large gathering. With the circling fan hardly containing the heat, Justice Janet Ocloo called the proceedings to order before a panel of twelve jurors.

The prosecutor, John Amoah, began by calling his first witness, Madam Beatrice Amoo, a businesswoman who lives next to the deceased. Madam Beatrice, as she prefers to be called, took her oath beaming with apparent self-esteem.

The prosecutor, in a confident manner of the pastor that he is, walked slowly to the witness. He stopped momentarily to survey the jurors before facing the witness. "Madam Beatrice, would you bestow on us for informational purposes the non-ambulatory geographic site of your habitual domicile?" Lawyer Amoah began.

"Pardon me?"

"Where is the territorial situs of your physical habitation?"

"I'm sorry I don't understand you, sir," Madam Beatrice said, her frown betraying her confusion.

Justice Ocloo asked the prosecutor to rephrase the question so the witness would understand.

"Where is the locative presence of your habitual abode?"

"Huh?"

Justice Ocloo shook her head, as though in disapproval of the prosecutor. She explained to Madam Beatrice: "Where do you live?" The Justice asked Prosecutor Amoah if that was what he meant. He said it was.

After Madam Beatrice gave the information, the prosecutor continued, "And could you expatiate on the intervening proximate relation of the two dwellings, yours and the victim's?"

After Justice Ocloo explained, Madam Beatrice said, "Her house was next to mine. I rented it to her."

"Accord then, of your familiar acquaintance with the victim?"

Justice Ocloo: "Do you agree, Madam Beatrice, that you knew the victim?"

"I knew her very well," said Madam Beatrice. "We were neighbors and I was her landlady. Sometimes when I needed something, I would go and ask her and she also used to come and ask me for little things, like salt and tomatoes when she'd ran out. She was such a sweet girl."

"And your social intercourse?

"Like I said, we interacted often; and she sometimes came over so I could plait her hair or she mine."

The prosecutor asked Madam Beatrice if she knew one Inspector Boateng.

"He used to come to the house very often," Madam Beatrice replied. "Sometimes when Akwele was with me and sometimes not. You see, Mr. Boateng often stopped by my house on Sunday afternoons. I knew his father. His father and I were very good friends until he died. I have always felt close to the family. I feel like a second mother to Mr. Boateng. And so I invite him home often and he comes with his friend Mr. Ofori."

"And what constitutes the vocational foundation of Mr. Boateng and Mr. Ofori."

"Huh?"

Justice Ocloo: "What work do they do?"

"Oh, they are both policemen."

241

"In view of the testimony thus far presented, shall I be accurate in synopsizing that by virtue of their being frequenters to the territorial situs of your domicile, you acquired close social intimacy apropos both Messrs. Boateng and Ofori?"

"Objection," yelled the defense lawyer, Ekow Dadzie. "The prosecutor is leading the witness."

"Overruled," Justice Ocloo said. "You may answer the question, Madam Beatrice."

Madam Beatrice said, "I'm sorry. I don't understand the question." Justice Ocloo explained the question.

"Yes," Madam Beatrice said, "I knew them well."

"Could you recount, Madam Beatrice, the occurrences of the afternoon now at issue?"

"Yes sir. On the afternoon in question, I invited Mr. Ofori and Mr. Boateng to my house. I prepared a meal and we ate and talked like we always do when they come to my house. I told them I was waiting for Akwele because she was supposed to plait my hair that afternoon. They were kind enough to help me take out a few chairs and put them on my verandah. In the meantime they started playing checkers."

"What transpired subsequently? Were your tympanic membranes activated in the negative by a squeal?"

"Objection," Lawyer Ekow Dadzie interjected. "Leading, suggestive."

"Overruled," said Justice Ocloo. "Did you hear a scream, Madam Beatrice?"

Madam Beatrice continued, "We heard a loud scream and then the words 'He has killed me.'"

"Objection! Hearsay."

"Overruled. You may continue, Madam Beatrice."

"All three of us stood up and moved in the direction of Akwele's house. That's when we saw a man rush out of Akwele's house and run away."

"And is that man present in the courtroom?"

"Yes!" Madam Beatrice said. There was a hushed murmur as the accusatory finger of Madam Beatrice pointed to the defendant, who sat with a rather impassive expression. He looked up at his accuser and then he looked down and shook his head. The Prosecutor asked that the records show that Madam Beatrice had identified the defendant, Koo Manu, as the man she saw running from the house of the victim, Akwele Oddoi.

Asked what she did next, Madam Beatrice explained that she and the two policemen rushed to Akwele's house. They saw her lying on her face. Policeman Boateng and Madam Beatrice attended to her while Policeman Ofori went in pursuit of Koo Manu. The defense counsel's objection that the reference to Koo Manu as the person seen fleeing Akwele Oddoi's house was prejudicial was overruled. Madam Beatrice then went on to say that the victim, Akwele, lay unconscious in her living room and wouldn't respond when they called to her. They saw a small pool of blood from her head region and a pestle was lying next to her.

She didn't think Akwele was dead because she was breathing. The defense counsel objected that the witness was not qualified to state an opinion as to whether Akwele was dead or alive, but he was overruled. The prosecutor asked what they did next and Madam Beatrice explained that they got some help and carried Akwele into her car and drove her to the Korle Bu Hospital. Why didn't she call an ambulance? "With all due respect, we all know that if I'd done that, she would have rotted before the ambulance arrived." The audience in the courtroom murmured its approval of that assessment, as the prosecutor thanked Madam Beatrice and Justice Ocloo invited the defense counsel to cross-examine her.

Lawyer Ekow Dadzie rose from his seat slowly. He looked tired as he started his cross-examination. "Madam Beatrice, is it correct to say that Mr. Boateng and Mr. Ofori were frequent visitors to your house?"

"Yes."

"On those occasions when they came to your house, was liquor served?"

"Yes."

"On the afternoon in question, did you serve Mr. Boateng and Mr. Ofori any liquor?"

"Objection. Irrelevant."

"Overruled. You may answer the question, Madam Beatrice."

"It wasn't as if we were …"

"Yes or no, Madam Beatrice, did you serve Mr. Boateng and Mr. Ofori any alcohol on the afternoon in question?"

"Yes."

"What kind of liquor?"

"I served gin, *imported* gin," Madam Beatrice said proudly. "I don't like the cheap local stuff." There was laughter in the courtroom.

"And did you consume any of that *imported* gin?"

The prosecutor objected that he didn't see the purpose of that line of questioning and the defense counsel replied that the perception of what happened that afternoon is important. "I think we are entitled to probe the sobriety or lack thereof of the witness." Justice Ocloo overruled the objection and instructed the witness to answer the question.

"Yes"

"So you served them gin when they arrived at your house?"

"Yes."

And you were drinking with them as you ate and they played checkers?"

"Yes."

"Madam Beatrice, how long were the two policemen at your house?"

After a short pause, Madam Beatrice responded, "They were there for about three hours."

The defense counsel turned to the jury and said, "So for three hours you and your visitors were drinking. *Three hours* of drinking *imported* gin." Then turning to Madam Beatrice, he asked, "Would you say that you are a drunkard?"

"Objection."

"Sustained."

"Let me rephrase that. Do you drink a lot, Madam?"

"Objection! Asked, objected to, sustained. Badgering."

"Overruled."

"Of course not. I only drink occasionally."

Lawyer Dadzie asked Madam Beatrice how much she drank over the three-hour period. She resisted until Justice Ocloo instructed her to answer. She had drunk roughly three glasses of gin.

"Then, Madam, being only an occasional drinker and having drunk *three glasses* of gin on the afternoon in question, are we not right in saying that your sense of perception was impaired?"

"I wasn't drunk."

"I didn't say you were drunk. But you don't dispute that you had drunk liquor. You say yourself that you only drink occasionally. Given all that, Madam Beatrice, is it not possible that your perception of events was not at a hundred percent?"

"It is possible."

"It is possible! It is possible that your perception was not one hundred percent."

"But I am telling you what I saw happen."

"What you *perceived*. But a perception impaired by alcohol. Alright, Madam Beatrice, let me ask you this. You have testified that your house is next to where Akwele lived. In fact, that you own that house."

"Yes."

"Very well, Madam, is there a wall between the two houses?"

"Yes."

"And how tall is the wall?"

"It's about five feet."

245

"So a five-foot wall divides your house and Akwele's. How can you see what goes on in her house?"

"You can see if you are standing."

"But if a person is running in the other compound and another is observing from your compound, you can only see at best from the mid-section of that person; perhaps from the elbows up, correct?"

"Correct."

"Plus there are a number of mango and guava trees inside your house, correct?"

"Correct."

"Madam Beatrice, is it not true that you did not see the face of the person who was running from the house of the deceased on the afternoon in question, and that standing in your compound, you simply saw, through trees, the back of a person running; and that you only saw this person from the elbows up?" There was a long silence as Lawyer Dadzie waited for a response. When none came, he added, "Well, yes or no, Madam Beatrice? Did you, in fact, see the face of the person who was running from the house of the deceased on the afternoon in question?"

"I ... you see ... "

"My Lord," Lawyer Dadzie said, "could you please instruct the witness to answer the question?"

"No," she said meekly, when Justice Ocloo instructed Madam Beatrice to answer.

"No!" Lawyer Dadzie bellowed, suddenly energized, and turned to the jury. "You did not see the face of the person who ran from the deceased's house on the afternoon in question. Very well, Madam Beatrice, given that you are a social drinker and had been drinking quite a bit on the afternoon in question; given that a wall separates your house from the deceased's; given that your own yard has a number of trees; given that you only saw the back of the person you claim was fleeing from the house of the deceased through these trees; and given that you did not see the face of this person ... Madam Beatrice, given

246

all these, is it not possible that the person you saw was not Mr. Manu, the defendant, but another person?"

After a few seconds of reflection, Madam Beatrice sighed heavily and answered, "It is possible."

"Thank you, Madam Beatrice, I have nothing further."

Justice Ocloo asked Prosecutor Amoah if he wanted to redirect. Looking quite subdued, Mr. Amoah asked Madam Beatrice if she had ever seen the defendant before the afternoon in question. She answered that she had seen him many times. He often came to visit his second wife, who lived behind the victim's house. Over the course of about a year or so, they had become quite well acquainted: Madam Beatrice; the defendant; the defendant's second wife; and Akwele, the victim.

The prosecutor then asked her, in language the Justice ended up translating, as to whether or not, having become so acquainted with the defendant over the year, she was confident he was the one she saw fleeing the home of the deceased. Madam Beatrice answered that she was confident of that. Justice Ocloo adjourned proceedings for the day.

ॐॐ

2

After my prior investigation, I wanted now to focus on Madam Beatrice. Who was she? My imagination had given me reason to suspect that there was more to her than was revealed in the courtroom. I considered going to ask her for an interview, but given what I'd learned so far, I was somehow doubtful that she would be cooperative. What if for that reason she deliberately stymied my investigation, or led me in the wrong direction? That night, I got my toes tickled to ease the tension and excused myself from home and drove around for a long time, thinking.

I thought of Ama Badu, my ex-wife, now sitting on the jury. What was she thinking? Had she noticed me in the courtroom or no? I remembered how she'd turned cold a few years into our marriage and (with the urge to finish what seemed like unfinished business) I felt I needed to see her again. I hated myself for it, but the truth is that I hadn't lost my feelings for her, even after all these years. Seeing her again in court only sparked those old feelings and I cursed myself twenty times twenty times.

Urged on by my thoughts, I knew I had to see her. I drove to her Ridge bungalow (where I used to live once). It was rather odd to see it again with the old images tormenting me with things past and potential lost. For a long time I couldn't garner the courage to enter it. Then, pushing all inhibitions aside, I drove into her driveway and parked in front of the house. Her car was parked there, but all the lights were out. I looked at my watch and it was only nine o'clock. Could I not disturb her a little even if she was asleep? I asked myself. I knew I was being unreasonable; but hell, sometimes reason unduly stifles necessary action. I parked my VW and went and knocked on her door several times. She didn't respond. Frustrated, I drove away, cursing her twenty times twenty times. But when I saw her sitting in court the next day, my anger fled and my affection started building again.

The next day, I retargeted my focus: Colonel Duah, now MP. I drove to Parliament House, flashed my press pass (restored after much doing). My intention was to bait him through a barrage of questions in the glare of public view. Inside Parliament House, a debate was raging on the Government's push for funds from the international monetary institutions. The opposition leader was berating the Government: "We do not need to turn to the cheap expediency of going to foreign governments and institutions year-in and year-out begging for alms. Why don't we regenerate internal forces, the power of the country, in an effort to crate our own wealth? Why must we keep begging for ..."

Colonel Duah rose from his seat and yelled: "The gentleman is talking nonsense. We need this money. Where else can we go? Will the gentleman finance the Government's projects with his own funds? Such foolish talk gets us nowhere."

The opposition leader shot back, "I'm afraid it's your stupidity that blinds you to the realities we face."

"My friend," said Colonel Duah, "if you want to fight by calling me names, say so. I'm a soldier. I will show you soldier power."

"I'm afraid you still think this is the army. We are not taking brawn here. We are talking brain. You have one. Use it. Or perhaps I'm mistaken?"

Colonel Duah jumped from his seat and charged towards the opposition leader, while the Speaker of Parliament tried to restore order by bringing his gavel down heavily. The scene was close to pandemonium as the Colonel bulldozed his way forward while other MPs tried to restrain him. "Foolish man!" the Colonel yelled. "Let me show him where power lies."

It took at least ten voluminous men to restrain the Colonel. In the meantime, the leader of the opposition had bolted. The Speaker adjourned proceedings. A still fuming Colonel Duah stepped outside. I followed him.

"Colonel Duah," I called and showed him my press card. "May I ask you a few questions?"

"Leave me alone. Can't you see I'm busy?"

"Busy doing what?"

"Enjoying the fresh air."

"Do you know Akwele Oddoi?"

Colonel Duah narrowed his eyes in threat, but he was speechless. I had to press my advantage. "Are you aware of the rumors that you had something to do with Akwele's death, your involvement with her?"

"What are you talking about?" Colonel Duah asked, but he was sinking, with a lack of confidence. I was beginning to believe the young man had told me the truth.

"Colonel, are you denying that you were involved with prostitutes?"

Sweat masking his face, Colonel Duah asked, "Who told you that?"

"It is common knowledge on the streets, Colonel."

A gathering was surrounding us at that time and the Colonel was looking cornered. "Let's be clear about this, you have said things that are completely false. What kind of yellow journalism is this? You are in dangerous territory. You better be careful." And with that he scurried away like a haunted animal. I had not baited the Colonel into a confession as I'd wanted, but he had showed me enough to convince me that he knew more than he was telling. I still had a lot on my mind when I wrote the next report for *The Accra Chronicler*.

WITNESS TESTIFIES MANU THREATENED TO KILL DECEASED

The Koo Manu trial continued today, with the prosecution calling to the witness stand Ms. Anaa Quarshie, a neighbor of the deceased. The prosecutor asked Ms. Quarshie to state her address and she indicated that it was in Dansoman. "And in relational proximity to the deceased's territorial habitation?" Prosecutor Amoah had to repeat the question several times and in the end Justice Ocloo had to interpret its meaning to the witness.

"Oh, it's diagonal to Akwele's house."

"And your acquaintanceship, of what time span?"

"What?"

"He means how long have you known her?" said Justice Ocloo.

"The five years I've been at that residence." Asked how she came to know the deceased, Ms. Quarshie said, "I used to visit her very often and she used to come to my house, you know, just as neighbors come to know each other. Over a period of five years I came to know her very well."

Asked if she knew the defendant, Ms. Quarshie said that she did. "About a year ago, he started visiting the house behind Akwele's. I later learned that he'd bought it for his new wife, Ama Owusu. We could see him and his wife often, sitting outside and eating or chatting."

"Please detail the associational content between the accused and the victim?"

"Huh?" The witness looked confused. Justice Ocloo explained.

"They were very cordial at first. Sometimes, when I was at Akwele's place, we would stand over the wall and chat with Mr. Manu and his wife, Ama Owusu. He would talk freely with us whenever his wife wasn't home. He was more quiet when she was around. But he was there by himself a lot because I understand he had the key to the house and he came and went as he wished. Then one day when he came over and his second wife wasn't there, Mr. Manu stood by the wall and yelled for Akwele. She and I were inside her house at that time. Akwele went outside and asked what he wanted. I don't think he realized I was in Akwele's house when he replied that he was developing a strong liking for her and wondered if they could get together."

"Objection!" the defense lawyer yelled. "Hearsay."

"Overruled," said Justice Ocloo.

"And the victim's oral counter?"

"Objection," Lawyer Ekow interposed. "Same grounds."

"Overruled. The witness may answer the question."

"Akwele said it wasn't wise to do that because Mr. Manu's wife was her neighbor, but he kept insisting that they should get together. He said he would make her rich, that he'd give her anything she wanted. Akwele kept refusing him till he got angry and said he wouldn't leave her alone until she gave in to him."

"And that transpired in what proximate measure to the defendant's *murder* of the victim?"

"Objection, my Lord, this is ridiculous on its face."

"Sustained. Be careful with your words, Mr. Amoah."

The prosecutor rephrased the question: "Ms. Anaa Quarshie, how proximate were that solicitation and confutation prior to the homicide?"

"Huh?"

Justice Ocloo explained, "How long did what you describe happen before the afternoon Akwele died?"

"About three months," Ms. Quarshie replied. The prosecutor then asked her if she had occasion to observe anything else between the defendant and the deceased. She replied, "Yes. At least three times after that Akwele came to my house and on each occasion she was sweating profusely and seemed very afraid. She told me the man had come to her room and insisted that they sleep together. She refused, but he kept insisting. Then as she moved from him he began to pursue her. He grabbed her …"

"Objection, my Lord, we are entering into a world where hearsay is the norm."

"Overruled. I will decide when we have inadmissible hearsay. The witness may continue."

"He grabbed her, but she managed to free herself and ran away. Then a few days later, she came to my house looking terrified and said the same thing had happened again. But the last time she came to my house was the day before she died. She told me that she'd run into the man the previous day and he'd told her his wife would be going to her home town the next Sunday afternoon. He would come over that Sunday so they could be together. She told me she was going to be very firm with him when he came over. She would tell him if he didn't stop pestering her, she would tell his wife. I advised her to do just that, otherwise he'd keep bothering and terrifying her."

The prosecutor had no further questions.

The defense lawyer rose. For a long time he looked at Ms. Quarshie as if he was not sure what to say. Then after a while he began, "Ms. Quarshie, you just told us that you knew the deceased very well. Could you tell us what she did for a living?"

"She was in business."

"What kind of business?"

"Objection, irrelevant."

"Overruled. Please answer the question, Ms. Quarshie."

"She sold food at the Makola Market."

"Is it true that she was often home during the day hours and left home at night?"

"That is true."

"If she were selling food at the Makola Market, wouldn't you expect her to be at home during the nights and do her selling during the day?

"That is correct."

"Then it is not correct to say that she sold food at the Makola Market, is it?"

"I don't know. I think she sold food there. That's all I can say."

Moving closer to the witness, Lawyer Dadzie said, "You claim you knew the deceased very well and you've known her for years. Yet you can't even say with conviction what she did for a living? Are we to believe that in her world alone the market came alive at night when everybody else was asleep, and went to sleep during the day when everybody else was awake?"

"Objection!"

"Sustained. Mr. Dadzie, you will refrain from such inflammatory speeches. If you have questions to ask, then ask them. If not, the witness will be excused." Turning to the jury, Justice Ocloo instructed, "Members of the jury, you will disregard the defense lawyer's last statement."

"Ms. Quarshie, is it not true that the deceased was a prostitute? A prostitute who made men think they could ..."

"Objection!"

"Sustained. Mr. Dadzie, move on."

"My Lord, whether or not the deceased was a prostitute is key to ..."

"Sustained! Now you will move on!"

Judge Ocloo instructed the lawyers to approach the bench. After she had spoken to them in whispers no one else could hear, Lawyer Dadzie returned to his questioning looking a little defeated: "Ms.

Quarshie, yes or no, did you ever see Mr. Manu raise his fists against the deceased?"

"No."

"Were you present in the house of the deceased during the afternoon in question? Yes or no?"

"No."

"So you have no way of knowing who struck the deceased, do you?"

"No."

"In fact, you don't even know if Mr. Manu was in her house that afternoon, do you?"

"No."

"You said when Ms. Oddoi came to you she said the man was after her. Did she say the man's name?"

"No."

"So it could be any man."

"I knew she was referring to Mr. Manu."

"So you are a mind reader?"

"Objection."

"Sustained."

"Ms. Quarshie, in fact, you have made up your entire story, have you not? I suggest to you that you are lying."

"Objection."

"Overruled."

"I am not lying."

"Ms. Quarshie, are you related to Ananias or Sapphira in the Bible?"

"No, I am not related to Ananias or Sapphira in the Bible."

"Then how come you have inherited the genetic traits of Ananias and Sapphira in the Bible?"

"Objection!"

"Sustained."

"Thank you. I have no further questions for this distant relative of lying Biblical characters. I feel obliged to point out the deceptive nature of the witness and draw allusions to universally and historically acknowledged liars."

"Objection!!!"

"Mr. Dadzie, I am warning you!" stormed Justice Ocloo. "The jury will disregard Mr. Dadzie's last statement."

"I am sorry, my Lord," Lawyer Dadzie responded. "I ask the court's forgiveness."

Visibly angry, Justice Ocloo yelled at the defense lawyer: "You better be sorry because one more such sly comment from you and I will hold you in contempt of court!"

Lawyer Dadzie returned to his seat.

బ∽ⅉ

3

Even amid the happenings around and within me, I was still fascinated by the distinguished old man, I observed him even as I tried to follow the proceedings in court. His continued intensity intrigued me a great deal. It appeared the trial held some lofty riddle to him that he had to solve. I felt obliged to find out. But after court, I couldn't muster the strength to follow him.

Instead, I drove back to Dansoman and parked close to where Akwele Oddoi used to live. I sat in my car and watched Madam Beatrice's house, not knowing what would happen next. My heart beat strongly, but I was in too deeply now to retreat. I began my watch around three o'clock. It wasn't until six that Madam Beatrice came out of the house. By then, night had almost fallen in Accra. Madam Beatrice looked around her quickly and walked to her car and drove off. I followed her at a safe distance.

Twenty minutes later, she arrived at her destination, a blue rectangular building of concrete. Madam Beatrice parked her car and walked in. I wondered what kind of place it was. What went on in there? The façade revealed nothing to me and for a few minutes I felt like going in after her to see for myself. But I knew I had to file my report for the day and it was getting late.

I was very curious, but, for the moment, I drove off and went and prepared my report on the Koo Manu trial:

CRITICAL DAY FOR MANU AS POLICEMEN AND FORENSIC EXPERT TESTIFY

On its fourth day, the Manu trial seemed to enter a critical stage as the policemen directly involved in the discovery of the body of the deceased were called by the prosecution. Prosecutor John Amoah first called Police Inspector Boateng to the stand.

Asked where he was on the afternoon of Akwele Oddoi's death, Inspector Boateng answered that he was at the house of Madam Beatrice. Madam Beatrice, an Accra businesswoman, had earlier testified that Ms. Oddoi lived next to her. As to what he was doing at Madam Beatrice's house, Inspector Boateng answered that he often visits her because she and his father were good friends and he took her as a second mother. He also indicated that he was there with another colleague, Corporal Ofori. Mr. Boateng revealed that he had known Madam Beatrice for about fifteen years.

After he understood the prosecutor's questions as to whether he knew the defendant, Koo Manu, Inspector Boateng answered loudly that he did. "Everyone in Accra knows Mr. Manu. He is a rich man with many cars. Yes, I know who he is."

Asked what happened on the afternoon of the murder, Inspector Boateng explained, "Corporal Ofori and I had gone to Madam Beatrice's house. After we ate, we decided to play checkers. We were playing outside when we heard a yell from Akwele's house. We all stood up. Reflex action, I think. Soon after, we saw the defendant run out of Akwele's house. All three of us hurried to the house. When we entered, we saw her lying on the floor in her living room. Lying beside her was a small pestle and next to her head was a small pool of blood."

At that point, the prosecutor went to his desk and uncovered a pestle, which he introduced as evidence for the prosecution. The small pestle, (a wooden instrument used to crush or pound food in a mortar) was about four feet in length with a diameter of about five inches.

Inspector Boateng went on to explain that he notified forensics immediately after they discovered Akwele. Madam Beatrice went and got a couple of neighbors to help carry Akwele into Madam Beatrice's car. Corporal Ofori went in pursuit of the defendant. They drove with Akwele to the Korle Bu Hospital.

Lawyer Ekow Dadzie began his cross-examination of Inspector Boateng by asking, "Mr. Boateng, do you personally know the defendant?"

"I know who he is. He is a very visible man in the city."

"Did you see him enter the house of the deceased on the day in question?"

"No. But we were in the …"

"Yes or no?"

"No."

"No, you did not see him enter her house. Inspector Boateng, you have just testified that you did not see the defendant enter the deceased's house and that you saw the defendant ran from her house. Did you in fact see the face of the person who fled from the deceased's house?"

"No, but …"

"You didn't see his face. You only saw his back, correct?"

"Yes."

"And you saw his back through a bunch of trees?"

"Yes."

"Inspector Boateng, do you drink on duty?"

Inspector Boateng looked puzzled and the prosecutor objected to the question.

"You may answer the question, Inspector Boateng," opined Justice Ocloo.

Inspector Boateng replied, "Everybody knows that a policeman can't drink on duty."

"Why is it that you are not allowed to drink on duty?"

"Objection! Irrelevant."

"Overruled."

"I don't know," Inspector Boateng replied.

Lawyer Dadzie asked, "Could it be that it's because drinking could impair your judgment, your perception, your ability to execute your duties as a policeman efficiently?"

"Yes, but I was off-duty that afternoon."

"Yes, I understand that. I am not blaming you for drinking. We all take a little, every now and then. But when you have drunk liquor and you have to perceive things and respond to them, no one wants your perception and judgment impaired by alcohol. Inspector, is it fair to say that perhaps the person you saw was not Mr. Manu? Is it not fair to say that, especially given your own admission that you don't know Mr. Manu personally and that you only saw the back of the fleeing person on that afternoon?"

"I am sure it was ..."

"Mr. Boateng, please answer my question. Yes or no, given that you had been drinking ..."

"I had been drinking but I wasn't drunk.'

"I didn't say you were drunk. Let me remind you of what you've agreed to. You can't drink while on duty because it might impair your judgment. You were off-duty, so you were drinking. No one faults you for that. After all, you can drink like a horse when you are off-duty, which is exactly what you did that afternoon."

"Objection!" yelled Prosecutor Amoah.

"Sustained. Mr. Dadzie, you will refrain from such incendiary statements."

"I'm sorry, my Lord, withdrawn. Mr. Boateng, I ask you again and please answer with a yes or no. Is it possible ... with the drinking that afternoon, the wall separating the two homes, the trees, the partial sighting of the back and not the face of the person fleeing from the house ... Is it possible that the person you saw leave the deceased's home was another person, and not the defendant? Another person, perhaps, who fits the description of the defendant but who is actually not the defendant? Yes or no?"

"Yes."

"Yes, it is possible?"

"Yes, it is possible."

"Thank you, Inspector Boateng."

The jurors had listened intently, but it was difficult to judge where their sympathies lay. As Inspector Boateng left the witness box another police officer who had been present that afternoon took his place. Testifying for the prosecution, Corporal Ofori corroborated the testimony of Madam Beatrice and Inspector Boateng. Corporal Ofori indicated that they decided upon discovering the deceased's body, that one officer should accompany the body to the hospital while another went in search of the fleeing defendant. They decided against calling an ambulance because they were afraid the ambulance would take too long, since from their experience they knew that the ambulance service had seriously deteriorated.

While the rest went to the hospital, Corporal Ofori ran to the street where his motorbike was parked. He started the bike and drove after the defendant. When he arrived at the defendant's home, he saw his Mercedes parked in his empty yard in front of the house. He immediately went to the car and checked the engine. It was hot. Besides, the car's key was still in the ignition of the defendant's Mercedes. Then he ran to the front of the defendant's house and knocked. He had to knock several times without any response. He was about to search for other means of entering the house when the defendant opened the door. Corporal Ofori identified himself and asked the defendant where he had been. The defendant seemed to take umbrage at the question and angrily asked Inspector Ofori to leave the house and not disturb his afternoon sleep.

Asked if he had seen anyone else in the house, the police corporal said that he had not. He further testified that the defendant was wearing shorts and a tee shirt, as if he had quickly put them on, especially because his fly was unzipped. Mr. Ofori said that the defendant looked very confused. Finally, against the objection of the defense lawyer, Corporal Ofori told the court that he had no doubt that the defendant had just been driving his Mercedes on the afternoon in question.

Amid dead silence in the courtroom, the defense lawyer began his cross-examination: "Mr. Ofori, on the afternoon in question, did you notice anyone enter the house of the deceased?"

"No."

"Did you see the face of the person who ran out of her house?"

"No."

The defense lawyer asked what seemed to be his favorite question: whether it was possible that, in light of all the circumstances, the person observed leaving the deceased's home was not the defendant. Corporal Ofori answered that it was possible, but he added quickly that it wasn't likely.

Defense Lawyer Dadzie then asked, "Did you see the defendant enter his car and drive off?"

"No."

"Did you see him on the street as you made for his home?"

"No."

"So, based on a vague suspicion, you drove straight for the home of the defendant. Is it standard police practice to go chasing into the homes of citizens, based on such unreasonable suspicions?"

"Objection!"

"Sustained. The witness will not answer that question."

"In fact, you had decided between you, Madam Beatrice and Inspector Boateng that Mr. Manu was the culprit and, therefore, without seeing his face, without any proof, you prejudicially barged into his house in violation of all standard police procedures and all basic rights and expectations of privacy and so rudely ..."

"Objection!"

"Sustained!" Justice Ocloo sounded angry as she said, "Mr. Dadzie, if you have no questions left, the witness will be excused. The jury will disregard Mr. Dadzie's last outburst."

Lawyer Dadzie asked, "Mr. Ofori, was it very sunny on the day in question?"

"Yes."

"A hot day that could make any engine feel hot." Before the policeman could say anything, Mr. Dadzie went on, "Now, Mr. Ofori, you have testified that Mr. Manu was wearing shorts and a tee shirt and looking confused. Now, isn't that description consistent with someone who has just woken up from sleep?"

"No, I don't think so."

"But is it possible that someone might draw a different conclusion? Someone who had no prejudgment whatsoever, who just happened to walk into the scene. Might that someone not conclude that Mr. Manu had just woken up from sleep?"

"I don't think so."

"Mr. Ofori, I am not asking what you think, I am asking you what someone else might conclude ..."

The prosecutor objected on the grounds that the witness could only speak for himself and not others. The objection was sustained.

Perhaps in the most damaging testimony of the day against the defense, the forensics expert, Alia Hassan testified that she had examined the pestle marked as an exhibit for the prosecution. She testified that the pestle had the fingerprints of the defendant on it. On cross-examination, however, Ms. Hassan agreed that the prints were found at the middle part of the pestle. However, other unidentified prints were found at the top part of the pestle. It is not clear what the defense lawyer, Ekow Dadzie intends to achieve by his line of questioning. Most legal experts believe, however, that he may be laying the groundwork for future testimony. Proceedings were adjourned for the day.

After I filed my report, my thoughts returned to Colonel Duah. I saw an opportunity. Perhaps there was enough to interest Ekow Dadzie in the Colonel. I drove to the lawyer's office the next day and told him what I knew. He had a pile of newspapers on his desk. (I had not yet read the morning's papers). Ekow Dadzie threw a few newspapers in my direction. I read the headlines:

MP ACCUSED OF MURDER

JOURNALIST POINTS FINGER AT PARLIAMENTARIAN

IS COLONEL DUAH A MURDERER?

"You have done a very reckless thing," Lawyer Dadzie said. "Don't you know who you're playing with? If you have any evidence at all, you should've gone to the police. Now that you've accused him in public, he will do two things: the first is to get rid of any evidence that might implicate him."

"You give him more intelligence than he deserves."

"Be careful."

"What are you going to do?"

"There's not a lot I can do now. I can't work on rumors. I need hard evidence."

❧

4

I hurried to the office after court the next day to prepare my report. But as I sat down to write, I found myself simply reminiscing and thinking about Ama Badu, the juror, my ex-wife, my longing for her rising like wave heaped upon tempestuous wave. I couldn't concentrate. It took me a long time to finish my report. It was late when I finished, and I was exhausted. I looked over at the report one last time, and sighing, handed it in:

DAMAGING TESTIMONY IN MANU TRIAL

The prosecution in the Manu trial rested its case after searing testimony from the pathologist who examined the body of the deceased, Akwele Oddoi. After the prosecution entered the report into evidence, Dr. Joseph Andane was asked to describe the results of his examination.

Dr. Andane explained that he found multiple fractures on the skull of the victim and a deep impression in the back of her skull. In his professional judgment, the pathologist said that a hard object caused the deep impression. A small pestle, for example, if struck hard against the skull could cause that impression. Asked what in his professional judgment was the cause of death, Dr. Andane said he concluded that the victim died from being struck repeatedly on the head, causing severe traumatic injuries to the skull. The resulting injuries to the brain caused swelling and fluid to accumulate in the brain tissue or what is technically referred to as the cerebral edema. The victim suffered a severe form of such edema and this led to increased pressure resulting in a total loss of blood flow to the upper and lower parts of the brain.

This disruption in the blood flow caused a complete stoppage of brain functioning: respiration, Dr. Andane explained, is controlled by the brainstem, which stimulates the diaphragm and intercostal muscles and make the lung fill with air. In addition, the heart is deprived of oxygen and it too stops working. The disruption in respiration and the beating of the heart results in death.

In summation, Dr. Andane explained that, based on his examination, the victim died as a result of the traumatic injuries to her head, which damaged her brain and, therefore, her ability to breathe and the capability of her heart to pump blood. He believed that she suffered these injuries because of being struck repeatedly by a hard object such as a pestle. He said that the damage to her head was so severe, he did not believe it was reversible. "Given the nature of her injuries, she died about thirty to forty-five minutes after they were inflicted. She was dead by the time she was brought to the hospital."

The defense lawyer, Ekow Dadzie, began his cross-examination: "Even if what you are saying is true, Dr. Andane, you were not present when any of the striking to the skull occurred, were you?"

"No."

"So your report is based on your examination of the deceased after the fact, is it not?'

"Yes."

"So you cannot say who killed the deceased, can you?"

"No, but that is not my duty."

"Doctor, in your report, you do not state that the victim was struck by a pestle, do you?"

"I do ..."

"Doctor, do you not state that the striking was by a hard thin and blunt object?"

"That is what I said. I did not mention a pestle specifically."

"So, in fact, that object could have been any hard, thin and blunt object, say a metallic pole, for example, could it not?"

"Yes."

"So, doctor, we don't even know for sure that it was the pestle, do we?"

"It was in all likelihood, a pestle."

"But it could have been something else?"

"Could have. Yes."

"Okay. It could have been something else. Now, Doctor, if the deceased could have been struck by another object, not the pestle placed into evidence by the prosecution, would someone not be able to hide the actual object used to kill the deceased, and instead make everyone else believe that the pestle was the instrument of harm?"

Prosecutor Amoah raised an objection that the question called for speculation outside Dr. Andane's testimony or expertise. The objection was sustained. The defense lawyer moved on: "Dr. Andane, based on your report, would you say that the injuries to the deceased could have been inflicted by a man of such moderate strength as the defendant?"

"Yes, if he struck hard enough."

"Are you sure?"

"Very sure."

"Dr. Andane, the defendant, as you observe him sitting in the court room today, is clearly of moderate build, wouldn't you agree?"

"I agree."

"Very well. So are you, and so am I and so are many members of the jury. So could a man of your build have inflicted the injuries?"

"Objection!!!"

"Overruled. Doctor, please answer the question."

"Yes," said Dr. Andane. "A man of my build could have inflicted the damage."

"In fact a man of the prosecutor's build could have inflicted the damage."

"Objection!!!"

"Sustained. Mr. Dadzie, you've made your point, now move on."

"I am done, my Lord." The prosecutor kept Dr. Andane on the witness stand for one more question which translated into whether the pathologist had any doubt in his mind that the pestle caused the injuries.

"I have no doubt," the pathologist replied. The prosecution rested.

In a dramatic turn, Mr. Dadzie declared, "My Lord, I wish to call as my first witness the Prosecutor, Mr. John Amoah."

The prosecution objected immediately. Justice Ocloo asked, "On what grounds?"

"My Lord, we have reason to believe that the prosecution is acting in cohorts with the police to withhold exculpatory evidence from the defense."

"And you choose this venue to make this request?" asked Justice Ocloo.

"My Lord, this information just came to my attention."

"I will hear your motion in chambers ..."

"My Lord, you need to grant me this request. We have reason to believe that Colonel Duah is responsible for the death of Akwele Oddoi and we have reason to believe the prosecution has not shared this with us."

An uproar of voices erupted in the courtroom.

"Objection!" yelled Mr. Amoah above the cacophony. "This is outrageous!"

"Counselor," said Justice Ocloo as she brought her gavel down. "You are in contempt of court!"

"For speaking the truth?" asked Ekow Dadzie.

"Bailiffs, remove the defense counsel from the courtroom. Mr. Dadzie, I will give you a night in jail to rethink your shameless shenanigans in the courtroom."

"My Lord," protested Mr. Dadzie, as the bailiffs seized him. "I only wish to bring to light Colonel Duah's involvement in the death of Akwele Oddoi."

"You are close to the brink!" yelled Justice Ocloo as she rose from her seat and pointed her gavel at the defense lawyer. "One more word and you will be sorely sorry."

Mr. Dadzie did not tempt the Justice any further as he was led from the courtroom to spend a night in jail.

I reckoned Ekow Dadzie had taken a calculated risk. He had put himself in jeopardy with the hope of igniting the Fourth Estate. After my accusations in front of Parliament House and his declarations in court, an avalanche of calls for an investigation into the Colonel's involvement, if any, into the death of Akwele Oddoi was unleashed by a body politic only now recovering from the brutalities of the just-ended regime. Colonel Duah had played such a role in the Government that he seemed to have become a scapegoat. The Ghana Bar Association held a press conference and called on the Inspector General of Police to investigate the matter. I suspected Lawyer Dadzie was somehow behind that call. He'd stepped down as its president, but he must have held great sway over the GBA still. The Chamber of Commerce issued a communiqué saying: "The fate of a great business leader is at stake. No stone must be left unturned. These allegations against Colonel Duah must be taken seriously. An investigation is warranted."

The allegations became the talk of the town. National talk shows and commentators questioned whether the police had done their job. One political commentator proclaimed: "Silence is golden, but the silence of the police over the matter is so deep it glitters too brightly, and we must look away or develop the blindness that has afflicted the police." In buses, bars and on the radio, the issue was raised again and again. Some members of the Citizens United to Save Bottom Power held a demonstration calling for justice. I wasn't sure how much of this was spontaneous. A few days later, however, the Commissioner of Police in charge of its Criminal Investigation Department announced that fresh investigations had been opened into the death of Akwele Oddoi.

ঔৡঌ

5

I found the courage to enter the blue building. And right away I knew it was a mistake. I wrestled with what I said and saw, and I felt like a complete failure. It was as if someone had taken a giant drainer and sucked out all my body's contents except sweat. Instead of discovering a story I could use to add spice to my reports on the Manu trial, I had uncovered a truth I wish I'd never known.

The circle was clear: Madam Beatrice, the matron; Akwele Oddoi, the victim, working for her; and my ex-wife, Ama Badu, the juror and also a ... hell, let me say it. A prostitute. But how? I couldn't believe it. How could it have come to this? Had I failed her as husband somehow and so badly that she felt she had to turn to this?

I felt tears coming as I drove home and replayed our conversation in my mind. I was very angry with myself for having pushed time to unfold its stories so prematurely. I tried my best to put away the discoveries of the night. I couldn't relive them without feeling deep pain. Perhaps some other day I would tell the full story.

I knew I had the power to cause a great deal of pain. In different circumstances, I would have jumped at the opportunity to reveal the secrets and sell more newspapers; dig deeper to find all the unconnected dots arrayed in my mind. But not now. I felt I'd dug deeper than I should have; that if I went farther, I'd regret it. I concentrated as best as I could as I sat down to prepare my report:

THE ACCRA CHRONICLER

MANU TRIAL CONTINUES AS DEFENSE OPENS ITS CASE

The defense in the Manu trial got the opportunity today to put its case before the jury. Defense lawyer, Ekow Dadzie, entered court looking very ebullient, in sharp contrast to his demeanor on the first day of trial. He refused to answer questions about his day in jail for contempt of court. Asked by reporters what strategy he intended to pursue, the lawyer smiled and said confidently, "The case begins today."

In court, however, Mr. Dadzie seemed more subdued when he began the direct examination of the defendant. Looking weary and beaten, the defendant, Koo Manu, sat in the witness box as his lawyer began, "Mr. Manu, did you know the deceased, Akwele Oddoi?"

"Yes," Mr. Manu said in a rather mellow voice.

"In what capacity did you know her?"

"She lived next-door to my wife, Ama Owusu."

"And did you ever talk to her?"

"Yes," Mr. Manu answered. "Sometimes when I went to visit my wife, I would start a conversation with her."

"And what was the nature of your conversations?"

"They were friendly discussions. I would ask her about her health and she would do the same."

"Mr. Manu, did you ever visit the deceased in her home?"

The defendant paused for a long time before replying, "Yes, I did." The courtroom audience murmured noisily and Justice Ocloo had to bring down her gavel and ask for silence before order was restored.

"And why did you visit her?" Lawyer Dadzie asked his client.

"She invited me over. Only twice. The first time was about six weeks before she died. The second time was the day she died." Another murmur broke in the courtroom and Justice Ocloo had to issue a warning that she would throw out the audience unless order was restored. When she had restored silence, Justice Ocloo asked Mr. Manu to continue. "I had spent the night with my wife, Ama. She left that morning to go to the market. So I was alone. I got up from bed and went outside. I was standing there when I saw Akwele. She came out of her building. I greeted her. She told me I didn't visit her enough. Then she asked me where Ama was. I told Akwele that my wife, Ama Owusu, was at the market. Akwele invited me over for breakfast. I was hungry, so I went over."

The defendant paused. "What happened after you went over?" his lawyer asked.

Clearing his throat, the defendant continued, "Akwele led me to the kitchen. She was making porridge. We ate when it was ready."

"And where did you eat?"

"We ate in the kitchen. She had some stools and a small table. That's where we ate."

"And after the meal?"

"We spoke for about five minutes. Then I left."

"While you were there, did you touch anything?"

"Objection," said the prosecutor. "Leading."

"Overruled."

The defendant continued, "I touched a lot of things. Before the meal was ready. And after we'd eaten. I kept touching things. And looking at them. Especially in the kitchen."

"Anything in particular that you recall?"

"Yes. There was a pestle. It was lying in the kitchen. I picked it up. Then I put it back on the floor."

"Did you do anything with it?"

"No. I just asked her what she was doing with it. She said she was going to pound some fish later on."

"In all, how long were you at her house?"

"About one hour."

"And what time was it when you left her house?

"It was about eleven in the morning."

"While you were at her home, did you quarrel with her?"

"No."

"Did you fight with her?"

"No."

"Have you ever quarreled with her?"

"No."

"Have you ever had any dispute with her?"

"No."

"Have you ever propositioned her for sex?"

"No."

The defense lawyer paced for a few seconds, looking as if he was contemplating his next question. Then he asked, "Mr. Manu, where did you go after you left Akwele's home?"

"I went back to my wife Ama Owusu's home for a while. Then, after about ten minutes, I left and went home."

"Was anybody at home when you got there?"

"No, my wife, my nephews, nieces, maid and three of our children were away. My eldest son wasn't home either."

"What did you do then?"

"I had been awake almost all night. I was very tired. So I took the papers and went to the bedroom. There, I read a little. Then I fell asleep."

"And at what time would you say you fell asleep?"

"It was about half past noon."

"And you woke up. Why?"

The audience laughed as the defendant answered, "Yes, I woke up. But that was because I heard knocking. At first it sounded faint. Then I became fully awake. And I could hear it was very loud. I got up and rushed to the door."

"Mr. Manu, did you kill Akwele Oddoi?"

"No, I did not. I would never ever do such a thing."

"Thank you very much, Mr. Manu."

The prosecutor rose from his chair and immediately started his cross-examination. Justice Ocloo asked the prosecutor on several occasions to rephrase his questions because the defendant seemed to be having a difficult time understanding them. Sometimes the judge, as she had done with other witnesses, had to rephrase the prosecutor's questions so that the witness could answer.

Prosecutor Amoah asked the defendant why he would break the oath he had made to his first wife and marry a second woman. Defense lawyer Dadzie objected immediately on the grounds that the question was irrelevant. He was overruled.

"I love Ama Owusu." Did he love his first wife, the prosecutor asked? "Yes," answered the defendant.

Then the prosecutor asked why the defendant would break the vows to his first wife that he had made in church.

"I didn't make any vows in church," said the defendant.

"No?"

"No. I performed the customary rites, and that is all. We had no vows in church."

Was it not expected, however, that he would remain faithful to his first wife?

The defense lawyer's objection was overruled.

"I am faithful to her. I only took a second wife."

The prosecutor reasoned that Mr. Manu had broken a sacred vow, whether expressed or implicit, to his first wife. If he could betray his wife in the face of God and man, then what couldn't he do? This question drew a very vehement objection from the defense lawyer, who was immediately overruled.

Sweating profusely, the defendant explained, "I have not betrayed her."

Why, the prosecution continued, would the defendant be so base as to marry a second wife? Wasn't there a tragic flaw in the character of a polygamist, a sinful nature? The defense lawyer objected, his fist chopping the air, as he said, "My Lord, my client is not on trial for marrying a second wife."

Justice Ocloo sustained the objection this time. Looking a little disarmed by the judge's decision, the prosecutor stared into space for a few seconds before beginning a long question. He suggested to the defendant that he had solicited Akwele, the victim, for sex. She had turned him down repeatedly. He kept pestering her. She complained to friends. On the afternoon in question, he had gone to her home seeking sexual favors. She turned him down. Then she threatened to tell his wife. That was the last straw. He was infuriated because she refused him; he was afraid Akwele would tell his wife. He had picked up the pestle and hit her repeatedly on the head.

"It isn't true. It didn't happen that way."

Seizing on that, the prosecutor repeated, "It didn't happen that way", and then asked that if it didn't happen that way, then how did it happen?

"I mean it didn't happen."

How would the defendant explain the policeman's testimony that he had seen his Mercedes parked in the defendant's yard, with the engine hot and the key still in the ignition?

"I don't know. I hadn't driven the car since that morning."

"Is your vehicle manufactured in Mars?"

"Objection!"

"Sustained."

"Withdrawn."

The defense is expected to rest its case soon.

ॐ∽

6

Ekow Dadzie came to see me, his lawyer's confidence apparently slipping. The police had started a lackadaisical investigation into the death of Akwele Oddoi. But Justice Ocloo refused to suspend the trial, claiming that as far as she was concerned, no formal investigation had been launched. "Tell me, honestly and frankly how you got wind of Colonel Duah's involvement in Akwele's death."

"I can't reveal my sources."

"Nii, this is a matter of life and death, a matter of humanity and justice. An innocent man could be sentenced to death. Think about it. Now's not the time for any high principle except justice."

"If it were just me, there'd be no problem. I promised my source I'd keep his identity confidential."

"Try and convince him otherwise."

"I'll see what I can do."

I found the man that night, and with the bait of money got him to agree to see Ekow Dadzie. Dadzie came to my house, and together we met the man at a prearranged rendezvous and then drove to a secluded part of town. In my VW, the three of us talked. Lawyer Dadzie probed the man, his story, what he'd seen, his memory, searching for contradictions. "I find your story credible. I need to have you testify in court."

"No!" the young man cried like he was wounded. "I can't put myself in trouble. What kind of palaver do you want to make for me?"

"Young man," Ekow Dadzie said. "A man might be killed for another man's misdeed. Don't you see the need to do whatever you can to help justice?"

"If I testify, I could die myself. Don't you see that?"

"I will protect you."

"How? You are not in power. Colonel Duah is."

They went on for half an hour. Finally, Ekow Dadzie named a price for the young man's testimony. They bargained over the price a while. After the young man agreed to testify, Lawyer Dadzie said, "If anyone asks you in court, I haven't paid you anything for your testimony."

I gasped. "You are asking him to lie?"

This is justified. And technically, he's not going to lie. This is how we'll work it out. I'll give you money. But that is for what you've told me so far, not for what you will say in court."

"What's the difference?" I asked.

"You ask too many questions," he said.

The next day, Ekow Dadzie came to see me, completely crestfallen. "Justice Ocloo turned down my request to call the new witness."

"Her reason?"

"That it will be unduly prejudicial."

"Can she do that?"

"It's her court. What happens on appeal is a different matter."

For several days I had gone to court to report on the trial of a man who had everything, but who seemed to have sacrificed it all for a prostitute. The strange revelations of people's hidden lives numbed me.

Even the dignified old man baffled me and I was annoyed with myself that I still hadn't been able to talk with him. Like seeing a great task for which the first step seems so hard to take. As for the defendant, I wasn't sure if he did it or not, but, in my opinion, the evidence against him was quite strong. I thought over that until I had a headache. I simply would have to wait for the jury's decision.

And thinking of the jury, I thought of the juror who masquerades with a public persona that masks another private life. I sat through court, observing and listening, this time with my eyes opened wider, my ears listening more closely, my mind working sharper. With as much calm as I could muster, I sat down and summarized the events of the last day of the Manu trial:

DEFENSE RESTS CASE IN MANU TRIAL

The Manu defense concluded its case today by calling the wives of the defendant and a pantheon of witnesses to testify to the defendant's good character. The defendant's first wife spent a relatively short time testifying. Mainly, she told the court that she had been married to the defendant for a little over twenty-five years. They had four children. The defendant, his first wife said, was a very loving man who cared for their children. Together, they had raised very good children and she had no cause to complain. "Has your husband ever been unfaithful to you?"

The answer was a big "No! Never!"

"Do you think he is capable of committing the crime he's been accused of?"

"No. Absolutely not!"

Upon cross-examination, however, Mrs. Manu did indicate that she was a little upset at first when her husband told her he wanted to take a second wife. But she had gotten over that quickly. She was adamant in response to the prosecutor's suggestion that she was still gravely upset. Why didn't the second wife live with the rest of the family, the prosecutor asked?

Mrs. Manu turned to the defense lawyer as if looking for help. The prosecutor asked the question again. Then Mrs. Manu burst out with this question: "Pastor-Lawyer Amoah? Why are you doing this to us? Have we not been good? Have we not come to your church all these years? Why do you stand there now and do this to us?"

The prosecutor answered that they were not in church and in a courtroom she had to answer his questions. Then the prosecutor turned to the judge, asking that she instruct Mrs. Manu to answer the question. Ordered by the court to answer, she said, "We didn't have her come live with us because I did not want her to live with us."

As Mrs. Manu looked down, the prosecutor asked rhetorically why a woman who was not eternally opposed to her husband's marriage to a second wife would oppose living with her. The prosecutor asked no more questions of Mrs. Akua Nsiah Manu.

The defense called Mrs. Ama Owusu Manu, the defendant's second wife. She also testified that the defendant had been good to her. She knew of no quarrel between her husband and the deceased, nor did she believe that her husband had asked for sex from the deceased. The prosecutor asked why she would live in such sin. What sin? "Polygamy?" It isn't a sin, she said. Changing course, he asked her if she loved her husband. She said yes. Did she rely on him for financial support? Yes. Would she do anything to protect him? Yes. Including lying to save him? No? You expect us to believe that? The objection was sustained.

The rest of the defense's case was spent calling character witnesses for the defendant. Among them was his old-time friend, Kwamena, who testified that the defendant was a loyal friend, through poverty and in wealth. Although he'd become wealthy, the defendant never turned his back on Kwamena, who remained poor. They were still as close as when they were both poor. In fact, said Kwamena, the defendant was always helping him, trying to get him well settled financially. He did not believe the defendant was capable of murder.

There was some drama in the court when the witness, Kwamena, got a little agitated and called the prosecutor a hypocrite. Rising from his seat, the witness exclaimed: "This case is over. I declare it over. *You* have no case. *I* rest my case." Justice Ocloo had to threaten the witness into silence.

Three more witnesses testified for the defendant. One of them was a business competitor who said that the defendant was a fair man. He couldn't have committed murder. The prosecutor, looking confident, didn't cross-examine those witnesses in any significant manner. The defense rested. The prosecution, perhaps signaling its confidence, declined to make any rebuttal, resting on its case-in-chief.

The case, it is now believed, will go to the jury tomorrow after the prosecutor and the defense counsel make their closing remarks. Some analysts believe that the case against the defendant, although mostly circumstantial, may be sufficient for a guilty verdict. "There are too many factors pointing to his culpability," said Kofi Minta, a famed defense lawyer. "I have seen convictions on less convincing evidence."

However, some commentators point out that all that is needed for acquittal is reasonable doubt. In this case, they say, the defense lawyer has done a good job of creating such doubt. "If I were on the jury, I would probably have some serious doubts about the defendant's guilt," said Adjoa Appiah, another famous lawyer. "The case is quite circumstantial."

So, will Koo Manu spend the rest of his days behind bars? Or will he walk out a free man? *The Accra Chronicler* will bring you the latest developments.

ॐॐ

7

Finally, I was bringing closure to this episode in my life that had taught me many things. I was ready to move on. In a way, though, I would always be caught in the events because of Ama Badu, the juror. It was as if discovering her secret drew me closer to her in a weird way. But I ramble …

After the lawyers gave their closing statements, I followed the distinguished old man again, this time knowing that I might never see him again. Because of that fear, I was determined to talk to him. I couldn't explain his power, why I had so much reverence for him. I felt a little weak as I caught up with him. He was dressed in a sharp suit made from a *kente* cloth. Willing away my uneasiness as much as I could, I asked in a shaky voice, "Sir, are you a relative of the victim?"

He shook his head no.

"Of the defendant?"

Again, the same gesture.

"Just an observer?"

He looked at me, blinked and began to speak in a voice so assuredly purposeful, it was as if he was speaking from a different world, into which he transported me:

Somewhere within history's womb a mother gave birth to her children Wrapped them in Ebony bands And saw that all was well But they met with a Virgin from afar And she set their sun steps forward And she set their sun steps backward.

Listen to the drums of yesterday Beating the history of its Eclipse

They came from east They came from west They came from north They came from south:

A virgin in her sparkling beauty Her eyes were emeralds Her nails, rare gems Her teeth were golden marbles Her landscape, mind-racking Her perfumes unsurpassed Not even by Arabia's best. She offered us her water And we drank with sweetness But tasted the bitter bile. She presented her delicacies And we ate with relish But soon tasted the feces within. Her handshake was a trip to heaven But also a cartel of thorns Her stare twinkled as stars But pierced like poisonous arrows And her beauty rippled our veins But in her embrace we struck stone Crushed within the paradox of the Virgin.

She carried her self-made thunder Her self-made lightening When her lightening flashed we shuddered When her thunder struck We fell down and died The land was lost as in a whirlwind A whirlwind of confusion Papa's abode lost its fusion Mama's home lost its dignity And the strength of Mother's gods Sapped by the avarice of her offspring And the stage was set For The Eclipse of Mother.

Now it rains snow

In the land of the sun.

But pray, my child, pray As an eclipse is transient So it begins to rain rain again So the sun smiles on Mother again So the sun smiles on her progeny again Like it never has in her past Her punctuated past....

The old man paused a little. Then he continued.

Her faults bemoaned I too will weep.

But today let me recite sweet verses like shining stars in bleak nights of despair Even if it belies her crimson sweat. In her, I see a belly laden with wealth A Road of Hope I will not let strained motions becloud a mammoth potential I want the rhapsody of the monsoon winds to trumpet sweet dreams To foretell progress Yes, I will write verses to her in hands of gold Even if her path becomes a medley of thorns I will see the silhouette of hope in it.

So let me go on then and sing songs in voices of gold

I will gather wise elders and let their gray hairs tell the tribute to their wisdom

I will gather the children too and let their forefathers begin to tell stories of old interspersed with proverbs Proverbs that mesh with the intellectual spice of sagacious words.

I will listen as they tell of her unwritten wealth of the ages pouring like a storm's rain I will watch the sojourner crouch in awe under the bellowing trees Yes, I will hear the songs of the ancestors and their beckoning progeny resonate in her face Urging her to sing songs Chant sweet verses.

And still write her verses in hands of gold.

I will let her limbs swoon me Stand proud like Kilimanjaro singing with the Kalahari across the Sahara Draining me and yet offering eternal oases.

I hear in her whispers of the azure Atlantic with its sweet sensuous simoons.

Yes, I will write these in hands of gold.

Her faults bemoaned I too will weep

But today let me recite sweet verses even if they belie her crimson sweat

The bloody petals that are her pain.

As I pondered the old man's enigmatic words, he walked away into the distant dusk. I went to my office a little annoyed that I hadn't extracted more from him. And I hoped so much to be able to meet him again.

I sat down and prepared what I hoped would be my final report on the Koo Manu trial:

CLOSING STATEMENTS IN MANU TRIAL

In a tense courtroom atmosphere, the heat rising to fever pitch as the general audience and the jurors seemed to hold their breaths, the prosecutor and defense counsel delivered their closing statements. The tension was unbearable. After several days of testimony, direct- and cross-examinations, objections, drama and eloquence, or the lack thereof, this was the day for the lawyers and the lawyers alone. Justice Ocloo called the court to order as both lawyers seemed determined in their dark gowns, but looking a little out of place in their wigs amid the heat.

The prosecutor spoke first. He rose slowly, radiating the full force of the state in his deliberate gingerly gait. *The Accra Chronicler* has reprinted portions of the closing statement:

Ladies and Gentlemen, arbiters of facts. We have hitherto been witnesses to proceedings bearing patent witness that on the afternoon in question, the happenings of which have been amply deliberated, the defendant, with the requisite malice aforethought caused to expire the hapless victim, Akwele Oddoi.

The defendant's proclivity for women, demonstrated by an impudent disregard for his first marital companion in a second marital union, undermines faith and confidence in hallowed matrimonial institutions. We see actions that are the functional equivalent of criminal conversation. What is to avert the extension of his sexual predatory tentacles to another powerless woman, especially witnessing his patent perception of the female species as procurable commodities? That he scorns the gripes of his wife and marries another underscores such nefarious tendencies.

With a penchant for soliciting women other than those to whom he is in marital union, it eventuates that he would want to acquire carnal knowledge of the victim. That women are feeling beings and not chattels, he completely scorned, reducing them in the despicable polygamous arrangement here demonstrated. You have been privy to testimony that the defendant completely ignored the protestations of the victim.

Recall the repeated failures of the defendant to seduce the victim, failure propelling him to anger. His anger aroused, the defendant, possessive of the requisite *mens rea*, extinguished the victim's life by striking her with a pestle held in his fore member. Let not the trickery of the defense that anybody else could have committed the crime mislead you.

Recall now the testament of sophisticated police officers and Madam Beatrice, which cannot be assailed by flimsy attempts to throw dust into your eyes. Remember now the confused appearance of the defendant, when accosted by a police officer, as completely consistent with a guilty deed. The heat of the engine, the key in the ignition. How explicated by the defense? None. Moreover, contemplate the instrument used to bludgeon the victim repeatedly to her demise: the pestle and the fingerprints of the defendant.

Ladies and gentlemen, in summary, the gravamen of the case is proved thus: a man whose carnal inclinations and whose consequent overtures to the victim are rebuffed and who in wrath slays her. And a man without an alibi except his sleep. In the face of such evidence, ladies and gentlemen, *me judice* and yours, there ought not be any other determination than guilty. The Government's burden is satisfied and the perpetrator must be severely penalized for his *mala in se*.

The courtroom was silent as the prosecutor returned to his seat. And then the defense lawyer stood up and started his closing statement, parts of which follow:

Dear jurors, there is only one verdict you can return. And that verdict is, not guilty. My Lord, fellow jurors, the prosecution's case reeks of misjudgments and misperceptions, factual tricks, legal fiction, verbal gymnastics, rash judgments and a disregard for simple rights. It flies in the face of common sense. It baffles the mind why the people's resources would be spent in persecution of an innocent man whose only crime, according to the prosecutor, is that he married a second wife.

I said at the beginning of the trial that we had to ask the question whether we had any reasonable doubt of Mr. Manu's guilt. We have now heard the prosecution's case and seen his evidence; and now we must ask ourselves whether we feel comfortable that the murder of Akwele was at the hands of this gentle and generous man who has been wrongly targeted by the police? This man, whose great contributions to society are unquestionable, who is kind to his friends, whose entrepreneurial spirit we all must applaud.

First, did Mr. Manu have any intent to kill the deceased? And second: did he have the opportunity to do so? The answer to both questions is clearly no.

Let's start with what the police officers said. What they saw, as they admitted before us, was the back of a man they thought might look like the defendant. But let's keep in mind that they had been drinking. Now, we all know what liquor can do to the ability to perceive things accurately. Additionally, all they saw, through trees, was the back of the fleeing person over a wall about five feet tall. In that situation, how can we say that they did not see the back of someone else, who had a build similar to the defendant's? I look like the defendant, so it could have been me. In fact, there are members on the jury with the defendant's build. You, too, could have been falsely accused. Just as the defendant has been falsely accused.

How about the fingerprints, we might ask? The fact is, Mr. Manu's prints were found in the middle of the pestle and not at the top. Now, if you were going to strike another person in the skull with a pestle, would you not hold the top of it?

[The defense lawyer walked to his chair and took out a pestle and proceeded to demonstrate how it would be done. He held the pestle at the very top and swung it in the air. "This is how one would use this," he said. Then he held the middle of the pestle and when he tried to swing it, the movement was awkward as the pestle hardly moved away from his body.]

No one would do it this way. This is entirely consistent with Mr. Manu's testimony that he was in the deceased's house that morning and touched things. He touched the pestle, but he did not strike anyone with it. Please recall that fingerprints were found at the top of the pestle that didn't belong to Mr. Manu. Plus, we are not even sure the pestle was used to kill Ms. Oddoi. There is no indication that any blood was found on the pestle. But as we heard testified, there was blood around the head of the corpse. It could have been any blunt object. Ladies and gentlemen, what kind of case is this? There are too many unanswered questions. The prosecution has constructed fiction and given us too many doubts.

Mr. Manu does not deny that he was in the house that morning. We heard him say that. But it was all in innocence. He is a good man, a friendly man. We heard his friends affirm that. There is nothing criminal for a man to accept an invitation from the neighbor of his wife for breakfast. There is no reason why he would want to harm Ms. Akwele Oddoi. He had no reason whatsoever. But did he even have the opportunity? Mr. Manu was in her house much earlier and left a long time before the incident occurred.

And Mr. Manu's demeanor on the afternoon in question is completely consistent with innocence. I know that for a while after an afternoon nap, I can be completely confused. I am sure we have all felt like that before. Wouldn't a man who has just woken from sleep look a little disoriented? Even, not properly dressed?

But the most shameful thing about the prosecution's case is the subtle attempt to have you convict the defendant because he married a second woman. The defendant is not on trial for polygamy. Are we now going to prosecute, in fact persecute, those of us who engage in that practice? Why don't we dig up all our forefathers and condemn them, then? And if we have moral objections, why don't we go from home to home and start prosecuting fornication, adultery, divorce?

No, this trial is about murder. The issue is whether or not the defendant is guilty of murder. And it is clear that the prosecution has no case. So what the prosecution has done is present a case that requires a gigantic leap over the facts, or the lack thereof. It is a case full of holes and doubts, untrue in all its particulars. Therefore, I submit to you that the prosecution has failed woefully to carry its burden of proof. The evidence is grossly circumstantial and untenable. There are too many holes in the story presented by the state. There are too many doubts. And that is because Mr. Koo Manu is innocent.

I am outraged that an innocent person has been murdered. And it behooves us to punish the perpetrator of the crime. But it would be equally unjust to convict the defendant, an innocent man. Please let us not commit a double injustice. Please return a verdict of not guilty, so that this good and innocent man can return to his family.

Ladies and Gentlemen of the jury, thank you very much for your time.

Justice Ocloo gave her instruction to the jury after the defense lawyer sat down. She instructed the jurors to determine first the facts from the proceedings and the proceedings only. Second, she asked them to listen to her instructions on the law and decide whether the state had met its burden of proving the defendant's guilt beyond a reasonable doubt. She reminded the jury that the defendant is presumed innocent until proven guilty beyond a reasonable doubt. Reasonable doubt, she explained, is difficult to define. However, she said that it was something akin to proof powerful enough that it leaves no hesitation in their belief in the defendant's guilt. At the same time, it didn't mean proof beyond all doubt. Justice Ocloo then asked the jurors to judge the credibility of the witnesses and decide what weight to give to their testimony. They also ought to decide whether the defendant had the criminal state of mind.

In summary, Justice Ocloo charged the jury with the duty to determine if the Government had proven beyond a reasonable doubt that: the defendant killed Akwele; that he did so either intentionally or recklessly, with extreme disregard for human life; that the killing was premeditated. She said that the jury's verdict must be unanimous. The jury retired to begin its deliberations.

EPILOGUE

THE PROSECUTOR

Several days prior to trial, night crept surreptitiously on me. I walked from my bureau in the church to imbibe the air palpitating angrily, the sprinting wind which seemed to shift speed wantonly, unpredictably chilly and then unpredictably warm. I deem it a therapeutic prescription to stand at nighttime with head abuzz and stare at the beguiling simplicity of the shadows, wherein licentious and untoward principalities spark their red-glaring seductions. So, therapeutic only if we refuse complete surrender to all that which abides in the night. I stood there unmoving for countless minutes till familiar with the alien shadows that seemed so unfamiliar moments prior thereto, I embraced it momentarily, still not surrendering to it.

If a society becomes morally neutral or blind so that the divine is eclipsed by heathen practices, then laws must bend to His will. Verily, only divine law is sacrosanct amid the unfolding idiosyncrasies of human frailty. Therefore, if the forefathers erred, I, by virtue of the power vested in me as prosecutor (and as a divine appointee of the Word) must pursue as a goal, an obdurate drive to God. It is not simply a divine imperative, it is a societal necessity, a Darwinian dictate, if you will. Those whose foresight compels this conclusion, I count myself as one. Let not the obscurantism of the forebears hijack the endless possibilities before us.

As expected, I thought, despite the *corpus delecti*, overwhelming both in law and in moral and social significance, the accused denied guilt. Steeped in archaic mannerisms, he projected surprise. Some have stymied and lambasted me with their salmagundi of excuses, even insults. But my will, divine, is of iron constitution.

The Sun by Night

It is a practical conclusion, this office, my dual career paths; each important to me and each uncompromising, working in tandem. They have said a pastor must not mix the sacred yearnings of religion with the secularism of legal practice, which imposes ethical dualities incompatible with Divine credo. They say that legal practice must perforce venture the practitioner thereof in the realm of deceit, that masterly massaging of truth, so that the end product approximates, even if implicitly, that cloak of deception and moral compromise. But I reject the notion that the two personas must clash. My credo is simple. God is my guide; Divine justice is my goal and, as a lawyer, I reach for justice and, as a pastor, I seek God.

Yet how somatic yearnings yield to unrighteous temptations. It was a regrettable action, the ramifications of which echoed devastatingly in my guilt. It hit in the night and with a far-reaching aftermath, this hiccup now blossoming into a baby. My Lord, I cried, why did you permit this to befall me? Why make me err so pitifully? Yet I discerned I could not set the onus on God. It was solely *mea culpa*. I sought absolution. But the facts. Oh the abominable facts.

When Stella and I concluded Bible lessons on Wednesday, I felt a robust famishment that induced me to solicit immediate nourishment. I intimated to Stella, whereupon she procured food from nearby and we sat down and dined. The trial weighed heavily; Stella was commiserating. I bestowed on her my approach for the second day of trial. She ventured to poke holes therein. She urged me to confidence. God will be my steersman: Yea, though I walk through the valley of the shadow of death …

Stella grinned, rose and came to me to rub tension from my shoulders. That motion on my shoulders ignited something deep … a licentious fervor overtook reason and I allowed myself the unconstrained imagination of Stella and myself in libidinous congress. And so it happened. Somatic congress. After the final puff, I pulled away and sobbed.

"What have we done?" Stella queried.

"Sin of blasphemous proportions in the House of the Lord."

Epilogue

"We shall be punished," she opined. "We must ask for God's forgiveness. We must do it now."

I concurred. First genuflecting and then fully on dual knees each, we beseeched God for forgiveness.

After, I pronounced, "This must never betide us again."

"It will never happen again," Stella affirmed.

I fasted the following day. Very difficult in light of preparation for trial.

Proximate to the closure of the jury's prolonged deliberations, Stella gave me the news. Pregnant: she conceived the union of our act in her womb. I thought hard and long that night. Then the day after the trial ended, I mused over events again. And I knew what I must do. This was a cruel but necessary event for me.

THE DEFENSE LAWYER

After having done my best for my client, I was, nonetheless, unsettled. It was a formidable case for me, although not because the evidence against my client was overwhelming. It wasn't, in my estimation. Knowing, however, that things didn't add up, I was torn. Unable to explain the heat of Koo Manu's car and the key in the ignition when the police arrived at his house, I still was loath to question my client's integrity. Normally, having an instinct one way or the other on the guilt or innocence of a client, I offer the client the benefit of my legal knowledge and skill. This time, however, although having enormous difficulty believing Koo Manu had committed the crime, especially after the young man linked Akwele and Colonel Duah, I still couldn't conclude that he hadn't. I had asked him, "How do you explain the engine and the key in the ignition?" I was hoping he'd express something convincing. A hope... unfounded?

But he'd said simply, "I don't know, Ekow."

291

"How can you not know?" He shrugged. "It will be very difficult to explain that to the jury, to be honest with you. I may have to simply ignore it. And that is dangerous."

Knowing I could attribute it to the sun, still the key in the ignition cast some doubt on that theory. Did he simply leave his car in the sun with the key in the ignition? Tough to believe. Pushing the sun theory too much, I feared, might be asking the jury to suspend reality a bit too much. I was going to have to hint on it, but not push it.

"We just have to take the chance."

Not desirous of arguing with that, I asked instead, "And how do you explain the flight from Akwele's house?"

"It wasn't me. I did not run away from her house. I have told you exactly what happened."

"The story doesn't quite add up."

"You have to believe what I'm telling you. I am not lying about that."

Looking as believable as he did, I wondered why I unquestionably could not affirm my belief in his innocence. Unanswered questions remaining, armed or disarmed, I had my case; and I had to perform at my best with what I had, and hope for the best.

Glad, however, that the trial had ended, I was desirous of taking some time off from work. A lawyer's most formidable task is the often futile attempt to separate his own feelings from a case he is handling, especially in a murder case and, in this case, especially because the defendant is a friend.

What surprised, nay perplexed, me the most was John's actions the day when I walked into court to hear the jury's verdict. Before entering the courtroom, he called to me, asking about my health. Not expecting that because of our chilled relationship, I paused momentarily before replying, "I'm very well, thank you."

I was expecting some sarcastic remark, but instead he said he would be honored if I would come to his church the following Sunday.

"Are you inviting me to your church?" I asked in disbelief.

"Yes," he said.

"I don't know if ..."

He said I should come. We had had our differences, but we could begin a new chapter. He was almost begging.

Memories came flooding back to me, and briefly recollecting sparks of our prior friendship, I said, "I'll be there."

Asking me to honor my promise regardless of the outcome of the case, he put out his hand and I took it. Then side-by-side, with the media hovering around us, we walked into the courtroom to listen to the jury's verdict.

THE JUROR

At first glance the defendant looked so familiar that I felt an uncomfortable closeness to him and immediately felt some sympathy for him. Yet I knew that he had a formidable case against him and that it would be very difficult for me to vote to acquit the man accused of murdering my close friend, Akwele.

As the trial itself began I wondered what my fellow jurors would say if they knew what I did at night, and in a sense I thought it interesting that I was judging the man accused of murdering a woman I knew so well. When I first got on the jury, I thought it was an opportunity for me to bring Akwele to life again and to punish her murderer. I was convinced that whoever the defendant was, he would be guilty, because I would find him guilty and I would do all I could to get the other jurors to find him guilty.

And yet that feeling of familiarity and closeness was so powerful when I saw the defendant that I began to feel as if I had a duty to him just as much as I felt a duty to Akwele, and that dual feeling perplexed me. I struggled back and forth during the trial and I couldn't convince myself completely that the defendant was guilty. And I wasn't happy with the prosecution's sometimes subtle and sometimes blatant attempt to shift focus from the crime of murder itself to the defendant's polygamy.

My worst fears almost materialized when my ex-husband, who was reporting on the case, began his investigation, which led him to Madam Beatrice and ultimately to me. He was clearly surprised to see me in the brothel the day he walked in. I knew that despite my vague disguise he recognized me. He looked at me for a long time before moving away from Madam Beatrice and then walking up to me and whispering my name.

"You do not belong here," he said, as his voice seemed to choke his throat and he began to sweat while I tried to remain calm.

"So what are you going to do now, Nii? Are you gong to tell the whole world about me?"

He was almost in tears when he said, "I wouldn't do that to you. Believe it or not, I married you because I love you. I know it's hard for you to believe in love. But there are some of us who do. I won't do anything to hurt you."

"I suppose I should thank you."

I wanted very much to assure myself that he would be true to his word and not reveal my secret to the rest of the world. In my desperation, I got the idea to tempt him into my world and let him share of it so that he would have its scent on him and make him incapable of looking at it with any detachment. He was still in love with me, and all I had to do was take him with me to a room and he would succumb to my power over him. So I began my teasing movement of the eyes placed high and close to narrowed eyelids and I effected my well-tested look of vulnerable surrender. Because I knew I had him, I reached for his hand and when he opened his lips to speak I put a finger over those lips and hushed him. Then I pulled him gently and started to lead him to a room where I would make him a part of me.

Epilogue

But the conquest had been too easy and I felt a sharp prick of conscience; I knew it was not right to entrap him so selfishly. And I felt if he was so vulnerable to me then perhaps if I went all the way with him, I might get him addicted and he would be incapable of extricating himself. But that was not my intention because I knew not everybody could handle the duality I lived without destruction. And because I still liked him at a certain level, I didn't want to risk destroying him for my own selfish ends. For those reasons I stopped myself and told him, "You need to go home to your wife."

He looked disappointed and relieved at the same time, and perhaps his own conscience was re-wakened by the opportunity I had given him to stop before he started on this path. He warned, "You should be very careful. If I could so easily discover you, anyone who puts in the effort can." Then he looked down as if in thought. "Who are you?" he asked with a puzzled look.

"Asking who I am is as futile as asking the question where does the human body begin and where does it end?"

He did not lambaste me and I was extremely grateful for that. And he did keep to his word and never published what he had found about Madam Beatrice or me.

That night, I spoke with Madam Beatrice about Nii's visit and even she had to agree that, given my role as a juror and her having being a witness, things were getting a little too close to home and that perhaps it was a good idea for me to take some time off for the moment. And that little grant of freedom could not have come at a better time, because I feared I was close to emotional exhaustion.

I realized why I felt such a closeness to the defendant on the last day of the trial, after the closing argument, when I saw the defendant and his son standing together as I was leaving the courtroom.

There was the defense lawyer and the defendant – and a younger man standing next to the defendant who looked exactly like him and whom I recognized.

And it was none other than the man who had told me his name was Kwamena and who had proposed marriage to me and who had asked me to give him my dress. And I strongly suspected then that it was not the defendant who killed Akwele.

I walked into the jury room with that the conviction of the defendant's likely innocence and with a knowledge that I could not share with my fellow jurors. And I knew that if it had to be up to me alone to prevent a guilty verdict, then I would do so. There were eleven other jurors: two schoolteachers, a mason, a broadcaster, a timber merchant, two businessmen, a boxer, two drivers and a trader. We briefly discussed the case with its evidence and witnesses and statements. We cast our first ballot and three jurors found the defendant not guilty and nine voted to convict him.

"How can anyone not vote to convict?" asked one of the teachers.

"He is not guilty," I replied. "There is nothing but circumstantial evidence against him and I say you cannot convict a man on such evidence."

"I agree," said the mason. "The policemen were drunk. How could they see anything?"

"They were not drunk," countered the boxer.

"Hey," said one driver, "we can't vote to convict unless we are sure he did the crime. Don't you have reasonable doubt?"

"I do," said I. "The testimony of policemen who have been drinking for three hours cannot be trusted, and besides they never saw the face of the person leaving the house."

"How about the hot engine and the keys in the ignition?" asked the broadcaster.

Said I, "The engine could have gotten hot from the heat of the sun and perhaps the defendant forgot to take the key out of the ignition and that is no crime."

We went back and forth and the numbers of those who had reasonable doubt increased from three to four. I continued to advocate the defendant's innocence, and all the while I was thinking why I was so strongly advocating for the defendant's acquittal when the person who had died was Akwele. But I was convinced that it would be better to let him go free than convict him when I so strongly suspected he had not done the crime, even though I was asking myself if it was possible that he somehow knew the truth. The deliberations got interesting when the broadcaster asked, "Why was the prosecutor picking on the defendant for marrying two wives? My grandfather had three wives, and the prosecutor thinks he knows better than us all by equating polygamy with sin. This isn't a case about polygamy."

"Very true. And by the way, did you understand the prosecutor? I was lost most of the time."

"I am glad you said that. I was afraid to admit it before because I didn't want to sound stupid."

"Yes. He speaks a different language. He doesn't speak our language. How can we vote in his favor?"

"That's nonsense. That's not what this case is about."

"It is all this case is about. This case that shouldn't have been brought in the first place." The jurors were evenly split after about three hours of deliberations, with six believing that the defendant was guilty, and six believing he was not guilty or that the prosecution had not proved its case. And so I prepared for a long day, and at that point I did not know what the eventual outcome would be.

That same day I discovered I was pregnant. I was feeling sick after the deliberations, so I went to see the doctor on my way home. The news pleased and displeased me at once: I had a baby whose father I was not sure of, and which I didn't expect, and so I felt repelled. But at the same time, this was a child of my own that I would raise and cherish and nourish into adulthood. I feared, however, that I would detest the child just as much as I would love him or her. This child was everyone's baby and really no one's and whom I would have to teach many things if I stayed strong enough not to abandon him or her.

THE DEFENDANT

Naturally, my family rallied around me. Akua held me warmly. For the first time since my second marriage. I felt her love. And I thought of all that could have been. The strain was still there. Perhaps less visible. But it hadn't gone away. Yet no one in the family believed that I had done murder. Nor would they want to see me imprisoned. So my wife Akua did what she could in court. I was so grateful to her. I knew it wasn't easy for her. I was struggling to heal my family. My relationship with my first wife. That had suffered so. I knew she blamed me for the events. I had to start all over again. Regain her trust and confidence. Remove the rust. I had to do the same with my children.

I was surprised when Pastor-Lawyer Amoah came to see me. It was the day after the jury's non-decision. I greeted him very coldly. He said he wanted to invite me to church. I told him that I had a new church. I didn't need his. He begged me. And he was almost in tears. He said I should come, if only just that Sunday. Why did he want me to come so badly? He had me intrigued. I said I would think about it.

I suppose that I should be happy. The jury could not agree. After several days of deliberations. Split six-six. They could not reach an unanimous decision. So they were dismissed. And I was free. I was happy in a way. But I was also very sad for two reasons. I did not commit the crime. But if the jury couldn't agree, then I had not been declared innocent. I would always carry a blemish. I had my freedom, but what will everybody think? That my lawyer got me off for murder?

Epilogue

The second reason is that a woman died. Her murderer should have been punished. But how could I say that? When a couple of days after the trial I found out who killed her.

Two nights after the trial, I couldn't sleep. I thought of Grandpapa. I got up in the middle of the night. I was still confused. Everything had happened so fast. How could an innocent man ever be accused of murder? Something was wrong. I wanted to yell. Tell the world that a terrible mistake had been made. I got a bottle of beer and sat in the living room.

"Papa," I heard Kubi's voice.

I looked up and saw him standing beside me. I had never seen him like that before. His eyes were red. He had not shaved. There was a small growth on his chin. There was also misery in his face. He looked very troubled. And I became worried for him. "Kubi," I said, "I am the one who just went through a terrible trial. You shouldn't worry so much. After all, the trial is over. God, you look like a thing on the street."

"He said softly, "I have something to tell you, Papa."

"What is it, Kubi?"

Kubi looked down. My heart beat badly. I couldn't handle another misfortune at that time. "Nothing can be so terrible that we can't solve. What is it?"

He waited a long time. Then he knelt in front of me. He began to cry. He had never done that before. "Papa, I know you are going through a difficult time. But I want you to know what happened."

I was surprised. "Why are you talking like this, Kubi?

"I am sorry," he kept saying. "But no one deserves better than mother."

He was confusing me. "Kubi! What are you talking about?"

Kubi explained. He explained his relationship with a prostitute. He said he'd lied to her about himself. He'd fallen in love with her. And proposed marriage to her. She turned him down. He was angry with her. Angry that a mere prostitute would turn him down. He wanted to take revenge. He wanted to make her suffer. But he found out he couldn't harm her. He just couldn't bring himself to do so. Instead, he preyed on other prostitutes. There was one in particular he followed for a while. Her name was Araba. He observed that she was into illegal drugs. He knew the man who supplied her the drugs. His name was Zogomi. The man liked to drive a red Peugeot. They formed a trio of sex and drugs.

And then things got complicated. Colonel Duah was named to the new Government. After the coup. The Colonel, who had frequented the brothel before, couldn't do so anymore. The Colonel and Kubi had been schoolmates. They'd lost touch. But one day they'd run into each other again. At the brothel. They'd renewed contact. After the coup, Kubi went to Colonel Duah. To see if he could get my release from detention. The Colonel said he'd try. But he asked Kubi to help him. To get Araba to him from time to time. Kubi complied. But Araba got too brave. She began to threaten Colonel Duah. That she'd reveal his secret to the world. Unless he paid her a hefty sum. Araba had been found dead soon afterwards.

Kubi on his part had been busy. He had earlier hired the drug dealer to follow the prostitute he loved. By stalking her. This way, she might feel insecure. She might need protection. Hopefully, she would turn to Kubi for protection. It was an insane idea, he knew. But he was desperate. In any case the drug dealer botched the stalking. Then he died in a car crash. Mission still unaccomplished.

But now Colonel Duah needed a new woman. He asked Kubi to help him with Akwele. The same way he'd helped with Araba. Kubi saw an opportunity for him there. Perhaps he could prevail on Akwele. To help him win the woman he loved. He would pick Akwele up. And drive her to an arranged place. There, Colonel Duah would take her away. And return her close to her home. The arrangement worked for a while. Then Colonel Duah had suggested, "Let's get rid of Akwele. She could cause me trouble. She knows too much." Kubi refused to participate. But the Colonel's proposition seeded an idea in Kubi. He realized how vulnerable Akwele was.

He started following Akwele around. He asked her to help him win the prostitute he loved. Akwele said she couldn't do anything for him. Kubi felt frustrated. One day he went to see Akwele. He had a knife in his pocket. He showed it to her. More as a symbol of power than anything else.

"What is it for?" Akwele asked.

"To kill," Kubi said. But he didn't mean it.

"Who?"

"You."

She laughed him off. But he followed her home the next day. She asked him to leave her alone. But he didn't. He told her to help him. He had power over her. Many nights afterwards, he followed her home. He wasn't sure why he did that. In a way, though, he felt jealous. It was as if he himself was a prostitute. Who saw Akwele as a competitor. On the afternoon of the murder, he felt depressed. He'd gone out for a while. I was asleep when he returned. He took some drugs. Then he drove my Mercedes to Dansoman to visit Akwele. He'd parked the car a short distance from her home. And he walked to her house. She let him in. She asked him why he was bothering her.

He was feeling very high from the drugs. He felt a need for gratification. He reached for her and she jumped and ran. He went after her. She seemed trapped. She went to the kitchen. He grabbed her. She pushed him away. He was enraged. He saw a pestle in the floor. He picked it up. He wasn't thinking. It was as if he was in a different world. A world in which he held great power. It seemed so surreal when he felt the urge to strike her. It was as if he couldn't control himself. She seemed afraid and she screamed. He hit her once. She seemed to yield to the strike. But not completely enough. She still struggled. He hit her twice. Then repeatedly. He threw the pestle on the ground. And then he ran from the house. He drove back home. But he was very afraid.

He had left the key in the ignition. Then he'd run into the backyard. He jumped the wall and ran away. He'd ran and gone to a park. He sat there for a long time. After all that, he could not go to the brothel anymore. Because he couldn't bring himself to. Despite a longing to go back.

The Sun by Night

He wanted to tell me earlier, but he was afraid.

I sat down for a long time. I didn't know what to do. He had just told me a very strange story. But everything made sense to me now. The accusations by the police officers, the unexplained prints on the pestle, the hot engine ... I trembled in anger and shock. For three minutes I couldn't speak.

"Get up!" I ordered him.

He stood up.

"I don't understand why. Why a prostitute? You have everything. And then to propose marriage to her. Did you think I would allow that? God, I didn't know you were capable. Of such foolishness. Such cruelty. What is the monster that I have made?"

"I am sorry, Papa," he said.

"Sit down!" I said and he sat.

I got up. I paced the room. I was thinking. Then I knew what I would do. "Your actions are stupid and monstrous. They cannot be excused. But this is what we will do. You will not tell anyone what you've told me. No one. Not even again to me. Not to your mother, your sister, your brothers. We will pretend you have not told me anything. I am giving you a second chance. The second chance that society will not give you."

But I couldn't get Kubi's confession from my mind. It tormented me. Day and night. To know that my son had murdered. And I was staying silent. And to know that Colonel Duah might be involved. My mind was in deep turmoil. I knew I'd promised Kubi that I'd not tell anyone. But I found that I couldn't live with myself. Yet what could I do? Call the police? How could I turn in my own son? What consequence on our already strained relationship? How about the effect on the rest of the family? Could I even face myself? Should I help my son? Continue to help him cover up? I sought the wisdom of Mother and Father. Of Grandpapa. I remembered the warning of Mother ... That I had ignored after her death. Papa's too ... I remembered the resurrection of Grandpapa. After my arrest. I got conflicting thoughts.

Epilogue

It was hard. But I willed myself to my own self. I found some clarity in that state.

I called the police. And I wept. Then I called Lawyer Dadzie. "My friend, you have a big case to prepare for."

The next day I read the following in *The Accra Chronicler*:

MANU ARREST REPORTED

Reports reaching *The Accra Chronicler* indicate that Kubi Manu has been arrested for the murder of Akwele Oddoi. The police have not disclosed the basis for the arrest. Readers will recall that Kubi Manu's father, Koo Manu, was tried for the murder of the same woman. The jury was unable to reach a unanimous decision in that trial. According to reliable sources, Kubi Manu made this terse statement after his arrest: "Though we escape, we die. That which is hidden scorches deeper than that which is revealed." *The Accra Chronicler* is investigating the matter and will bring you the latest developments in this unfolding saga of the Manu family.

We were summoned to the police station. Lawyer Dadzie and I. When we arrived, the police greeted us warmly. "Your son wants to talk to you," we were told. "You and the lawyer."

Kubi seemed calm when we entered. For the first time in a long time, he hugged me. As adult-to-adult. I was moved by that gesture. Of forgiveness. But it was he who asked for my forgiveness. "Papa," he said, "I'm sorry for all the grief I've caused. I have thought over things a lot. Last night, I said everything I know to the police. They have my signed confession."

Lawyer Dadzie gasped. "Your what?"

"I confessed."

"Confessed? Without a lawyer present? Without talking to me first?"

"Lawyer, we are past legal nuances. Your role now is not to defend my innocence. I will enter no such plea. I'm not innocent."

"No matter what you think you've done, in the eyes of the law, you may be innocent. There are defenses we can put up for your benefit. We need to explore alternatives: self-defense, insanity…"

"I'm not interested. But I don't want to die. I need to live because I don't want to die. But I also need to live in order to repair the pain I've caused, do what I can to mend broken fences. I also want to spend every day in penance. By strengthening my own life, I will pay redemptive tribute to those whose lives I've so corrupted. Lawyer, your role is to save me from a death sentence."

"You are making a big mistake."

"Please, let us not debate this." Kubi turned to me. "Papa, when I confessed to you, I left out some details. I want to fill them now."

Kubi gave us a rejoinder to his earlier confession to me. Colonel Duah and Kubi went to the same secondary school. Even in those days, they were friends. Despite a four-year age difference. They shared similar tastes. Duah became a mentor of sorts. Then Duah graduated. Kubi would not see him until many years later. They were reunited at Madam Beatrice's brothel. But after Duah became part of the Government, he had to be careful. Kubi helped get Araba to him. Colonel Duah had a particular liking for her. They formed a quartet: Kubi, Colonel Duah, Araba, and Zogomi, a drug dealer. They gathered in obscure motel rooms. They did drugs. There were other women, but Araba was Colonel Duah's favorite.

But after Araba made demands on him, Colonel Duah got angry. He fumed that she'd blackmail him for money. He allowed it to continue for a while. Then he had no patience left. He invited Kubi to his home. He showed him a cabinet. In it were notes from Araba demanding money from him. In her broken English she had scrawled a few words. Colonel Duah said he couldn't suffer her demands any longer. He summoned Zogomi. He asked him to liquidate the problem. Days later, Araba was dead. Not long afterwards Zogomi died in a car accident. Form then on, Kubi's confession was consistent with what he'd told me.

"What are you going to do?" I asked the police officer in charge.

"We got a search warrant early this morning. When we went to search Colonel Duah's house, he wouldn't let us in. I think he still believed he was untouchable. But these are different times. We are supposed to be under a constitutional democracy now. And you know how the lawyers and their friends have been making noise about this matter. The CID Commissioner has given instructions not to fool around with this investigation. Anyway, we had to force ourselves into his house. There, we discovered the letters referred to in Kubi's confession. But that's not all. We found a knife with dried blood on it. But he absconded before we could arrest him."

The next day, the following item appeared in *The Accra Chronicler*:

MEMBER OF PARLIAMENT ARRESTED

The arrest is reported of Colonel Duah (Rtd.), Member of Parliament and a former cadre in the erstwhile Revolutionary Council. Colonel Duah was arrested in connection with the murder of an Accra prostitute. According to reliable sources, Colonel Duah was apprehended after a tip from a close acquaintance. On the basis of incriminating evidence discovered at his residence, the police were ready to effect an arrest, but Colonel Duah bolted. He was arrested at Nsawam last night, disguised as an old woman. He is now in police custody.

It was with a very heavy heart that I went to church. At Pastor Amoah's invitation. It was a brilliant Sunday morning. Pastor Amoah stood there, Bible in hand. It was amazing. One day a big lawyer. Another day a pastor. I was a little nervous. I wondered if he would chastise me. I was afraid he would talk about polygamy and murder. But I was completely wrong. I believe his entire congregation was surprised. By what he said next.

"Dearly beloved," he began. I listened intently. For the first time in a long time, I understood him. Every word he said. I didn't have to guess his meaning. He said that we ought to thank God. The God who gives life. It is He also who takes life. He had been thinking of what he'd say. About a week ago, he didn't know, he said. Pastor Amoah said he'd been involved in a lot of things. Then he mentioned the word "Fornication." And there was absolute silence in the church. He said the Bible forbids fornication. It is a sin, he barked. He said he had preached against fornication many times. With the cross hanging over his head, he'd preached. He wanted to repeat it: "Fornication is forbidden."

And then he confessed. He had committed fornication right there in the church.

There was complete silence. It was bothersome. Pastor Amoah repeated his confession. He said he could understand our surprise. We couldn't believe that a preacher would do such a thing. He who warns against the desires of the flesh. He wanted us to be angry with him. He wanted us to berate him for betraying us. He had done a wrong thing. He made no excuses for it. So he wanted us to be disappointed. But he didn't want us to condemn him.

Pastor Amoah paused to wipe sweat off his face. He was only human, he said. He wasn't God. He would keep striving to get closer to God. But our best deeds are like filthy rags before God. He said all have sinned. All have fallen short of God's glory.

So as a human being, he would make his mistakes. That he'd betrayed us, he asked for our forgiveness.

It was a surprising but refreshing sermon. There was mixed reaction after church. There were those who blasted Pastor Amoah. A preacher should be above us. This was beyond pardon. Then there were those who thought we should move on. A pastor was like anybody else. We ought to admire his courage. For confessing in church. A huge section of the congregation was gathered outside the church. One member of the congregation turned to me. He asked what I thought about the matter. I picked up a stone and held it out to the gathering.

I heard neither hue nor cry for the stone.

No frenzy to reach for a slab.